Ivy C[...]

"Werewolf Ivy Cole [...] [...]nd
blessed with a deadly [...] [...] horror
fiction. Gina Farago's gripping novel is sure to please genre
fans and mainstream readers alike."

—Elizabeth Massie, Bram Stoker Award–winning author

"An intriguing morality play, featuring sharply drawn,
engaging characters and loaded with rural southern atmosphere. With her stark descriptions, authentic, colloquial dia-
logue, and characters possessed of dreadful secrets, Gina
Farago gives us a tale with both dark, subtle undertones and
wild, graphic action—kind of like Flannery O'Connor meets
The Howling."

—Stephen Mark Rainey, author of *The Lebo Coven*

"Fast-moving . . . Fiction has a new, thoroughly engaging
leading lady . . . Farago's novel immediately captures the
imagination with its setting in the deep dark North Carolina
mountains and its action spanning those mysterious nights
when the full moon shines and wild creatures go wilder. We're
looking for a sequel and looking hopefully out the window for
the next full moon." —*Greensboro News & Record*

"It is rare when an author has the ability to let the reader see,
hear, feel, and smell so vividly what they are reading. Farago
lets the mind's eye travel beyond the printed page so one may
experience this well-written story. At last, an unusual and
entertaining book for werewolf enthusiasts!"

—Robert Harris, actor, *Cabin Fever*

"What's not to like about a sweet thirties-something southern
belle who feeds on the entrails of her enemies under a full
moon? This is the kind of book that can make you cry, giggle,
throw up, and stroke your chin page to page."

—*Insidious Reflections*

Ivy Cole
and the
Moon

Gina Farago

BERKLEY BOOKS, NEW YORK

THE BERKLEY PUBLISHING GROUP
Published by the Penguin Group
Penguin Group (USA) Inc.
375 Hudson Street, New York, New York 10014, USA
Penguin Group (Canada), 90 Eglinton Avenue East, Suite 700, Toronto, Ontario M4P 2Y3, Canada
(a division of Pearson Penguin Canada Inc.)
Penguin Books Ltd., 80 Strand, London WC2R 0RL, England
Penguin Group Ireland, 25 St. Stephen's Green, Dublin 2, Ireland (a division of Penguin Books Ltd.)
Penguin Group (Australia), 250 Camberwell Road, Camberwell, Victoria 3124, Australia
(a division of Pearson Australia Group Pty. Ltd.)
Penguin Books India Pvt. Ltd., 11 Community Centre, Panchsheel Park, New Delhi—110 017, India
Penguin Group (NZ), Cnr. Airborne and Rosedale Roads, Albany, Auckland 1310, New Zealand
(a division of Pearson New Zealand Ltd.)
Penguin Books (South Africa) (Pty.) Ltd., 24 Sturdee Avenue, Rosebank, Johannesburg 2196,
South Africa

Penguin Books Ltd., Registered Offices: 80 Strand, London WC2R 0RL, England

This is a work of fiction. Names, characters, places, and incidents either are the product of the author's imagination or are used fictitiously, and any resemblance to actual persons, living or dead, business establishments, events, or locales is entirely coincidental.

IVY COLE AND THE MOON

A Berkley Book / published by arrangement with NeDeo Press

PRINTING HISTORY
NeDeo Press hardcover edition / September 2005
Berkley mass-market edition / October 2006

Copyright © 2005 by Gina Farago.
Cover illustration by Johnathan Barkat.
Cover design by Monica Benalcazar.
Interior text design by Stacy Irwin.

Grateful acknowledgment is made for permission to reprint from *The Werewolf Book: The Encyclopedia of Shape-Shifting Beings*, by Brad Steiger, Visible Ink Press (January 2005), copyright © 1999 by Visible Ink Press.® Reprinted by permission of Visible Ink Press.

ISBN: 0-425-21256-4

BERKLEY®
Berkley Books are published by The Berkley Publishing Group,
a division of Penguin Group (USA) Inc.,
375 Hudson Street, New York, New York 10014.
BERKLEY is a registered trademark of Penguin Group (USA) Inc.
The "B" design is a trademark belonging to Penguin Group (USA) Inc.

PRINTED IN THE UNITED STATES OF AMERICA

10 9 8 7 6 5 4 3 2 1

For my husband, Karl,
thank you for believing...

Acknowledgments

Along the path of researching and writing this novel, I have worked with some wonderful folks who stand out as deserving special recognition. They were helpful beyond my expectations.

To the staff of Wolf Park in Battle Ground, Indiana, particularly Gale Motter, Monty Sloan, Pat Goodmann, and Holly Jaycox, I give a heartfelt pat on the back for your love of and commitment to the beautiful wolves in your care, and a special thank you to Gale and Monty for taking the extra time to introduce me to Deneb and Alyeska.

With sincere appreciation, both for the law enforcement information he provided and the brave men and women whom he directs, I thank Sheriff BJ Barnes of the Guilford County Sheriff's Office. His answering of my endless questions about police procedures and his publicity efforts on my behalf afterward went beyond the call of duty.

To Andrea Monroe Weaver, a lifelong friend and gifted writer, I thank you for your untiring enthusiasm, professional help and advice, and unfailing support, the latter of which has benefited me not only over the course of writing this book but in all the years before.

With much heartfelt gratitude, I thank my mother, Lois Sutphin, my best friend, Kym Goins, and my husband, Karl, for believing everything is possible and encouraging me to strive for it. And to Barbara, Glenn, and Terry Bane, many, many thank yous are in order for your meticulous editing, creative vision "outside the box," and candid guidance and insights. The occasional kick in the pants to get this thing finished didn't hurt either. Without you, this book would not have been possible.

Last, but never least, I thank the wolves themselves: Deneb, Alyeska, Chetan, Tristan, Renki, and all their brothers in the wild. The teachers, the warriors, the survivors. I have learned a lot. . . .

Prologue

When darkness falls on a mountain, it does not descend slowly, like the sinking of a great black ship over the peaks. Rather, the light is just gone. The forest, by the shade of midnight, becomes irregular, indiscernible—a spot of dropped ink, opaque and black.

Things crouch there, in the dark, hidden. Eyes watch from treetops or hollowed trunks close to the mossy floor. Slithering and creeping take place unhindered. Rustling leaves in the wind become stalking footfalls, and twigs that snap betray unseen threats from behind every tree.

There is care to take in the woods at night, alone . . .

Clifford Hughes, self-proclaimed ladies' man and handsomest employee at the Doe Springs Post Office, tore through the thick underbrush, unmindful he had fouled his pants. How long ago was uncertain. Seconds, minutes, an eternity. It didn't matter. Panic drove the man onward. An iron band of terror wrapped around his laboring chest, squeezing the wind out of him but propelling him blindly into branches and limbs that seemed all too determined to hold him back. Vines curled like nooses to grasp at his collar, and the ground melted up to his ankles in a leafy quicksand. A shoe wrenched loose, but Clifford left it, only to go sprawling as a log rose up from the forest floor, bashing his knees. He scrambled to his feet and continued running, leaving a trail of blood droplets through the ruined legs of his postal uniform. A spiderweb netted his face and he batted at it wildly as his body pitched forward a second time, sending his bulk face-first into a bed of moss.

Clifford looked up, bits of dirt and leaves clinging to his

scratched face. He drew a painful breath and realized the
rock wedged under his ribs may have done some damage.
Clifford's eyes darted around, but he was alone. Slowly, he
pulled himself to a sitting position. Breath hitched on what
was surely a broken bone. He touched the sore rib and winced.
Holding his side, he staggered upward, a damaged man
climbing an invisible ladder to unsteady feet.

· The forest was still. Clifford strained to hear something—
anything—beyond his own shallow breathing, but even the
chirring of crickets and frogs had ceased. He turned in a circle, gathering his bearing. At some point the footpath he
thought he was following out had disappeared, swallowed up
by feathery clouds of bracken ferns. In front of him, behind
him, to the left, to the right . . . it all looked the same: a black
wall of towering tree trunks and its suffocating screen of underbrush. Boulders crouched among the laurel thickets like
gravestones, or something else. A moving branch, the wind?
Or the—Clifford couldn't bring himself to think the word. It
was impossible.

Clifford stumbled forward, aware of the noise he made.
Sweat dripped in his eyes but his hand came away red when
he wiped it. *Jesus Christ, I'm going to kill myself trying to
get out of here,* he thought. Hysterical laughter bubbled up
behind the notion. He redirected the energy down into his
legs, willing them to keep going. This was the right way. It
had to be. Clifford shambled through the trees, drunk from
the pain in his ribs, his head, his knees. From trunk to trunk,
he made his way, praying to the good Lord that what pursued him had tired as well.

Ahead of him—a break in the trees. He had made it! ·

Adrenaline and gratefulness mingled to push Clifford forward once more. He broke into a jog, then a run. *Thank you,
God. Oh sweet Jesus, thank you.* Safety lay in front of him at
last, out of these cursed woods. His truck was there, the
house, a telephone.

Clifford rushed into the clearing and stopped, bewildered.
A woman's torn clothes lay on the ground. The stream bab-
bled to his right. A belt lay at the toe of his dirty sock—it was
his own, fallen off when he'd first fled this place.

He was back in the glade he'd attempted to escape. Sweat and blood stung Clifford's eyes once more, but he made no move to wipe it. He strained to see into the shadows, but all was still.

He froze. The sound came from behind him. It was close. Clifford heard the thing padding softly toward him. It rose up on powerful hind legs and breathed gently against his neck. Its breath was earthy and sweet, like the leaves and soil of the mountain.

"Please . . . no . . . " A fat tear rolled down Clifford's cheek. He slowly turned.

Part One

"Sometimes there are folks in this world
who just deserve a good killin'. . . ."

Chapter 1

How could a monster have come to Doe Springs?

Sheriff Gloria Hubbard sat at her desk, a stack of grisly photographs and a hurriedly typed police report in front of her. Her hands trembled slightly, out of frustration more than anything, as she held the brief and photographs of the latest victim, Clifford Hughes.

"Sheriff, are you all right?" Deputy Jonathan Meeks hovered in the doorway, the peppering of gray along his black sideburns seeming heavier this morning. He was only thirty-six, but today they all looked older. "I brought you a cup of coffee." The deputy placed the cup on her desk, then settled his still-athletic frame in the seat across from her. He glanced at the stack of reports between them, waiting but not expecting much in the way of an answer. Scraping another body off the forest floor last night had not been easy on any of them.

Gloria nodded and took a drink of coffee. The liquid burned all the way to her stomach, a familiar and comforting feeling this early in the morning.

"I was looking at the board." Gloria nodded at the five-by-five bulletin behind the deputy's head. It should be blank, this small-town crime board, a window of brown nothingness into which she could focus, the pores in the board a distraction to lead her mind away from the new set of photos in her hand. But, instead, it was a crowded place, filled with the faces of folks she'd known since childhood. They stared back at the sheriff, a few of them she'd had the privilege to call friend. "I was thinking Clifford's picture would be up there with the missing if we hadn't been—lucky—this time."

The word hung between them. *Lucky*. Lucky to have

found one so quickly, she meant. For Doe Springs had not seen luck for a while now, this rural town, perched on a crest within the Blue Ridge Mountains of North Carolina. What a difference a year could make. One short year. Gloria recounted the first of the losses one by one, a daily ritual that did nothing in the way of bringing them back or easing the pain of how they left this place. Delaroy Cox, found wedged facedown in the rapids of the Crippled Bend River, his body decimated by water and the creatures that inhabited it. The sheriff's two deputies had hauled Delaroy's overturned raft and bloated body ashore while the man's skin slip-slided off in sheets behind them. Randy Mabe, fallen from a bridge, his skinny broken frame discovered by wife Eleanor, who'd been out looking for her drunken husband all night. Alice Tripper, train fatality. Jerry Flint, heart attack, found high up in a chestnut oak, his hunting rifle empty and clutched tightly to his chest. Macy Wyatt, their only apparent suicide—frozen to death in her own root cellar, the door bolted tight from the inside. The missing persons list had shrunk as bodies turned up, like Clifford's, but the postal worker's pictures would not go on the wall with the accident victims and the unaccounted for. There was a special place for those reports: in the stack of files now growing thicker along the edge of the sheriff's desk.

"Doesn't make much sense, attacking livestock all this time, then going for people too," Meeks tried again. He didn't like the sheriff this way—quiet, withdrawn. She'd been holed up in here since they got back from the woods off Route 7.

"No." Gloria took another sip. She put down the photographs and cradled her mug thoughtfully. "If only livestock had been the end of it, and not the beginning. When Merle called us last November, I never believed here we'd be, six months later, dealing with this. It seemed like a minute ago we were at the farm." They'd found Merle's Herefords scattered about their pasture like gutted confetti. Merle, standing in his raincoat underneath an overcast sky, ranted and waved his arms, then fell oddly silent when he realized there was nothing the police could really do; heavy rains washed away any prints before they got there. A fluke, they'd assured Mr. Trent, something wandering through with an overzealous appetite but most likely moved on.

Until Dennis Largen's pigs in late December.

"Four."

"What's that, Meeks?" The sheriff steered back to the present again, her coffee mug growing cold in her hands.

"I said Mr. Hughes makes four." The deputy eyed the files lying on the sheriff's desk, their pages peeking out browned and bent from handling.

As if I don't know that! Gloria put the cup on her desk and massaged her temples. The pecan-colored hair pulled back in a tight ponytail felt slick, and the edges of her forehead, where hair met skin, were taut with the strain of her worry. A migraine was brewing, and there'd be no stopping it.

"Another full moon this time too," Meeks continued, pointing out the obvious. "You know what folks are saying. Are you a superstitious woman, Sheriff?"

She was not. Gloria did not believe in curses or wives' tales or the thing under the bed. As the rumors grew wilder, her resolve grew stronger to fix whatever was broken in her town. But the police were no closer to knowing what they were after than they were months ago, when the first body turned up. Sadly enough, a girl no older than seven discovered the remains. Sneaking off to play in Daddy's cornfield traumatized what up until then had been a typical farm daughter's life. The torso lay in the field just a few feet from a well-traveled road leading out of Doe Springs. Barely beyond childhood himself at age twenty-one, the transient had apparently been hitchhiking when whatever roamed the mountains came upon him. The little girl's screams echoed across the corn, then a deafening silence swallowed the cries as she sat in the back of the sheriff's car engulfed in her mother's arms. The frightened woman rocked her daughter, whose eyes looked only inward at the horror she'd stumbled across.

Two other attacks followed, but the similarity to the ravaged livestock pointed to the same culprit. Patrolling Doe Springs's one main street and cross-stitch of back avenues was a regular nightly habit now, regardless of the cyclic lunar connection. Nonetheless, May's full moon, gently named the Flower Moon in Native American lore, rose over Appalachia pale as milk glass last night, and with it came a frantic call from a hunter on the outskirts of town. The dispatcher's voice, filled with cold radio static and dread, had driven the sheriff's heart into her stomach and her Jeep into a ditch. She'd sat at the wheel, cursing God and the devil all in the same breath. Then she'd headed south into the country to find what was left of their postal service's only deliveryman. Number Four.

"Superstitious? Don't be ridiculous, John." Gloria straightened in her rollaway chair, the springs supporting her back whining from old age. The report in front of her blurred for one dangerous moment, and the sheriff wiped her eyes with an unladylike rough hand, a police officer's hand. *How could a monster have come to Doe Springs?* she wondered again. Why her little mountain haven, of all places? There was nothing here but farmers, good ole boys, and a miniscule collection of townspeople. Nosy, yes. A little too imaginative? Maybe. But good folks, all of 'em.

Maybe not all of them. Clifford Hughes's pictures stared up from the desk, the Polaroids fanning out to blend into an ochre haze. The man's usual cocksure expression was unidentifiable in a mask of eyeless gore. Deputies had been to the Hughes house a half dozen times to pull the brawny alcoholic off his wife, Patricia, but Clifford was smart enough to be lounging in his battered recliner whenever law enforcement arrived. It was always the neighbors who called, and Patricia never pressed charges. The girl was young and pretty; why she stayed with such a violent man (and a well-known womanizer to boot) was perhaps more of a mystery than his death.

Gloria secretly thanked God over and over when a call came through with a name she did not recognize or was not close to in some way, like Hughes, other than their attempts to arrest him. Knowing the victims, another downfall of small-town life, made sleeping impossible and living a numb experience between grief and exhaustion.

"Sheriff Hubbard?" Deputy Melvin Sanders poked his head through the office door.

"What is it, Sanders?"

"The body is on its way to the medical examiner's office. We couldn't find everything." Melvin looked apologetic and drawn. The short, dark hair on his head was wet, an attempt to clean up at the office, the sheriff supposed, but the effort only made him look mobsterish. The bruise-like circles under the deputy's eyes, however, mirrored her own.

"I know, Sanders. I was there, remember? It's just like the others."

"No, ma'am, it's not the usual. There are personal items missing this time. Mrs. Hughes swears she doesn't have them and Mr. Hughes never took them off."

"Well, for God's sake, tell me what they are." Gloria's patience was worn clear through. After wading through last night's bloody muck, she was in no mood for beating around the bush. The "usual," as her deputy put it, was the condition of the kills. Every site they'd investigated had revealed the same: a body ripped to bits, the pieces strewn within feet of each other, and the organs—gone. It was consistent with what they would expect from an animal attack. Predators favored soft tissues. But whatever had come down from the mountain had a vicious appetite as there was rarely ever much left for the police to collect aside from bones.

"Two rings are missing from Mr. Hughes's possession: a wedding band and a silver Harley Davidson signet. And also a gold chain." Sanders filled up the sheriff's doorway, waiting for a command or a reply of some kind.

"Type it up, and get a picture of the missing jewelry from the widow, if she's got one."

"Yes, ma'am. I did that already—this morning while I was at the Hughes house." Melvin cleared the distance from door to desk in two strides. He was a big kid, Gloria observed, to be so polite all the time, even in the most stressful of situations. Experience would take that out of him, though—Gloria felt forty-two going on a hundred, and while courteousness was still a valued small-town attribute, it became harder to muster it up the older and less tolerant she became.

The new photos landed atop the stack from the previous night, juxtaposing death and life in a glossy finish. Clifford on his wedding day, his bride sliding the gold band onto his hand. Clifford outside a biker bar, shooting the camera the bird, the Harley Davidson ring front and center.

"Thank you," Gloria managed.

"Uh, Sheriff?"

"What is it, Deputy?"

"I don't know of any animals that like to wear jewelry."

Gloria attempted a smile, but it sat crooked on her exhausted face. "I'll make a note of that, Sanders. You and Meeks go get some breakfast now. It's going to be a long day."

Chapter 2

Ivy Cole sat at the Hughes's kitchen table with her dear friend, Patricia. It had been a horrific night for the new widow, and Ivy consoled her the best she could. The call came that morning, much earlier than Ivy had expected. Usually her work was not discovered for days, sometimes weeks, and on most occasions since moving here, not at all. But bodies had been turning up left and right over the past year, and even Ivy couldn't take credit for all of them. Maybe a curse had fallen over the town. Lord knows the little she did to eradicate riffraff could raise such a ruckus, especially since she was so careful about disposing of the evidence.

But not well enough lately. And certainly not this time. Ivy had barely crawled into bed when Patricia's weepy voice on the end of the phone line pulled her enervated body from underneath the covers once more. A deputy had been at the

Hughes house since four, a deer hunter, of all people, the culprit to blame. Ivy grumpily wondered his name and address while she pulled on yesterday's skirt, still rumpled on the floor. But the hateful thoughts passed as soon as she drove up to the ramshackle two-story farmhouse, lit up like Christmas even after the sun had cleared all traces of a foggy dawn.

When the police finally exited after questions and condolences, the big deputy tiptoed out like he was navigating gravestones in the front yard. Southerners were respectful of the dead, even from a distance, and widows were particularly venerated. Patricia would soon have enough suitors to replace any pleasant memories she might conjure up of Clifford after the funeral, but Ivy guessed the girl would be hard-pressed to think of even one.

Now, in the officer's absence, there were only the two women and a big empty house. Low-slung ceilings cracked and bowed over rooms that stank of Clifford Hughes and his penchant for Wild Turkey. The living room itself was a zoo of dead animals the man had killed over a lifetime, their glassy, dust-coated eyes haunting even to Ivy. She steered her friend from the plaid sofa and its Winston-Light pockmarks into the slightly friendlier kitchen. Perched in wood-backed chairs cushioned by frilly heart pillows Patricia had made herself, they talked and stared and cried the morning away.

At ten-thirty, Ivy scrounged through the splintering cabinetry for a skillet to begin some breakfast. The refrigerator was overstuffed with meat, eggs, butter, cheese, milk—even though the house was falling down around them thanks to Clifford's slack attention, Patricia knew better than to ever let the food stock get low. Clifford's appetite could change for blood if his stomach was ever made to feel neglected.

Ivy stood over the frying bacon and eggs with a spatula. Tendrils of blond hair escaped from a messy knot at her neck only to cling to her cheeks and forehead, glued there by stove heat. Somewhere upstairs, a clock ticked loudly, and Ivy, in between consoling her friend and cooking this grease-sputtering meal, considered going up there and smashing the annoying thing. But that would be unexplainable and crazy, so Ivy swiped sticky hair from her eyes instead and wished there

were more to the air conditioning in this house than an open
window and yard-sale fan. But even her own house had no
central A/C; up on the mountain, you didn't need it. Unless you
were cooking enough bacon and eggs to feed an army. An
army of one who might down a forkful if the cook was lucky.
Ivy didn't dwell on it. This was Clifford's food, and getting it
out of the house would be a good cleansing. If most of it
ended up in the pigs' trough, so be it. It was fitting, in a way.
She flipped the food onto a plate and set it in front of Patricia,
who had not moved since Ivy placed her there hours before.

Patricia started to lift her fork, but then a new spate of
tears streamed down her face and off the edge of her chin.
They dripped over the food and set up around the edges of it
with the grease. Patricia'd alternately cried and laughed since
Ivy had arrived. It was hysteria, the weary deputy had whispered before leaving. But Ivy knew better—Patricia didn't
know whether to be sad or completely grateful, and the guilt
was eating her up.

"You're not having nothing," the girl sniffled. She plucked
at pillow lace and didn't even glance at her meal. The eggs
sat under the watery deluge, turning Ivy's stomach.

"I had a huge supper last night, darlin'. I'm not the least
bit hungry. But you need to keep your strength up. Please finish your breakfast." Ivy nudged Patricia's plate closer. The
girl needed to eat. She was a nickel shy of a hundred and
shrinking fast. Ivy swore Patricia had weighed a good one
hundred twenty-five when they met.

"I can't. How can I eat after hearing . . . what happened
to him." Patricia's brown eyes grew wide as the egg yolks.
Flecks of green near her pupils competed with the amber,
but the colors were backlit by a swollen ring of red inflam-
mation that looked dangerously close to pinkeye. Ivy studied
the peculiar state of Patricia's eyeballs as the girl continued.
"Torn apart, they said, Ivy. Parts of him—gone." She hissed
the last word and grasped Ivy's hand in a quivering claw.
Raggedly chewed fingernails bit into her friend's skin, leaving irregular half-moons along the palm.

Ivy pried her hand from underneath the distraught younger
woman's. "Now listen to me, missy. You just put that right

out of your head. Doe Springs is suffering from too much melodrama, and the police have fallen right into the drama pit with it. People are talking crazy enough without you jumping in after them. That deputy should be ashamed of himself for stirring such a vile pot this early in the morning. I've half a mind to file a complaint." She considered it seriously for one moment, then shook her head. There was enough fuss in this town without adding the spectacle of a lawsuit against the sheriff's office. But really, they were making such a big to-do about it all. Nobody even liked Clifford, for heaven's sake. "Anyway, I'm sure it wasn't nearly as gruesome as you're picturing it, Patricia. Don't let your imagination get away from you."

Patricia lapsed into giggles at that point, then clamped a hand over her mouth. Tears trickled down her fingers in their endless unfaltering flood. Ivy was growing tired of the boomeranging emotions, and upstairs the incessant ticking was wearing on her last nerve as well.

"Stop that, Patricia. Get a hold of yourself. You're not acting rationally."

"Rationally!" Patricia screamed suddenly, startling Ivy in her seat. "My husband of six years was disemboweled last night not a mile from this house and you want to know something?" Patricia took a gulp of air, her red-rimmed pupils growing insanely large. She spit the words at Ivy: "I'm happy! This is the best thing that's ever happened to me, so I must be the most horrible person in the world—worse than whatever creature did that to him." Patricia slumped like a battery-dead doll, the outburst stealing the last of her energy. The flood finally ended with the revelation, and now she stared spent at the Formica tabletop.

The confession was out. Ivy, even though knowing it to be true, was relieved. Each time, the fear was the same: What if she'd made a mistake? But looking at Patricia's swollen lip, the cut around it crusty from where she continually sucked at the wound not allowing it to heal, was the only reminder Ivy needed to know what she did was right. Whether Patricia admitted it or not. But she did admit it, and the modest confirmation was gratifying.

"Oh no you're not, sweetheart. No, you're not . . . " Ivy
held the sobbing girl as her eyes focused past the peeling
kitchen walls and the sagging farmhouse and the modest
stretch of garden beyond it to someplace far away, where
deep woods held secrets and the dead cycled back into the
soil to feed the forest womb.

At a quarter till noon, Ivy put Patricia to bed and promised to come check on her later that evening. Just before going, Ivy sneaked upstairs and located the noisy little clock.
She smashed it soundly, then scraped the shattered pieces
into her pocket.

Ivy began walking home—it was only two miles and she
could pick up her van on her second visit later. A walk could
clear her head and her hair of the smell of cooking grease.
She avoided the route that passed by the last place Clifford
Hughes ever saw alive. It was too beautiful a day to be
dredging up more thoughts of *him*.

Ivy bent down and removed her sandals so she could
enjoy the gritty dirt road on bare feet. The evergreens and
rhododendron closing in on each side of the narrow, twisting lane dwindled down into a pasture of sweeping grasses
the color of butternut. Rising above them, the Appalachians
arced and rolled across the skyline. This was a far cry from
the lower Los Angeles home she'd left a year ago, but the
isolating landscapes and pine-boughed privacy were a welcome respite from the cramped California streets.

It had long been time to get back to her roots anyway. But
one never really left the South, no matter where travels
might take them. A girl born below the Mason-Dixon carried
that stamp in her heart for life. Blue mountain fogs and
sweet magnolia haunted dreams regardless of where the pillow on which Ivy rested her head lay.

Her whole life she'd clung to the memories of her childhood in North Carolina, ten years that were broken into frag-
ments of flight about the world as she and her mother,
Catherine, followed William Cole's growing business from

one upstart to the next. But always to return to the safe haven of the mountains . . .

It had seemed all too brief, those backwoods romps and firefly chases and knee-high wadings in cow-muddied creeks, before a move across the ocean to Catherine's native Germany and, finally, a hasty flight back to the concrete-bound permanence of New York (without her mother, this time), where Ivy spent her teenage years wandering across graying landscapes and wishing for the verdant green from her youth. After leaving her father's Manhattan apartment at eighteen and traveling all over the United States, the gently misted rises of the Blue Ridge finally called Ivy home. It was not the same mountain town of her past, but she needed to come back to the South a stranger. In time, she would be accepted as a local. Maybe in the next twenty or thirty years. But Ivy was young. She could wait.

A breeze caught Ivy's long skirt, playfully tossing the hem around strong, trim calves. And that brought Clifford right back around in her mind again. It was those legs which had lured him out to that desolate spot in the first place. It had been so easy, as they always were. Ivy would have let him go—tried to reason with herself early on that there must be some good in him somewhere for Patricia to have married such a beast in the first place. But Patricia's latest busted lip, poorly concealed by a childlike application of tan makeup and lipstick, sealed ole Clifford's fate. It's not like Ivy didn't give him a fighting chance. She always gave the condemned an opportunity to repent, a moment to reflect and see the ill of their ways. It was the Christian thing to do. But Clifford did none of those things; he ridiculed Ivy instead. The man brought it on himself really.

"What's this?" Ivy stopped abruptly, her attention snatched back to the present. She breathed deeply, the dust from the road redolent with dandelion, and something else. That smell, so familiar. It was the scent of something near death.

Ivy turned a slow circle, inhaling the late spring air and listening. Eyes and ears, sharply focused, swept the valley, the rhododendron thickets, the tops of bristle-brushed hemlocks lording over an understory of mountain laurel. But the effort was overdone. Ivy dropped her gaze to the roadside. A furry gray mound lay in the ditch not five feet from where she stood. It looked dead, but Ivy could hear the slightest gurgling breath.

She approached the animal cautiously. Sometimes her presence startled small things. The combination of human and—the other—confused and frightened them. Ivy bunched her skirt between taut thighs, then, dropping to all fours, she crawled to the roadside.

It was a mutt of some kind, and a mangy one at that. Another mangy mutt. Ivy sighed. They always were, to some degree. Her house was overrun with them already—strays and the injured, like this one, that she'd scraped from the road during the course of her travels across America. It was getting difficult, moving from location to location with a growing entourage of pets. The world was getting decidedly more pet unfriendly, and it was hard to hole out a place for oneself anywhere when the application read "Single woman, no children, seven dogs." And counting. If she took this lost soul home, her pack would total eight. But this was her house now, not a rental. That settled it.

"My pack." Ivy smiled slightly, amused at her own joke. She put her hand on the dog's matted side, his skin raw and prickly from the sores. He raised his pitiful head and whined.

"You're all right now, little fella. Ivy's found you, and everything will be just fine." Ivy ripped off the lower half of her billowy skirt and gently slid it under the dog like a sling. The dog did not resist when she cradled him.

A car pulled up alongside just as Ivy slid on her shoes and began walking again.

"Hello, Miss Cole."

Ivy turned to the pleasantly deep voice. Then it dawned on her whom it belonged to.

"Hello, Officer. Didn't I see you at the Hughes house just this morning?"

"Yes, ma'am. I'm patrolling the area. I saw you walking." It was Deputy Sanders, driving slow with the windows down.

"That's right. I'm walking." And she kept walking. This was no time for an inquisition. She was sore enough at the Doe Springs police, and keeping it in might be a problem if he insisted on conversation.

"Ma'am, I don't think, after what happened last night, that you should be out here on a back road walking alone." Deputy Sanders kept pace with the woman and her bundled package. A gentle cologne drifted out of the patrol car and mingled with the sweet smells of the valley. Ivy sorted the scents until it came to her: The officer smelled like fresh laundry on a summer breeze.

Ivy stopped walking and faced the window. Her ripped skirt, alarmingly short, dragged the deputy's eyes south against their will. He hit the brake, sending dust swirling around them and into the car.

"Deputy Sanders, how old are you?"

"Uh, I'm twenty-eight, ma'am."

"First of all, then, you can quit calling me ma'am. I'm only three years older than you. Secondly, do you see what I've got here?" Ivy leaned against the door and folded the makeshift blanket back.

"It's a dog?"

"Yes, Deputy, and he's sick with mange and possibly run over too. Why don't you run along and scare some other poor women to death with ghost stories. I've got work to do."

Deputy Sanders pursed his lips. He'd intended to give Miss Cole a ride, not aggravate her. The woman was walking again. He pressed on the gas and crept along beside her. "Miss Cole, I regret having to give news like that, but hiding the truth from Patricia Hughes wouldn't do her a bit of good. Our newspapers may not be all big city like from where you come from, but that makes it worse. A dead body to a small-town reporter is like possum to a coonhound. There's no calling them off till they get the last scrap. Folks need to know what's going on around here so they can look out for themselves. Do you understand that?"

Ivy didn't slow down, but he'd piqued her interest. "How do you know I'm from the city?"

"We local yokels know a thing or two." Deputy Sanders didn't smile, but Ivy could tell he wanted to.

"Well, you don't know everything. Just because I lived out from under the shadow of the Confederacy for a while doesn't make me an outsider. I know how things work down here. And I also know how the rumormongers twist up a tale to make it bigger than the facts themselves. It wouldn't kill you to keep at least a few of the gories to yourself."

Deputy Sanders chewed on that without comment. He drove alongside Ivy but decided to leave her alone otherwise. She stared straight ahead and tried to pretend the police car was not cruising beside her like an old faithful dog.

After five minutes of listening to tires crunching on gravel, Ivy's patience gave out. Her arms were giving out too. The fifteen pounds clutched to her chest were starting to feel more like thirty. Ivy wheeled around and yelled over the car hood. "For crying out loud, are you going to follow me like this all the way home?"

Deputy Sanders, dark eyewear and stoic expression in place, nodded. "Yes, ma'am. If I have to."

"Fine. Since I'm in an awful lot of danger out here wandering about this deserted road, why don't you give me a ride to Dr. Hill's office?"

"Yes, ma—yes, Miss Cole. I'd be glad to."

Chapter 3

Doc Hill scratched the terrier mix behind the ears. "He's a scrapper, this one." The vet went to the sink and scrubbed his hands. The stray had just enjoyed a medicated bath and was now drip-drying on a fluffy towel. Ivy took another towel and began rubbing the dog gently.

"I don't know what I'd do without you, Doc. You're a life-saver, over and over," Ivy said, as the little terrier peeked from the rolling folds of terry cloth.

How many times had Ivy stood here in this very spot with one dog or another, watching Doc give vaccinations, remove stitches from a neutering, administer a heartworm check? When Ivy first rolled into town after that long haul from California, finding a veterinarian had been priority number one. She'd picked up Hansel the golden retriever (finally, a companion to complete Ivy's dachshund, Gretel) en route. With six dogs already cramming the back of the aging minivan, Ivy knew it was a risky endeavor to introduce this happy-go-lucky bundle of energy with hundreds of miles left to go. But she couldn't just drive away and leave the golden bounding up the median between I-40 and snapping at butterflies. How he made it across the first stretch of seventy-five-mile-an-hour traffic was a mystery anyway, but Ivy seriously doubted he'd make it back across unscathed. She pulled over, the aging van dragging a groaning U-Haul behind it, and chased the dog down. Ignoring the honks and hoots whizzing by just feet away, Hansel and Ivy played a ten-minute game of tag before the dog finally came to her. She hoisted the sixty pounds of vigor into the passenger seat, unsettling Aufhocker, the only member of Ivy's family who'd been with her since her teenage years in New York and was not a stray. The chaos following the new arrival's introduction warped Ivy's nerves to such a degree, she debated setting the dog back out herself. But the Great Smoky Mountains put an end to the retriever's rowdiness—between the Tennessee border and Asheville, North Carolina, butterflies churned up with grass in a vile yellow mucous that sprayed the front seat of Ivy's van, along with a good splattering across the dashboard and the driver's right arm. Dripping but fighting not to be mad, Ivy pulled over to the first gas station coming into Doe Springs to clean up. Dr. Jacob Hill stood across from the frazzled woman at the pump station, filling his own minivan with super unleaded.

"If I'm a lifesaver, you're an angel," Doc Hill said, standing beside Ivy once more. His girth crowded the space between examination table and wall, nudging Ivy slightly to the side. The vet's neatly trimmed beard and snow-capped forehead reminded Ivy of her first Christmas in Germany, when Uncle Stefan dressed as Saint Nick.

"There are some blessed dogs in this world because of you, Ivy. You're up to, what, eight now?"

"Yep. I guess I should be thinking of a name. I've run out of creative ones. Maybe just a simple Rex would do. How would that be, boy?" The dog reached up and licked Ivy's chin.

Doc Hill laughed, a deep resonance from his considerable belly that rang like a church bell. "Then Simple Rex it must be."

Ivy lifted the terrier from the examination table and set him on the floor. The vet tech, Doc Hill's seventeen-year-old daughter, Bonnie, had fashioned Rex a leash from hair ribbons to use till they got home.

"Thank goodness he wasn't hit by a car," Ivy said.

"That's true, but he's still got a long ways to go. Malnourished, wormy—and that's the worst case of mange I've ever seen." Doc Hill put a hand on Ivy's shoulder. "Now you go on out through the kitchen with him. Betty will have his medications ready for you, and grab some of her cookies before you go. I think she made chocolate chip today."

Since Doc's closing of the practice in town and continuance in the comfort of home, Mrs. Hill busied herself with baking nonstop for all the patients who walked through the door, human and canine alike. It was having a good effect on her husband. The burden of eating the homemade confections now fell on multiple shoulders instead of the good doctor's alone. He'd dropped thirty pounds since Ivy was last in with The Duchess (a feisty basset-beagle conglomeration) for an ear infection four months ago. Another fifty pounds and they could all quit worrying about such nonsense as strokes and heart attacks.

Bonnie came back in the room, hands on her hips. "The Parsons are here again. Mrs. Parson is in the laundry room. Oh, I mean, the *waiting room*." The girl rolled her eyes and walked back out.

Doc Hill frowned. "Let me see what Mildred wants this time. I think we're finished up here, Ivy, but call me if his skin's not showing signs of clearing in a week or two."

Ivy and her new companion walked down the wallpapered hallway, escorted by family portraits spanning three generations of Hills. Smiling faces and grinning animals adorned the walls on either side, crowding the passageway with a motley assemblage of relatives, pets, friends, and four-legged patients, Ivy and her black shepherd Aufhocker among them.

Ivy emerged from the parade into a country-blue-and-white kitchen. She'd smelled cookies long before Doc mentioned them, but he was wrong—they were peanut butter, not chocolate chip, and Ivy's favorite. She'd had no intention of leaving without one or three.

Betty stood by the stove, a pileworn oven mitt in one hand and a bag labeled "Rex" in the other. Silver hair wound up into a perfect bun high on Betty's head. Clear gray eyes matched the platinum in her hair and sparkled with kindness. "Come on in, dear. Let's see the latest family member."

Rex came around the counter, his skin even less appealing against the spotless white linoleum. Betty took off the oven mitt and knelt eye level to the dog. "Scrawny fellow." She gave him a hug, then sighed. "I've been reminding my husband for ages that he's retired, but what can I do? These little guys need him more than the golf course, I suppose."

With a final pat, Betty stood up and offered Ivy a plate of golden-brown perfection, still warm.

"Peanut butter—my favorite!" Ivy munched on a cookie while Betty wrapped a couple more in a napkin for her. Ivy put them in her skirt pocket. The shards of clock rattled, reminding her of an evening date with Patricia.

"And for you." Betty gave Rex a homemade doggie biscuit that looked better than the cookies.

"I need to get on home now. I promised I'd go check on Patricia Hughes this evening," Ivy said around crumbs.

Betty's sunny smile suddenly inverted itself, followed by a knot of worried wrinkles on her brow. The tight bun capping Betty's head jerked forward a fraction. "It is true what they're saying? The Devil of Doe Springs again? It's all over the local news today."

"The Devil of Doe Springs?" Ivy shook her head. "We've gone from cursed to being possessed by the devil. I swear, Betty, the media will have us carrying garlic and staring into crystal balls before this is all over with."

"But four human attacks so far, plus what happened to Angus Shepherd's cows recently—and all the animal attacks before then . . . " Betty wrung the last bit of life out of the ragged oven mitt.

"We live in the mountains, Betty. Things like this happen in the wild every day. Just so happens now it's happening here too. It's nothing more than a mountain lion or a bear, mark my words."

"That's what the news was saying. Doesn't make us feel any better, though. We're keeping all of our animals in the barn at night and the kennel outside locked up too. But it's not the what of it that's giving this town the jitters, Ivy, it's the when. Don't you find it odd?"

"The full moon thing?" Ivy lit into another cookie and chewed as if she were thinking real hard about it all. "How can the police be entirely sure about that? They're finding these people after the fact. An estimate is a guesstimate, and both of those can be wrong."

"But not last night. How is poor Patricia? I'm going over there tomorrow with some food."

"She's . . . inconsolable. Her family is coming in tonight to stay with her. They've got a long drive, all the way from Alabama."

"That's good to hear. That sweet girl is all alone now, although being with Clifford was no . . . " Betty cut the disrespectful thought. "Anyway, I'm about afraid to leave my front porch. You need to watch yourself, Ivy, out there in the country all by yourself."

"I'm far from alone." Ivy looked down at Rex. He wagged his inflamed tail. "I've got eight guardian angels watching my back. No devil will be sneaking up on us."

"Even so, you be careful. Doc thinks a whole lot of you, you know. We all do. Oh! Your blanket."

Betty left the kitchen and came back carrying the rest of Ivy's skirt. "I don't suppose you can reattach this?" she asked, eyeing the remnants Ivy still wore.

"No, I think this skirt is done for. It'll make a fine rag." Ivy took the fabric and Rex's bag of medications. Before leaving the kitchen, she turned back to the older woman.

"Betty?"

"Yes, dear?"

"No devil would ever harm you or your family. I've just got a feeling about that."

Betty smiled. "I hope you're right, dear. I hope you're right."

Ivy and Rex stood on the Hills' front porch. The sun was going down and Ivy still needed to get back to Patricia. Where had the day gone?

Deputy Sanders pulled up in his patrol car just as she made it to the bottom of the steps. "I've come to give you a ride home, Miss Cole. You said it would be about thirty minutes," the deputy explained. He'd removed the dark sunshades, and his eyes peered at Ivy through mesmerizing denim blue.

Ivy contemplated her choices: Walk home, a good five miles now, carrying Simple Rex; bum a ride from Bonnie, the seventeen-year-old blonde with an attitude; or endure a brief trip through the country with Doe Springs's finest. Ivy's anger of the morning melted into fatigue. The exploits of the previous night were catching up, and suddenly the latter option seemed the handsomest of the choices, in more ways than one.

"Deputy, you are a knight in shining armor today," Ivy said. "I could use a ride. If you don't mind, you can drop me out at Patricia's. I need to get my van anyway. Thank you so much."

"It's my job, ma'am." The deputy's cheeks pinked slightly, and he turned his head.

Ivy expected an "aw, shucks" that never came. "Can you give me one minute? I forgot something."

"I'll wait right here."

Loud voices had drawn Ivy's attention. They'd started the moment Deputy Sanders's car pulled up, then lowered to whispers. Ivy could hear in Doc's tone that something was wrong.

Ivy walked quietly through the garage and stood in the laundry/waiting room. Doc's office lay just beyond it. Rex, mimicking Ivy's stealth, was soundless, but the irritated voices wilted his tufted ears, and his tail tucked deep into his tummy.

"I should call the SPCA," Doc Hill said angrily. "This is the third time this cat has come in with suspicious injuries."

"I told you what happened," a woman's voice snapped.

Ivy pushed the swinging laundry door slightly. The sliver of view showed Mildred Parson in a fuchsia windsuit, one long-nailed finger pointing evenly at the Doc's chest, the other manicured hand wrapped around an empty pet carrier. A gawky boy, about eleven, stood beside her. His lips protruded from freckle-stamped cheeks, and a cow-licked shock of red hair loomed over his forehead like a rooster's comb.

"Yeah, she told you what happened. Are you deaf?" he said.

Doc Hill ignored the child. "These are burns, Mildred. They look like cigarette burns. I'm not buying your excuses anymore. I can walk outside to Deputy Sanders right now—"

"You wouldn't dare."

"—or I can keep this cat. It's up to you."

"You can't keep my cat, you crazy old coot!" Jeffrey screamed.

"That's enough out of you, young man." Doc Hill's quiet whisper mushroomed to just south of a yell. "Go wait outside while I finish talking to your mother."

Ivy let the laundry room door slip quietly shut. She had never heard Doc raise his voice before, had never been aware he was capable. Jeffrey huffed into the garage, his face twisted up as if getting ready to cry. Ivy moved from the shadows and caught the boy's arm as he passed.

Jeffrey squealed and tried to jerk away, but Ivy held fast. "Hello, little boy. Jeffrey, is it?"

"Yeah, that's right. Who are you?" A spit bubble formed underneath the boy's pouty lower lip.

"I'm a concerned friend, Jeffrey, terribly concerned. I heard what happened in there. Heavens, that's a lot of fuss over a cat. Is everything all right?"

"No, it ain't all right. Now lemme go." Jeffrey jerked his arm but Ivy held fast. The boy stood there, looking up at her. "What do you care?"

"Well, I overheard some things by accident. Pretty mean of that old vet to threaten your mother and want to keep your cat like that, wasn't it?"

Jeffrey wiped his mouth with the sleeve of his free arm. "Yeah. He's a . . . " The boy's face screwed up, "a asshole!"

Ivy chuckled. "Yes, somebody like that certainly would be, wouldn't they? Who does he think he is, trying to tell you what to do with your own cat. It's your property after all, right? I mean, look at Rex here."

Jeffrey looked at the pitiful dog. "Tabby's my cat. I can do what I want."

Ivy knelt down eye level to the boy. She smiled. "So tell me, Jeffrey, what really happened to that bad ole kitty cat anyway?"

Jeffrey looked about the garage, up at the ceiling, down at his feet, anywhere but Ivy. "Nothin' . . . it was an accident. Just like Mom said."

Ivy shook her head. "Ah, now come on. You can tell me. I promise I won't tell another soul. Especially not him." Ivy jerked her head toward the vet's office; she could still hear the animated prattle of Mrs. Parson defending the cat's wounds.

"It wasn't me," Jeffrey said softly.

"What's that? I didn't hear you." Ivy's fingers clamped tighter on the boy's fleshy arm. His skin emanated cola and chocolate. Would he taste as sweet?

"It was my stepfather. He doesn't like the cat. It climbs on his things and sheds on his clothes."

"Did your stepfather hurt the cat, Jeffrey?"

Jeffrey was lost in the layout of the garage again, his eyes roving everywhere but into the face of the woman who was questioning him.

"Did your stepfather burn the cat, like the doc said?"

Jeffrey snatched his arm out of Ivy's grasp, and she let him have it. But he didn't run. He stood there, looking around, seeing nothing, avoiding her. Finally, his gaze landed on the toe of his worn-out tennis shoe and stayed put.

"Yes," he said quietly.

"With what, Jeffrey? How did he hurt the cat?"

"Cigarettes. It was cigarettes . . . this time." Jeffrey said it with the dusty sigh of an old man, an old man relieved to be rid of an even older secret. "He hates the cat. He hates all of us. But I hate him more."

Ivy sighed herself. The sullen, arrogant boy was gone. A lonely, confused child stood before her.

"Have you ever hurt the cat, Jeffrey? Answer me honestly. I'm sure your mother taught you not to lie."

Jeffrey shuffled his feet.

"One time. I kicked her, really hard. Frank was yelling and yelling and I went to my room and the cat . . . I didn't mean to hurt her."

Ivy took Jeffrey's arm again and drew him close. A predator stirred in her belly, but its focus had shifted. "I believe that, Jeffrey. I truly do. Does your stepfather ever hurt you or your mom?"

Jeffrey squinted at Ivy, the makings of a lie struggling with the cold hard truth. The cold hard truth, as it turned out, was a relief. "He doesn't hit us or nothing. He just yells. A lot. And then he leaves, which is the best part. But he always comes back. If he did hit us, maybe Mom would leave him. But he only takes it out on Tabby." Jeffrey shrugged, a sad waffling of the shoulders that was more hopelessness than indifference.

"Your stepfather—his name is Frank Parson?"

Jeffrey nodded. Ivy drew the boy closer still, till their noses almost touched.

"Jeffrey, I want you to listen to me very carefully, do you understand?" She tightened her grip. "You will not hurt any more animals ever again. You will love them and protect them because they are helpless, the same way you feel helpless when your stepfather is mean. Bad things—very bad things,

Jeffrey—happen to little boys who hurt animals. And I don't want anything bad to happen to such a good boy as you."

Ivy's breath blew hot on the child's face; her usually green eyes glittered bright orange into his. Jeffrey's own eyes grew wide and his mouth dropped open. A tinny squeak escaped him.

Ivy let the Parson boy go, and he dashed out of the garage. A few moments later, Mildred Parson strode out, catless.

Chapter 4

Dear Journal,

This pen sits heavy in my hand tonight. I had no sooner crawled into bed, a long night of business attended to, when the phone rang. It was Patricia. Some hunter has stumbled across Clifford already. The sheriff's office is stirred up again, and the media are dubbing our "menace" the Devil of Doe Springs. I am not flattered.

But I was sloppy, careless. Clifford should have been chalked up as another runaway no-account. After weeks in the woods, what little remained would have been swept under Mother Nature's carpet. Moss and insects could claim the scraps I left behind.

Maybe, deep down, I wanted him quickly found. I don't know. But a point needed to be made. What good is justice if no one can witness it? Like the thief who took off through that cornfield with a pillowcase full of my mother's things: the silver platter, the mantel clock . . . How lucky he must have felt to discover an empty, unlocked house in the middle of the night. It saddens me to have taken one so young— never would I have pursued him for money. But Mama's things . . . so little I have to remember her by.

*So Patricia knows she is widowed and not simply aban-
doned. I left her eating tonight, a good sign. She will be fine.
She will be better. Hopefully, my dear friend can sleep well
knowing that her nightmares are over. Perhaps, past the
grief and the guilt, there is a crocodile smile filled with the
teeth of revenge: Patricia has the knowledge the bastard got
just what he deserved.*

*On another note, a newcomer has joined my growing
family: Rex (or Simple Rex, per Doc), the terrier mix. I drug
him out of a ditch, and now he's sleeping peacefully at my
feet. Something Betty said to me when I took the sick little
dog in—Angus Shepherd's cows. Mauled, like the other animals? Somehow I missed this bit of news. All these animal
attacks are disturbing me. I truly want to believe it's a mountain lion. I tell it enough to other people, hoping to convince
myself. But there is a niggling fear in the pit of my gut that it
is not. Is it possible there is another in my town and I have
overlooked him?*

*I will call my new good friend Deputy Sanders tomorrow
to glean some details. Deputy Sanders, hmmm. A deliciously
handsome young man. But it is Frank Parson who is food for
thought. A bad husband, a worse stepfather, and an animal
abuser to top it all. I see by the calendar, Moon, you are full
June 22.*

Ivy pulled up a floorboard underneath her braided bedroom
rug and slipped the fat, dog-eared journal into the hole. Rex
padded over and peered inside.

"It's my entire life in this hole, Rex. Every important
memory, every significant event. And no one to share it with
but you guys. Speaking of which, I'll let you meet the rest of
the gang when your skin's cleared up. There are going to be
some mighty long faces tonight when only you get to share
the bedroom." Ivy patted the dog's head.

Rex's tail thudded on the hardwood, an almost human
smile of delight on his face. He was not accustomed to feeling
this special. He'd been a throwaway dog his whole short life.

Ivy moved to replace the floorboard when a glint of gold

and silver drew her eye back into the hole. She pulled the jewelry out to examine it. Red flecks speckled the chain and rings. Ivy tsk'ed at her neglectfulness, but then, she'd never taken souvenirs before.

The woman carried the items to the bathroom and ran them under the faucet. With the blood washed away, the jewelry gleamed. Two rings. A gold chain. Ivy studied the biker ring and dismissed it. The gold chain too. But the wedding band . . . Ivy held it to the bathroom light, and remembered the mark that ring had left on Patricia's life, remembered the night Clifford Hughes lost his . . .

They met at the Laundromat. Having just moved into her new home, Ivy had yet to purchase a washer and dryer. She traveled light when she moved *(ran),* and household items too heavy to carry in her arms felt more akin to anvils than necessities. She'd spent twelve years traveling from one place to another with no more baggage than personal effects and a growing entourage of dogs. Laundromats had simply become an extension of home. Ivy could settle down in a quiet corner and while away a whole afternoon, doing no more than listening to the rinse cycle and observing human behavior up close and personal.

But perhaps it was time to make the leap. She was a home-owner now—isn't that what homeowners did? Buy things like washers and dryers and lawnmowers? Ivy was pondering this exciting notion when a young woman struggled through the door, laundry piled so high it obscured her face. She fumbled with the knob, then jammed a hip against the cheap metal screen, all the while balancing the impossible load.

Ivy watched the scene over the top of an old issue of *Southern Living* she'd found lying in a chair, ironically flipped to an ad for Maytags.

"Do you need some help?" Ivy asked, as the top third of the clothes tumbled to the floor.

She leaped up to grab the basket before the rest of the laundry followed the first. Laughing, she and the girl wrestled it to the counter.

"Whew! Thanks a lot. What a mess." The girl went back to the door and scooped up the rest of the fallen garments. Ivy bent to help her.

"Hi, I'm Ivy Cole. I just moved here." She stuck out her hand, but the girl stayed bent over the pile on the floor, her long brown hair hanging in her face.

"It's nice to meet you. Thanks again," the girl said. She grabbed the socks the other woman had collected, then walked back to the counter and busied herself sorting.

"Here, you dropped this too." Ivy was beside the girl again, holding out a change purse. "Can't do much laundry without that."

No response. Dirty boxers turned over and over in the girl's hands as if manually wringing them prewash might help. Ivy glanced at the nervous fingers at work while trying to see through the thick bangs shielding the lowered head. "I'll just lay this right here. Nice to meet you." She set the purse on the washer and turned back to *Southern Living,* where visions of sparkling Maytags awaited.

"I'm Patricia," the girl suddenly said. She lifted her chin and bangs parted over a bantam-egg-sized bruise that had healed from purple to sallow. The girl smiled shyly, as Ivy's own smile faltered.

"I'm Patricia Hughes," the girl said again, sticking out her hand. And a friendship was born.

Ivy watched the bruises travel all over her young friend's body for a year. But no amount of pleading or common sense could persuade the girl to leave.

"Marriage, till death do us part, Ivy," Patricia told her once.

Ivy had smiled. That's all she needed to hear.

A year after Patricia Hughes met a pleasant blond woman in the town Laundromat, Clifford Hughes was on his way to meet the same woman at her home. The message on Clifford's desk last week requesting a late delivery got a loud "go to hell"—till he saw the name scribbled at the bottom of the note. Then he'd waited days for that package to arrive so he could deliver it personally. Not that anybody else would do it; he was Doe Springs's only deliveryman after all. But just in case somebody decided to be extra nice in the P.O. and save him a late trip out to the Cole house on their way home, he'd pocketed the note and gone through the packages as soon as he got to work each day to make sure he grabbed it before somebody else could.

And today, that package arrived.

Clifford whistled as he flipped the latch on the picket fence and made his way across the cobblestones to the front door. Violets and geraniums strained inward over the porch steps to grasp at his ankles, while bleeding hearts, with magenta blooms the size of quarters, dripped over their potted confines to tickle the big man's forehead as he passed underneath. Brushing plants aside, Clifford made his way to the door. This mellowing two-story cottage buried in a jungle of spring flowers might be his last delivery, but he was in no particular hurry. None a'tall. With any luck, he'd catch a glimpse of the good-looking lady who lived here. Ivy. His wife's best friend.

Clifford rang the doorbell and a chorus of angry barking greeted him from inside.

"Damn dogs. No wonder she's still single," he muttered. The man shifted the light box to the other arm and prepared to knock, when a voice called to him from behind the house.

"Hello! Hello—I'm out here."

Clifford, still whistling, stepped off the porch and walked around back. The woman was kneeling in a deep cluster of lilies alongside the dog fence, her back to him. Torn-off blue jean shorts rode high on each cheek facing Clifford, and the whistle momentarily caught in his throat. He coughed to clear it, and Ivy turned with a bright smile.

"Evening, Clifford. I see you've brought me something." Ivy peeled off her gardening gloves and wiped a tendril of long gold hair from her face. She'd left it down purposely this evening. A faded pink-checkered shirt was tied halter-style at the woman's waist, a flat belly button winking just below the knot.

"Uh, yeah. Here ya go," Clifford said.

Ivy took the box full of newspapers she'd mailed to herself a few days ago and signed at the bottom of Clifford's clipboard. The burly man pretended to study the signature, stalling for time and another stab at conversation. Ivy saved him the trouble of both. "Thanks a bunch for delivering this after hours," she said. "I hate to put you to the trouble."

"Well, that's okay. I am off the clock, though. Wouldn't have done it if you weren't such good friends with Patricia and all."

"I owe you one, Clifford, I really do. Hey, I bet you could use a drink. I know I sure could. Working out here in these flowers all afternoon has wrung every bit of water right out of me. I've got some fresh lemonade in the icebox." Ivy cocked an eyebrow and let the last sentence linger between question and suggestion.

Clifford pretended to check his watch. "I guess I've got a minute. It's sure hot enough. Too hot on this mountain for May." The man punctuated the comment by wiping his forehead with the sleeve of his post office uniform. Sweaty patches reeked from the armpits of the starched shirt, and Ivy bit her tongue to keep the gag held at the bottom of her throat. A nose such as hers could not handle the likes of Clifford Hughes in this close proximity. But maybe it was more psychological than anything—evil had its own mental stench, and looking upon those brutish fists, it was Patricia's pretty face Ivy saw exploding at the end of them.

"I'll get some glasses!" Ivy said. The words squeaked out sudden and shrill, rising too quickly from behind images she needed to keep buried if the farce were to continue. Clifford didn't seem to notice, and Ivy quickly brushed by him, leaving the scent of lilies in her wake. Clifford swiveled his head on the trail of springtime perfume and followed it back to the front porch.

"I'd invite you in, Clifford, but it would cause quite a ruckus. My babies aren't used to strangers, and we don't have much company." The dogs had started howling again the minute Clifford approached the porch. Ivy disappeared into the house with her delivery, and the dogs went immediately quiet. A moment later, she came out with two mismatched glasses and a frosty pitcher of lemonade.

"I just made this, this morning. It's your lucky day," Ivy said.

Clifford eyed the woman up and down. "It certainly is."

They shared a seat on the porch swing and sipped the drinks. Beads of condensation dripped from Ivy's glass and trailed down a bronzed leg. Clifford watched the droplets, and Ivy marveled that he was too primitive to even disguise it.

Clifford looked up from his hard study of Ivy's thigh. "Must be a pretty important package for you to need me to come out here after work and all."

"Oh, it is, Cliff—can I call you Cliff? Or is that only reserved for Patricia?"

"Call me anything you want. She don't hold a patent on my name."

Ivy laughed. "Right. Anyway, I knew when I left that note for you, you wouldn't let me down. Patricia says all the time how dependable you are."

"She does?"

"Yep." Ivy sipped her drink, but the lemons had gone sour on her tongue. She forced the conversation on. "So, where are you off to after you leave here? I'd hate to be keeping *you* from something important."

"Only my supper, but Patricia will wait. She's used to me coming in at different times. Sometimes these deliveries take me clear across the county." Clifford debated trying to impress this little snip of a gal with the daily exploits of a deliveryman, but realized his effort would fall short. He changed the subject instead. "You know, you don't come out to the house like you used to. And you hardly speak when you do. I was starting to think you didn't like me."

"Oh, be serious." Ivy swatted his arm. "You've got that entirely wrong." *Dislike is too mild a word, you defective excuse for a human being.* "I just don't like to step on toes is all."

"What do you mean?" Clifford didn't really care. Ivy's

thigh rested against his, and the swaying of the porch swing was creating friction.

"You know. Something being taken the wrong way—a look, or something somebody says. Wives can be pretty jealous over their husbands, especially the really handsome ones. I learned a long time ago to tread lightly on another woman's territory."

Clifford puffed up at the compliment. He set the lemonade glass on the porch rail and stretched his arms overhead. Muscles flexed and bunched under the brown postal shirt, reminding Ivy of the wrestlers on television, posturing for the camera.

"Well, looks like I'm in your territory now," Clifford said. He looked at Ivy, who was staring at her lap, a cute little embarrassed smile on her face. He relaxed his arms, considered draping one around her shoulders, but went for the lemonade glass again instead.

"I never knew you noticed anything about me," he continued. "Most the time when you're at the house and I come through, you and Pat got your noses buried in some book or craft project. Patricia drives me nuts with her stupid hobbies. But don't worry about Pat. She knows better than to say squat to me about anything."

"What do you mean?"

"I don't mean nothing, other than I can take care of my own wife." Clifford downed the rest of the lemonade. Ice rattled in the empty glass and Ivy offered him more.

"No thanks. I'm done—with the lemonade." Clifford looked at Ivy to gauge her response. She'd been sending signals the moment he got here. The clothes, the lemonade, the important package that just had to be delivered after hours. Hell, the woman didn't even have a real job, why was after hours such a big damn deal?

But now he knew. He could read 'em, all right. From the first moment Ivy set foot in his house, he'd felt something off her—a vibe, an energy, something—that hit him hard and stayed with him all this time. He'd just never been able to pin down the draw. Looks like it was his lucky day, no joke: Clifford found out the draw was mutual.

The deliveryman looked down at his wife's best friend. Emerald eyes gleamed up at him from underneath dark lashes. The hue shifted for an instant. Clifford blinked.

"Something wrong?" Ivy asked.

"This late sun, it's messing with my vision." Clifford wiped his eyes.

Ivy nodded. "Yes, it is starting to get late. . . ."

She took a deep breath to gather herself. Then she lifted her hand and slowly, deliberately, placed it on the man's knee. "Cliff, if you don't have to rush off just yet, would you like to take a sunset walk with me? There is a beautiful spot not far from here and there's something . . . amazing . . . I want to show you."

Clifford Hughes gazed at the hand on his knee, followed it up the slender arm to the curve where her delicate neck disappeared into the open V of the pink shirt, and beyond it still to the softly beating pulse in her throat and the chin tilted upward toward his face. He held a beefy arm out in front of him. "After you, little lady."

The woods closed around them, and Clifford was starting to wheeze. Soft loam seeped around his heavy feet, sucking them into the ground and tugging at his heels with each step. Branches picked at his hair and smacked his shins as he tracked behind Ivy, who bounced along the path as if at the county park. This was not what he'd had in mind for a sunset stroll. "How much farther? I thought you said a little walk, not a freakin' hike."

Ivy didn't answer. She flitted ahead of him, yellow hair swishing back and forth with her bobbing head. Clifford thought she might be singing to herself.

"Dammit!" A mosquito squared off with him, perching obnoxiously on the end of his nose. Clifford swatted at it, then went after the gnats that'd discovered the sweaty patches puddling outward from his armpits toward his back and chest. What's worse, he smelled himself, an annoying development, considering the circumstances. Jesus Christ, couldn't they have just used her bedroom? She could have put the dogs outside for thirty minutes, it wouldn't have killed 'em. Now he stank and his hair swooped and dived across his forehead like fighting barn swallows. The clammy hands continually running through to straighten it only worsened the mess. To hell with it. If this was her idea of seduction, she'd get what she asked for. Some women liked a little grime on a man. Pansy office types were not this broad's cup of tea, otherwise he sure wouldn't be here.

Ivy continued on, ignoring the grunts and crashing of the man behind her. She practically skipped, she felt so alive. "We're almost there," she called back. "Just a bit longer."

The forest finally opened up to a small glade severed by a stream. Evening was falling into night, and the forest tuned up to greet it. All around the odd couple, crickets whirred on fiddlers' legs, and frogs croaked from the creekside. Amid the night play, Ivy twirled around and around, her laughter floating over the trees.

Clifford leaned against a poplar and fought the urge to bend double. He'd thought himself in shape, but apparently thick arms alone meant nothing in the way of athleticism. Breath whistled raw in his throat, as the emerging cool night air replaced the warmth from the setting sun, and the shirt clinging to his back was a chilly second skin. Clifford stared at Ivy. "Woman, have you lost your mind?"

"I assure you, I am quite sane, Clifford Hughes." Ivy stopped her playful dance and stood in the middle of the glade. Man and woman faced one another across a silence of assumption. Clifford pushed away from the tree. It was time to get down to business.

Ivy moved first. She walked to him, her eyes pinning his in a look he could not fathom in the dwindled light. Ivy stood before her best friend's husband and took both of his large hands in hers. She pulled him to the center of the clearing.

Clifford stood there, facing Ivy, holding her dainty hands in his calloused ones, and waiting. A minute passed and nothing. He released Ivy's hands and reached to touch the gold hair, but she ducked away.

"What did you bring me out here to see, Ivy?" Clifford reached for her again but she sidestepped him.

"In time, Clifford, in time. I just need to ask you a few questions first."

"Questions?" Again he reached out and she avoided him.

"Yes. They're easy questions and all you have to do is answer them honestly. I don't like to be lied to." ·

"I'll tell you whatever you want to know. Just come here first." Clifford lunged forward, but Ivy darted easily away. She remained at arm's length, a teasing smile on her face.

Clifford put his hands on his hips. He was too old and too tired to play games in the middle of the woods. "What is this? Look, I said I'm not in a rush, but I ain't got all night neither." *Let's get on with it.*

"Do you want your surprise or not, Cliff?"

"Yeah, but—"

"Then shut up and listen."

Clifford's spine snapped straight. "I don't like your—"

"Question one: Why does Patricia have so many bruises every time I see her?"

"What?" Clifford's brows dipped to hood his eyes.

"Black eyes, broken fingers . . . Tell me why."

Clifford wasn't sure he was hearing right. "You're asking me about Patricia? Hey, I didn't just hike fifty miles to the middle of nowhere to talk about her. I don't know what kind of kooky game you're cooking up here, but I'd rather just skip all the chitchat. Why don't you come on over here and let's forget about talking for a minute."

Ivy sighed. "I want to know what's wrong with your wife, Clifford."

"You're just bent on talking about my wife, huh? Okay, fine." Clifford rubbed his chin and shook his head. "What's wrong with Patricia. Let's see, I've been trying to figure that one out from the first day I married her. But no matter how hard I try, Ivy, fixing Patricia just doesn't seem to be within my capabilities. Ah, well, what can you do?" He shrugged and grinned at the same time. "You know, you're a beautiful woman, Ivy Cole. I never could quite get what a piece of work like you would see in a mouse like Pat. Then I s'posed maybe you hung around 'cause you felt sorry for her, her being all timid and, well, let's face it, she ain't the sharpest knife in the drawer. But now I know what's really going on. It's all right—you can drop the good-friend act. I'm not going to tell Patricia a damned thing, and you two can go on putting together your little needlepoint kits and chumming it up just like always. I know a thing or two about discretion, and this ole boy don't kiss and tell. So relax."

Ivy half-cocked a smile of her own. "Why, Cliff, looks like you've got it all figured out. You are the smart one. I can certainly see what Patricia has seen in you all these years. There's no mistaking that. Unfortunately, she just hasn't figured out how to get away from it yet. I'm going to help her on that one."

Clifford stopped grinning. Ivy's words ran around like riddles, but he thought he sniffed a threat. Or an offer, he couldn't decide. "You want to tell me what this is all about, lady? My patience is wearing thin, and you won't like me near as much when my patience wears thin."

"I don't want to test your patience. I just want some simple answers to some simple questions. Can't you humor me? Then I'll show you your big surprise. You haven't forgotten why we came out here, have you?"

"I'm not sure what I'm doing here now. Why don't you remind me?" Clifford grabbed for Ivy again, but only air closed in his fists. Anger rippled across the man's face in a quick, contorted wave. He pushed it down inside himself, but it sat there, roiling in the pit of his stomach.

"One more time, Cliff—how does Patricia get all those bruises?"

Clifford's face slacked, devoid of anything but a dare to challenge him. "She's clumsy."

The ridiculous lie didn't matter. The indifferent tone told Ivy clear enough this brute, this thing, didn't care what she believed. It was the story he used over and over, the perfect cliché to hide every wife beater's transgressions. The words came from Clifford Hughes with such robotic ease, Ivy was less sure he knew what they were as much as they were the programmed response to an oft-asked question he was tired of answering.

Then she would push him to the next level, prick the

thorn underneath the skin till she got a real reaction, good or bad. "She's clumsy. Clumsy enough to put belt marks on her own back? Clumsy enough to pull out a nickel-wide chunk of hair she was so self-conscious about she wore a baseball cap for months? Or how about clumsy enough to bust up her own cheekbone bad enough, she's got a permanent dent underneath her eye? She says you told her it looked cute—like a dimple. No, I don't think so, Clifford. I'll tell you what I think. You're a liar. You're a wife beater and a cheat. And I'll tell you something else, Clifford Hughes, and you listen real good now, you hear?" Ivy leaned forward and let the words roll like nettles off her tongue. "I knew you weren't a real man from the moment I laid eyes on you."

The thorn had reached the quick. The tree frog chorus faded into the background as blood pumped harder in Clifford's ears. Red flushed up the man's neck and enveloped his cheeks, washing out the ruddy tan of his skin. Words he could barely hear through the pulse pounding in his head hissed through gritted teeth. "I told you, I take care of her when she needs it."

A cockeyed admission. It would do. Ivy nodded slowly. "Question two, Clifford." Ivy paused. Inside, a part of her was hoping, hoping this time would be different—that, when given the opportunity, people, even bad people, would do this one simple thing that could, perhaps, start to turn it all around: repent. But the other part, the other side to her gentle nature, watched with cold hungry eyes, and waited. . . .

"Question two, Clifford. Are you sorry?"

Clifford clenched and unclenched his jaw; fists opened and closed in unified rhythm—telltale signs that would have sent Patricia Hughes running. But this one only stood there with her arms casually crossed, staring him in the eye as if he didn't loom a good nine inches over her head and could toss her ten times as far. She was way too small to be poking the bull with a stick. But problems like this could arise with mouthy women. Clifford had seen it before. Sad, sad, sad how they forgot their lot. And as close as this gal might be to Pat, it looked like the little wifey didn't share everything with her best buddy here. *Looks like the little wifey left out the most important thing to learn of all, and that was when to shut your mouth—life lesson number-fucking-one.* A storm was coming, and it was getting ready to knock down some serious female attitude. Just who the hell did this bitch think she was?

"Just who the hell do you think you are? Did Patricia put you up to this? If she did, you're both going to get a hurting like she's never seen." Clifford took another step forward. This time, Ivy didn't move. Dark was on them now, and somewhere behind the canopy of trees, a full moon climbed steadily upward. But Clifford could see Ivy clearly. Her hair, her bright eyes. She seemed to glow, illuminated by a soft ivory halo of lambent light.

"You're not sorry at all for what you've done." Ivy bowed her head. It would soon be too late to let him go, but it didn't matter. There would be no reprieve for the condemned again this night. If she could not save his despicable life on earth, the least she could do was release his soul to a higher power. And save Patricia's.

"I don't have to be sorry for what I do, Ivy. Is this my big surprise? To come out here, get all weepy, and say I'm sorry? For what!" Spittle rained down the front of Clifford's shirt. "Spineless whiners get what they deserve. And now, Ivy, I've got a surprise for you. You don't play these kinds of games with a grown man and expect to get away with it."

Ivy, still lost in her own crestfallen meditation, did not notice the fist that snaked out to finally close hot and tight around her wrist. Shocked, she jerked back, but Clifford clamped the other arm around her waist. Afraid now, she searched heaven for the moon only to find it still too frightfully low to do her any good.

"Stop squirming, Ivy. Don't act so innocent. I know this is why you really brought me out here." Clifford grabbed a fistful of that sunny hair and yanked backward. If this was the way she wanted to play it, fine with him. She'd been teasing him from the get-go; he sure as hell wasn't going back empty-handed. Ivy screamed and he placed a rough hand over her mouth, a ring—a wedding ring—digging hard into her lips. Then he knelt, dragging the woman with him.

She clawed and scratched at his chest, but Clifford's two hundred forty pounds were like a cement wall pushing against her, a compactor pressing her toward the ground. The two fell into the dirt as the moon's northernmost rim peeked above the treeline. Adrenaline roared through Clifford, the spike in his blood like a chemical rage. He fumbled against the woman's body, ripping at clothes while she slapped and flailed, unknowingly urging him on.

Ivy frantically looked past the man's shoulder at the black sky above. It yielded nothing as Clifford's weight crushed her into pebbles that dug between her shoulder blades and the length of her torso. In his ruthless urgency, the hand covering Ivy's mouth inched upward, pinching her nose. Air whistled past the thick fingers in the wail of a slowly dying balloon. The weight forcing the air from her lungs and the effort to breathe past Clifford's hand were making her light-headed. Stars flickered brightly and started to dim. *I'm going to suffocate.* The thought scurried through Ivy's mind like a frightened mouse. Like a timid, nervous little mouse.

Patricia's sweet face replaced the monster's sweaty grimace above her. And beyond that, a paler face rose high and strong at last, bathing the clearing in its saving grace.

Something shifted inside Ivy, a mental bending that chased the frightened thoughts away. Colors churned behind slitted lids, reflecting the moon's glow and breaking it into a kaleidoscope of fractured light. A warm, slow orange burned behind green irises, and underneath Clifford's meaty palm, a thin smile uncoiled. Lips parted and bit down hard.

"Dammit!" Clifford jerked his hand back and sat up. His shirt flapped open over a belt that dangled halfway off. The belly above it bulged soft and vulnerable. Ivy scooted backward from the release of his weight, then kicked the man in the stomach and crawled away, struggling to regain her feet. Her shirt blew behind her in tattered shreds, and Clifford grabbed for it, missing. On his feet again, he lunged and tackled Ivy from behind, straddling her slight frame. He grabbed both wrists and pinned them to the small of her back. Then he leaned down, close to her ear: "I like to play rough, Ivy. Just ask Patricia."

Ivy lay completely still. Her breathing slowed to a soft and even rhythm. Moon-white hair covered her face in a tangled mass.

"That's better. Be a good girl for this ole boy." Clifford lifted his weight slightly and rolled the woman underneath him onto her back. What he saw did not quite register, and his jaw—and grip—went slack.

The face staring up at Clifford had subtly changed. Her nose seemed longer, her cheeks flatter. The blond hair seemed—how was it possible?—shorter.

"What the hell?" Clifford looked down. The small frame between his thighs a moment ago was moving, sliding. *Lengthening.*

Clifford tried to jump up but only managed to stagger backward and land on his tailbone. He sat there, mouth agape, mesmerized. The woman before him twisted and writhed. The full moon overhead washed over the clearing in a white mist. Shapes swirled in the shadows and seemed to whisper his name.

"Ivy?" Clifford said softly.

A moist clicking of joints unhinging and rejoining again. Tendons stretched, and cords of sinew twanged. Snapping bones, subtle, like twigs. Then a gentle whishing as the marrow reknitted, thicker, stronger. The spine bowed out, vertebrae visibly cracking against the skin, only to be concealed beneath a blanket of emerging white fur.

The thing in front of Clifford Hughes unfolded itself from the hunched and painful contour on the ground. It squatted on massive haunches to face the human. The white fur coat shone silver in the moonlight, but the fangs dripping from the edges of its muzzle shone brighter still.

Orange eyes fixed on Clifford. *I . . . see . . . you.*

Clifford Hughes screamed. He was on his feet and running hard back the way he came.

The wolf rose to all fours. As the prey ran off ahead of her, she lowered her head to the forest floor and breathed it in. The smell of fear marked an easy trail, and she picked up cadence to a steady trot. She could travel this way all night, her bicycling gate covering ground tirelessly. There was no hurry now, only night and the forest and a hunger soon fulfilled.

Spring's second full moon draped light over the Appalachian wilderness like a heavy yellow pall. Underneath the quiet veil of sleep and darkness, the wilds of the mountains petered out to the edge of a small backyard overgrown with the season's flowers. Beyond the natural garden lay a tidy cottage fronted by a white picket fence. The wooden fence behind the house was more substantial. Corralled inside, a motley group of dogs lay sleeping close to the door, awaiting the morning and their mistress's hand to feed them.

Among the domestic pack, one stirred. A black shepherd nearly the size of a Dane rose to its feet. Nose to air, it padded to the fence and stared through the confining slats. Across the yard, a bastion of trees melded to shield what lay within them. But something lurked there, the dog knew. Something beautiful and dangerous and strange.

The watcher observed the cottage from the treeline for some time. Apparently satisfied, it moved from its cover, wading through a wavering patch of blue phlox. As the shadows peeled back and blossoms parted, the wolf's white coat grew visible, drizzled in golden pollen and dew. Flickering moonlight played among the watery facets, highlighting the glacial shades of the dense fur, its layers like striated bands of blue-white ice. Closer the wolf drew, and the shepherd could see queer vermilion stripes splashed along the animal's flanks and coating the rim of its jowls. Already the blood had dried into spiky turrets. A wallow streamside had left the shallow pool pink, but the wolf still held evidence of its task.

The shepherd stood still, head slightly raised into the heady scent coming toward him. An intoxicating sanguine essence carried across the wind, drowning the perfume of the wildflowers. The wooden barrier rose flimsily between dog and wolf. Whimpering slightly under the shadow of the animal before him, the shepherd lowered his head, his body curling into a ball and his tail tucking up between his hind legs. Ears flattened against skull, he peered upward, avoiding the other animal's direct stare.

The wolf studied the lesser canid, then gently leaned its head over the wooden fence and dropped something inside the confines of the yard. The dog lowered his nose to the gift, then tentatively reached to receive it. When the wolf over him did not move, the shepherd snatched the offering and trotted away, the meaty bicep and forearm dangling from his jaws. The other dogs began to rouse and joined their companion to feed.

The pack attended to, the wolf's attention drifted above the dogs to an attic window, unseeing to what roamed within the yard beneath it. Miniscule splits in the outer walls trickled down from the window, drawing the wolf's eyes to a riverstone foundation. The siding, its white color aged to cream, showed the weathering of hard winters, but the cottage's green shutters had been painted and only recently opened to welcome warmer days. A wind chime pealed from underneath the facing eave, and the wolf cocked its head to listen. Despite age and wear, the house had swayed with a thousand country breezes and been a stalwart of comfort against natural forces to someone who loved it and had loved it for a long time. When that person passed on, the house, too, passed—sold to a tenant heralding residence for little more than a year. This new presence in an old shell invigorated the structure in ways of gardens and painted shutters and chimes. The wolf knew this, but in the haze of its canine brain, the information seemed more instinct than a carefully acknowledged fact.

Shepherd forgotten, the wolf skirted the side of the sleepy little home, then jumped the white picket fence from a standstill. Sharply clawed feet click-clacked up cobblestones toward the porch steps. The wolf nosed the geraniums and overstuffed violet pots that narrowed the stairway to a one-person passage. Ahead of it, a screen door cloaked a sturdier interior one, crisscrossed by beams in a rustic maplewood X. But both were slightly ajar, the screen propped open by a carefully wedged tennis shoe. The wolf looked back once toward the sky, where nighttime began to lose its grip on the murky dark of early morning. The moon would soon slip soundlessly down the inky canvas to be replaced by a cheerless day's sun. And Doe Springs's postal deliveryman would not be there to greet it. With one last look, the wolf nosed the doors open and slipped inside.

Chapter 5

Ivy awoke with the sun seeping through her gauzy curtains and spreading like melted butter across the coverlets. She smiled and stretched, then draped a hand over the edge of the bed. It was immediately beset by kisses.

"Good morning, Rex."

Ivy sat up and looked at the digital clock. Eight thirty-seven. It felt good to sleep in. She'd been more exhausted than she'd realized from the adventures of night before last. And nothing beat wallowing around in a soft bed on a lazy morning in your own house. This long into it, and she still woke up marveling that she was finally settled in a place where landlords could not raise her rent on a whim and neighbors would not complain about barking dogs. There were no neighbors.

Throwing off the covers, Ivy shook out her pillow-tossed hair and yawned wide, another huge smile erupting behind it. *Sunny days bring glad hearts....* Mama loved saying that to her only daughter, and it was entirely true. Sunshine could cure just about anything and there was plenty of it pouring through her attic-bedroom window.

Ivy hopped out of bed and slid into a pair of gray sweatpants and a black tank top bought at a thrift shop when she lived in New Orleans. The word *Wicked* stretched across the chest in red letters, a bespangled Mardi Gras mask in the shape of a wolf's eyes and muzzle hanging off the points of the *W*. What a hoot. Some things in this world were too perfect to pass up, especially at a buck ninety-five.

Opening the door, Ivy was greeted by a lumpy carpet of calico fur crowding the small upstairs landing between bedroom, bathroom, and stairwell. Seven heads popped up simultaneously, seven tongues rolled out in one collective, happy pant when Ivy emerged. She closed the door on Rex and waded through the pack on her way down the stairs. The dogs tumbled down after her in one excited, bumbling knot on their race to the back door and breakfast. Demanding the most attention, Hansel, the I-40 golden, nearly tripped her with his exuberant affection, and Ivy grabbed the handrail before she herself toppled down the last three steps. (Gretel, the dachshund, had shown no interest whatsoever in her loud counterpart. The little dog stayed a good hound's length away from the retriever and his stampeding feet at all times.) Aufhocker hung behind the mob, allowing them to run through the kitchen and out the back door ahead of him. He passed Ivy coolly, head cocked in the other direction on his way to a yet-to-be-filled food dish. Ivy suppressed a smile. His dignity was bruised enough and she would not add insult to injury.

"It's just until his skin is clear, Auf. You don't want the mange, do you?" The dog buried his nose in the water dish outside and lapped loudly, ignoring the words. He had never been banished to sleep in the hall his entire eighteen years with Ivy, mange or otherwise. Damaged pride would take some time to heal, just like the "interloper's" unsightly skin condition.

Ivy left the shepherd to sulk but returned minutes later with a bag full of chow for the hungry crowd. Then she turned her attention to Rex's breakfast before jumping in the shower herself. The water felt good on her skin. It was going to be a glorious day.

Until the doorbell rang.

Ivy slipped on a pair of jeans and a button-down white shirt. She toweled her hair and left it to lie damp across her left shoulder. Outside, the dogs were on a mad tear, biting at the fence and howling, and Ivy quieted them first before answering the front door.

Sheriff Gloria Hubbard and Deputy Melvin Sanders stood on Ivy's porch, looking very official. Behind them, Ivy could see the sheriff's off-white Jeep Cherokee parked alongside the picket fence.

"Good morning, Miss Cole. I'm Sheriff Hubbard, and I believe you know Deputy Sanders." Gloria stepped into Ivy's view and extended a hand.

Ivy gave it a firm shake. Police here were different from those in Los Angeles. There, there were no formalities before business. They just barged in and let you have it.

"Yes, we met yesterday at the Hughes's," Ivy said. "Is something wrong? Is Patricia all right?"

"Mrs. Hughes is fine. Her family is taking good care of her. We just need to ask you a few questions. Do you have a minute?"

I just need to ask you a few questions, Cliff. "Sure. Come on in."

The police stepped inside the foyer and followed Ivy to the living room. Sanders perched by the sheriff on the edge of the yellow sofa, his back Popsicle straight. He pulled out a notepad and balanced it on one knee.

Gloria noted Sanders's fix on formality and suppressed a roll of the eyes. The boy needed to lighten up. An officer's demeanor affected that of those around him: witnesses, victims, criminals, or even ordinary folks under routine visits like today. Perhaps she should have brought along the more seasoned Deputy Meeks. He was newer to the department, up from Montgomery County eleven months ago, but had been in law enforcement a solid fifteen years. Nevertheless, Ivy had met Sanders already and Gloria thought the woman might be more at ease in his presence. But looking at the serious expression on her young deputy's face, he appeared more intimidating than congenial. Ironic, considering the tender heart that beat beneath the badge. She tucked a mental note in the back of her mind: Talk to Sanders per interview techniques.

"That's a beautiful mantel clock," Gloria said, redirecting her attention to Ivy and ice-breaking small talk. It was a habit left over from growing up a good girl in the rural South. "And fireplace, too, I might add."

"Thank you," Ivy said, seating herself in a sage-colored armchair across from the two officers. "The clock has been in my family for generations. It doesn't work anymore; I keep it out for sentimental reasons. As for the fireplace, the previous owner of this house said it was constructed from river rock collected on the property."

"This is interesting." The sheriff picked up an old book from the oak coffee table. It was black with a word stamped in the worn leather jacket.

"Lykanthrop." Gloria looked at Ivy with raised brows.

"That's an old spelling of lycanthrope. It means were-wolf," Ivy explained.

"May I?" The sheriff leafed through the tome. Uneven lines of calligraphy swirled and looped across the aging tea-colored pages. The text was a foreign language, most likely German, the sheriff surmised. Black-and-white drawings, finely sketched in ink, showed scenes of shape-shifting creatures with hunched backs and sharp claws and fangs. An illustration near the back of the volume caught her eye. It was a pack of enormous hounds set upon a peasant farmer and rending him to bits.

"Not much of a children's book, is it?" Gloria said.

Ivy laughed. "A very adultly illustrated Grimm's, if I had to make a comparison. I have a taste for European legends and myth," she explained. "The book is very old, a collector's item. I loan it to libraries when they do rare book exhibits."

Gloria nodded politely. She set the book down. The interest in European literature did not surprise her. It was a small town—in fact, the sheriff knew quite a bit about Miss Cole already. The woman's "new" status made her a target of broad speculation, making the sheriff a recipient of town gossip by proxy. Fortunate for many of the curious minded, Patricia Hughes and Betty Hill, good souls both, were not tight-lipped when it came to anything in Doe Springs. But why should they be? Ivy Cole, according to the girl and older lady, was a wonderful, considerate person—a good Samaritan to lost dogs everywhere, and to lost young wives as well. Her story was simple and tragic and lonely. An only child. No immediate family. Both parents deceased, first her mother, a sweet little German lady (hence, the European connection—how exotic that made Ivy seem to the locals, even though her Southern accent rivaled the sheriff's own), then her American father, a North Carolina man, years later but while Ivy was only still in her teens. Ivy herself, wandering about the U.S., looking for . . . what?

A home, she'd told Patricia, who'd told Lynette at Etta's Diner, who'd told the sheriff at her morning coffee right after Ivy had moved into town last spring. No secrets here, and the information flew at you whether you wanted it or not. Sometimes it was sensory overload, knowing the details too soon. Made first impressions impossible for the person at hand.

Gloria already had an opinion of Ivy Cole before she'd even answered the door. Anybody who loved dogs and lost causes that much had to have a good heart.

"Sheriff, can I get you and your deputy a drink? I've got homemade lemonade, tea . . . "

Somebody else apparently knew the "good girl" rules as well. Deputy Sanders looked like he might pipe up, but the sheriff cut him off. "No, thank you. We're fine," she said.

Ivy braced herself for what was coming next. She'd been through this routine before, but she was never comfortable in the role. Lies did not roll easily off the tongue, as she ranked liars right up there with thieves, miscreants, and misfits in general. Hypocrite did not sit well in her vocabulary either. However, with amenities exchanged, there was nothing left to do but get to the point, which would most likely involve a fair amount of lying and misfitting and hypocriting all together. This was the game those such as herself had to play sometimes to survive. Ivy sighed. Where had all the sunshine gone?

"What exactly is it that can I help you with, Sheriff Hubbard? I told Deputy Sanders everything I knew yesterday, which unfortunately wasn't much." Ivy glanced at the deputy, but he was lost in his notebook, scribbling.

"We're just working out the details today, Ivy. May I call you Ivy?"

You can call me whatever you want.

Ivy shook her head to clear it. *Get out of my head, Clifford Hughes!*

"No, I can't call you Ivy?"

"What? No, Ivy is fine. I'm sorry, I've been an addled mess since yesterday. When Patricia called to tell me what happened . . . And then for it to have happened in the woods right down the road from here . . . "

Gloria nodded sympathetically. "I know you don't want to keep hashing this out, Ivy, but the location of the bo—of Mr. Hughes is what we need to talk to you about. Now, you said yesterday Clifford dropped off a delivery around—," Gloria looked up from Sanders's notes, "six forty-five p.m."

"That's right," Ivy said.

"Just curious—what was it?"

"A platter."

"A platter? Doesn't seem like an emergency item."

"Of course not. Why would it be?"

"There was a note from you requesting a late delivery of this item, to be delivered to you personally, in fact."

"Oh, the note. That's not an emergency, Sheriff—that's leftover paranoia from living in Los Angeles. You see, it's not just a platter. It came from my uncle in Germany and he had it engraved for me. I had to work a crazy schedule this week, and knowing it was coming, I didn't want something that special left outside by the fence. Since Clifford is . . . was . . . my best friend's husband and they live so close by, I didn't think he'd mind running it over here after hours."

"You didn't want to swing by Patricia's one evening and pick it up yourself, maybe save Clifford the trouble?"

"Sheriff Hubbard, I wish to goodness I had."

Gloria's eyes squinted slightly. She looked at Ivy for a moment too long, then continued. "Okay, so Clifford dropped off the platter. Then what?"

"Well, he left." Ivy shrugged her shoulders. "That's the way these things normally work, isn't it?"

"Normally, yes." Gloria smiled. Ivy didn't like the look of it. "You and Patricia have been friends now for how long?"

"A little over a year. We met at the Laundromat after I first moved here."

"So you knew Clifford pretty well?"

"Not real well. I steered clear of him whenever possible. He wasn't very friendly. To be honest with you, he made me nervous."

"Nervous? In what way?"

Ivy regretted saying it. "He was a gruff man," she continued. "He wasn't very nice to Patricia."

"And you didn't like him because of that?"

"No, I didn't." Say little, volunteer nothing. Ivy looked at the sheriff pleasantly but dutifully concerned.

"She must have confided in you quite a bit," Gloria said.

"She told me some things about their relationship. She felt the need to explain away what I could see for myself. I quit buying the 'I fell down the stairs' bit early on. But for the most part, Patricia didn't like talking about family business when we were together. I think what made us close was the escape the friendship provided."

"What exactly were some of those things she told you about her relationship with Clifford?"

Ivy's forehead wrinkled. "Sheriff Hubbard, I don't see how revealing Patricia's confidences is any help. You're the police—I know you've been to her house several times this year. You know what she was living with."

"And that worried you."

"Of course it did. What kind of friend would I be if it didn't?"

"Not a very good friend at all," Gloria said. Ivy and Sheriff Hubbard stared at each other. Deputy Sanders cleared his throat.

"Let's get back to that evening," the sheriff continued. "Clifford dropped off your package. Did you talk for a while? Maybe you asked about Patricia."

"There was no real conversation. I said to tell his wife hello, signed for the delivery, and he left."

"Did he tell you where he was going afterward?"

"Why would he?"

Gloria looked exasperated. "Miss Cole—Ivy—we're trying to establish an order of events for that evening. Your house was the last stop on Clifford Hughes's route. His truck was found between here and his home, a matter of a couple of miles, and his body lay just a few hundred feet into the woods. If he left here around six forty-five heading for home, we can't explain how the medical examiner put the time of death hours later, well after dark. There's a missing piece here that we were hoping you could help us with." Gloria softened her tone and waited for Ivy Cole to admit to what she was suspecting. The sheriff didn't come here to badger the poor woman, just fill in the gap in her timeline.

"He must have gone somewhere else in the meantime. I have no idea," Ivy said.

Gloria sighed inwardly. At least, she hoped it was inwardly. She pressed on with her questions, while Sanders sat silently listening. Good, strong backup with no interference. Gloria liked that in a deputy. "Were you home all that evening after Clifford left?"

"Yes, I was. All evening." Ivy sat poised in her armchair, the blankly pleasant expression still in place. Cooperative and helpful, through and through. How boring.

She listened to the persistent sheriff with her ears but let her eyes and thoughts drift over to Deputy Sanders. Tall. Obviously, by the uncomfortable bend in his knees. The sofa sat too low to the floor for his height. Dark, closely cropped hair, barely shy of a military cut in length. Clean shaven to a fault—a tiny knick on his neck from the razor, a hint of razor burn by the left ear. Faint crinkles around the denim eyes and set mouth. Ah, Deputy Sanders could smile after all. Smiled often and wide, by the evidence on his face. Below his lips, a half-inch scar marred the square chin, maybe something left over from childhood, or perhaps something obtained in the line of training or duty. Brown uniform, starched and creased in the proper places. Big hands clutched the notebook, the fingernails clean but not entirely neat, as if trimmed with whatever might be handy—scissors, a pocketknife. He was turned out, professional, but not fussy. Ivy liked that in a deputy.

She looked up from her last observation to see the man staring at her too. But so was the sheriff. *Oh, the sheriff!* Ivy's attention zipped back to the moment and the pesky questioning that saw no end.

"You didn't hear anything? Your dogs didn't bark at anything or behave strangely?"

Ivy did a mental backup, before blue eyes and square chins, to their last topic. That evening. After Clifford left. Right. "Nothing unusual. They always bark off and on through the night—we've got a lot of deer and nocturnal critters that like to get in the trash cans from time to time."

"Even with the dogs in the yard?"

"Most the time I keep them in the house at night. It makes me feel safer. That night they were in."

Gloria drummed her fingers on her knee, thinking. Then she said, "Ivy, about how many dogs do you have?"

"I now have eight, thanks to my newest addition yesterday." Ivy glanced at Deputy Sanders. The firm set of his mouth relaxed and the crinkles bent slightly, then he was buried in the notebook again.

"Would you mind if I see them?" Gloria asked.

"No, I don't mind. They're in the backyard."

The two officers followed Ivy to the back porch. The dogs leaped to their feet at the sight of the strangers and started barking. Ivy raised her hand in the air and lowered it, palm down. The dogs went to their bellies in unison and were quiet.

"I'm impressed," Gloria said. "That's quite a feat."

"It's what I do for a living," Ivy said. "I'm a dog trainer and behaviorist. I give classes at the community center twice a week, plus I give sessions in people's homes. It wreaks havoc on a normal schedule, working around other people's lives, but I love it. I get to meet a lot of neat folks—and dogs—that way. I've found that it's usually the owner, not the dog, who has the problem anyway, so you have to work with both to get a constant barker or incessant chewer straightened out."

"Business is good for that sort of thing, here in Doe Springs?"

"I get by."

Gloria nodded again. She had heard of Miss Cole's magic dogs. She'd even considered taking her own unruly chocolate lab to one of the clinics. Time didn't allow for such things, though, not when you're chasing your own tail in circles over missing persons and mishaps and maulings. Gloria looked out over the yard. "You've got some big ones there, well, except for the dachshund. How did you get so many?"

"They're all strays but one." Ivy pointed to the huge black shepherd at the bottom of the steps. "He's been with me a long time."

"You must really love dogs," Gloria said.

"I have quite a soft spot for them. They're my family."

"I'm a dog fan myself. I have a lab at home. Not much of a guard dog, though. You say you keep all your dogs inside at night?"

"Usually I do, especially with whatever is loose out there."

"You don't think a pack of . . . one, two, three . . . I only see seven, where's number eight?"

"He's inside, in the bedroom. Until his mange clears up I can't introduce him to the rest. And no," Ivy finished the sheriff's thought, "these dogs would not defend themselves. They'd all run for the house like big cowards if someone— some*thing*—called their bluff."

Gloria seemed satisfied. Spring sun beat down on the trio, promises of an early summer in its touch. The dogs continued to lie obediently, but their attention never shifted from the intruders. Shielding her eyes with her hand, the sheriff peered past the yard to the woods beyond. "How much property is with your place, all told?"

"Just this lot to the edge of the trees."

"Know who owns the rest of it?"

"Jack Lutsky. He parceled this off for me."

"And how much would that be, the total property?"

"About two hundred acres."

Deputy Sanders jotted it down. Gloria turned to Ivy. "Well, thank you, Ivy, for the information. I hope you will be careful out here by yourself. You might be safer if you left a few of your biggest dogs out at night. Barking can be a big deterrent to wild animals, and the place we found Clifford Hughes was not far through those trees. Whatever did that to him may still be around."

Gloria eyed the dogs one more time, then the officers walked back through the house. Gloria stopped in the kitchen. "Is this the platter, Ivy?"

Ivy came around beside her. "Yes, it is."

The sheriff picked it up and looked at her reflection in the ornamental silver. A woodland scene with great horned bucks was etched into the metal. High over their heads and the tops of the trees, a daintily engraved full moon shone down on the argentine deer. Gloria squinted at faint lines flowing behind the tree trunks. She could barely make out three forms hiding among the forest, watching the bucks. They were wolves, the lines of their lean bodies blending like ghosts within the picture.

Gloria flipped the plate over to an inscription on the back: *um elfe kommen die wolfe, um zwolfe bricht das gewölbe.* "This is a beautiful piece of work, I have to say. It looks to be very old."

"My life seems to be a study in personal antiques. Everything I cherish most goes way back in my family. This platter once sat on my mother's Christmas table when we lived overseas. Uncle Stefan had it inscribed before sending it to me. He is Mama's brother. You can see why this is a very special gift."

"I'd say so. Do you mind me asking what the inscription says?"

"Not at all. It reads 'Much love to you, my sweet niece. I miss you.' "

"Well, that's very nice." Gloria set the platter down, where it thunked solidly against the countertop. "Hefty thing, isn't it?"

She continued to the front door, Sanders and Ivy behind her. Ivy stopped the sheriff in the foyer. Sanders had made it out onto the porch, where the hanging plants presented some problem. One rested above his head like a terra cotta hat with mad green hair erupting from the top of it. He slumped to keep from bumping into it.

"Sheriff Hubbard, before you go, may I ask you something?"

"Sure. Shoot."

"I heard that Angus Shepherd lost some cattle recently. Was it—you know—the same as what's happened to the people?"

"Similar, yes." Gloria looked at her simply, but Ivy could see from the closed expression the details would not be forthcoming. Apparently only the police were allowed to ask the questions in this game.

"Do you have any idea what it could be? The local news is coming up with all kinds of strange stories—escaped lion from a zoo, a hatchet-wielding maniac . . . ," Ivy paused, hoping the sheriff or even Deputy Sanders would fill in the blank with the police's theory.

"There are a lot of rumors out there. But as soon as we find out for sure, the whole town of Doe Springs will be the first to know," Gloria said.

And that was that. It was just last night Ivy had contemplated calling the deputy to find out what she could. Now, amazingly, two-thirds of the sheriff's office had spent the better part of an hour at her house and she'd found no way to get an inside scoop on anything. She'd fielded questions, and they'd offered nothing. A man of few words to begin with, Deputy Sanders was a man of no words in the sheriff's presence. And apparently the sheriff had very little she wanted to give up about this. How frustrating. Would it be too forward to make that phone call to the deputy after all?

Gloria joined Sanders on the porch. "Have a good day, Ivy. I hope we didn't take up too much of your time. If you think of anything else, anything at all that might be helpful, let us know. Thanks again."

Deputy Sanders nodded to Ivy, then he followed the sheriff

down the steps as Ivy closed the door behind them. Gloria slid behind the wheel of her Cherokee while Sanders settled into the passenger side. She looked at the cozy cottage, the rambling flowers and fence. Neat and tidy and warm, everything in its place, yet wild at the same time. The radio bleeped, pulling the sheriff from her observations. It was Meeks.

"Well?" he asked. "Was it like we thought? Clifford had a fling before stopping off to take a—to relieve himself in the woods on the way home?"

Gloria pondered another moment before answering. Fingers drummed on the steering wheel in staccato four counts. "Sanders, find out who Ivy Cole's vet is—ten to one, it's Doc Hill—and talk to a few of her clients. I want to know exactly what kind of training she does. See if there is any guard dog work in her background." She spoke into the radio. "Meeks, I want you to talk to Jack Lutsky this afternoon. See if he heard anything, and see what other farms his property backs up against. Then I want you to visit Patricia Hughes. Find out exactly where she was the night her husband was killed."

"Sheriff, you don't think Patricia could have had anything to do with this? It was an animal attack, pure and simple." Meeks's voice was punctuated by static but she heard the disbelief loud and clear.

"We're merely covering our bases. What is it, Sanders?"

The deputy had his notebook back out and was tapping his chin with the pen. He said nothing about Dr. Hill and giving Ivy a ride. Instead, he asked, "What are you thinking, Sheriff? Those dogs looked tame enough."

Gloria nodded thoughtfully. "Yes, yes they did. I'm just thinking, though, if Miss Cole would lie about the platter, she might just lie about something else."

"What platter?" Meeks said.

"The one in her kitchen that, according to Clifford's parcel records, only weighs ten ounces."

Ivy drew the curtain back and watched the officers leave. They'd sat in her driveway several minutes, the woman staring at her house.

The woman. Sheriff Gloria Hubbard. Ivy said the name aloud to see if it felt keen on her tongue. It did not. In fact, Ivy would like the sheriff under different circumstances. She was a sharp tack, that one. Ivy would have to keep an eye on her. But just an eye. For now.

Chapter 6

"Ivy! What a nice surprise. Come on in, sugar." Mrs. Ava Pritchard, or the Widow Pritchard to those who knew her from a distance, waved Ivy inside the grand Victorian, which was twice as old as the widow herself. Ivy stepped through the heavy cherry door and gave the woman a hug with her free arm, the other hand holding a plastic food container. Today Ava wore gardening overalls rolled up at the cuff and a bright yellow shirt, but Ivy would be surprised to see her in much else considering the elderly lady's love for the personal arboretum hugging every corner of her house. The customary loose bun poked over the horizon of Ava's head, a lethal-looking ruby pin jabbed through the center of it. Pearl-gray tendrils escaped from the jeweled bit of metal and swept around sun-dappled skin, which should have been as wrinkled as the dried-apple dolls Old Man Brigham sold in his feed store. But it wasn't. Instead it stretched nearly smooth along her cheeks and forehead, giving the widow an air of timelessness, like an antique defying its age under the many layers of dust life had laid over it. Genteel even in her old work clothes, Widow Pritchard was pure Charleston, misplaced on a mountaintop. But Ivy knew things about the widow, despite her refined and kindly manner. She was strong as a hickory switch and could bite just as sharp when provoked.

"What's that you're carrying? I think I smelled it thirty minutes ago," Ava said, her vocals strumming an elegant debutante accent, dripping honey and belying deep country roots.

"I have brought you a blueberry pie, Ava."

"Oh, that sounds just lovely, sugar. A visit from my favorite girl with my favorite pie in tow. Homemade, I hope?" Ava knew better, but she liked to tease Ivy about her aversion to the kitchen. Always too thin despite her healthy appetite, the girl's cupboards held more dog food than rations from the Pig and Poke Grocery.

"Would I come over here with anything less? I was taking a stroll behind my house a few days back and stumbled across the fullest bush of blueberries you've ever seen. I thought of you right away, and here I am."

Clear hazel eyes sparkled under dainty diamond-rimmed glasses, and Widow Pritchard's brow arched over the top of them. "Little early for blueberries, isn't it?"

"All right, you caught me. I picked the pie up on the way over here."

"I'll take blueberry pie any way I can get it." Ava grasped Ivy's free hand and led her down the hall. "Let's eat in the sunroom. It's too gorgeous to be closed in by all these dreary walls. We'll take a shortcut through the kitchen and grab some plates. Just so happens I've got fresh whipped cream in the fridge too."

Snipped bluebells overran the kitchen, and Ivy moved a vaseful aside to make room on the counter for the pie. A pitcher spilling blue blossoms found a new home by the sink. Ivy put two plates in its place on the tiny breakfast table, then she rummaged through the refrigerator for the cream.

"Ava! What is this?" Ivy pulled out a half-eaten roll of cookie dough and pointed it at the elderly woman.

"Just a little guilty pleasure is all. You wouldn't deny an old woman that, would you?"

"This isn't on your diet. Your doctor is not going to be pleased."

Ava crossed her arms. "That old busybody doesn't have to know everything. Now put that cookie dough back where

you found it and let's go sit down. I wish you'd told me you
were coming; I'd have picked up a bit."

Ivy looked around the pristine room. "You do live like
such a pig, Ava. Next time I'll be sure to call ahead."

The ladies carried plates, forks, cream, pie, a knife, and
linen napkins toward the bright spot emanating from an
opening near the end of the wallpapered hall. Ava ordered
the addition after her husband, Jeb, passed on years before.
Ivy, snowbound in South Dakota, could not make the funeral of a man who was a stranger to her, a man who had
begged Ava to disown the friendship with her sister Una's
stepchild.

Despite their differences on that matter, Ava and Jeb had
loved one another very much. Jeb's memories haunted every
room of their home of sixty-four years, and the sunroom became the only place in the house where Ava could get away
from the sorrow, forget the biggest chapter in her life and
concentrate on the tiny sliver of oneness she was carving out
for her last years alone on this earth.

Ivy sliced the pie, then settled in a wicker chair beside her
aunt. Peace plants and Easter lilies crowded the giant glass
window rising above them, and the garden beyond pressed
against the opposite side of the glass, a carnival of bloomed
faces staring in.

Ava took a small bite of blueberries and waited. She'd
known Ivy a long time, long enough to sense there was a
point to the visit other than sharing a good grocer's pie. But
Ivy continued to nibble quietly until Ava could stand it no
more. She wiped her lips with the linen napkin and very casually said, "Ivy, I just have to ask you, is it true about the
Hughes fellow? That he was chewed up and spit out just a
stone's throw from your house?"

Ivy set her fork down, relieved. She'd not been sure how
to broach the subject, but Ava had saved her the trouble.

"Yes, it's true. Everything you heard. They found him all
over the place." *What a mess I made,* Ivy thought. She remembered wallowing in the creek afterward to rid her coat
of chunks of flesh and clotted blood.

Widow Pritchard pushed her plate away and settled her

chin atop the tips of her fingers. "He was a bad apple, that one. What comes around goes around, yes?"

Ivy nodded and pushed her own plate away, the pie nearly untouched. She traced an imaginary design in the glass tabletop while Ava talked.

"I don't suspect Cliff will be missed that much," Ava continued. "Especially not by Patricia. I bet she thinks whatever did that to Clifford Hughes did her a big ole favor, that's what I think."

"I know it. But I talked with her on the phone this morning and she's still terribly upset."

"Of course she is! It just happened. The girl is shell-shocked. Even when you hate a person, there's the attachment of proximity you have to turn loose. They shared the same house, shared the same bed, shared all the ups and downs of a marriage. He was her husband, good or bad, for several years, and there will be a grieving process just the same. Give it time, Ivy. Patricia is going to blossom in ways you didn't think imaginable." Ava tilted the younger woman's face up to meet her eyes. "Is that what's bothering you?"

Ivy nodded. Patricia was a dear friend, and the only close friend she'd ever done a favor for. All the other times, Ivy was not present to witness the intimate aftermath. Rather, she got to savor the results of her work from afar: in newspaper articles or television or gossip. But the outcomes always seemed good from that distance—widows and widowers got life insurance settlements, abused children got safe foster homes, neglected animals got food in their tummies and veterinary care. Wasn't that better than their lives before? Shouldn't folks be shouting from their rooftops in appreciation? Ivy thought so. Naively, she realized now. She'd overlooked the most basic of human emotions: guilt, and the fear of being alone.

Ava shook her head. "Now listen to me, child. Sometimes there are folks in this world who just deserve a good killin', and Clifford Hughes was right there in the ranks of them. Make no mistake about that. Whenever you see Patricia in a state of some kind, you just remember how she lived and what all she went through. You might even remind her of that

a few times because she's bound to start blurring facts in her
head now that he's gone. You know, the self-flagellation routine: 'Well, maybe it wasn't all that bad, maybe he wasn't
the most wicked man to walk the face of the earth, maybe I
did bring it on myself a bunch of the time. . . . ' Blah, blah,
blah—nonsense! He was evil, that's all there was to it, and
that's been done away with in a tidy manner. In fact, sugar,
there are others around here that I wouldn't care two cents
if they got eat the same way." Ava tickled Ivy's chin before
letting it go.

Ivy looked up and smiled slightly. How the widow loved
to tease her. But the cheering up part was working. She
could always count on her aunt to shoulder the burden of
doubt and turn it into something positive. "And who might
that be, Ava?"

"Oh, I've got a list, chickie. I could point some fingers,
name some names. There's not an indiscretion in this town I
don't know about."

"Actually, that brings me to the real reason I'm here. But
thanks for reassuring me on the other thing."

"Any time, sugar. We Southern gals got to stick together.
Now, what is the real reason you're here? I was starting to
feel privileged that you just wanted my company."

"I always want your company, but I need your wisdom
just as much. There's a man in this town I need some information about. Frank—"

"Parson. Banker. Married to Mildred, a sour gossip and
none too bright. She works at a salon downtown. Her son, Jeffrey—hell on wheels, but with some guidance he'd straighten
out all right. Does that about cover it?"

"Just about. Tell me more about Frank. What do you think
of him?"

"Not a lot, not often. But seeings we've only got one
bank, our paths cross from time to time. I'm sure you've
seen him too. Skinny, balding right on top. Colors in the
pink patch with some kind of spray-on hair replacement
from a can."

That jogged Ivy's memory. The name may have escaped

her, but the painted bald patch was hard to miss. "Anything else?"

"Affinity for the ladies and long lunch breaks. Wednesdays in particular." Ava leaned back in her chair. That was enough. She could feel Jeb's disapproving gaze through the glass, beaming in with the spring sun and trying to shame her for encouraging a force that was older and stronger than humankind itself.

"Ava," Ivy looked at the lady sideways, an eyebrow cocked, "is Frank Parson on your list?"

Ava smiled, her perfect eighty-seven-year-old teeth gleaming. "Ah, sugar, everybody is. Except for you. Anybody who brings me such good pies would never make that list."

"Ava, you are a little devil," Ivy said.

"You don't know the half of it, dear," Ava said and winked.

Chapter 7

Deputy Melvin Sanders stood in his bathroom and stared into the mirror. He stooped to see himself in the beveled glass. One of these days, he promised himself, he would raise the blamed thing to eye level. Or buy a taller house. How many times had he cracked his forehead on the doorjamb coming home after a late shift?

Melvin sighed and sprayed the shaving cream into his hand. Working the lather over his face, he began to shave, as he did every day, sometimes twice a day if he was feeling compulsive. Ancestry demanded it. Melvin's paternal line evolved from pure grizzly mountain man, coupled with a

twist of Scotch-Irish on his mama's side. Put the two line-
ages together and sparks flew. That's how they made Melvin,
his father kidded. Melvin never cared for the joke.

Melvin tapped the razor under warm running water and
made the first long stroke down the stubble on his cheek.
The day's agenda played through his head in tune with the
whish-whoosh of the razor: Five-thirty a.m., rise and shine.
Check. Five thirty-five a.m., jog to Watershed Mill and back.
Check. Six-fifteen, shower and shave. Working on it. By six
forty-five a.m., cereal and then on the road with a thermos of
hot coffee, black. Today would be a busy day, and danged if
he weren't getting a late start. These all nighters out in the
woods were taking their toll. The whole police force—all
three of them—were walking around like something from
Night of the Living Dead. Even Melvin's usual seven-mile
run was clipped to six today. Short-winded, he'd practically
limped the last half-mile home. Tired, and getting old too.
Thirty wasn't all that far away.

Melvin flicked bristly foam into the sink and started on
the other cheek. The blade pressed a straight line from side-
burn to cleft in chin, and the schedule resumed. First stop, a
meeting with the town's retired vet, Doc Hill. Subject: Ivy
Cole's ferocious pack of retrievers, shepherds, mutts in general, and, oh yes, the dachshund. *(But what a pretty name,
isn't it? Ivy, Ivy, Ivy.)* Early afternoon—a trip one town over
for an appointment with a Mrs. Ruthy White to discuss her
dog, Chippy, a student in Miss Cole's Tuesday class at the
community center. The two trips combined seemed like a
waste of a day, a day that could be spent back in the woods,
searching. Searching. For what? No stray hairs found on any
of the bodies, human or animal alike. No retrievable saliva,
no prints around the attack scenes. DNA results, nil. Autop-
sies, forensics, all the science that had been thrown behind
their effort . . . worthless. Whatever was out there defied it
all. It's as if a specter blew down from the clouds, gobbled
whatever lay beneath it, then ascended back into oblivion
leaving nothing but fleshy bits and pieces as the only proof
of its coming. Cursed. A simple enough answer. If it quacks
like a duck . . .

The razor briskly hopped across Melvin's upper lip as he thought it out. Unfortunately, police officers didn't deal with curses, they dealt with real life and evidence. And the sheriff's instincts had paid off before, so he wouldn't question her methods today. Like she told Meeks: just covering all the bases. Melvin would rather be chasing vets and dogs than going back out to question Mrs. Hughes, that was for certain. The first visit had been horrible enough. The way her big doe eyes welled up at the news, then she'd crumbled against his chest in sobs. Melvin stood there, the unwavering oak, patting the woman's bony shoulder and wishing there was something real he could do. Condolences and I'm sorrys were a waste of breath; he felt phony uttering a single one. Not that he didn't feel it, he just knew it meant nothing to the one suffering in grief. So he stood quietly as the tears stained his uniform, until her friend, Ivy Cole, pulled up in a broken-down van and relieved him of his awkward predicament. She came right in and took over, cradling Patricia in her arms much as she'd held that scrawny little terrier hours later. Patricia had quieted in her friend's embrace, and after a few short questions, Melvin reluctantly left. Reluctantly. Because of *her.* Not Patricia—the friend. It was definitely not the right time to be thinking thoughts like that. Inappropriate. Highly unprofessional. Shame, Melvin. *Ivy. Not Mrs., but Miss.*

"Ouch!" A bead of blood welled up on the young officer's throat, turning the white foam around it pink. Melvin topped the blood with a dab of toilet paper. Red quickly seeped through in an irregular splotch, gluing the paper securely to his neck. Melvin watched the tiny dot of crimson spread to the raggedly torn edges of Charmin, and Clifford Hughes's mangled body popped into his head.

"Poor bastard," Melvin said to his reflection. It was hard not to think about the bodies all the time. They came at him from every direction—while driving the car, when eating a meal, after cutting himself shaving and patting the drop of blood before it could mar his collar. They invaded sleep, then devoured it till there was no such thing. Melvin knew every line in his ceiling, every flake of plaster that had worked loose around the walls. Nights were spent relishing the mundane when sleep evaded him and he sought to evade what had chased it away.

Before the town went all to hell, Melvin had been a police officer here for three years and living out his master plan. Doe Springs was exactly the kind of place he'd been looking for after finishing training in his hometown of Asheville. He'd grown up with a Mayberry notion of where he wanted to settle down: a community where folks all knew and cared for one another, including their police force, whom they regarded as friends as much as lawmen. Leaving the excitement of a larger city's crime behind was the trade-off for the family life he hoped to build someday—and landing the job in Doe Springs, with its picturesque streets and outlying farms, was all he could have hoped for. He liked and admired his boss, Sheriff Hubbard, from day one. So sure of his future here, Melvin bought this modest house on Dogwood Avenue just six months into the job. Next, he'd find a sweet wife, raise three sweet children (one girl and two boys to watch out for her), and later be the most wonderful grandfather in the world—all right here. It was the simple life of his dreams. Until the nightmare started exactly three years and one month later. It began subtly enough with the rise in accidents and assumed runaways; but then the bizarre animal mutilations came on their heels followed by the human attacks.

Melvin remembered seeing the first body, lying in a cornfield outside town. It took a long time collecting him. The sheriff, Deputy Meeks, and himself fanned out, combing dirt and corn and rocks looking for enough puzzle pieces to put the victim's identity together. A finger discovered twenty feet from the biggest mess yielded a clear enough print for ID. Only twenty-one years old, the man was a parole violator drifting through town. Background checks revealed a file already full of petty larceny and burglary charges. The boy was a bad egg, but he met a worse fate out on a lonely stretch of road in the corn. Cursed. Cursed in Mayberry.

Melvin almost walked off the job that day, but police work and obligation ran too deep in his bones for desertion. Besides,

it was just another animal attack, they thought. A one-time
fluke of an accident befalling people instead of livestock, an
accident like all the other quirky accidents visiting the area. A
boy in the wrong place at the wrong time, set upon by a cougar
or a bear. Or even, maybe, a pack of wild dogs.

Dogs. Dog behavior. Trained dogs. Ivy's face crowded
out corpses and Melvin's introduction to the Devil of Doe
Springs. The way she cradled the injured little pup, so lovingly, protectively. She would be great with kids. He pictured her again, walking down Rural Route 7, the long hair
falling to her waist and the tan legs rising upward to meet it.

"Jesus, Melvin," he told his stooped reflection before
splashing cold water on his face. He had to get moving. After all, it was going to be a busy day.

Deputy Sanders pulled up the gravel driveway and in behind
a green minivan. Grassy hills tumbled outward from the
sprawling farmhouse in front of the vehicles, not a neighbor
in sight. An aging red barn stood sentinel behind the home,
and beyond it, a couple of horses grazed lazily to the peaceful humming of bees. It was an ideal place for retirement,
but Doc hadn't realized it yet. Hardened, muddy ruts ran
alongside the drive where clients found parking in the yard
on busier days. Melvin bet a parking area would be added
long before the vet hung up his stethoscope for good.

Melvin stepped out of the patrol car and resisted the urge
for an early morning stretch and yawn. A brindled Great
Dane, dragging Bonnie Hill behind it, bounded around the
corner of the house to greet him.

"Whoa, Samson! Whoa!" Bonnie, Doc's only daughter,
slid to a halt in front of Sanders, the Dane already licking his
hand.

"Hi, Samson." Deputy Sanders patted the big dog's velvety head. "And hello to you, Miss Hill. Is your dad inside?"

"Hi, Deputy Sanders," Bonnie said, looking up at the officer through a splash of straight blond bangs. A row of perfect
white teeth, recently freed from two years of braces, connected the girl's round apple cheeks in a wide grin. "Daddy's

looking for you. He didn't schedule any appointments till the afternoon, so you can stay as long as you want."

"Isn't your father retired?"

"So he keeps saying, but we haven't seen any proof yet."

"Well, I don't need but a few minutes of his time."

Bonnie and Samson trotted after Deputy Sanders into the house.

"Good morning, Melvin!" Betty Hill waved from the kitchen. "There's some fresh coffee here, if you like."

"Thank you, ma'am." The words jogged his memory. Melvin saw his own thermos of hot coffee still sitting on the kitchen counter at home. Getting absentminded on top of everything else.

"I'll get it!" Bonnie let go of Samson and raced around Deputy Sanders into the kitchen. The girl's ponytail bobbed happily behind her, and Melvin remembered how much fun it was being a kid: football games, milk shakes at Bernie's Burgers, the prom.

"Here, take your father some as well." Betty handed the steaming mugs to her daughter. Painted dogs chased painted cats round and round the cups. "He's in his office, Melvin. Just go on in. Um, Deputy," Betty pointed below her chin, "you've got a little something . . . "

Sanders touched his neck. The piece of toilet paper still clung there from his shave. "Oh. Thank you. Again." He stuffed the bit of paper in his pocket. Betty smiled and turned away, busying herself with making more coffee. The timer dinged on the oven and Melvin left her, bending over the hot stove and retrieving something that smelled absolutely wonderful.

Bonnie gave Melvin a mug, then grabbed his other hand and led him down the hall. He paused in front of a wooden-framed photo tucked within a myriad of others. Ivy Cole smiled out at him. Wisps of hair blew around her face in the outdoor scene, which looked like it could be Montana or the Dakotas. She knelt with her arm around a big black dog, the one he saw in her backyard yesterday.

Bonnie tugged at the end of Melvin's arm, but gave up

when he didn't budge. She walked back beside the deputy to stare at the picture too.

Melvin motioned to the five-by-seven with his coffee. "You must know Miss Cole right well to have her picture up here on the wall."

Bonnie shrugged. "Yeah, I guess so. She's pretty cool. Lived all over and stuff." Bonnie pulled again on the three fingers filling her hand. "The office is down here. Daddy converted the entire den."

Melvin took one last look, then allowed Bonnie to drag him away from the photograph. The girl knocked once on the door at the end of the hall and turned the knob. Doc Hill turned at the sound of them coming in.

"Hi, Daddy. He's here!" Bonnie announced.

Sanders stepped around the girl and held out his hand. Doc Hill peeled off rubber gloves and shook the offered hand firmly, a big bearded smile stretching across his face.

"Good morning, Melvin. Come in, come in." Doc said, stepping back. The office was also an examination room, all in one, and the stainless steel table and countertops gleamed. Lemon and bleach competed in the air, and Melvin knew he'd interrupted a morning of cleaning, the preparation for the workday ahead.

Glancing at Bonnie, Doc said, "Is that for me, or have you taken up decaffeinated over hot chocolate?"

"Oh, yeah! Your coffee. Sorry, Dad."

Doc took the cup and Bonnie stood there suddenly aware she had nothing to do. She moved to pick up her father's gloves and continue the scrubbing, but he interrupted her. "Bonnie, why don't you go take Samson on a walk."

"I already did that."

"Then go help your mother clean up breakfast."

"I already did that too."

"Bonnie, go do something somewhere else so I can talk to the deputy in private."

Bonnie frowned. "Bye, Deputy Sanders. If you'd like a sausage biscuit before you leave, stop by the kitchen—"

"Bonnie!"

"Okay, Dad, geez." She gave the deputy one final bright smile as she edged out the door, closing it reluctantly behind her.

"Teenagers," Doc sighed. "Here I am sixty years old and father to a beautiful girl who suddenly has every adolescent hormone firing at once. What was I thinking?"

Deputy Sanders laughed and took a sip of the dark brew. Hazelnut.

"Now to what do I owe the pleasure of your visit, Melvin? I'm assuming you've not run out and adopted an animal yet."

"I'm still working on that part, Doc. My schedule doesn't allow for much more in my house than fish. And even taking care of fish right now might be risking their lives."

"You've got your hands full."

"You can say that again."

"This about Clifford Hughes? I don't know that I can contribute much beyond what I did last time. Never seen anything like that from an animal, Melvin. Hope to never see anything like that again."

"Don't worry, Doc. I didn't come bearing pictures this time. Actually, I need to ask you some questions about a client of yours, Ivy Cole."

"Ivy?" Doc set his mug down and leaned against the exam table. Then, remembering his manners, he pushed a rolling stool the deputy's direction. Melvin set his own empty mug atop the green vinyl, but remained standing.

"I know Ivy as well as a person could through office visits," Doc said. "All told, though, that's been a lot of visits. She's got a lot of dogs. Been bringing them to me since she first moved to Doe Springs."

"And when was that exactly?" An unnecessary question. Melvin already knew the answer, but routine questions were habit.

"A little over a year ago."

Melvin pulled out a notepad and pen. "How many has she brought in all together?" Eight. Melvin wrote it before the vet answered.

"Including the latest, eight. Most were her pets when she moved here, one she found on the way, and the last one

I believe you've met in person. That was real nice of you to give her a ride, by the way."

"Yes, sir. Now, about the dogs. What are they like, the ones she's had the longest?"

"Sweet-natured animals, every one. Ivy is a dog trainer with a gentle hand, and it shows in her work. I've referred plenty people to her. Don't know how many actually make it to a class, but I hear she's doing okay for herself."

"You've never noted any aggressive behavior out of her dogs or any you know she's trained?" Melvin held his pen ready over the paper.

Doc Hill scratched his head, mulling that one over. There was one day, an incident, a moment . . . It was Doc's day off, but Ivy called to see if she could bring in her shepherd, Aufhocker. Seeing's how Ivy was new in town and the dog only needed routine vaccinations, Doc told her to drop by. *Betty, gone with Bonnie . . . where?* Doc couldn't remember, but it didn't matter. The point was they'd left Samson outside like they always did on his day off, and Doc didn't think of it until he heard the commotion out front. What he saw still amazed him. The black shepherd and his Dane rolled in a snarling tangle on the ground. Doc grabbed the broom by the door, and started to run out, then stopped. Ivy had stepped around the side of her van and walked in the middle of the gnashing teeth. Her lips moved, but she spoke too low for the vet to hear. Immediately both dogs fell back. When Doc Hill finally came out, Samson was licking the woman's hand and the shepherd lay at her feet.

"Aggressive tendencies?" Doc Hill came back to the question.

"No. Nothing out of the ordinary. They're protective of Ivy, but that's only natural. Dogs bond close to their owners."

Melvin tapped his pen on the notepad, waiting. The good vet looked like he might have something to add, but the thought sucked backward before it could come out. What did emerge was another broad smile and a shrug of the shoulders, dismissing any further exploration of the question.

"Let's get back to the other dogs, the newer strays she's

picked up along the way. Maybe they're not trained as well. What about them?"

"Good pups, all of them."

"Ever come in with any out-of-the-ordinary injuries? Bleeding or torn gums? Missing hair? Bite marks or signs of fighting?"

Doc Hill didn't know whether to laugh or get angry. "Deputy, I'm not an idiot. I swear it sounds like you're implying something here, and I don't like to make wrong assumptions. Just ask me outright, son."

"Ask you what, sir? I'm just gathering information about some of the animals and people in the vicinity of the attack a few nights ago."

"All right, then, I'll save you some beating-around-the-bush time. Do I think Ivy is caring for a pack of murdering hounds over there? No. Do I think the dogs she's picked up have ever hurt anyone? They couldn't catch their own tails, let alone bring down Hereford cattle. A loud yell wilts half of them—Clifford could have managed that and a big boot in some canine ribs besides. Eight dogs don't make a wild slavering pack of monsters, Deputy. It just makes eight poor, lost, unfortunate animals that were lucky enough to come across an angel's path like Ivy's. If you want to see suspicious injuries, come with me."

Melvin, pocketing the notebook, followed the vet through the laundry room and garage to a simple structure not much bigger than a garden shed. Behind it stretched a chain-link run ending in a twelve-by-twelve pebbled turnout. Doc flipped on the light inside the one-room building. A few scattered cages lined one wall. "This is the kennel for overnight visitors too sick to go home. Right now, fortunately, we're running plenty of vacancies. However, we just got a permanent admission."

Doc led the deputy to a small cage on a shelf four feet off the ground. A pillow and bunched-up blanket hid something huddled in the far corner. Doc reached past food dishes and a stuffed mouse to pull out a raggedy-looking tabby cat. It hung in the vet's hands like a broken toy. "When she's feeling better, we'll introduce her to Samson and hope they don't tear the house down."

"I saw Mildred Parson bring this cat in," Melvin said.

"You didn't see this." Doc turned the cat on its back and tucked it in the crook of his arm for support. Cigarette burns marred the soft tummy. "She's declawed. Couldn't defend herself if she wanted to. If you're itching to arrest somebody today, go on over to Frank Parson's house and ask him to explain this cat."

Thirty-five minutes after the interview with Doc Hill ended, Deputy Sanders was in another part of the county sitting uncomfortably on the edge of a plastic-covered couch with a teacup balanced on one knee and his notebook on the other.

"Chippy, down. Good boy. Now stay!" Ruthy White, standing in the middle of her living room floor, whipped her head around to Deputy Sanders proudly. The helmet of tight brown curls around her face snapped back into place at the end of the motion. Ruthy was a housewife with empty-nest syndrome, and Chippy was her latest project since the last kid left home. Nester, Ruthy White's husband, sought shelter from his eagerly attentive wife at the Moose Lodge most days.

"I could never get him to do that before. He'll sit there all day if I don't release him," Ruthy said.

Chippy the pug lay at his mistress's feet and stared up at the officer through Mr. Magoo eyes.

"Quite impressive," Melvin said.

"Aren't you going to write it down?" Ruthy looked at the officer's notepad. Melvin set his teacup on the end table and then carefully wrote "Dog obeyed all commands. Quite impressive."

Ruthy beamed. "It's all because of Ivy Cole. You should see what she can do with most these dogs. Is the police department in Doe Springs considering getting some dogs, Deputy? Because if you're looking for a trainer recommendation, I can give one wholeheartedly."

Melvin nodded thoughtfully. He'd sat in Mrs. White's living room for the better part of twenty minutes now watching Chippy perform a variety of duties and tricks. He'd retrieved bones, a Frisbee, and his plastic food dish, strangely labeled

Kitty. He'd rolled over, played dead, shook hands, barked on cue, and danced on his stubby hind legs. Melvin was all Chippied out, and a little lie didn't seem like a bad idea if it would get them to the point. "Yes, we have considered starting our own K-9 unit, but I don't know that Miss Cole would be the right trainer after all. I mean, teaching dogs to sit, stay, come—all those things are important. But police dogs need special training. They have to be fearless. And they have to learn to bite. Does Miss Cole do any kind of training like that, that you're aware of?"

Ruthy sucked air through her teeth as she thought about it. Flecks of red lipstick dotted her pearly whites, which Melvin suspected might be a partial plate. Finally, the woman shook her head. "I don't think so, Deputy Sanders. I've been to a lot of her classes. It's all manners stuff. Making dogs good citizens and the like. Most of her students are like Chippy: house dogs and overly spoiled pets that need a little straightening out. She teaches them how *not* to nip and bark. Not the kind of training that brings a criminal down, huh?"

"No, I'm afraid not. Mrs. White, you mentioned Ivy is good with most dogs. Does she ever have problems with some of them?"

Ruthy paused too long, and Melvin suspected a negative thought peeped from behind the merriment in her head but was hesitant to come on out. Just like Doc. Apparently Ivy inspired loyalty in people as well as dogs.

"In Chippy's class," Ruthy finally said, "there was only one dog she couldn't do anything with. He seemed like the sweetest thing but turned vicious every time Ivy got near him. His owner was so embarrassed, said the dog had never behaved that way in his life. They left after the first session and never came back. That was months ago, back when Chippy only knew how to chew up my favorite slippers and pee on the carpet."

"Hmm. I guess even the best teachers get a problem student every now and then. What kind of dog was it?"

"Let me see, it was something foreign sounding. Fancy. I'd never heard of it before. Didn't know the owner either. One of those *Yankees*." Her voice lowered on the last like a dirty word. Outsiders were swarming over the mountains in locust droves, trying to escape their polluted city lives, and locals didn't take to it well. Hospitality was running in short supply anymore, and Ruthy seemed none too bothered the man was gone from the class for good. Funny, considering Ivy had rolled into their neck of the woods all the way from Los Angeles. But the Southern accent gave her a leg up on the competition. Being from Out West was easier swallowed than from Up North to most folks, no matter from which region of the South they themselves hailed.

"That's all right. Doesn't matter." Melvin fingered his notebook and rooted about his brain for any more questions. "Just curious, Mrs. White, does Ivy Cole ever bring any of her dogs to the classes with her? Maybe for demonstrations or the like?"

Chippy, thinking he'd been forgotten amidst the conversation, started to rise. Mrs. White nailed him with a don't-even-think-about-it-buster glare and the pug flattened out belly to carpet once more. The glare softened as it traveled from dog to deputy. "You know, she does bring her dog Alf with her once in awhile. For the first class, she used him to show us what our dogs could learn. Now when she brings him he just sleeps in the corner. Big fella."

"I believe I've seen him. That's the only one she's ever brought?"

"Yep."

"Do you know about any of his training?"

"Like the guard dog work you're talking about? Hmm. I know Alf can do everything Chippy just showed you and better. Well, except for the dancing thing. I've never seen him do that. A big dog I suppose wouldn't. And he is an awful big dog, a hundred fifty pounder if he's an ounce. I guess he's a good guard dog by nature of his size—anybody seeing a shepherd like that would think twice before taking him on. If intimidation is half the job of a guard dog, then yes, I suppose she uses him like that. Living alone like she does, she'd need something for protection." Mrs. White paused at the last thought and looked Melvin up and down. "You're single, aren't you, Deputy Sanders?"

"Uh, yes, ma'am."

"You know, Deputy, my Hannah is in her fourth year of college at Western Carolina, and I bet you two would have a lot in common."

"Oh, well, yes, ma'am . . ."

"You need to drop by next time she's home from school. I'll be sure to tell her all about you."

Melvin flipped the notebook closed and tucked it in his pocket. Interview terminated. All good cops knew when it was time to beat a hasty retreat.

He glanced at his watch and effected a disappointed frown, which he hoped looked convincing. "Looks like I'm about late for a department meeting, Mrs. White. I've taken up enough of your time, anyway. Thank you for your help. Bye, Chippy."

Melvin stepped over the pug, and Mrs. White followed him to the door. "You take care, Deputy Sanders. I'll tell Hannah you stopped by!"

Melvin strode to his car. He started the ignition, just as Mrs. White came running around to his side and banged on the window. He slowly rolled it down, fearful a phone number was about to be thrust into the vehicle.

"Borzoi," Mrs. White said. "I just remembered the breed of that dog, and it was a borzoi—also called a Russian wolfhound."

Chapter 8

While Deputy Sanders conducted an interview with a lonely homemaker and her praiseworthy pug, Frank Parson was in an interview of another sort. The bank buzzed with lunch-hour activity, and he was a minute shy of kicking everybody out, especially this fat prude sitting in front of him. He was bank manager, he could do what he wanted. The latter part of that thought floated wistfully under Frank's painted pate; it was a fantasy he clung to in moments like these. But reality was this: Twenty-five minutes of his time—of his lunch hour *on Wednesday,* no less—were wasted, and he would sit here for another hour with this vapid smile molded on his face, if that's what he had to do. It's what bankers did, if they wanted to get paid, manager or not.

"I just don't know which way to go, Mr. Parson," the fat prude said. "CDs, IRAs, stocks versus bonds. It's all so confusing. Could you explain your 401(k) roll-over options again?"

The air whistled in Frank's narrow nostrils as he breathed in and expelled carefully. Calm was fighting to elude him, but good God almighty, managers should not be forced to put up with aggravation such as this. It was hard enough running a bank. Yet things like this always happened, especially at the worst of times, and today was no exception. After forty-five minutes with Ed, the assistant manager had given up and passed the buck, sending this addle-brained woman the chief manager's way. An answer to her hundredth redundant question forced its way through thin lips: "I don't think I could possibly make it any clearer, Mrs. Butterwart. Surely after everything Mr. Ripple and I have explained to you—"

"That's Butterwert, not wart."

"Of course, excuse me." Frank glanced at the wall clock and saw the minute hand click on over to twelve twenty-nine. Lunchtime, almost half over. Oh, the things he could be doing right now. A mental hand glided over Cheryl's smooth thigh. Would she still be waiting for him at the restaurant after this long? She'd better be. "Here, why don't you take some pamphlets home and think it over. Maybe have a friend or relative help you make a decision. Then come back in and see us, and we'll be happy to set you up an account." Frank walked around his desk and reached for the woman's elbow to assist her out. Before he could grasp the fleshy protrusion, she snatched it away. Her bulk remained wedged between the padded arms of the office chair, and he doubted he could pry her out alone. She was rooted, and he was stuck.

"But Mr. Parson, I really wanted to do something today. I said this morning when I got up, 'Now Greta, you are going down to that bank today and getting all your financial affairs in order.' I've put it off for so long. You see, after my husband passed away, I just let all this go until one day I woke up and said, 'Now Greta, you have to pull your life together. . . .' "

Pink painted lips formed words of a sort, but all Frank could hear was the time and his patience slipping away. The smile plastered to his face melted into a grimace. Click! Twelve-thirty. Click! Twelve-thirty-one. By one o'clock, his afternoon would be ruined. It would be a-whole-nother week before he could see Cheryl again, and that was iffy. The husband was getting squirrelly as of late. He'd miraculously sprung a pulse and started taking interest in his wife's comings and goings. Maybe Frank could call up Rhonda for drinks tomorrow after work instead. Not as good-looking as Cheryl, for sure. Horse-faced came to mind. But the things that woman could do . . . Working at the mill may have stunted her career creativity, but she more than made up for it in the bedroom. And no husband. Hmmm. Mildred would be with her sewing circle tomorrow night. . . .

" . . . and I thought, 'Now Greta—' "

No, he really wanted to see Cheryl. She was the sweetest piece of cake in the county, and this was Wednesday after all. He deserved a little special dessert after putting up with this bank and that wife and her bratty kid and this whole freakin' town for umpteen years of his miserable life. *But how to get rid of Buttwart* . . .

"Mrs. Butterwart—"

"Wert, it's Butter*wert!*"

The muscles in Frank's neck tightened. Anger wadded up into a snug knot at the base of it and shot straight up the spinal pipeline to throb behind his eyes. Suppressed stress, his doctor had said of the migraines. Too much tension bottled up. It needed an outlet. The quack had refused medication and recommended yoga. What was this world coming to?

"Ma'am, this is my lunch hour and as much as I've enjoyed hearing all about your personal revelations, I have to leave. My apologies. Now you take these pamphlets, go home, and read them over thoroughly. They'll tell you everything you need to know and some you don't. Study them, Mrs. Butterworth. Study them!" Frank reached for the elbow again and took a firm hold. He hauled the woman to her feet and stuck a handful of leaflets in her shiny patent leather purse. Elbow still in one hand, Frank grasped the office door with the other and pushed her through. Mrs. Butter-whatever-it-was turned to speak, but he cut her off:

"Study them!" Frank slammed the door. A trickle of sweat beaded down between his eyes. Frank pulled a crisp white handkerchief from his suit pocket to wipe it, only to see it come away black. Damn. His hair was running. No time to mess with it now. He had less than thirty minutes to make it to the restaurant, gulp down some food, and drive out to the Motel 6 on the interstate. If he called ahead, he could get the food to go and eat in the car on the way over. Frank picked up the phone.

A polite tap-tap on his door.

"Jesus Christ!" Frank slammed the phone down. "What is it?"

A teller poked her head in. "There's a lady here to see you, Mr. Parson. Says she wants to open a savings account."

"Tell her to see Ed. I'm on my lunch break."

"She doesn't want to see Ed. She asked for you specifically." The teller paused, then added, "She's a real looker too. Name's *Miss* Cole." The teller eyed her boss smugly when he came to the door. There was a good ten bucks in it for her if he accepted the appointment. Two other tellers watched the office from across the room, both hoping Mr. Parson would make good on his Wednesday "lunch."

Frank looked over the teller's shoulder. A blonde in a tailored white suit sat in the reception area perusing the *Farmers' Almanac*. Frank looked at the clock. Twelve-thirty-six. Ah, to hell with it. He'd never make it now anyway. "All right, send her in. And have somebody get me a cheeseburger. I'm starving."

Chapter 9

Sheriff Gloria Hubbard drummed her short nails on the weathered desk in front of her. It was merely a habit, not signaling impatience or irritation. Moreso, the fingers played in cadence with her thoughts. Rapid, steady, methodical. Right now, she was thinking and drumming hard as she listened to her deputies seated on the other side of the desk's mound of familiar paperwork, itself a growing fortress dividing her from the rest of the world. But she didn't feel safe behind it. *Smothered,* she thought. *I'm smothering under this paperwork of the—*

". . . dead."

"What's that, Sanders?" The fingers stopped drumming as Gloria realized her concentration had wandered off into distraction.

"I said we can safely assume that lead is dead. A dead end." Sanders put the notepad back in his pocket.

Gloria nodded thoughtfully, turning and tossing every word of Sanders's account to the rhythm of her fingers, which had revived into a lively da-da-da-*da* in front of her. According to Sanders, the vet did nothing but sing Ivy Cole's praises, and by the same token, Ruthy White claimed she could all but walk on water. The sheriff's youngest deputy, interestingly enough, seemed relieved to put the Ivy Cole issue to rest. Yesterday turned up just about what Gloria expected: not much. It had been worth a shot.

Gloria turned to Deputy Meeks. "What have you got?"

Jonathan Meeks, who did not have a notepad, relayed the meeting with Jack Lutsky first.

"Mr. Lutsky was gone on the night of Hughes's death. His house isn't too far from Miss Cole's, but he drives a truck and he's away a lot. That night he was hauling a load up to Illinois. There is no Mrs. Lutsky—he lives alone and shares his time between the house near Miss Cole's and his mama's place in town. So, other than Ivy's, there are no other households in the vicinity that could have heard anything."

"What's the nearest property bordering Lutsky's, east of the Cole house where Clifford's body was found?"

"Andy Talbot's sheep farm. I've spoken with the Talbots already and they didn't see or hear anything that night either."

"All right. Anything else?"

"Well, there was one interesting thing Lutsky said."

"And what was that?" the sheriff asked.

"He said Miss Cole paid him cash for the house. He offered to owner finance it for her, but she wrote him a check the same day she came to look at the place."

"Sounds like Ivy has a buck or two tucked away somewhere. And Lutsky offered to owner finance the house, just like that? I know Jack, not well, but enough. That doesn't sound like him," Gloria said.

"I get the feeling he's sweet on her."

"Well, isn't everybody." Gloria maintained Meeks's gaze, but Deputy Sanders looked away.

"What about Patricia, what did she have to say?"

Meeks scratched behind his ear and shrugged shoulders that stretched the limits of his uniform. "Says she went to the grocery store about four, then came straight home and started making dinner. She was looking for Clifford to be home around five-thirty or six."

"Then she didn't know he was going to Ivy Cole's for a late delivery?"

"Nope. Said he never mentioned it to her and neither did Ivy."

"So what did she do when Clifford didn't show up for dinner?"

"Nothing. Said she put his plate in the oven and went to bed. I got the impression she'd learned not to ask questions when her husband didn't show up at the house on time."

"A pattern she was used to?"

"Yeah, that's the way I figured it."

"What time did Patricia go to bed that night?"

"Around ten, right after she got off the phone with her mother."

"And she still wasn't worried about Clifford? She didn't try to reach him on his cell phone?"

"No, but she was on the phone, all right. Talked with her mama in Alabama for the better part of two hours—I'd hate to be footing that bill. I checked the phone records and it pans out. They were on the line from seven-forty-two to nine-thirty-eight, to be exact. Then she went right to sleep until Sanders here knocked on her door."

An alibi: phone records and a dear sainted mother in Alabama. The unconcern for a husband who didn't show up for dinner would, in itself, sound peculiar, if Gloria didn't know the circumstances. But since she did, it was nothing to go by. For all she knew, Patricia went to bed that night grateful to have her mother to talk to and grateful some other woman might be suffering through her husband's attentions in the meantime. On the other hand, why didn't Clifford or Ivy Cole mention the late delivery if there was no hanky-panky involved between them?

"When was the last time Ivy and Patricia spoke, prior to the late delivery?"

"Two weeks before. They'd aimed to go shopping for some kind of arts-and-crafts thing and ended up having words instead. Patricia said Ivy got aggravated with her. She hinted around that Ivy was after her to leave Clifford again. That seemed to be a common argument between them, and Patricia was sick of hearing it. They ended the day early—"

"And have been mad at each other ever since, until now. Hence, Ivy would not have told Patricia about the late delivery or bothered with trying to pick the delivery up at Patricia's house."

"Yeah, I guess so. All kind of makes sense now, if you think about it." Meeks leaned back in the rickety office chair and it groaned with his weight. Not quite as tall as Sanders, Deputy Meeks was a powerfully built man in his own right. Approaching middle age, he was still in peak shape. Looking from one deputy to the other, Gloria was glad she had these two watching her back.

"Yes, everything ties up pretty conveniently, doesn't it?" Gloria said. "We're back to square one. Nobody knows anything, nobody heard anything. For months we've hiked through the woods tracking a wild animal or animals that leave no trails, no prints, and not even complete bodies. And who now, perhaps, may have an affinity for jewelry. Good job, gentlemen. Dismissed."

Gloria picked up her phone and pretended to dial. Sanders and Meeks sat where they were, uncomfortably at attention.

"Go on now, fellas." Gloria's tone softened. The deputies shuffled out of the office, and she was immediately sorry she'd snapped at them. They were all doing the best they could. And it clearly wasn't good enough. Not even close. Clifford Hughes was the fourth victim in Doe Springs. Soon the SBI would be champing at the bit to get involved. City thinkers in city suits, nosing around in her business, tromping through her woods and her files, pretending to offer assistance but instead, stamping a big fat letter F on her forehead for another failure to add to her short list of only one.

But Gloria couldn't think about the past right now. About Annie and the years before Doe Springs. There was a time and place for that grief, and it was in her nightmares, but not here, in the waking hours when all her focus had to be set on the *(curse)* case before her. *I'm a good cop, dammit. I am!* Her whole life had been devoted to it. Doe Springs, male dominated and more than a little red behind the collar, had trusted her enough—a woman—to take over the job of sheriff five years ago after leaving the Albemarle police force *(and Annie)* to come home and make it on her own. She wouldn't let them down. But the local trackers, the biplane scouts, the Malinois driven all the way over from the Asheville K-9 division, even the Cherokee Indian who claimed to have psychic connections to animals, had come up with nothing credible or definitive, no finger pointing to a solution and saying with assurance, "This here's your culprit and you can catch it like this. . . ."

The sheriff had hoped if they couldn't catch whatever haunted the backwoods and alleys of Doe Springs, it would eventually migrate elsewhere or die of natural causes. Maybe a truck would hit it on one of its moon-shrouded sojourns down from the Blue Ridge. But then Clifford Hughes turned up and the town feared the cycle was fueled all over again.

The cycle. The full moon connection became obvious quickly. Gloria researched the moon's influence on animal life, interviewed numerous biologists and zoologists, but found nothing related to what was happening in Doe Springs. The only person with any kind of theory at all was the crazy old Indian. "It's a werewolf," he said, before they packed him up and carted him back to the reservation.

Gloria had her own theory. The Devil of Doe Springs was human, not an animal at all—a human working *with* a viciously trained four-legged companion. This person was intelligent, a loner, someone living near the town who could come and go unnoticed and train in the privacy of their home, but with no immediate neighbors to pry. Someone talented with animals, an intuitive animal whisperer, if you believed in such things. Maybe someone who hadn't lived here long, say, a year thereabouts, when the first bit of trouble had started. Someone with an interest in the moon and its cycles, maybe even collected rare books on its folklore. Someone, perhaps, like Ivy Cole.

"That's ridiculous," Gloria muttered. She rubbed her eyes and realized she still held the phone in her hand. She dialed for real. A man's deep Southern drawl answered, surprising the sheriff. She'd expected the answering machine, then she could quickly change her mind and hang up. She considered it anyway. Then a picture of Clifford's mangled corpse and another full moon on the horizon resigned her to speech.

"Hello, Tee? This is Gloria. I know you're sitting there with your feet propped up enjoying life in Montana, but slide your boots on, cowboy. I need your help."

Part Two

"Fairy tales have been written about you. . . .
But I never believed they were true."

Part Two

Chapter 10

The sheep barely stirred as the night breeze picked up. It was early, three-twenty-two a.m., and they slept unafraid, lulled into security by the presence of their guardian Border collies and the farmer's house at the bottom of the hill. They were fat sheep, a herd of thirty strong, accustomed to all the sweet grass they could eat, a barn for shelter, piles of hay and corn thrown into their pasture in winter. The price paid in return was the loss of their wool once a year, a small price, indeed.

The collies also slept, their guard not once challenged in all of their time on duty. An occasional fox played fair game for entertainment but never proved a threat. It was a comfortable life for sheep and dog alike.

Tonight the full moon illuminated the pasture, deepening shadows within the thick stand of trees surrounding it. The farmer's house and barn stood dark below where the sheep huddled together, their black faces disappearing into irregular mounds of grayish-cream wool trying to recover from the spring shearing. Occasionally an ear twitched or tiny hooves shuffled to regain balance, but otherwise, the breeze and flowing grasses were all that stirred on this quiet June night.

The oldest Border collie, Sadie, raised her head. Her younger companion still slept, but the hairs prickling on the back of her neck woke her. She never completely slept. She was seasoned, a real sheepherder before becoming so old her original master gave her away. Now she lived here, mostly as a pet, but her instincts had not left her. There was a tang on the air this night, and the scent prickled her graying muzzle. Not unpleasant entirely. But entirely wrong.

Sadie softly rose to her feet. She scanned the herd—her herd—painfully aware the night vision of her birth had retreated somewhat as the summers accumulated behind her.

The sheep still slumbered in tight knots, their bodies knit like pulled wads of cotton. At the bottom of the hill below the pasture, the house too, still slept, its paned eyes sightless coal squares in the white framework. Opposite the sheep on the other side, the tree line and a cluster of boulders walled in the pasture, a natural rock-and-timber border uninteresting to grazers of sweet Junetime grass. Nothing stirred there, or anywhere that the dog could tell. Sadie's gaze dropped to Baxter, her younger companion. He remained curled nose to tail, puppylike and undisturbed. Perhaps she'd been mistaken. Sadie sniffed the breeze again. No. Something carried on the wind.

Sadie's hair bristled, rising into a black-and-white ridge along the ruff of her neck. A low growl escaped through the beginnings of a snarl, a posture she had not taken since encountering a black bear many years ago. He had lumbered along the edge of another pasture she tended when barely older than Baxter. She ferociously barked and lunged at the heels of the large animal through the fencing, but her threats went barely noticed. The bear had not been interested in her or the sheep; he was after a blackberry patch a good two miles away and did not even turn to acknowledge the dog's presence on his purposeful trek to those plump, ripe riches. Nevertheless, Sadie, trembling with a charge of fear and adrenaline, had trotted back to her unmolested herd, victorious. Her master of the time had arrived by then, gun in hand, to reward her with *Good dog, good dog* and a welcome pat on the head.

But this smell was not of the bear or any other animal Sadie had encountered in her fourteen years of guardianship, and the growl clearing her throat intensified. The noise roused Baxter; he stood beside her, suddenly alert. Both dogs lifted their heads into the breeze.

Sadie took off at a trot across the grass, Baxter on her heels. She circled the herd, nose to the air, then the ground, then the air again in rhythm with her footfalls. Baxter emulated his senior, fighting the uneasy quaking of his juvenile heart. He smelled it now too, but it was alien to his limited experience. Breeding told the collie to wait, listen, discover, as the old dog did. But canine intuition pawed at a different level of breeding: survival instincts. Right now they were screaming *run*. Baxter ignored thousands of years of evolution and continued the purposeful exploration around the herd perimeter, only to run into the tail of his leader, who had abruptly stopped and faced the woods again.

Nothing moved along the bouldered tree line, but the smell uncoiled from that direction. It wafted on a steady stream toward the canine pair like a filmy oil, which clung to the hairs of their noses. Old rotting meat quarreled with their master's chicken coop in their fine-tuned muzzles, but yet, it was neither scent. There was a dankness to it, like plowed dirt after a rain.

Something ancient began to well within the elder Border collie as recognition slowly dawned. This was not a foreign stench after all. It was old, older than her breed, predating her furthest ancestors. An unexpected yearning diluted the dog's concern—to leave her post and join the visitor, running free into the night, a pack of two beneath a cornflower moon. There was primal kinship here, but despite the sudden enlightenment, Sadie did not sense benevolence emanating from the strangeness in the forest. She sensed nothing at all except a scent that belied another's camouflaged presence and a draw to it that caused fear and longing to wrestle side-by-side within her well-trained sheepherder's brain.

The dog's aging eyes once more swept the jagged silhouette of limbs and rock laced into a curtain of purple on black. The full moon overhead spotlighted her and her companion but revealed nothing. But what her eyes could not see, her nose told her well enough. She looked harder, breaking the search down into its parts starting ground up. Left to right, right to left, the grass, a tall stand of Queen Anne's lace, the rocks large and small and larger still, the tree trunks . . .. Sadie's head whipped back to the left.

She saw it. The massive shape hunched, unmoving, on the edge of the woods. A boulder, she'd first thought, just like all the others clustered at the base of the trees, but with two sparks of light like pebbles afire, which had flared out of the rock, then died away as the intruder blinked or turned its head. It had been there the whole time, watching them.

Baxter followed Sadie's gaze. Orange eyes stared out of the boulders, two perfect pupils that blazed brighter before disappearing again. The woods were dark once more, but the hunched shape was still there, its outline barely discernible. Something was among them, and whatever its intentions, Baxter suddenly did not care. This was no fox or wandering house cat or lost neighbor's dog come calling. This was not easy game or a night's simple entertainment. The hair along Baxter's back puffed out like porcupine quills, and his once proud tail melted between his hind legs. A tinny whine escaped him, then crescendoed into a piercing howl that broke the night. Behind the dogs, the sheep jolted awake. Confused, the animals lunged into each other, while their dog barked and howled at the trees. Sadie joined him then, adrenaline charging through her old veins. A sheep slammed into her side, twisting her haunches out from under her. A surprised yelp clipped her baying short, but she was up again and racing toward the tree line, unmindful of the blood streaming down her injured leg or the fact her once peaceful herd was now stampeding down the hill toward the barn, Baxter right behind them.

The house at the bottom of the hill snapped to life, first with a light in the upstairs of the house followed by the glare from the porch's one bare bulb. A man stood beneath the dim glow, hastily buttoning his pants over the tails of his nightshirt. A big gun dangled from a strap over the man's shoulder.

"Sadie! Baxter!" Andy Talbot came off the porch, squinting up the hill as his sheep came galloping toward him.

"What the heck?" The farmer stepped into the yard. The moon lit up the field in front of him, and he walked forward without a flashlight. The sheep huddled barnside now, crowded into the small adjoining paddock. Out from behind the frightened herd, something rushed toward the old man, and he attempted to unshoulder the gun, wrangling strap and barrel until it was free and pointed at his attacker. The shape emerged from the shadows into the light of moon and porch.

"Baxter! What are you doing down here, boy? What's going on?" The dog heeled at the farmer's feet. Andy laid a hand on the collie's head. "You're shaking like a quake, fella. Where's Sadie? Sadie!"

He heard her, barking at the top of the hill. "Sadie! Sadie, come on down here, girl!"

The barking paused, then resumed louder than ever. Andy moved to shoulder the gun again, but the pitch of his dog's voice advised him different. *Better check it out, I reckon. Ain't like her, ain't like her a'tall.* Andy skirted his sheep—none hurt, far as he could make out—and began trudging up the hill. The earth was pitted from the trampling of one hundred twenty panicked feet. *Make that one-twenty-four.* Andy looked back at Baxter, who remained within the circle of the porch light.

At the top of the hill, the farmer bent to catch his breath, his seventy-year-old heart complaining loudly in his chest. He pushed off his knees and straightened up, the gun clasped firmly in both fists. Sadie bounded back and forth a ways in front of him, close to the woods and raising Cain.

"Hey now, hey now, easy there. What do you see, Sadie?" Andy approached his irate dog much like sneaking up on a quail in the grass. She had yet to acknowledge him, and a nasty thought crept right along with Andy as he crept toward his beloved pet. *Rabies.*

Sadie stopped barking and whipped around to face the farmer. Andy stopped and stood upright, the blood in his face running cold. Sadie's lips were peeled back showing all tooth and an inch of gum. Foam dripped from her lower jowl, and her hind leg was wet, with urine or blood or something else, Andy could not tell.

"Sadie? It's me, girl. Don't you recognize me?" Andy held the gun like a protective bar out in front of him, but at the sound of his voice, Sadie's expression relaxed. She ran to her master and barked up at him, then raced back to the edge of the woods, doing the same.

Andy's breath escaped in a loud whoosh—he hadn't realized he'd been holding it when Sadie raced toward him. Both dogs had given him a scare tonight, and he was starting to feel like a foolish old man. Nevertheless, something had them all stirred up bigger than shoot, and he stared hard into the woods to try to see what. The forest revealed nothing he hadn't seen for the past forty years: trees and rocks. Andy wished he'd brought that flashlight after all.

"A fox out looking for my chickens again, old girl?" Andy didn't think so. His dogs would've chased a fox off without waking him or stampeding the herd. Especially Sadie, the smarter of the two. She didn't go ape like this over foxes, and Baxter loved to chase them, not run away with his tail between his legs. This weren't no ordinary behavior from his dogs; this was pure spooked.

Andy swallowed, but his throat had turned to desert. Grit clogged his gullet just over the rise of his bony Adam's apple, and he coughed. His mind's eye focused in on a newspaper lying open on the workbench back at the barn. He'd saved the paper, but Margie wouldn't let him keep it in the house. Too morbid, his wife had said, as she tossed it out back onto the burn pile. Andy had snagged the front-page news out of the flames, then spread the charred print across the bench in his shop to read again and again. Clifford Hughes, their very own deliveryman and Margie's cousin's neighbor, the latest victim just one short month ago. In the woods. Torn to pieces. Definitely another animal attack. Just like all the others. *Under a full moon.*

The old farmer tilted his head back, his knobby chin pointing straight toward the sky, the moon a giant blue-yellow cheese wheel hanging just over his head. He swallowed again with no luck. *Dry mouth, sweaty hands, you are an old fool. That's what Margie would say.* Andy tried to laugh, but he choked on the effort. The loaded gun did not feel reassuring in his hand. Not at all. Nothing moved in the trees, yet Sadie was still berserk.

Andy mustered his courage and walked toward the woods. The boulders drew closer, black figures in the dark. He held the gun at belly-level, but the barrel trembled. Standing before the frightening black forms, he hollered over top them: "Anybody there? Anybody out there? I got a gun, so you just get on out of this place, you hear me?"

Only the wind answered, swirling the grass around Andy's ankles and rustling the leaves in the trees. Sadie ceased the relentless barking and jogged from boulder to boulder, sniffing each one from top to bottom before moving to the next. An unsettling whine scraped up her throat, raw and thin, as she traveled between the rocks.

A bright light shone behind Andy, cutting the forest all around. Andy turned to see Margie behind the wheel of their pickup, perched right where hilltop and hillside met.

"Get in this truck right now, you crazy old coot," she yelled.

Andy looked at his wife's frightened face and didn't argue. He turned as casually as he could muster casual and forced himself to walk all the way to the truck. Baxter hung out the passenger window but scootched to the middle of the seat when Andy got in.

"What's up here, Andy? Did you run it off?"

"Nothing. Dog's gone all peculiar over some rocks. Must be the full moon."

"Yes, the full moon. Let's get back inside." Margie reached for the gearshift, but Andy stayed her hand.

"Wait a minute, Margie, where'd Sadie get to? She was just beside me. We got to get her."

"What we got to get is to the house. Sadie knows her way."

Andy leaned out the window and whistled. "Where the heck is she? Drive on up closer to those rocks."

"We're going to the house—"

"For Pete's sake, woman, just drive on up to those rocks. I don't want to leave her up here."

Margie's lips thinned, but she held her tongue and wrestled the long stick shift around in the floorboard. The gears grumbled, but with a final knock and a yank, Margie wrenched the Ford back into first gear. The truck lurched forward as her bedroom-slippered foot slid off the clutch.

"There . . . she is . . . I . . . see her," Andy's voice hiccupped with the bump of the truck across the field. Sadie still ran from one boulder to the other, nose to the ground. Andy leaned out the window. "Come on, girl! Come on, Sadie, let's go to the house!"

The Border collie stopped and listened. She turned her head to her master calling just as a flash of movement barreled toward her from the other side.

Andy's eyes widened as something large and burly ran toward his dog. *"No!"* he thought he yelled, but it was his wife's terrified scream that jarred him. Andy grabbed for the shotgun, but Margie, with no trouble this time, slammed the truck in reverse, knocking the gun to the floor. The truck flew backward down the hill and away from the terrible howling that followed them.

Chapter 11

Sheriff Hubbard dreamt hard, of a moonlit forest path and something bearing down on her fast, its breath hot on the back of her neck. She ran blindly, the rocks on her bare feet slowing her escape. She rounded a corner in the path, sure the creature would take her down now, but up ahead, blocking the way, crouched another beast. Its eyes glittered orange as it lunged toward her. . . .

A jangling noise sent Gloria bolt upright in her chair. Disoriented, she knocked the desk clock to the floor before realizing it was the phone that had woke her. Annoying. Not the phone. Her. After endless sheet-twisting, insomnia-ridden nights in her own bed, she had drifted off here in the office after patrolling the streets for most of the night. The plan had been a quick cup of eye-opening caffeine, then back on the road. There could be no sleep on a full-moon night. But somehow the old swivel chair with its cracked vinyl had done what her Sealy Posturepedic could not. For how long? The clock lay broken on the floor and the phone still rested in her hand, unanswered.

"Sheriff Hubbard," she said into the receiver through a tangle of her own hair. She swiped it away to better hear the caller, but it was unnecessary. The receiver shrilled in Gloria's ear, a hysterical voice screeching on the other end of the line. "Mrs. Talbot, is that you? Calm down. Mrs. Talbot, calm down!" Half of what the woman said made no sense, but Gloria understood enough. "Mrs. Talbot—Margaret!—I am sending an ambulance. Stay inside the house. I will be there in fifteen minutes."

Gloria arrived in time to see the EMTs carrying Andy out on a stretcher, his wife running alongside. An oxygen mask covered his face. When he saw the sheriff, he ripped it off and tried to sit up.

"Don't make us buckle you all the way in, Mr. Talbot." The paramedic holding the stretcher at Andy's head motioned for another to come fix the unwilling patient's mask.

"Sheriff! Sheriff!" Andy batted the young woman's hands away from his face. "Margie, tell the sheriff everything. Don't you come to the hospital till you do."

The woman attempted to secure the oxygen mask over Andy's nose and mouth once more. "I'm fine! Let me out of this thing, I have to see the sheriff." Andy struggled with the straps around his waist as the technicians hoisted the stretcher into the back of the ambulance. The ambulance doors slammed shut and with sirens blaring, it headed for the Doe Springs Emergency Medical Center, a brick building with a fancy name and only half the size of the elementary school. Locals called it the hospital and it worked well enough. Serious emergencies were carted all the way to Asheville, but Andy Talbot looked like he needed the police, not a doctor.

Gloria weighed out going after the ambulance or approaching Mrs. Talbot, who stood shivering and clutching her nightcoat. Wild white hair clouded haggard cheeks—ash locks blending on ashen skin. Margaret watched the ambulance's taillights until they disappeared. Her watery eyes wandered up the hill in front of the house. "We better get inside," she said.

Gloria made a pot of coffee while Margaret sat motionless at the kitchen table. Her head was turned sharply to the right, staring out into the blackness beyond the kitchen window above the sink. *Stricken* ran through the sheriff's mind looking at her. The demeanor was Patricia Hughes all over again, when Sanders told her what had happened to her husband. But there were no casualties this time, no tattered fleshy pieces to sift from the debris of the forest floor. Mr. Talbot was lively and well on his way to the clinic, while the Mrs. sat here safe in her kitchen, shaken for some reason but no worse for the wear. Perhaps it would not be such a bad night after all. Perhaps the moon's tides were changing for the better. Perhaps.

Gloria set a cup of coffee in front of Margaret, then seated herself across from the elderly lady with her own steaming mug. And waited.

"I saw it," Margaret finally whispered, still transfixed on the window and its sightless view.

Gloria strained to hear the hoarse words. "You saw what, Mrs. Talbot?"

Margaret turned her head to face the sheriff then. Sallow light from an ancient overhead fixture jaundiced the woman's pale skin and poured shadow into the creases of her cheeks and forehead. She leaned across the table toward Gloria, who found her own self pulling away from her, her and her hands drawn into clawed fists and the witchy white hair streaking around her face like frozen lightning. *Stricken* was replaced by *crazy* in the sheriff's mind, and the next words from the old woman's mouth should only confirm the notion, had it been a saner time and place, a Doe Springs before last year and its own brand of crazy that had been hoisted upon it.

Mrs. Margaret Talbot hissed, "I saw *it*. Up the hill, by the rocks." She abruptly sat back in her chair, a queer smugness about her, as if to say, *Now what do you think about that?*

"You have to be more specific, Mrs. Talbot. I couldn't make out what you were saying on the phone."

"The Devil of Doe Springs! Are you daft, woman?"

The words hit Gloria and bounced right back off. For a minute she wasn't sure she'd heard correctly, and she dared not hope too much. For all she knew, Margaret could be in shock and spouting off anything at all. Did anyone check the elderly wife's vitals before roaring out of here with her agitated husband?

Gloria put her elbows on the table and clasped her fingers together under her chin. They fought to free themselves and begin the da-da-da-*da* drumroll, but Margaret did not need any more distraction. Gloria would get this statement as gently as she could while suppressing her own growing excitement at the possibility the woman was suggesting. "Tell me exactly what you saw, Mrs. Talbot."

Margaret took a deep breath to speak, but only a thin rattle and wheeze exhaled from her parted lips.

"It's okay, Mrs. Talbot. Take your time."

Margaret nodded and took another deep breath, gathering herself for what Gloria prayed would be a clear and accurate description of the plague on their town. The popular theories ticked off in the space of pause between the women's exchange. *Mountain lion, bear, pack of wild dogs, cannibalistic lunatic . . .*

"Sheriff?"

"Yes, Mrs. Talbot, I'm listening."

"I need to be with my husband. I thought he was having a heart attack. And Sadie, our dog, is dead." Margaret put her head in her hands and a sudden flood of tears disappeared down the sleeves of her nightcoat. "Go away, go away. I need to get to the hospital."

Gloria sighed as the woman's shoulders hitched with each sob. She quietly got up from the table and went outside to her car. She could needle Mrs. Talbot all morning and get nowhere. Time was wasting. It was nearing six a.m. already; she needed to get up that hill and search for tracks immediately. With any luck, the animal might still be around. Gloria considered going to look without backup; but Margaret's horrified face made her think better of it.

I saw it. That's what she'd said. Nobody had seen it and lived. A mistake on the old woman's part? Possibly. A fallen log crouching ominously, a dead tree looming forebodingly— all very likely. Most likely, in fact. Seventy-year-old vision in the dark in the wee hours of the morning was not the most dependable source. The newspapers and local television had done much in the way of inspiring imaginations. Bogeymen and monsters were popping up all over Doe Springs in unlikely places: toolsheds, lettuce gardens, back porches, tractor barns . . . every report without a body had been either a crank call or a case of mistaken identity. Big friendly hounds and rotten stumps were taking it hard in this town these days. In one instance, a neighbor's escaped donkey had caused more than a smidgen of panic for a young family, before Sanders showed up with a halter and a carrot.

Tonight could be the same, Gloria reckoned. But there was presumably a dead dog up there next to those woods, and something killed it.

Gloria grabbed her radio and called dispatch (a.k.a. Shirley, office administrative assistant and part-time detention officer) for Sanders and Meeks to meet her at the Talbots'. She would have Meeks drive Margaret to the hospital after they completed their search. The woman shouldn't be behind the wheel of a vehicle right now. Later the sheriff would make a trip to the medical center herself and get a statement from Andy. Gloria suspected they'd taken the wrong person away in the ambulance.

Deputy Sanders followed Sheriff Hubbard up the hill to the woods. Meeks radioed in that he was on his way, but Gloria couldn't wait. She'd snagged Sanders the second he stepped from his patrol car, and now their high-powered flashlights scoped the ground. The lights were unnecessary in the pasture as the sun began spreading over the horizon, but the woods ahead still loomed dark. Anything to see would most likely be there, hidden in the veil of dawn's gloom.

"What exactly are we looking for, Sheriff?" Sanders asked.

"I exactly don't know. The Border collie, dead or injured, is up here somewhere, along with something else that scared the bejesus out of the Talbots. Margaret mentioned rocks. Let's start over there."

The officers passed the flashlights across the boulders and into their many tight crevices. Torn-up grass and paw-prints ran around the base of the rock-bordered timberline in erratic patterns. Deputy Sanders knelt for a closer look and the sheriff dropped down beside him.

"Medium type dog, probably the collie," Sanders said. "It was tearing after something through here, that's for sure."

"Could have been a rabbit or fox using these crevices as a hidey hole," Gloria said.

"Yeah."

"Yeah." Gloria stood up and shined the flashlight into the woods. She crow-hopped over the smallest boulders in front of her and heard a heavy thud as Sanders did the same. Sanders headed left to examine the ground along the rocks on this side while she went farther into the trees. Her dream flickered in the back of her mind as the woods closed off behind her and a narrow path revealed itself under her light's beam.

"I've found a trail of some kind. Looks like a deer path," Gloria called. Sanders didn't answer.

"Great." She unholstered her gun, the cool metal heavy in her hand. A little woman with a great equalizer, that's what her instructor had said when he taught her to fire her first weapon. She'd blown the firearms instructor (and the target) away with her natural skill. Her class called her Crackshot, and she carried the nickname as proudly as the .45-caliber Glock. In moments like these, Gloria was thankful for the extra backbone two and a half pounds of metal could provide. Fiery eyes glared from her nightmare, and she understood perfectly how creatures of all kinds could be conjured up in these woods by sheer will alone. For a moment, she half-hoped Mrs. Talbot *was* crazy.

"What have we here?" The sheriff bent to examine a bit of fur on the ground. It stuck to the barrel of her gun when she nudged it over. The long black-and-white fringes of hair were less congealed on the other side and the sheriff could make it out. It was an ear. A Border collie's ear, by the looks of it. *Where there's a will, there's a way; where there's an ear there's a . . .* "nother one. So where's the rest of you?" Gloria stepped around the piece of fur and followed more hair down the path. A paw, a leg, a slick and squishy balloon that might be a bladder. Nothing else.

Gloria put the back of her hand across her nose, sending the flashlight beam helter-skelter through the trees. The warm copper smell of blood mixed with a sourness that tickled her nose like pepper. It rose not only from the remains, it was all around. She'd smelled something similar once, on an animal rescue case. A dozen dogs and almost as many cats left locked in an abandoned trailer. Neighbors complained of a foulness leaking from the sagging aluminum structure like a drunk oozing booze from his pores. Urine, feces, and rotting carcass overcame Gloria's team quicker than an onslaught of gangsters when they'd burst through the door. The officers had gone right back outside, staggering and coughing, while a stream of scraggly animals ran past their feet.

Crashing came through the woods toward her. Gloria pointed her light and swung the weapon around in one broad sweep, a surprising jolt of fear kickstarting her heart and overpowering the stench.

Sanders broke through the trees, Jonathan Meeks behind him.

"Whoa, whoa, whoa! Get off the trail." Gloria holstered the gun and waved the deputies to the side. Sanders looked sheepish. "We didn't know where you went, Sheriff."

"I found the dog." Gloria swept her flashlight over the ground.

"What's that God-awful smell?" Meeks said.

"Could be scat, or urine. I think it marked its territory. If it left a pile anywhere, we need to find it."

"That's new. It's never done that before." Meeks looked around as if the scent would turn tangible and save them the trouble of hunting for the source.

"Maybe it's our lucky day."

"Sheriff, point your light back this way. I think there's a print here." Sanders's own flashlight was aimed a foot off the trail.

Gloria squatted next to Sanders's boot and pushed a mound of dew-wet leaves aside. Meeks and Sanders leaned over her.

"It's a print. More light, give me more light!" Gloria suppressed snatching a deputy's flashlight herself. It could belong to anything, any animal, maybe even another print from the Border collie. But today was different already—a sighting, a smell, a trace of this thing that had eluded them. This morning, it had finally messed up.

"Doesn't look like any pawprint I've ever seen. I can't believe you saw this, buried under these leaves and all," Meeks said, looking at Sanders.

"Like the sheriff said, it's our lucky day. What do you make of it, Sheriff?"

"Give me your hand." Gloria grabbed Sanders's wrist and pulled him down beside her. "Spread out your fingers and place your palm over top the print. Careful, don't touch it."

Sanders's hand hovered a hair above the fresh track as instructed. He looked up at the sheriff and Meeks.

"That's impossible," Meeks said.

The four toes of the pawprint stretched beyond the deputy's fingertips; four long, thin indentions dotting the tip of each one could only be claws. A rounded triangular pad protruded outside the perimeter of Sanders's palm.

"What animal leaves a print larger than a man's hand?" Sanders said.

"A damned big one," Gloria said. "Either of you know what you're looking at?"

No one spoke.

Gloria shined her light farther along the path. "All right. We'll come back when the sun's all the way up and follow this trail out. I need a cast of the track—Sanders, you're in charge of that. Go back to the office and get what you need. Meeks, gather up Margaret—she's in quite a state, I have to warn you—and drive her to the medical center. I'm going on ahead to get a statement from her husband, Andy Talbot."

"What about . . . the dog?" Sanders said.

Gloria sighed. "Take an ear and leave the rest. If we're truly lucky, the son-of-a-bitch might come back for seconds."

Chapter 12

Sheriff Hubbard strode through the front doors of the "hospital." Four understuffed and overused mismatched couches welcomed patients to a sit-down in the waiting room. The seats were still empty at this hour—no sign of Andy either. Wired on little sleep and a lot of anticipation, Gloria walked through the couch lineup to a small reception desk that doubled as the entrance to the nurse's station. A woman in her mid-twenties and starched whites rose to greet the approaching sheriff.

"Good morning, Millie. I'm here to see—"

"Mr. Talbot! I know! He's been waiting for you, Sheriff. He's spouting off some mighty weird tales in there. I hated to leave him to come out here and run the desk, but it's my turn to do it—you know, play receptionist instead of do what I spent all those years in school to do—so here I am. But is it true? Is it all true?"

Millie strained across her desk toward the sheriff, the pleading sparkle in the girl's eyes reminding Gloria of someone. It came to her: her Labrador, Chester. He got the same look when she held up his squeaky toy.

"I can't confirm anything until I talk to Andy myself. What room is he in?"

Shoulders slumped and the sparkle died. Even the sterile bleached white of her uniform seemed to dim. "Oh. Okay. I'll just have to read it in the newspaper this afternoon. He's in Room 2B. I don't even know why he's here, really. He's healthier than I am. Anyway, go on in. They should be finishing up in there."

"What's this about the newspaper, and who's finishing up? The doctor?"

"Oh no. Dr. Lesten's with another patient now. Andy's

been moved out of emergency already. He's just down the hall. I reckon he'll go home as soon as his wife gets here. Dr. Lesten says Andy's a tough old geezer. A little elevated blood pressure is all he's showing for a night like last night."

"So who's in there now?"

"Artie Crimshaw. He's getting Mr. Talbot's story for the *Doe Springs Gazette*. They're running a special afternoon edition, isn't it exciting? Anyway, I'm sure you can go on in if you want to."

"I think I'll do that. Thanks."

Gloria huffed the short distance to Room 2B. Two more nurses stood outside Andy's room, trying to look as casual as eavesdroppers could. The door was open a crack, revealing a quilted bed with Andy Talbot in it. Beside him sat a portly man in a rocking chair with a tape recorder on his lap.

"Break it up, ladies." Gloria pushed past the two nurses and into the room. "Hey!"

The man jerked his head around but kept the handheld mike aimed Andy's way.

"What are you doing here, Art?"

"I'll be out of your way in a minute, Sheriff Hubbard."

"You'll be out of my way right now. I haven't even had a chance to get Andy's statement yet. Who told you he was here?"

"Relax, Sheriff. You're sucking all the cozy out of Mr. Talbot's room. It's a small town, news travels fast here. Specially when you've got a police scanner." Artie pushed black-rimmed glasses a notch up his nose and turned back to Andy.

"Oh no, you're finished now. Get out."

"What's the problem? Mr. Talbot said he'd be glad to talk to me." The reels in the recorder kept on spinning.

"That's right, Sheriff Hubbard," Andy Talbot said, propped upright against two hand-embroidered pillows and looking considerably better than when Gloria saw him last. "I'm feeling fine now. Don't worry about me."

"It's not you I'm worried about. Beat it, Artie, I'm not playing around. And use some discretion when you print that. Your piece on Clifford Hughes terrified the whole town."

"Well, pardon me for saying it, but they should be terri-fied," Andy said. "They need to know what I saw."

"I couldn't have put it better," Artie said. He clicked "stop" on the recorder and stuck it in a leather satchel. "Thank you, Mr. Talbot. I think I've got all I need now anyway. Sorry, Sheriff Hubbard. Didn't mean to step on any toes this morn-ing, but it's the story of—"

"Out!"

Artie slung the satchel over his shoulder and nodded good-bye to Andy. He crab-stepped through the doorway past Glo-ria, who grounded herself like an oak and dared him to touch her. The glasses slipped once again down the sliver of carti-lage cutting his round face, and for a fierce moment Gloria saw herself snatching the pop bottle bottoms and smashing them on the floor.

Get a hold of yourself, Gloria! The sheriff rubbed her forehead and let the anger ride out on a controlled sigh. Artie was only doing his job. They'd worked side by side many a time with nobody pitching fits. He undercut her today, but there was no law against a reporter talking to an old farmer in obvious good health before she could get to him.

Really, she couldn't much blame Artie for not waiting to talk to Andy, good health report or otherwise. Stories of a lifetime didn't usually land in the laps of small-town re-porters, or small-town policemen either, for that matter. Things like this were only read of in books. But this after-noon, it would be read in the *Doe Springs Gazette,* and there wasn't a thing she could do about it. She just hoped good sense and an iota of taste would be foremost on Artie's mind when he told Andy's story for the local audience.

Gloria filled the seat Artie vacated. She would worry about the afternoon edition, well, this afternoon, when her office would be flooded with more calls and visitors than she'd care to handle. It was turning out to be an excellent day to track monsters in the woods after all.

Gloria effected a smile and hoped it looked friendly and reassuring. "Hello, Mr. Talbot, how are you feeling?"

"Better. Would you like some breakfast?" Andy motioned

to a plastic bowl on the bedside table. "They tried to feed me some kind of bran mishmash an hour ago, but I didn't make seventy eating like that. Fatback, grits, and caffeine—now that's a healthy breakfast. Southerners grow up on grease; the minute you try to take that away, our bodies go all to pot. These new-fangled city doctors don't know half of what they're talking about."

Dr. Lesten was forty-seven and had practiced in Doe Springs ten years. New-fangled city doctor seemed off the mark, but his hometown was Raleigh, so there you go. "No thank you, Mr. Talbot—"

"For Pete's sake, Sheriff, call me Andy. I've only known you since you were knee high and falling out of my crab apple tree."

Gloria smiled. "Okay, Andy. I'll cut to the chase. Tell me everything that happened last night, starting from the time the dogs woke you."

Andy started to speak, but the walkie on Gloria's belt beeped. She sighed again.

"Just one minute, Andy. Yes?" she said into the radio.

"Sheriff Hubbard, Sanders here."

"What is it? I'm with Mr. Talbot right now."

"I'm sorry to bother you, but you're not going to believe this. I don't even know how to tell you."

"Spit it out, Sanders."

The deputy's voice came through a crackle of static, but Gloria heard it plain enough.

"It's gone, Sheriff. The pawprint we found. It's just . . . gone."

Chapter 13

"Did you read it yet?" Patricia Hughes whispered into the phone. She stood outside in her backyard with the phone cord stretched to its limit through the metal screen door behind her. Around Patricia's feet scurried ten ducks, snapping at her ankles and each other while awaiting the afternoon snowfall of breadcrumbs that refused to come. In Patricia's left hand, where the breadcrumb pail should have been, was a rumpled newspaper.

"Hello? Who is this? I can barely hear you," Patricia's best friend Ivy said on the other end of the line.

Patricia glanced back at the house and raised her voice a notch. "I said did you read it yet? I've been dying to talk to you for over two hours. Where have you been?"

"I just got home. Me and Rex took a hike. What an amazingly beautiful day, Patricia. And Rex! He was full of himself today. His mange has cleared and he feels—"

"The newspaper, Ivy, *the newspaper*. Did you read the story yet?"

"What story? And why are you whispering? I can still barely hear you."

"You're not going to believe it, Ivy. The *Gazette* ran a special afternoon edition today. Last night . . . the full moon . . . you're just not going to believe it!" Patricia's voice leaped an octave and scattered the ducks.

"There was . . . another attack?"

"Not just an attack—there was a witness!"

"Patty, what are you doing out there with the telephone?" An older lady stood at the screen door, her nose and blue apron pushed up close against it.

"Nothing, Mama, everything's fine. I was on my way out to feed the ducks when the phone rang is all. You go on back in. I'll be there in a minute." Patricia smiled at her mother and shooed her away. "Go on, I'll be right there."

The woman watched her daughter through the closed screen a moment longer before turning away.

"That was Mama," Patricia said to Ivy. "She watches me like a hawk, her and Aunt Thelma both. I can't get a minute's peace, and I don't want them to know about what's happened. They'll find out soon enough as it is, and then they'll never go home. I mean, it's the end of June already! Daddy thinks Mama's left him for good and I'm starting to wonder myself."

"Tell me what's happened, Patricia." Ivy's voice had gone from light to dark in the course of the interruption. Patricia didn't mince the details.

"Old sheep farmer Andy Talbot saw the Devil and lived to tell about it. His wife saw it too. It ate their dog before running off. There's a long interview with Andy and some quotes from Margie, plus a picture of their farm and the woods behind it. There's also a picture of the sheriff looking none too happy. You think she would have at least smiled— she made the front page!"

"It killed a dog?"

"Yes, a Border collie. She was trying to protect the sheep, poor thing. Want to know what it is, Ivy? Are you ready for this? It was . . . Ivy? Are you there? Hello?"

Ivy sat down lightly on the edge of her yellow couch. Patricia's last sentence faded and then clicked out as the phone slipped into its cradle on the end table. Rex bounded into the room, his mustache dripping with water from the dog dish. The terrier's happy panting paused at the sight of his person, and he trotted over to nudge against her hand.

"We've got a problem, fella. A big problem." Ivy scratched Rex's ears, raising the tufts that topped them into scruffy turrets. Across the room, the mantel clock faced the pair, its age-crackled face frozen forever at midnight. But Ivy could still hear it ticking, would forever hear its last chime resonating through a windblown house and across the glass scattered in diamond-glitter shards across a hard wooden floor.

Patricia's phone call took Ivy back there, to a brief moment just before the chime of midnight and the broken glass and the Christmas packages scattered like litter throughout the living room. Back to a cottage in the countryside an ocean away. She was a small girl again, with blond hair tied in ribboned pigtails and a holiday dress of green satin bunched around her legs like a crinolined blanket as she sat curled in the soft armchair. The room was warm from the fire, and on the mantel sat the new clock, a gift from Ivy's German grandmother, passed down from generations in their family. The house was quiet with all the relatives gone hours ago, save her mother tidying the kitchen. The clock's ticking and the crackling fire worked their magic on the child, and little Ivy's chin sank toward her chest. The chair she nestled on drew her down into its velvet cushions and into the depths of a sleep she'd fought most of the evening. But her eyes closed with a will of their own, the sleep so nearly claiming her, when the howling began . . .

"Ivy! Ivy, are you in there?"

Ivy jerked at the voice, yanking a terrier ear in the process and eliciting a wounded howl much gentler than the one of her nightmares. The other dogs were tearing up the backyard as someone banged on the door.

"What now?" Ivy looked out the window; her friend's frantic face peered back at her. "Patricia, what in the world are you doing?" Ivy said through the glass. She went to the door and let her friend in.

"You scared me to death, Ivy. I didn't know what happened." Patricia stood in the foyer looking around.

"We just got disconnected, you didn't have to come all the way over here to check on me."

"Sorry I overreacted. I'm a nervous wreck. Here's the paper." She thrust it at Ivy. "Hurry up and read it. I've got a confession to make: I was coming over anyway, you just lit a fire under me."

Ivy held the paper like it might bite. All of a sudden another peaceful, happy, unbothered day in the country had turned to dust. "Well, come on in then. You look great, by the way. I think your mama's cooking is doing you some good."

Patricia's formerly hollowed cheeks filled out into a plump, dimply smile. "I've gained six pounds in a month. I'll be dieting by fall if this keeps up." She was proud of it. Looking good and feeling good. Ivy smiled too. Widow Pritchard had been right: Patricia was blossoming in her own good time. Next year the girl would be a whole new person, a complete person, perhaps with a better beau than what she was used to. Ivy would have to watch her, though. Girls like that tended to follow patterns, and offing two of her husbands might be over the top. One had to use discretion in beau finding and beau eliminating . . . discretion in all things, really. Ivy feared there would be no discretion in the acts she was about to read of, and the probable immaturity of those acts dismayed her.

Ivy carried the paper to the kitchen table and spread it out. Patricia flanked her friend and stared at her the whole time she read, gauging reactions. The headline "I Saw the Devil!" spread across the front page in giant block letters. A grainy picture of an elderly man accompanied the story. Below that, the Talbot farm and Sheriff Hubbard's scowl filled a black-and-white frame. In the background, Ivy could make out Deputy Sanders and another deputy heading into the woods.

Ivy scanned the article, the good farmer's horror touching a chord within her as well. Andy Talbot's story unfolded, detail by detail. The barking, the stampede, then the attack on the Border collie.

At first I thought I was seeing things. Just two bright orange sparks like lit matches flying out of the woods toward my dog. Then I saw the rest of it. It was a wolf, a giant black wolf, bigger than a bear. I saw it plain as day in the headlights of the truck. It hit my dog hard enough to roll her several feet, then it was on her again. I tried to get hold of my gun, but Margie hit the gas and I lost it. The last thing I saw in the headlights as we backed down the hill? That thing stood up on its hind legs and snarled at us. I swear as I sit here, I think it was grinning.

Ivy stopped reading. She turned to Patricia, who was still standing within kissing distance. "And you believe this?"

Patricia raised her eyes from the page to her friend. "I don't know what I believe, Ivy. But Cliff is dead, and I wanted to know what did it. And now I do. All the whispering in town, Ivy, all the dirty looks I've gotten. You don't know what it's been like around here since Clifford got . . . since Clifford passed away. Not everybody's been crying for poor widowed Patricia. Oh no. Some folks thought I had something to do with it. I've heard the rumors, I'm not deaf. Even the police have hinted at hateful things. But don't you see now? This proves it, Ivy. These busybodies have something they can put their finger on. A werewo—"

"Don't even say it. It's too ridiculous. This isn't the Dark Ages, Patricia, this is the twenty-first century. But whatever the Talbots saw, consider yourself exonerated. Now go home, darlin'. I've suddenly got a headache that could pound an acorn flat. Come back over tomorrow and we'll have a picnic. It's an excuse to get you out from under your mama's house arrest."

"No. I want you to go with me now."

"Go with you where?"

"To Andy Talbot's. I want to see this place for myself. I need some kind of closure, Ivy, and this might give it to me."

"You don't need closure, you need rest. Clifford's only been gone since May; in a year's time this will all be behind you and you'll be in a totally new place with yourself. Now run on home. We'll talk tomorrow."

Patricia looked heartbroken. "I know you're right. And I can't explain it. I just think that maybe there will be some trace of this thing left, some hint, some essence that I can connect with. Have you ever had someone you were close to killed, Ivy? Do you know what that's like?" Patricia shook her head impatiently and backed away from her friend, clearing the personal space but leaving a void in its wake. Ivy felt the withdrawal like a gentle hand caressing her bare arm, down the tender skin of her wrist, and out the length of her fingertips into emptiness. Yes, she did know. She understood the desire for a connection, the need to make sense of the seemingly senseless, the restless call of revenge. Ivy could tell her these things, could put a The End on that portion of Patricia's story right now. All questions answered, all loose ends tied up, all guilt forgiven. Times like these, the secret uncoiled itself and kicked Ivy hard in the back of the knees, wanting to come out. Wanting to *share*.

"There will be nothing to see, Patricia," Ivy said.

"It doesn't matter. I just want to go." Patricia hung her head and the voice rising from the down-turned chin was small, a child's whisper. Ivy noticed something else for the first time then. The once-mousy brown bangs that would have shielded the girl's hurt expression were gone, the hair brushed back from her face opening her to the world. New streaks of auburn tinged the drab hue with lively highlights. The weight gain, the hair—it was a start. A good start.

"All right. We'll ride over there. I'll take Auf with us— he's pouted all day because Rex got to go on the hike and he didn't."

"Thank you, Ivy, so much."

Ivy walked to the backyard and let the shepherd slip into the house. Rex scrambled across the hardwoods to the big dog and tried to lick his muzzle, but he held it aloft, out of reach. Ivy shook her head at Aufhocker's aloofness. He was definitely one not to share anything, merely to tolerate, but of that, he did well. Rex gave up on kisses and danced around the black shepherd, wagging his tail. The little terrier's mange had cleared quickly, thanks to Doc Hill's healing touch. But there would be no helping Andy Talbot's dog. The downy hairs along the backs of Ivy's arms bristled. *A wolf that stands upright. Bigger than a bear. Fiery eyes. But only eats animals. First pigs and cows, now the dog.* Ivy knew it would have gone through most of the sheep if Talbot hadn't interfered. Soon it would gather its courage to satiate its true hunger. But for now, it was still a fledgling, finding its way. Ivy glanced at the wall calendar on her way back through the house with Aufhocker. It would be nearly a month until the full moon again. She'd intended to savor Mr. Frank Parson that night, as this past full moon he was away on business. How unfortunate for Ivy and the Parson family all way round. But Mr. Parson would be getting still another reprieve. The next full moon, Ivy would be hunting bigger prey.

"It's a zoo. A freaking zoo." Gloria sat on a log and wiped her face. Meeks and Sanders hovered over her, sweating through their uniforms and trying not to complain. Crashing and calling sounded all around as townspeople trekked through the trees, looking for Andy Talbot's devil.

"Water, Sheriff?" Meeks handed her a plastic bottle and she took a swallow before giving it back.

"I should've run the whole lot of them off when they first showed up," Gloria said. The deputies didn't respond. They stood stoic, wiping sweat and swigging water as flies buzzed around their heads. The officers had been at it since daybreak, searching the field, the woods, the boulders. They had backtracked and sidetracked and scoured every inch of Andy Talbot's alleged wolf site. Gloria joined her team after talking to Talbot in the hospital, only to be doubly aggravated to find Artie Crimshaw already at the farm and snapping pictures by the time she arrived. Along with the *Doe Springs Gazette* Special Afternoon Edition came the crowds. The police officers had been swamped by the curious, the angry, the religious, and the superstitious. Somebody plunked an oversized crucifix down in the middle of Margaret's geranium bed, and she sent Andy out to fetch it off the lawn right after they arrived home. "Wrong creature, nitwits!" Andy had yelled at a group of four making a beeline across his driveway and to the pasture.

Gloria considered turning the gawkers and well-meaning away right when they started arriving, but after an exasperating morning getting nowhere but winded, it seemed pointless. Besides, a few extra pairs of legs walking these endless loops couldn't hurt. They'd already spent most the day on the trail out the back of Talbot's property, following it until it forked and reforked a half dozen times, branching into new paths that crisscrossed and doubled back and wound around in a dizzying maze. Then they stumbled across this leg, which, perhaps, actually led somewhere. Andy Talbot had ventured up the hill a few times to offer advice to the officers (and tell them exactly what he thought about the hordes tromping across his yard), but of the trails, he had little to say. "Loggers mowed those paths out eons ago, back when horses moved the logs. Mostly hunters in there these days. I haven't been in them woods for twenty years."

And now, with only a few hours' light left, there was nothing to show for the day's hard work. For all their efforts, Sanders was right: There was not a track to be found anywhere. Even the scent marking was gone. Instead of angering Gloria, it only confirmed her suspicions. Some person had come back and covered up the tracks after they'd left. She should have made Sanders guard the site and sent Meeks to the office for the plaster cast materials, but what was that cliché about hindsight?

"Sheriff Hubbard, we may have found something over here." Law Thornton stood over Gloria, a shovel in his hand.

"What're you going to do with that shovel, Law?" Gloria squinted up at the man. The good townspeople of Doe Springs had shown up with pickaxes, shovels, rakes, and shotguns. It looked like a mob scene from *Frankenstein* or a bizarre gathering for *Better Homes and Gardens*.

"Shoot, Sheriff, you never know when you might need a hefty garden tool." He pretended to swing it like a bat. Gloria didn't smile, so he set it down. "Anyway, we've found something off this here trail finally. You need to come take a look."

Gloria rose to her feet. Her back cracked loudly but the younger men in her company knew better than to comment. "Okay, Law, show me what you got."

The officers followed Law fifty feet through the underbrush to a section of dense, low-hanging pines. Snuggled in behind them was a structure of some kind.

"Is it a cabin?" Deputy Sanders moved closer, the pines blocking most of the late-day light.

"More like a shack, I'd say." Law leaned on his shovel. "We didn't go in it yet."

"We?" Deputy Meeks said.

Two men came from around back of the small building. "Yeah, us. I'm Sam and this here's Riley. We're Law's cousins. We been looking to get in there but can't."

"Yep," Riley chimed in. "Windows're boarded up and the front's stuck tighter than a virgin's—uh, sorry, Sheriff."

"Shut up, Riley." Sam shot his cousin a look that would have killed a lesser man on the spot. "What he's trying to say is, we put some powerful gription to the boards but couldn't pry one loose. Brought the wrong tools, I reckon." He looked at his trowel with disgust. It was the only thing his wife would let him leave the house with.

"Hunter's cabin, Sheriff?" Sanders asked, ignoring Sam and his disappointment in choice of investigative instrument.

"Abandoned one, maybe. Let's take a peek. Law, looks like we've found a use for your shovel. Go apply some *gription* and open that door for me."

Law's eyes lit up, excited to have a job. He squared up in front of the doorknob, jaw set and attention focused on the target. He swung, and the reverberation from the blow rocked clean up to his elbow. The door edged grudgingly away from the jamb and the doorknob bounced on the ground.

The men crowded the doorway behind Gloria. Light entered from behind them, and the only movement was the dust swirling with the intruding draft. The cabin housed only one room with a table, chair, and worn-out cot. Stuffing dangled from its mattress. A fat woodstove sat in the middle of the back wall surrounded by a few spiderweb-covered logs. Shadows crouched low in the dingy corners, and Gloria imagined two orange eyes peering at them. Andy Talbot's eerily similar description of the animal in her dream played back in her head.

"What's that smell?" Riley pulled the neck of his T-shirt over the lower half of his face. Gloria doubted it smelled any better in there.

"Stinks like a pig farm in here. Nothing to see anyway." Sam stepped back into the pines, Riley behind him.

"I recognize it," Gloria said. "We smelled it this morning." She walked to the middle of the room and turned full circle. Cobwebs on the ceiling. Cold ash in the stove. The sheriff walked to the table and traced her finger across the pitted surface. Then she knelt by the cot.

"Law, bring your buddies back in here. I want some help getting this cot outside in the light."

"Yes, ma'am." Law jumped to attention and went to round up his kin.

"What is it, Sheriff?" Sanders hunkered down beside her.

"Probably nothing, Deputy. But there's animal hair all over this cot and I'd like to take a better look at it."

"Could just be rats or raccoons using the bedding," Meeks said.

"Probably." Gloria stood up. "But I don't know how they're getting in, if that's the case."

"Maybe a hole in the wall behind the woodstove. I'd say this cabin's been abandoned a long time, except for the critters."

"No, I don't think so, Meeks," Gloria said.

"Why's that, Sheriff?"

"About everything in here is covered in cobwebs and dust, everything but the table and chair. And look at the floor. Pretty clean. Couldn't have been that long ago when someone was here. And I don't think the possums out this way have taken up housekeeping."

Law and the cousins came through the door. They picked up the cot and carried it out.

Gloria continued. "We need to talk to the hunters in town. Whoever uses this shed may have seen something—an unusual track, a den . . . Hunters are in the woods a heck of a lot more than we are. Meeks, follow up on that, and find out who owns this land—Andy's farm ended at the tree line. By the direction the crow flies, we're not too far from Jack Lutsky's two hundred acres either. We also need to follow this trail completely out to see where it ends. Sanders, you're in charge of that. But we're losing daylight, I don't think we can go much farther on it this evening."

"Sheriff, with all due respect, shouldn't we get the trackers and the big guns back out here?" Sanders said.

"I've got that part covered, let me worry about it."

Sanders and Meeks pinged glances off one another. They
had not been informed of any new plans for trackers or otherwise. But they let it slide. Sanders had been with the sheriff long enough to know when not to push her, and Meeks
was a quick study.

"I don't know what Andy Talbot saw last night," Gloria
continued, "but I can tell you this—whatever animal we've
got running around out here, mutant wolf or otherwise, I'm
sure the real killer is the person behind it. Now let's go. I want
to get some hair samples off that cot and to the lab today."

Deputy Sanders walked a stone's throw behind the sheriff,
Meeks, and the Thornton cousins, who'd laid claim to the
ruined cot and were carrying it out of the woods with them.
They were heading back to the Talbot farm, and the longer
they walked, the bigger the entourage that followed. People
were tired *(frightened)* as the light waned. Melvin was too
deep in thought to pay fear much mind. Sheriff Hubbard
seemed certain a person lay behind the killings. That only
made sense to Melvin too. The missing jewelry. The cov-
ered-up tracks. The disappearing pawprint from this morning. But why kill people, then attack animals sometimes
too? Were they just mishaps? Maybe the big dog *(okay,
maybe it is a giant wolf, but standing on hind legs? Too* Little Red Riding Hood *for this old boy)* . . . maybe the big dog
escaped sometimes and the owner loved it so much he hid its
transgressions to protect it.

Ivy Cole came back to mind. Dog trainer, behaviorist. He
should go talk to her again. Maybe she could shed some insight into what kind of canine could do such a thing. There
were plenty of strange dogs out there they'd never heard of.
What was that one Ruthy White mentioned?

"Sheriff!" Melvin trotted to Sheriff Hubbard's side.
"About the tracking thing. Maybe we've not been using the
right trackers. Now that we know what we're looking for, we
can specialize."

"I told you, Sanders, I've got that covered." Gloria plowed

straight ahead, exhaustion and heat and the possibilities within the cot hair pushing her into single-mindedness. She wasn't in the mood for theorizing at the moment.

"I know you do, but hear me out. Something Ruthy White said to me when I went out to her place."

"About Ivy?" The sheriff's steps slowed a beat, and the cot pulled ahead. Law, Sam, and Riley had started to squabble over whose turn it was at the small bed's helm, all the glamour of police work sucked from the moment with the realization hard labor was in order. But the labor was self-imposed for whatever reason a Thornton might have for wanting a bedraggled, rodent-eaten cot. Law, whose idea it was to take the bed in the first place, seemed to be doing more directing than carrying, and the other two cousins were getting fed up. Meeks intervened in the argument while the sheriff and Melvin drew farther behind.

"No, not about Ivy—one of her clients. He owns a . . . um . . . a Bonsai," Melvin answered, watching Meeks grab hold of the metal bed frame and nudge Riley aside, a policeman on the verge of fed up himself.

"A what?"

"I don't know. Maybe that wasn't it. Ruthy also called it a Russian wolfhound."

"As in, hunts wolves, right?"

"That's what I gather from it."

Gloria squashed the hundredth mosquito against the back of her neck. By now it must look like a Buick grill at midnight with its high beams on. "Go ahead and check it out. Couldn't hurt. Nothing could hurt at this point."

"I'll drop in on Miss Cole first thing tomorrow." Melvin rubbed his chin. Looks like he'd need another shave before calling on the Cole residence again.

"Well, speak of the devil and there she is," Gloria muttered. They emerged from the woods to see Ivy Cole walking toward them, Patricia Hughes leading the way. The huge black shepherd heeled at Ivy's side.

"Hello, Sheriff Hubbard," Patricia said.

"How are you, Patricia?"

"I'm doing okay, thank you. My mom and her sister are still up. Daddy went home a couple weeks ago. He had to get back to work. But they've all been a big help."

Gloria smiled, the tiny crinkles around her eyes softening her face. "I'm glad to hear that." And she was. It was getting harder to face the families, leftovers of tragedies she seemed powerless to stop. But Patricia looked anything but tragic. There was a glow about her, in her skin and the copper tint to her brown hair. The last of the bruises had faded, leaving behind a fresh-faced young girl who had a shot at a normal future, as normal as it could be after losing a husband the way she did. "In fact, Patricia, I don't think I've ever seen you look better. Tell your mama to keep up the good work, and let me know if there's anything we can do."

"We've come to help you, actually. With the search."

Gloria glanced from Patricia to Ivy. Her eyes wandered down to the shepherd and his considerable paws before climbing back up to address the comment. "Ladies, we appreciate it, but half the town's turned out today, thanks to Artie Crimshaw. We're calling it an evening. Patricia, you need to go home and be with your family. You've been through enough."

Melvin watched Miss Cole as Patricia and Sheriff Hubbard spoke. She was focused past the sheriff, at the people still trickling out of the woods. Her dog stood at alert attention, staring in the same direction. The lips curled back slightly from his teeth, and Ivy put a hand on his head. Together they walked to the tree line and the last stragglers went around them, giving wide berth to the dog.

Melvin walked to Ivy's side. "Good evening, Miss Cole."

She smiled. "Deputy."

Ivy continued to stare into the dimming light, and Melvin stood there like a schoolboy with his hands in his pockets and nothing to say. He cleared his throat, but Ivy spoke first.

"I read the story in the paper today. Of course you knew that. That's why we're all here, isn't it, to find some mystical fairy-tale creature? Very fascinating stuff."

"We've even had some out-of-towners with cameras stop by. The story made the wire."

"So we're getting famous. At least there's an upside."

"Hello, Deputy Sanders! Hi, Ivy." Bonnie Hill stood in front of them, a girlfriend flanking each side. They all smiled brightly at the deputy.

"Hello, girls," he said. "What are you doing out here? Shouldn't you be in school or something?"

"School's out for the summer, Deputy, you know that," one of the other girls answered, "but you can arrest us anyway. Or maybe just Bonnie."

Bonnie's friends broke into giggles. Hot pink embarrassment inched up Bonnie's neck and flushed the skin of her cheeks.

"We've got to go," she said quickly. "I just wanted to say hi. And we did. So now we've got to go. Uh, bye, Deputy Sanders. Bye, Ivy."

"Bye, Deputy Sanders," the other two girls chorused in high-pitched singsong voices. More giggles as the trio fluttered away, and one loud "Will y'all *just shut up*?" from Bonnie.

Ivy looked at Deputy Sanders, the amusement in her eyes now embarrassing him.

"Kids." Melvin shrugged and redirected his gaze back toward the woods.

Ivy nodded and continued to rub her dog's head. "May I ask how the hunt went today, Deputy?"

"Badly. If there was a track out here anywhere, it was trampled. On the other hand, fifty pairs of eyes have to be better than three."

"You sound frustrated."

"Wouldn't you be?" It came out sharper than he'd intended.

Ivy ignored it. "That story in the paper—it's hard to believe. A wolf that stands on its hind legs and grins at people?"

Melvin sighed. There would be no shaving and cologning and a-calling for tomorrow. Ivy Cole was here, and he could just as well take care of business standing in the middle of a sheep pasture as he could in her living room, perhaps over a cup of coffee and some flowers he might have taken over as a gesture of . . . hmmm . . . goodwill. Melvin pulled out his notebook and pencil.

"Uh-oh. This looks like it's getting official. I must have asked the wrong question," Ivy said.

Melvin paused, notebook in mid-flip. "Actually, it was the right question. There are some canine behavior issues I'd like to go over with you, if you've got a minute."

"I don't. I'm hungry and standing here with my stomach growling at you is unladylike. Come by my house a little later, Deputy Sanders. You can take me to dinner and I'll tell you anything you want to know." Ivy started to walk away, then turned back. "And, Deputy, do me a favor, would you? Leave the notebook at home."

Chapter 14

Deputy Melvin Sanders had not been on a date in a long time. He was young, single . . . and busy. School was serious business, way back when; all those tests and tables and texts to memorize in preparation for his big day—not graduation, but the moment he could enter the Asheville Police Academy. When the basic law enforcement training finally arrived, life became even more serious. There was no room for slackers in the military-like environment of the academy. And now, of course, the work itself was deadly serious, no pun intended. There just weren't many free moments in Melvin Sanders's life to get out there and test the waters like other men his age. While his buddies were chasing skirts, Melvin was chasing criminals and hauling them into jail.

But it could be lonely, this line of work. Fulfilling as it was to the soul, it was leaving his heart a little empty. Melvin knew about those pitfalls long before he ever enrolled in the academy. There was a master plan in place for tackling that loneliness as well. With the goal of officer of the law tucked securely under his belt, Melvin's next sights were set on acquiring his family, starting with a loving wife who would understand what it meant to be married to a man who might or might not come home after a day on the job. It was a tall order to ask of a woman—dealing with that kind of stress while raising their children as well.

For these reasons, Melvin also took women and commitment seriously. He'd had only three girlfriends his whole life: one in kindergarten, whom he swore he'd grow up and marry; one in high school, whom he swore he'd marry as soon as they graduated; then one while he was in police training, whom he swore he'd marry as soon as he got a good job. That seemed to be his problem: Melvin Sanders was the marrying kind, and girls these days weren't.

"You're as faithful as an old hound dog, Melvin," Clarice from high school told him once. "And just as dull." Even Melvin's pre-adolescent love had left him for a chubby faced first grader named Roy. But Melvin couldn't help liking doing things by the book. Perhaps that's why police work was a well-fitting suit. Ironically, now that he wore the honored uniform, women were at him with innuendos and outright shameless offers all the time. But his standards had remained the same: wife material, or no material at all.

Melvin stooped before his bathroom mirror and pondered these things as he ran an electric razor over his face. This was a different situation entirely, however. Not a date really, just an interview at a comfortable hour for the interviewee. She was hungry. He was hungry. They would share a meal and some info over a burger—*God, no, not a burger, I can do better than that . . . a steak at least*—and that would be the end of it.

Melvin went to his closet and leafed through the metal hangers. Starched white shirts and camel khakis lorded over a row of shiny boot-camp-worthy shoes. "Geez, Melvin, you *are* dull." He contemplated wearing his uniform but reconsidered. Miss Cole didn't appreciate the formality of his notebook, how would she feel if he showed up with the gun and badge? Wasn't that what Gloria—er, Sheriff Hubbard—was trying to teach him? Loosen up with people?

Melvin snatched a pair of trousers and a shirt, rattling the hangers hard enough to send them to the floor. He reached for a tie, thought better of it, and slammed the closet shut.

Ten minutes later Melvin stooped in front of the full-length mirror in his bedroom. Satisfied, he grabbed the bouquet of flowers he bought on the way home from Talbot's and headed out the door.

Melvin stood on Ivy's front porch, clutching the flowers in one white-knuckled hand. He'd remembered to duck coming up the steps this time, avoiding the low-hanging pots and another embarrassing episode of "green hair." He rang the doorbell and was greeted by a chorus of barking.

"Hello, Deputy Sanders."

Melvin turned. Ivy stood behind him in jeans and a simple peasant blouse that hung off one shoulder. Her hair was up, but wisps of it hung around her face.

"Hello, Miss Cole." He tried to think of all the lines he'd rehearsed on the ride over, but all he could manage was, "You look nice." It was a lie composed of gross understatement. She was the most beautiful woman he had ever seen.

Ivy came up the steps. "Thank you, Deputy. You're wearing casual well tonight. I half expected to see you show up in your uniform." She stepped around him and opened the front door. "Come inside and sit a spell. I have to feed my last two dogs and then we can go. I'm so hungry I could eat—anything! I hope you're as starved as I am."

Melvin followed her into the living room and stood awkwardly in front of the couch. He wasn't sure whether to sit or stand or maybe even offer to help with the last of her chores.

"I'll just be a sec." Ivy started to leave, then eyed the flowers and waited. Melvin absently fiddled with the petals and looked about the living room, everything still in its place, just like the sheriff had observed on their first visit a month before. The lifeless clock on the mantel read twelve, but he knew it was going on seven. He hoped it wasn't too late to get in somewhere decent to eat. The sidewalk started rolling up in Doe Springs around six; by nine you could count yourself lucky to get cold pizza at Marty Dupont's Citgo, appetizingly named the Gas and Gulp.

"Deputy Sanders, did you bring those for me, or have I caught you red-handed with something from my garden?"

For an instant, he looked confused, then the tense line of his mouth broke into a slight grin. "Yes. These are for you." Melvin handed her the flowers, suddenly aware he'd crushed the stems in his death grip. The blossoms flopped to the side and Ivy caught the injured bouquet before it dove headfirst on top of the coffee table.

"I guess they don't make flowers like they used to. Those were in good condition when I bought them, I swear it," Melvin said.

"They're lovely. Or were. Thank you. I'll put them in some water. Make yourself at home." Ivy cradled the flowers with both hands and disappeared toward the kitchen.

Melvin sat on the edge of the sofa in the same spot he'd sat during his first visit here, his second encounter with Ivy Cole and under the worst of circumstances. He wished their initial meetings had been under sunnier conditions, like at a softball game or maybe their carts colliding at the grocery store. Maulings and mayhem were hardly romance inducing, and tonight that would be the topic once again. Perhaps if they addressed it early, their dinner conversation could venture into happier themes.

Melvin was debating how to break the ice on business without breaking the chances of an untroubled dinner afterward when he noticed the stare-down from across the room.

"Hi, little guy. You look considerably better than when I saw you last." Melvin stretched out his hand to the terrier peeking around the armchair facing him. The dog didn't move. Melvin leaned farther forward, and a whine escaped Rex's throat. A movement to their left brought his attention off Melvin, but it was not Ivy returning to the living room. The black shepherd stood at the end of the hall, watching man and dog from the shadows. With a quiet *woof*, Rex turned and scampered in Ivy's direction, leaving the deputy alone with the true guardian of the house.

Melvin sat back slowly, the dog's black chinquapin eyes

never leaving his. "You're Alf, ain't ya, buddy—the guard dog Ruthy told me about. You remember me, don't you? We met up close and personal this afternoon."

"It's Auf, not Alf. A-*u*-f." Ivy came back in, the flowers blooming amazingly upright from a crystal vase. She set it on the coffee table beside the leather-bound book *Lykanthrop,* then settled herself in the chair across from Melvin, one foot tucked underneath her. "It's short for the German name Aufhocker. Do you know it?"

"Sorry. English is my first, second, and third language, and sometimes even then I don't get it right. He's a beautiful dog, though. Don't think I've ever seen a German shepherd that big before."

"He's a mix, just like everybody else in this family, myself included." Ivy pointed at the dog, then swept her hand to the right. "Auf, go—kitchen. Dinner's waiting." Aufhocker immediately broke the rigid posture and trotted away. "I don't know what I'd do without him. He was a gift from my Uncle Stefan, given to me not long after I moved back to the States. Stefan shipped him all the way from Germany. He said that no matter what happened or where I went in this world, I would always have a friend to watch over me. And it's true. We've lived all over, and Auf's been right there beside me, ever since I was a child."

"Your uncle must love you very much. Funny, Auf doesn't look that old." Melvin studied on the dog's age for a minute before realizing what he'd said. "Well, that came out every which way of wrong, didn't it? I told you English gets me in trouble."

Ivy didn't reply. She sat in her chair watching him, herself perfectly at ease while he fumbled through the conversation. Desperate to change channels and segue into the business at hand, Melvin lifted *Lykanthrop* from the coffee table and leafed through it.

"I don't think your sheriff cared for my book," Ivy said.

"Sheriff Hubbard's not one for fantasy. She's a just-the-facts kind of lady. But truthfully, now, these pictures don't keep you up at night?" Melvin held the book up to show a half-man, half-wolf prowling a winter-bare forest. Ahead of the creature, illuminated by the full moon's light, stood a little girl.

"That's one of my favorites. It's interesting you picked it."

"Why's that? A favorite, I mean."

"Loss, Deputy. This sketch shows the imminent loss of innocence. You're familiar with the tale *Little Red Riding Hood;* it's the same concept on a more mature level. Here the predator is identified more directly: man as beast. The children's version shows just the animal form, but the implication is the same in both stories."

"So the beast is man and the wolf is a metaphor. I never would have thought of it like that."

"Oh? What do you see then?"

"I see a kid about to be eaten by a monster. But that's just me."

Ivy laughed. "You have to go deeper than that. If you look closely at the carnage in these sketches, the wolf is as much a victim as the people are, if you know anything about the true nature of wolves."

"How is the wolf the victim here? Looks like to me the folks in these pictures are in a heap of trouble." Melvin flipped to another page where a wolf hunkered behind a rock awaiting to spring on a maiden gathering water by a stream.

"What you're seeing is art based on stereotype. The wolf has worn the cloak of villain for centuries. Easy to see how that might happen—there weren't many biologists running around in the Middle Ages. In reality, Deputy Sanders, wolves are nothing like myth and folklore would have us to believe."

"How's that?"

"Well, in lots of ways. They are loving parents and loyal mates. They play like silly pranksters and touch each other often for the joy of companionship. And their language, Deputy Sanders—have you ever heard anything more beautiful than a wolf's song? That's only one of the ways they speak to each other. The slightest expression change in the eye or the nose or even the way they hold their tails can convey a world of meanings to anyone wise enough to pay attention."

"Ah, I get it now. The kinder, gentler wolf has been overlooked in stories." Melvin held up the sketch in *Lykanthrop.*

"I bet this gal by the stream is really about to leap over that rock and throttle the poor wolf with her water jug, right?" Melvin waited for Ivy to laugh at his joke. The hard set of her mouth and the way her jaw slightly ground told him a smile was not forthcoming.

"You don't have to be sarcastic. I'm trying to give you another point of view here. On the flipside of what I just said, wolves are still predators. They can be zealous social climbers within their own hierarchies and obsessively compulsive in defending their territories, both to the extent of brutal violence. Do you see any similarities to anything, Deputy, in all I've just told you?"

"I'm not a quick study on some things, Miss Cole, but I take it you're likening wolves to humans."

"That's right! I think the fear of the wolf is really the fear of ourselves."

"That's a different approach to the idea of murder, I suppose."

Ivy's brows jumped up a notch and her voice rose with them. "It's not my view on *murder,* Deputy Sanders. Did you not hear what I just said?" Ivy flipped her hair in what Melvin could only read as disgust. She leaned forward and aimed a long, slender finger his direction. "Did you know that warrior cultures in Europe honored the wolf, but when society shifted to corralling their food instead of hunting for it, suddenly the wolf was an enemy? It was okay for wolves to share their forests with men for meat, but when animals, and I'm talking about livestock here, became property, suddenly people didn't want to share anymore. Wolves were a threat to the purse strings. Then the church jumped in at some point and declared wolves to be evil. Aligning them with the devil made it even more acceptable to kill them. It became the moral thing to do!"

"Ivy, I didn't mean—"

"You know, you should study up on your facts and get to know a person better before you make broad, sweeping statements about murder. I'll tell you about murder. Man and wolf have been brothers for thousands of years. Wolves taught men how to hunt; they would lead entire tribes to the location of bison and deer. Many cultures in Europe and Native American tribes felt such close ties to wolves, they believed our ancestors were wolves and we evolved from them. Yet, bring the settlers to America, and within a couple hundred years, we've nearly wiped wolves out of existence here. They've been burned alive, poisoned, left in snares to bleed to death, strangled as puppies, had their jaws torn out or wired shut so they'd starve, lassoed and torn apart by men on horseback, had their tendons severed only to then be set upon by dogs. . . . We have tortured and killed many a wolf in this country, Deputy Sanders, and for what? So men can control more of the territory, hunt more of the wolves' game, and wear their magnificent pelts. Now *that,* Deputy Sanders, is murder." Ivy sat back, staring with a brittle, stone-chipped gaze her guest hated to see.

"I stand corrected," Melvin finally said. He set the book down and folded his hands in his lap. They had arrived at a crossroads between work and pleasure. Miss Cole was riled, much like the day he first met her. It was not a place he wanted to go to again, not when things were starting to get less awkward between them. Yet one insensitive comment, and he'd backed them right up to where they'd started. At this point, he could take one turn and send them out the door for a nice dinner and hopefully let sleeping dogs *(wolves)* lie, or he could plow ahead into the reason he was really supposed to be here, which could possibly create even more tension. Melvin pictured the morrow and Sheriff Hubbard's face. Sometimes it was hard being a cop.

"I respect all that, Miss Cole, I truly do. Nevertheless, Andy Talbot thinks it was a wolf that killed his dog, and we feel certain it's the same animal that attacked Hughes and the previous victims. It's hard for me to feel sympathetic or see another viewpoint right now. But while we're on this subject, I was wondering if you would take a look at something for me. Being so knowledgeable about canines, I think you can help us."

Melvin reached into his back pants pocket and pulled out the little notebook. Ivy sat up even straighter, stony gaze still in place, and Melvin felt the remainder of a good evening flying right out the window. He flipped the book to the middle and held out a sketch of his own for Ivy to see.

"What is it?" Ivy asked.

"It's a pawprint we think might belong to Talbot's wolf. It's not to scale; the track we discovered was bigger than my hand."

Ivy switched on the lamp by her chair, then leaned forward and took the pad to scrutinize. "It's a mistake."

"What do you mean?"

"I mean this cannot be a wolf print with the paw shaped that way. Either you've drawn it wrong or you're after a different animal, one I don't recognize."

"Explain to me what's wrong about it."

"The toes look right, as far as shape goes. But the claws are impossibly long. No wolf has claws like that. I'd say that's more akin to a bear's claw length. Plus the pad of the foot is irregular. It's basically triangular like a wolf's, but too elongated." Ivy handed the notebook back.

Melvin flipped the page to a blank sheet and fished a pen out of his shirt pocket.

"What can you tell me about scent marking? We believe this animal marked the Talbot kill site."

Ivy sighed and crossed her arms. "Wolves mark by urination, defecation, and scratching up the ground. They do it to set the limits of their territory, warn off other wolves, and let members of the pack know where they are. Boundaries are very important to wolves in the wild. Gregarious animals they may be, but one pack will readily kill a wolf from another pack who crosses those invisible lines into taken territory. Your animal is claiming his territory and warning anybody else who might be thinking of coming into it."

"You say 'he.' You think it's male?"

"Females do sometimes scent mark, but it's more prominent with the males."

"Back to territory, could the male be attempting to claim it from another animal? A challenge?"

"Interesting question. You think there could be more than one out there?"

"I don't know. We've considered it. But to leave no

tracks—it seems impossible. But the whole thing seems impossible, so . . . "

"So you think someone is covering them up."

"I didn't say that. Miss Cole, as a trainer and dog behaviorist, you tell me—what are we dealing with here?"

Ivy shook her head. "Deputy Sanders, I train poodles, pampered pets. Something like this is out of my league. I know a smattering about wolves because it's my job to know canids in general. But I've given you all I can."

"I'm just asking for your opinion. Do you think we have a rogue wolf on our hands or not?"

"And what would the 'not' be then, if not a rogue wolf? Something even more sinister perhaps, like a trained animal?"

"You're pretty quick. We could use you at the sheriff's office. But yeah, something like that."

Ivy clasped her hands. "Okay, Deputy, here's what I think about the Devil of Doe Springs. Based on the pawprint, I don't know what it is, other than it does resemble a wolf's print in some ways. The sporadic behavior we've seen from it, if it is a domesticated animal, tells me it's not killing for food or sport."

"Why then?"

"It's training. Learning. Getting smarter."

"The animals, like Talbot's dog, are practice?"

Night had fallen on them at last, and Ivy's eyes glittered in the lamplight. Her bronze skin was radiant under its golden glow. The drawl in her voice wound through the air like spun sugar, and she answered the question with peculiar relish. "Yes, that's right. Your case started with animal kills last year and escalated to humans, if I remember correctly. It used the animals in the beginning as teachers; now it is using them to hone its skills, stay sharp. Humans are the true prey, obviously."

"Then you think it will attack only humans eventually, and the animal mutilations will stop. Dogs don't train themselves, Miss Cole. People train dogs for that kind of behavior, right?"

"It was the wolf that first taught man to hunt, Deputy Sanders, not the other way around."

"But the missing tracks and jewelry . . . "

"Missing jewelry? So we have a thief and a killer on our hands?"

Melvin knew he'd made a mistake. He needn't worry about hazards of the job; the sheriff was going to kill him herself. "I would appreciate it if you wouldn't mention that to anyone. There are some things we don't leak to the general public about the cases."

"You have my word, Deputy Sanders. This isn't the kind of chitchat I have with friends over Coke and a Moon Pie, believe me. My compassion for wolves would not be popular in any company right now. But I hope you understand that my feelings toward these animals precede the tragedies that have occurred here. Whatever animal has done these things is not the one I defend."

"And I hope I didn't offend you. It's all right to be on different sides of the coin, I hope." Melvin picked the book up again. "Do you mind if I borrow this?"

"Taking up an interest in folklore now?"

"There's always hope for conversion. The things you've been talking about, some of the information is from this?"

"I wouldn't know. The book is in German; I only look at the pictures and draw my own conclusions."

"You don't speak German?"

"Dad was into complete Americanization of his only child. Even when Mama and I lived in Germany for a brief time, we spoke only English in our household. It was one of Daddy's crazy rules, even though he was back here in the States on business most the time. No foreign accent to muck up this Southern twang. But all that's a-whole-nother story for a-whole-nother time."

"I'd like to hear about it one day." Melvin hefted the book but did not set it down.

Ivy wasn't interested in her story, only the one Melvin held. "That's the only book of its kind in existence, Deputy Sanders."

Melvin read Ivy's face clearer than he would ever be able to muddle through this ancient text, could see the gears turning over from yes to no and back again. It was an expensive item, he shouldn't have asked her for it. He barely knew her, but being a police officer, he assumed everyone would find him trustworthy.

Surprisingly, she said, "Please take extreme care. I don't like it out of my sight for too long."

"I'll guard it with my life." Melvin tucked the book under his arm. "Hey, now I think *my* stomach's growling. Where would you like to go to dinner?" Time to end what had come to feel like a formal interrogation. A little evening left was better than none, and he thought a café over near Pine Knot served up until ten o'clock, if she had no suggestions. Plenty of time left to salvage the date and lighten up the stiff tone their conversation had taken.

"You know what, Deputy Sanders? If you don't mind, I believe I'll call it an early night. We've covered your questions. I believe that was the point."

Melvin's jaw went slack, and disappointment tarnished his lawman poker face. Ivy stood and Aufhocker appeared between kitchen and living room. He went to Ivy's side. They both walked to the door and turned to look back, staring at the deputy.

Melvin followed them to the foyer. "Good night then, Miss Cole. Thank you for your time, and the book. I'll enjoy looking through it. Maybe I can broaden my cultural horizons. And maybe we can go to dinner another time, when I return it? I'd like to see you on a first-name basis for a change."

"Yes, maybe. Enjoy the book."

Melvin stood there a moment longer, but Ivy's pleasantly blank face razed his hope. The night was over. He ducked out the door and she closed it before he'd made it off the porch. Melvin felt a bit like a dog himself just then, one with its tail tucked between its legs. He got in the patrol car and a thought hit him. He hadn't even asked about the Bonsai. Looks like he'd have to call on Miss Cole another time, but not tomorrow. Melvin started the car and drove away.

Ivy leaned against her door and listened as the deputy's heavy steps moved off the porch, then the car roared off down the road. She slid to the floor, back against the wall, and Auf sank down with her. Rex reappeared and immediately crawled into her lap. She stroked the dogs' heads and pictured Deputy Sanders leaving her yard, the sacred book in the crook of his arm. He couldn't read it, and even if he could, what difference would it make? No one would believe it. Man's disbelief was her greatest ally, always had been.

As for *the other* who had entered her town, there would be consequences. The pawprint was unmistakable, and what a fool he was to have left it. Inexperienced. Ineffective. Clumsy and reckless. That's what she really wanted to tell the persistent deputy. The wolf had made no human kills as of yet—those were hers, the remains left behind as points to be made. But he would, and his choices would be impulsive, not knowledgeable or controlled. He was most likely a mindless creature in the throws of the moon; how she despised their kind. Let the officers pursue the animal mutilator. If he was lucky, his foolheartedness would get him shot before she had a chance to deal with him.

The officers. Ivy saw Sanders's disappointed face and the way his shoulders squared up a little straighter to disguise his crestfallen walk to the car.

"I have to chase away another one, don't I, Auf? It's a curse, not getting close. But I like him, don't you, fella? Huh?" Auf answered with his cold black stare, and she knew no outsider would ever be welcome in his domain. She turned her attention to the terrier in her lap, whose own eyes had grown droopy under her massaging fingers.

"But that's the problem. If I had to defend us . . . " She let the thought trail away. The good deputy would find his killer wolf, and he would show no mercy. And neither could she.

That night, as the moon waned on its odyssey to new, two killers fitfully slept. One, a blond woman, tossed and turned in her dream-fright, fighting the coverlets for her life. The dog, Rex, stood over her and trembled. The woman's scream turned to a howl before she slumped, still sleeping, into a small and exhausted heap.

In town, another sat bolt upright in his bed, sweat from his own nightmares slickening his body. His hands shook, and he raked them through his dark hair. Out there, somewhere in the night, a sound drew him from his slumber. It was the agonized call of a kindred spirit. He looked at the calendar across from the bed. Not too much longer now, he would find her.

Chapter 15

Sheriff Gloria Hubbard cleared off her desk, for the most part. She gathered paperwork in both arms and refiled it on the floor in the corner behind her. Then she poured two cups of coffee, black. She set one on the far side of the newly clean desk, then sat in her chair to wait. He'd called from the airport before leaving Montana and again thirty minutes ago en route to the office. If Gloria's calculations were correct, her ex-husband would be walking through the door right about—

"Hi, beautiful. How've you been?" Tee Hubbard stood in the doorway, filling it up with a bigger-than-life smile and beat-up cowboy hat. It was the same hat he was wearing when they met twenty years ago. She thought he might have been born in the damn thing.

"Hello, Tee. Still overdressing for every occasion, I see," Gloria said.

Tee laughed and brushed a hand over his Wranglers, looking only slightly newer than the hat. Nevertheless, every female eye in the department had followed him into the sheriff's office. Gloria was always too well aware of that fact, even when her husband remained oblivious. Ex-husband, she corrected herself.

"Come 'ere and give me a big ole hug, woman. I've just flown across the country, it's the least you can do."

"How about a cup of coffee instead? Have a seat, Tee. It's good to see you."

Tee Hubbard sat down, snatching the cowboy hat from his mop of caramel blond hair and redepositing it in his lap. He took the coffee but didn't drink, just studied his former wife across the desk in front of him.

"You look good, Glory. It's been too long. I wish you'd called me sooner."

Gloria took a long drink from her mug before answering. "It's not a social call, you know that. I appreciate your coming."

"You must be in a desperate predicament to get in touch with me." The lines around his eyes crinkled, and an amused sparkle parted the seriousness behind the irises' stormy gray.

"You can get off that high horse, cowboy. I called because you are the best, not because I'm desperate. We need a tracker. The local boys I'm dealing with don't know a groundhog from a grizzly bear. Did you bring Zeke?"

"Yeah, I brought him." Tee set the mug on the desk. He'd had enough Sanka on the flight in. "I was hoping there could be some gab on getting reacquainted before heading into the long haul of why I'm here. But that's my Glory, all business."

"We covered a lot of ground while we were together, Tee, and a whole lot hasn't changed since then. Only thing's different is I'm sheriff now, and my life was looking pretty good until last year. Meanwhile you've been soaking up the Big Sky and enjoying your early retirement. Does that about sum it up?"

Tee leaned forward and crossed his hands on the desk. Gloria kept her own firmly wrapped around the coffee mug. She tilted back in her chair, away from him. He sighed.

"How've you been, Glory, really? Since Annie? I haven't slept in five years."

"I don't want to talk about that, Tee. Not now, not ever. It has nothing to do with what's going on here."

"Fair enough." Tee took new interest in his hat, flicking the brim and collecting his thoughts in its considerable well. When nothing brilliant stirred in the felt Stetson, he resigned himself to hitting the books. Fraternizing would come later, after work. It had always been that way with them, before marriage and during. Their drive to right wrongs pulled them together, then, sadly, pushed them apart. He'd reflected on that for far too long, out there under the Big Sky. Riding into clear coral sunsets and fishing in sparkling glacial streams had never managed to erase the face of the woman he'd left behind. But someday he'd learn to let bygones be bygones. Right now there was a case to solve, and she'd needed him enough to overcome the past and call him. He wouldn't let her down again. "So tell me, just what is going on here? What are we tracking?"

"You haven't heard the stories? We're getting real popular in the news these days, specially around full-moon time."

"Montana's a long way from everywhere, Glory. Fill me in."

"Read this." Gloria released the security of her coffee mug to slide the latest newspaper article across the desk. Tee scanned it with the look of a man addressing *The National Enquirer.*

"Then there's this." Gloria scooted a large sketchpad behind the newspaper. "This is about as good as we remember it. My deputy used his hand to size the track."

Tee held the newspaper in one hand and the sketchpad in the other. He shook his head. "Somebody's playing with you. This isn't an animal track. Doe Springs got its own version of Bigfoot running around?"

"You might say that, only this Bigfoot has a penchant for postal workers. The dog in that article isn't the half of it. We've had four human fatalities, the latest of which was a delivery man for the P.O., and several animal mutilations. They were all livestock except for the Border collie. We're pretty sure the dog interfered with an intended sheep kill. To top it off, we've had a run on kooky accidents and disappearances in the past year too. At first I thought we were having a rash of runaways. Now I don't think so."

"And the accidents?"

"Who knows? When it rains it pours. We've taken bad luck to the extreme around here. The media went from denouncing us as cursed to branding us as a stalking ground for werewolves." Gloria spent the next twenty minutes rehashing the whole lurid mess, recounting the fog that had settled over their sweet mountain community and its escalation from bad to worse, including their frustrated efforts to find the Devil of Doe Springs and its phenomenal ability to leave no traces at the attack sites. "Except once. This pawprint. We might have a hair sample too, but the lab will be awhile getting back to us on that. We can't explain the missing jewelry either, unless the thing simply ate it by accident."

Tee turned the sketch around, scrutinizing every angle and curve. He had retired, true enough, but only officially. Covering his ranch from horseback and tracking through the Rockies for the sheer pleasure of it ate up many a day since he'd left Appalachia way back when. It was better that way—tracking for recreation—with nothing at stake but the joy of spying on a mother bear holed up with her cubs or an elk camouflaged in conifers. If they never materialized, he rode home none the worse for the wear. On the job, it had been a-whole-nother story at the end of a fruitless day.

"Give me a pencil," Tee said.

Gloria rolled one at him, and he immediately began altering Sanders's rendering.

"Here, what's this look like to you?" Tee put the sketch between them. He'd drawn in fresh lines, pulling the bottom of the paw pad upward into a truer triangular shape and bringing the claw indentions closer to the toes.

"A wolf. Or a big dog. But the only wolves in North Carolina are the red wolves that were released a few years ago on the coast. I don't know much about wolves, but I know those aren't capable of what we've seen, even if one did manage to migrate this far. That would be unlikely, wouldn't it?"

"Out West wolves travel hundreds of miles, some have even gone thousands. But no, even the bigger gray wolves wouldn't do what you're talking about. There's never been an unprovoked wolf attack on a person in this country.

I find it impossible you'd start seeing it in North Carolina, even if wolves hadn't been killed off here a century ago."

"But you said they can travel great distances. What if—"

Tee cut her off. "Look, my spread is over five hundred acres south of Glacier National Park, Glory, and I've ridden every inch of it. I've only seen two wolves passing through the whole time I've lived there. There aren't that many of them, and they tend to stick close to isolated areas. Even if a gray wolf did manage to find its way to the South, it still wouldn't do what you're telling me. They're scared of people, with good reason. The two I saw probably ended up shot."

"I thought that was illegal in Montana."

"Only if you get caught, and the laws change on that every day too."

The look in Tee's eyes hardened for an instant, and Gloria figured trigger-happy ranchers chafed her ex-husband in uncomfortable places. When he'd left his Blue Ridge Mountain home, he'd headed west for secluded country and Mother Nature living at her wildest, two draws Gloria could not compete with and would never deny him. Leaving the crowded violence of the East behind to go where people were few and animals roamed plenty was exactly the therapy he needed after losing Annie. Illegally killing anything on four legs, in Tee's way of thinking, was a sacrilege.

"So we've got something akin to a wolf print, but you don't think it's canine. What do you think?" Gloria said.

"I didn't say that. What I said was, I don't think it's a wolf or a dog. I'm guessing it's both."

"A hybrid. Why so?"

"Size and intent. Hybrids sometimes outgrow their wolf-dog parents, and the wiring in their heads can get all mixed up. Not all of them; some hybrids can be gentle as rabbits. But if the wires do get crossed, hybrids fear people less, that's the dog in them, and they're more likely to attack livestock and children than a purebred animal. They're not being mean—they're being instinctual predators."

"Well, that computes, but no children have been killed and none are missing, far as I know. Thank God." Annie's

school photo burned in the sheriff's head like the afterimage
of a picture just taken. The sheriff had never laid eyes on the
little girl save for that photograph, a little girl long dead but
still heavy in Gloria's heart. Why did Tee have to bring her
up earlier? He'd been here half an hour and had already sent
an arrow zinging into her chest. When would he learn to let
bygones be bygones, even if it was just for show? She could
keep up the farce of being okay as long as nobody threw it in
her face. But Tee never let her get away with that stuff. Fake
wasn't a habit he was in, and one he couldn't abide in others.

"You still with me, Glory?" Tee'd been talking but stopped
when he saw the fingers start drumming on the beat-up
wood table and the marble look in his ex-wife's eyes, telling
him she saw faraway places and he was no longer part of the
scenery.

"I'm listening, Tee. Go on. You were saying something
about hybrids and France?"

"Yeah. I said it doesn't have to be kids, they're just small,
easy targets. In the 1700s a pair of wolf-dog hybrids killed
about sixty-four people in France before they were hunted
down. The male weighed in at a good hundred and thirty
pounds and was just five inches shy of six feet long, nose to
tail. He could easily take down an adult. Few purebred wolves
reach those sizes. Even adult gray wolves rarely make it
over one-twenty."

Tee squinted at the article again, but fought the urge to
fish out his specs. "This Talbot fellow says the animal he saw
was black. The pawprint is in line with that. For whatever
reason, black wolves tend to have bigger feet than their
lighter compadres. What I've redrawn here," Tee pointed to
the sketch, "is five and a half inches long by four wide—
that's to gray wolf scale. We can start with that as a realistic
guesstimate, anyway."

"Tell me what you think about the kills themselves. This
ought to help you get a better idea of what we're dealing
with." Gloria rolled to the corner and picked the top envelope
off the pile. Tee went through the photographs of Clifford
Hughes with the manner of an accountant reviewing stats.

"They're all about the same," Gloria said. "Bodies gobbled up. Few remains. Hughes was the only one with missing effects, though. We've found wallets with money, keys, even jewelry at the other three sites," Gloria said.

"Uh-huh." Tee nodded and put the victim's photos away. There would be time to go over these in detail later. He'd need to see all pictures, all sites, talk to plenty of locals.

Retirement slipped behind him as gears shifted into high and his faculties sharpened on the grindstone of a new challenge. Zeke's senses would reawaken too, the second Tee stuck an article of clothing under the old bloodhound's nose. They'd made a fine team back in the day.

"Critter's got some bite." Tee placed the envelope on the desk between them with more reverence than his words belied.

"Tell you anything?"

"Maybe. The bones in the body, they were eaten too?"

"Anything it got a hold of, it was able to mangle. And did. Could a hybrid do that?"

"Well, take a big domestic dog, German shepherd, for instance. He's got a seven hundred and fifty pound bite on him."

"That's a lot of pressure per square inch. Seems like overkill for downing some Purina."

"Maybe so, but I wouldn't want one clamped down on my arm, just the same. Wolves, on the other hand, aren't out there eating kibble. They're taking down big prey, like moose and bison. Now we're talking a bite pressure of one thousand five hundred pounds per square inch. Hearing what I've heard and seeing the little I've seen, I think your elderly witness, Mr. Talbot, might not be too far off on his thinking."

"A werewolf. Good. I'm glad I flew you out here. Thanks, Tee."

He ignored her. Glory could have some bite too, when she wanted. He'd rather tangle with the Devil of Doe Springs man to man than take her on, on a bad day. He continued: "Which brings me right back around to my original assessment: crossbreed. If you think a person is behind this, and I feel like you do, a hybrid is going to be more trainable. Wolves do what wolves will, but dogs listen. Wrap up the strength and intelligence of the wolf with the tractability of a domestic dog, and you've got a powerful package to reckon with."

Gloria pursed her lips, thinking. "Okay, I'll buy all that. But let's go back to the pawprint we found. Sanders drew an accurate picture of it. It was not like how you changed it."

"What I drew is how I think the track started out. I'd say your culprit is the one who changed it. He's messing with you to throw you off course."

"I thought about that, but it doesn't make sense. Why go to all that trouble when we're not even on the course to begin with? There's nothing to throw us off of."

"Sick minds like to play games, Glory. Whoever left that pawprint out there fully intended for you to find it. He tampered with the proportions to fiddle with your head because he's bored."

"Great. So even killing isn't enough of a thrill anymore."

"Think about it: You've got an old farmer who has the town believing there's a werewolf lurking around, no evidence to speak of, and now this crazy pawprint. That's a whole busload of recognition for somebody. His ego must be spinning."

"Because he thinks we're the biggest idiots on the mountain, right? Life must be peachy when you're a psycho."

"Honey, you wouldn't have called me for anything less."

Gloria let a smile get past her. "Maybe I have missed you, Tee. Just a little."

Chapter 16

Deputy Sanders bounded up the brick police station steps and strode through the short hallway en route to the sheriff's office. The previous evening had weighed heavy on him through the wee hours, manifesting itself into a terrible case of heartburn by sunup. A roll of Tums and a skipped morning run put his stomach under control again, but his mood was none the better. The nondate with Miss Cole could not have been more of a disaster if he'd walked in and given one of her dogs a good lick with the toe of his shined-up shoe. Today he was back in uniform and considerably more comfortable. They still needed to go over some things, but he swore after slinking off her porch like a sad, whipped pup he'd wait a few days to call. But. But, but, but. If his nerve was up and his stomach acid down by lunchtime, he might try again. Sheriff Hubbard would be asking about that Bonsai, and he'd better be able to spout some answers. *Better that I mend whatever I screwed up early, lest she forget about me altogether, isn't that really it, Melvin old pal?* He shook the thought off. Deputy Meeks was ahead of him, standing outside the sheriff's office and looking quite suspicious.

"Whatcha doin', John?"

Meeks jumped at Melvin's voice and wheeled around. "Christ, you about gave me a coronary. Do you always sneak up on people?"

"Only when I catch them eavesdropping. What's going on?"

"Big trouble, that's what." Meeks backed away from the office. "And it flew in at six-thirty this morning."

The door abruptly opened. Sheriff Hubbard stood forehead to chin with Meeks. He backed up a step.

"Good morning, Deputies. Glad you're both here. This is

Tee Hubbard, professional tracker. He's flown in from Montana and his retirement to help us out."

Tee stepped around Gloria and offered his hand to the two men.

"We're putting Tee up at Musket Dobbins's old place. The number is on my board in the office."

"Department's going all out, then. You might wish you were sleeping in a patrol car after a few nights over there," Meeks said.

"Welcome aboard anyway, sir," Melvin followed up, giving the man's palm a firm squeeze before releasing it.

"It's not that bad. I couldn't find any other rentals in a pinch." Gloria shot the deputies a look. "Tee's driving an old blue Ford pickup on loan from Musket, so don't have it towed if you see it in the parking lot. And he'll be working with a bloodhound, Zeke. Zeke's reputation exceeds Tee's when it comes to finding the unfindable. I'm going to get them settled, then we're heading to Talbot's to look around. Sanders, don't worry about hiking that trail out. We'll take care of it with Zeke while we're over there."

"Sheriff, I need to talk to you about some things before you take off," Melvin said.

"It'll have to wait. The longer we're off the trail, the cooler it gets."

"This might help. I spoke with Ivy Cole and showed her the pawprint. She says she's never seen anything like it, dog, wolf, or otherwise. She also had some theories on the animal's motivation."

Gloria nodded. "We've come up with a couple theories ourselves. I'll brief you on Tee's conclusions when we get back. Have Delores make duplicates of everything and bundle it up for me. Tee's got a lot of homework tonight." Gloria turned to Meeks. "Call the lab today and see what's going on with the hair samples. I know it's early yet, but it'll let them know I'm anxious. If they do know something, radio me ASAP. If it's anything besides raccoon, Zeke will find it useful."

The sheriff and Tee were out the station before the deputies could respond. Meeks stood beside Melvin, hands on his hips and a frown on his face. "Hubbard and Hubbard. Not a coincidence, is it?"

"Nope. Looks like the cavalry just rode in," Melvin said. "Don't look so happy about it."

Meeks relaxed his matronly stance, but the scowl remained molded in place. "We can handle it without some cowboy poking his nose in. We've already had a psychic Indian—it's turning into a circus around here."

"It's been a circus. Terence Hubbard is a local legend, John. He worked for years with the Special Investigations Division in Charlotte and he's tracked for police departments all over North Carolina, including the SBI."

"How do you know so much about him?"

"We learned about Hubbard at the academy, him and that old dog he totes everywhere. When it comes to intuition, he's as close to a real psychic as we'll ever get."

"If that's so, why hasn't the sheriff brought him in sooner? We had trackers out in the woods months ago, and she never said a word about him."

"There's a lot of bad water under the Hubbard bridge. Even I don't wade in that creek. But from what I've heard, theirs was more a clash of the Titans than a marriage. Sheriff's got a strong will, and Tee's got a strong ego. They finally parted ways after a case they did together went sour."

"So that's the one. I'd heard something about that too." Meeks hesitated at Sanders's slack-jawed expression. "Hey, I might have only a year of Doe Springs under my belt, but small towns are small towns. I had the lowdown on this place a week after I got here. But gossip isn't where I heard the most of it. Before moving, I worked not too far from where it happened. Uwharrie area, right? A family camping in the park woke up to find their tent minus one little girl. Daddy went hunting for her and found nothing but a big bloody inkblot just a stone's throw from their Volkswagen."

"That's one way to put it, yeah." Melvin didn't care for *bloody inkblot*. It was good the sheriff sent her youngest deputy to break the news to victims' families when she was unable to make the call herself. Meeks didn't talk much, and when he did, the too-candid side of his nature walked the edge of obnoxiousness. Perhaps too many years in this line of work had dissolved tact into taciturn. Even the loudest voices went quiet and the softest hearts morphed into granite after years of tragic bombardment. There was plenty to toughen up an officer and run an extroverted character into a cynical introvert that had nothing to do with slavering menaces in the forest. Scraping a family off a curvy stretch of country road could destroy a young nature forever and launch a person straight into old-man-hood in the blink of an eye. Melvin couldn't fault Meeks on his disposition. He found his own center wasn't the tender well of twenty-two anymore, when even an injured animal caused an ache that hurt for days.

They didn't talk about these things, the three of them. It was understood without discussion. And Melvin didn't need psychic Indians or intuitive cowboys to tell him about the sheriff's pain, either. He saw it clear enough in the dark bags under her eyes, the new gray that showed up in her hair, hair which she was lax to color before it parted the chestnut strands like a chalk line. Who had time to worry of matters such as appearance when merely getting dressed in the morning and teeth brushed could be an accomplishment? Gloria Hubbard had traversed a long hard road before she ever climbed up the ladder to The Sheriff of Doe Springs. She'd told him once that being at the top of the heap wasn't such a victory anyway; it just meant she had a bigger pile of crap underneath her to reckon with.

"The little girl was never found," Melvin finished for Meeks. "Neither was the abductor. For all Tee's experience, he and the bloodhound found nothing, and the park rangers wrote it off as a cougar attack. But Sheriff Hubbard couldn't let it go at that, even after she and Tee were sent home."

"That's irony in a nutshell, isn't it? Sheriff must be living it all over again with what's happening here. And now the family reunion completes it."

Melvin debated sidestepping the spit of disgust he thought might follow Meeks's last statement. He'd always suspected Meeks was sweet on the sheriff; Tee's arrival must be a hard pill to swallow. A shallow smugness settled in

Melvin against his will. He wasn't the only one with girl problems. "I don't know, Meeks. Forget it. It's all hearsay anyway. She never talks about it. Whatever happened between those two, I'm glad Tee's here. We need all the help we can get. If he's as good as they say, we might get somewhere."

Meeks's brow furrowed even deeper and he faced Sanders. Jealousy was ugly on his usually handsome face. Melvin didn't know whether to be concerned or laugh out loud.

"What is it?" Melvin said finally.

Meeks blew hard through his nostrils, then abruptly turned away. "I'm going to call the lab and see if they know anything yet." He strode off, leaving Melvin to wonder for the second time in as many days if he had done something wrong.

Deputy Sanders slid behind his undersized desk, crammed into a corner cubicle. His knees hit the top of it, but he was accustomed to the cramped position. It was a small station, too small perhaps for the likes of him. Six-foot-five in bare feet, he launched upwards in ninth grade and never looked back. Size kept teasing at bay but made everyday life uncomfortable at best. The world was made for the average— his cubicle, his house, cases in point.

Relieved of hiking duty, Melvin turned his attention to Miss Cole's book. It lay spread in front of him, ringed by photos of his parents from different stages of their lives: picnicking in West Virginia, when his dad worked in a coal mine shortly after they were married; smiling wide in front of their very first house in Asheville when Melvin was three; eating ice-cream cake on their twenty-first wedding anniversary, one short year before fate claimed them both—his dad, a heart attack, followed soon after by his mother's stroke. Above the wood frames poked a wilted potted plant, courtesy of Shirley, whom he feared had a crush. Melvin guessed he'd better replace the dying arrangement before she noticed and got her feelings hurt.

Melvin tucked distractions away and focused on the pages in front of him. Last night after the date disaster he fell asleep with the tome open on his lap. It would not be a light read, even if he had been fluent in the language. The text was penned in, he had no doubt, quill and ink. While some paragraphs flowed in graceful calligraphy, others appeared written by someone different altogether, with narrow scratchy marks or bold strokes ending in splatters that smeared across several lines. Ivy was right about one thing: the surreal beauty of the sketches. These were done with great care and detail. Whoever the author or authors of this book had been (and none were listed, that he could determine), they were truly artists.

Melvin flipped to page twenty and unseated his blank parking-ticket bookmark. The black ink sketch depicted a barren country road. In the distance hunkered an old village, asleep beneath a dim full moon. A traveler walked the road, unaware that behind him, from the direction of the city, crept four black figures illuminated only by moonlight rippling along their hackled backs. The caption beneath the sketch read *Barenhauter, Greifswald, 1643.* He turned more of the aged parchment pages, looking for—well, he didn't know what he was looking for. Something familiar. Then there it was, a word he recognized staring up off the page: *Aufhocker.* The picture with the text was similar to the Greifswald drawing—a weary traveler, alone at night on a deserted road. Deep clouds partially hid the full moon, and bare winter trees stretched like skeletons' hands over the man's head. Standing on the road before the man was a giant black dog.

"Aufhocker, it's you." Melvin remembered Ivy's hand on the shepherd's head, calming him at the Talbot farm, then the standoffish greeting of the hound in her house. Melvin snatched up the book and carried it to the sheriff's computer. He looked up the word *Aufhocker* online. He received one hit, a brief paragraph:

Aufhocker—The Aufhocker was a great black dog of German folklore. It sought lone travelers as it hunted by night, oftentimes at crossroads. Upon discovering a human victim, the Aufhocker would rise up on its hind legs and bite the person's throat.

"The sheriff might get worked up if she saw you using her computer without authorization." Meeks was back, leaning in the office doorway with his arms crossed. His composure had returned, the earlier irritation tucked away like Melvin's own distractions to be dealt with at a more appropriate time. "You know she warned us before about those video games."

The halfhearted joke warranted a halfhearted chuckle, but Melvin couldn't manage it. Shorter than he'd intended, Melvin answered, "I'm working on the case, Meeks. You'd think we could get more than one computer around here. It's the next millennium."

"Tightfisted taxpayers. What can you do?" Meeks walked behind Melvin and read the Aufhocker paragraph. "Falling for the werewolf hysteria that's sweeping our cozy neck of the woods?" He clawed his hands and made growling noises.

Melvin sighed. He thought about bringing up Tee one more time to somber the other deputy and send him sulking off again. Instead, he said, "I'm doing research on myths and legends. It could help us draw up a profile down the road."

"A profile. Good thinking. While you're doing that, I'll be down at Brigham's Feed talking to some hunters about the Talbot woods. A couple of them boys spend more time with rifles wedged in their armpits than they do making a living."

"And some of them make a living with rifles wedged in their armpits. Dad put squirrel on our supper table a time or two when I was growing up."

"Must be an acquired taste. I always preferred bigger game myself. But you've got to love the South. Everybody has a gun and an excuse to use it." Meeks checked his watch. "I'm heading out."

"Need me to go with?"

"Nah, I got it. We don't want pesky police work to interfere with story time." He clapped Melvin on the back before turning to walk off.

"Hey, John, what'd the lab say about our hair sample?"

Meeks paused at the door. "Nothing square yet. Seemed

put out we called a'ready." Meeks spied *Lykanthrop* by the
keyboard. "By the way, where'd you get that book you're
reading?"

"I borrowed it from Ivy Cole."

"Looks like it's about to fall apart. How's it relate to the
case?"

"Doesn't. I thought it would be handy for my research—
I'm working on a theory."

Meeks nodded. "Uh-huh. Seems like everybody's got a
theory but me. Let me know when you get it all figured out.
I'd like to get home on time for once."

Chapter 17

"No, Deputy Sanders, we've never displayed this book here.
I would remember it. Are you taking up book collecting? It's
a fine hobby, book collecting." Prudy Township looked up
at the handsome young deputy and batted mascara-caked
lashes through her spectacles. Melvin found his feet heading
to the Doe Springs Public Library for his lunch hour instead
of Etta's Diner. Now he stood here, Ivy Cole's book in hand
and librarian Prudy Township moony-eyeing him through,
bless her sweet aging heart, Coke bottles so thick he wondered if she was blind without them. It was an unsettling
thought, considering he'd seen her on the road more than
once with nary a spectacle about her.

"No, ma'am. I borrowed it from a friend. She is a rare book
collector and I thought she'd lent this one to the library before,
for exhibits and the like. I must have misunderstood her."

"Honey, it's Doe Springs—we don't do much exhibiting
of anything in these parts. If you came in and checked out a

book from time to time, you'd know the ropes around here, not to mention it'd give an old gal something to do twixt and between shelving these dusty old volumes by herself." Flap, flap, flap went the lashes. Melvin could all but hear them, beating against the glass like tiny bat wings on tiny bats vying for escape.

"Yes, ma'am, I do need to do that."

"Oh, but you'd about have to stand in line these days, Deputy. We've had a run on books here lately. Folks can't get enough reading in between lunch breaks and water cooler gossip. Werewolf stories, vampire stories, monsters of all descriptions—my entire Halloween section is wiped out. Everything from abominable snowmen to the Loch Ness monster has grabbed attention from one yahoo or another. We're hard-pressed to conjure up a Casper read-aloud for the kiddies anymore."

She acted exasperated, but Melvin could tell she was putting on. Prudy Township hadn't had this much activity in her library since she joined the staff thirty years ago. She was busy at last and eating it up.

"I've learned a few things myself," she continued. "This information might help you out too, Deputy, so pay attention." Prudy pulled a thin hardbound from underneath the counter. "Dug this out of the sociology section. Nobody thought to look over there." She adjusted her glasses and read to Melvin: " 'To ward off wolves from your village, it has been found effective to bury a wolf's tail at its entrance.' And 'To protect livestock from attack, bury wolf dung in the farmyard to keep the predators at bay.' Seems like wolves don't like their own posteriors so much. I tell you the truth, Angus Shepherd, Talbot, and the rest of them farmers should've been readers. A whole bunch of mess could have been avoided." Prudy turned several pages. "Now, if we're dealing with a bona fide werewolf, page fifty-seven says mountain ash, rye, and mistletoe will protect against one of those."

Melvin picked up Prudy's book, thus ending his education. "Mrs. Township, this title says *Legends and Remedies of the 18th Century.*"

Prudy shrugged. "Don't make no difference. Verna is drawing up a poster with a lot of these tips on it to hang on the door."

Melvin sighed. "Mrs. Township, I wish you and Verna wouldn't do that."

"Too late. That girl's got a mind of her own. I can't do nothing with her. That's the last time I take on an intern from the high school."

"Verna graduated fifteen years ago."

"See there? I've held true to my word. I'll tell her you don't want the poster, but I don't see why not. If guns and dogs don't cow this thing, what harm's hanging up a little mistletoe going to do? Don't know where a body can find a wolf's tail, though, but that's their problem."

The train had run way off its track. Melvin tried to steer it back around before the whole conversation was lost. "Anyway, Mrs. Township, I need your help. Do you know of anybody who can translate the text in my book? I think it's all German."

Prudy thumbed through *Lykanthrop* and zeroed in on one of its paragraphs. "Yes, it is. I recognize a word here and there, but my college German is rusty. The pictures are drawn right nice. You studying up on werewolves too, Deputy Sanders? I might can rustle up some stuff out of archives in English and you wouldn't have to bother with translation." She stroked the book's worn spine. "Someone put a lot of time into making this book, even down to the cover. Texture is unusual, a leather of some sort. And the pages are hand-bound, but a book this old would have to be."

"How old do you think it is?"

"Couldn't say with any accuracy. But I think I know the gent who can. I've got his business card around here someplace. He's a retired professor-turned-book dealer, and if I'm not mistaken, he speaks many languages, German among 'em." She pulled a shoebox from behind the reference desk. "Our high-tech filing system. Excuse me a minute." Prudy flicked cards onto the library counter like dealing a hand in Vegas. She stopped at number nine. "Here it is." Prudy held up an elegantly scripted card, which read "Alfred Toomey, Rare and Used Books of Asheville."

"Thanks a bunch, Mrs. Township." Melvin reached for the card. Prudy pulled it back before he could take it.

"Now don't be a stranger around here, Deputy Sanders. The library is a fine place for learning and socializing both." Flap, flap, flap.

"Yes, ma'am." Melvin snatched the card and nodded good afternoon to Mrs. Township. On the way to the parking lot, he stuffed Toomey's number in his pocket and pulled out his notebook in the same motion. Across the narrowly lined paper he jotted "Call Alfred Toomey ASAP." Standing by the patrol car, he pulled the notebook out again. He added: "And Miss Cole."

Chapter 18

"Miss Cole? Miss Cole!"

Ivy jumped awake and grabbed at the annoying thing pecking her shoulder. Mildred Parson, startled as well, jerked her acrylic-tipped finger away.

"Excuse me, Miss Cole, but you fell asleep. If I leave you under that dryer any longer, your hair's going to fry and there will be no fixing it."

"I'm sorry. I didn't mean to grab you like that. You scared me." Ivy wondered at the beautician's own frizzy bleached bob, perhaps the casualty of this very thing.

"My fault entirely." Mildred's lips attempted the long un- familiar haul upward into a pleasant expression, but they didn't quite make it, lodging themselves instead under her nose in the scrunched curl of a snit. Which, judging by the grooves radiating from her mouth, was an entirely familiar expression. Mildred lifted the dryer's glass bowl so Ivy could rise and follow the woman to her station. It was a pleasant day to be in the town's only salon, the Clip and Snip, getting a brand-new summertime 'do.

Ivy settled into a cool vinyl chair, and Mildred pumped the seat up six inches with short bursts from her sandaled foot. "Some real pretty hair you've got. Natural color?" she asked, removing the damp towel from around Ivy's neck and replacing it with a drape that covered her lap as well.

"Yes. This is my first time in a salon, believe it or not."

"You don't say. I was coloring and perming my hair when I was sixteen. Most women can't leave it alone till they've about done themselves bald. I've come close a time or two."

Ivy didn't find that encouraging. She was glad she'd signed on for a styling and nothing more. "My hair's easy, that's why I've kept it this way."

"Uh-huh. An upsweep will look good on you. Must be a special occasion, to get you in a beauty shop and all curly to boot." Mildred went to work freeing her client's hair from its pink captors. She gave the curlers a tug before releasing the ringlets completely. *Pluck!* A roller dropped in a chrome pan. *Pluck!* Another roller in the pan, a few strands of blond hair still wrapped around it. Ivy winced at each little sting to her scalp.

"As a matter of fact, it is a special occasion," Ivy said. "I've met a wonderful man, and today he's promised to take me somewhere romantic for my birthday. I'm meeting him at the motel in an hour and we're spending the whole afternoon together." There. The scene was set. It was not Ivy's birthday, but the meeting was arranged sure enough, although the rendezvous at the hotel certainly would not be what Frank Parson was expecting. Thus far Ivy had not let him touch more than her hand—and at times she felt even that challenged her integrity—but, as of today, leading him on and fending him off at the same time would, mercifully, come to an end.

"I see. Good for you!" Mildred continued plopping rollers into the pan, but the rhythm had slowed. There was gossip afoot involving the new girl, a motel, and a man, and

Mildred would not miss a word of it. Evanda, working on a ten-year-old's bowl haircut in the adjoining station, was leaning their direction and Mildred shot her a look. The exchange was not lost on Ivy, who dreaded the humiliation she was about to heap on the unsuspecting woman in front of her coworker. Hadn't Mildred been through enough with this horrible marriage? Seeing the frazzled woman at Doc Hill's and then talking to her in person made the misery in her life all too palpable. It wore in the lines under her thickly applied makeup, the flashy cut of her clothes, the fake nails with polish chipping from the ends. The air about Mildred Parson was a farce of *I'm put together and doing just fine, see?* but the real picture of the woman told a different story. Maybe Ivy should wait, pick a different time, figure out a better way. . . .

Snatch! Blond hair trailed away from Ivy's scalp and floated into the pan on the last roller.

"Ouch! That really hurts." Ivy would reach up and rub her sore head, but fighting through the big drape that reached down to her knees was too much trouble. She felt a bit like the child seated a few feet away: small, trapped, and at the mercy of a distracted woman with scissors.

No. No scissors. If Mildred produced any of those, Ivy was out of here to take care of business the old-fashioned way. She'd rather take her chances outwitting the police on another missing person than living through a bad haircut.

"Relax, dear. If I can survive a highlighting through a rubber cap, you can survive this. Now, finish telling me about your man." Mildred began brushing out the curls with a slightly gentler hand, no scissors in sight.

Ivy relaxed and considered what to tell Mrs. Frank Parson. She could fib again, create a romance out of thin air that would send both Mildred's and Evanda's heads spinning and their tongues wagging for days. Life would go on as usual for Mildred for the time being, but so it would for her husband as well. A redheaded kid's crestfallen face and a kitty with scars on her belly replaced Ivy's reflection in the beauty shop mirror. Frank Parson was scum, and Mildred Parson was hurting her head again.

"Okay. Let's see, he's handsome, in an offbeat way that I like, and very smart. He's got a good-paying job—he's high up there on the food chain, a manager. And he acts crazy for me when we're together. It would be such a perfect thing, except . . . "

Mildred licked her red lips, a Pavlovian response to the promise of delicious revelation. But the sentence sailed off, incomplete, through the blue yonder, leaving tendrils of smoky possibility behind it in that one glorious word.

"Except? Come on now, you can tell me. I've heard them all standing over this chair. Nothing can surprise me anymore."

How could Ivy deny her? "Oh, all right. Everything is great, but he's so secretive about us. He'll only see me certain times of the week, insists we go out of town for dinner because he says the restaurants are better, won't introduce me to his friends, things like that."

The brush ceased its task through Ivy's locks to wave in her face instead, Mildred looking sternly wise on the other end of it. "Have you ever asked him why?"

"Sure I have, and he has a bushel of excuses. But they're lame, even I realize that. You don't think he's ashamed of me, do you?"

Mildred twirled the brush around, then pointed it again. "I seriously doubt that. You're looking at the situation through love-blind eyes, deary. It's obvious what your Romeo is up to."

"It is?"

Mildred let her own suspenseful moment play out. She pulled Ivy's hair atop her head and secured it in a ponytail. Then she began pinning pieces in a lovely halo of curls about Ivy's head. Finally, she answered: "I hate to tell you this, but there is only one explanation for this type of mysterious behavior. Your fellow is stepping out on somebody, and you're the other woman."

"No!" Ivy's crushed expression in the mirror looked ridiculous, even to her. This was so beneath what she could do, what she was about. Slinking around with a married man, now playing the dumb put-upon blonde with a broken heart. Ivy would have preferred to simplify the whole matter by giving the wife and child Frank's head on a platter, but with Deputy Sanders on her very doorstep and a rogue wolf invading her territory, this was the best she had time to offer right now—truth without revenge (or a nice life insurance settlement, which tended to go a long way in relieving a long-suffering spouse's grief). The third act was under way, and it was time to finish it. The climax. A person like Mildred Parson could appreciate Ivy's efforts at theater. The woman obviously lived for the dramatic.

"He wouldn't do that," Ivy protested in her whiniest little girl voice. "He's a banker—they have to be honest. Besides, he told me flat out he's single, has never been married, ever."

"Did you say a banker?" Mildred pulled the bobby pins from their holding place between her teeth. She needed a clear mouth and a clear head for this conversation. It was getting way too good. "How about that? My husband is a banker too. I bet I know your boyfriend. Oh Lord, it's not Ed Ripple is it? It is, isn't it? I thought that little weasel was up to something. His wife's in my sewing circle. Lord, Lord, that woman will lose her mind when she finds out. I dread having to tell her. Ivy, I don't mean to fuss at you here, but everybody in town knows Ed's married with a passel of young'uns—he has a 'My kid's an honor student at so-and-so' bumper sticker right there on his car. And you meet at the motel? Um-mm-mm." Mildred and Evanda shook their heads sadly in unison. The ten-year-old in Evanda's chair had fallen asleep, only half a bowl crowning his head.

"I've seen Ed. Believe me, I'd never go out with him," Ivy clarified. "I said my boyfriend is the manager, not the assistant manager."

Evanda's high-plucked brows managed to arch a millimeter more. She stared at her friend, wide-eyed, and waited for the storm.

Ivy marched down Bloom Street, picking bobby pins out of her half-finished hair and muttering to herself. Curls stood up in wild strands where Mildred had clawed at Ivy's head before she could scramble out of the chair and through the door, that crazy woman screaming at her back the whole way. *Stupid, stupid, stupid, what I did. I will never go into a beauty shop ever again.* Bobby pins pinged on the sidewalk and into its grassy cracks as Ivy threw them down. Mildred had been clutching a fistful of gold hair and diving for the scissors when Ivy ran for her life. Frank Parson would be in for a big surprise when Mrs. Parson blew through the motel door with gale force this afternoon. That was probably better justice for ole Frank than anything Ivy could do to him, although she wasn't so sure that now, after meeting his wife, the two didn't deserve each other. But for Jeffrey's sake, and that of any other pets they might acquire someday, Ivy hoped Mildred would beat the sense out of her philandering cat-abusing kid-yelling husband, then pack up Jeffrey and get out.

A car slowed behind Ivy and her blood boiled. She whipped around. "I'm warning you, Mildred Parson!"

Deputy Sanders parked beside the street and got out to stand beside his vehicle. He had seen Ivy a few blocks back, stomping along and flinging things to the ground. It was a littering offense, but now, by the look of her, he thought he could let it go.

"Are you all right, Miss Cole?"

"I'm fine. Don't I look fine?" Ivy's hair stood pinned at odd angles while random loose pieces lay jagged down her back. Tied around her neck and dangling to just above her knees was a long plastic sheet of some sort. The deputy stared over the top of his car hood, not sure of what to say. Once again.

"Never mind." Ivy turned around and continued walking, muttering, and flinging. She heard the car rolling slowly behind her. Exasperated, she turned around again. "Haven't we done this before? If I didn't know you were a deputy, I'd swear you were stalking me."

Melvin pulled himself together. "No, ma'am. You just don't look . . . like yourself. I thought something was wrong. Are you sure you're okay?"

Ivy started to snap at the deputy again, then stopped. She looked down at the sorry shape of her beauty shop wardrobe, felt the mangled remains of a good hairdo gone bad, observed the tiny metal pins strewn in a zigzagging trail behind her. Laughter bubbled up and spilled over so hard tears came to her eyes. She untied the plastic drape and shook out the rest of her hair. Wiping her eyes, she smiled at Sanders with genuine pleasure. "Yeah, I'm sure I'm okay. Now. Thanks for breaking the moment."

"Glad I could help. Just doing—"

"Your job, ma'am. I know." Ivy rolled up the drape and tucked it under her arm. She felt tons better all of a sudden, the tension spent on the tail end of her laughter.

"Well, all right then." Melvin paused as if to say something else, but the words that did finally make their way out were not what Ivy expected. "Have a nice day." The deputy stepped back into his patrol car.

"Deputy Sanders, wait." Ivy came around to the officer's window before he could drive off. "About last night, I think I was rude to you. I'm sorry."

The crease between Sanders's eyebrows widened slightly, a sign Ivy thought could mean relief; at the very least he was staying put to hear her out. She'd made a mess of last night, inviting the deputy over and then running him off in the next breath. Where was the hospitality in that? Ivy'd been raised better. She hadn't even offered him a drink, for Pete's sake. And what did she expect anyway? Sanders was an officer of the law, sworn and bound to protect all citizens, even the rotten ones who deserved every last bad thing they got. Just doing his job, ma'am. She'd try hard to remember that next time. No, no next time. Guilt alleviated, she should be getting on home. She'd apologize one more time, then figure out where she was. The hissy fit had clouded her brain and landed her on an unfamiliar street. *Where did I park that van?*

"I'm the one who should say they're sorry, for offending you," Melvin said, catching Ivy off guard. "Anyway, I haven't been on a date in a real long time—chalk it up to inexperience if it will help my cause any."

Ivy didn't expect an apology but appreciated it just the same. They'd made up, were friends again. "So it was a date? I thought you were on official business."

"I guess that's how it ended up. We never got around to the date part. I'd like to try that side of it sometime, if you're willing to give a good old country boy another shot."

You shouldn't, Ivy. You know you shouldn't. "I believe in second chances, Deputy."

Melvin couldn't hide pleased well, not even with the dark shades and firm set of his mouth. Ivy saw his whole demeanor lighten as if the sun had come out and shined on an otherwise gloomy day. Her day was looking a whole lot better too, even though against her better judgment, against her own will, she'd invited the enemy into her house again. *We're just friends. What's the harm in that?* Plenty, perhaps. Ivy would beat herself up for it later, but later was down the road and this was the here and now. And the here and now was looking pert near perfect, catfight in the Clip and Snip aside. She admitted the cold hard truth to herself: Some things really were out of her capacity, and letting this man be was one of them.

Ivy spied *Lykanthrop* in the passenger seat. It was a good time to change the subject, before things wandered into touchy-feely territory. "How's the reading coming? Are you socially and artistically enlightened yet?"

"Not yet. Right now I'm just carrying the book around to impress the ladies. They like brainiacs who read all day and speak like foreigners. Or so I've been told. Are you impressed?"

"Very. Tell me what you've learned."

"Not a danged thing. Actually, I just like looking at the happy pictures."

"There are plenty of those. You should be feeling suicidal by now."

"Yes, and the sleepless nights are a plus too."

They smiled at each other, punctuation on the end of a conversation that had just run itself out.

"Well, I guess I should get on home. It was nice talking to you, Deputy Sanders. Drop the book by whenever you're finished with it."

"I'll do that. Miss Cole, before you take off, I wanted to ask you about one of your former clients, the one who owns a Bonsai."

"I don't recall training any Bonsais, Deputy."

Melvin's brows closed back together, reunited in thought. "How about a Russian wolfhound, do you remember working with one of those a while back?"

"The borzoi. Yes, I do. The man came to just one class with his dog. It had a mean streak. They were only in the session for thirty minutes, and the dog bit me. They left right afterwards. I think the poor man was too embarrassed—or afraid of a lawsuit—to stick around and let me work on fixing the behavior."

"Ruthy didn't mention all that."

"You talked with Ruthy? Sweet lady, and Chippy is a very good student. I kept the bite private from them and everyone else. I didn't want to upset my class, but that dog had some real issues. Were you checking up on my sessions for some reason?"

"Talk in passing, ma'am. Ruthy's proud of that pug—she fills anybody's ear who will listen about the dog's training and all the goings-on at the community center."

"That would be Ruthy, all right."

"Can I get the name of the dog's owner anyway? I want to bend his ear a little about the breed. A wolfhound might come in handy with what we're up against."

"Wow, I cannot remember his name off the top of my head. I'd have to go back through my registration forms from months ago. But it wouldn't matter anyway. He wasn't a permanent resident of this area, and I heard that before he went back to Vermont they had to put the dog down."

"How come?"

"One of my other clients was telling this story. Let me think a minute." Ivy stared at patches of sky through the maple over her head. She pursed her lips thoughtfully and counted leaves until a convincing amount of time had passed. "Oh, now I remember. He came home all tore up one evening. They thought he'd either been in one heck of a dog fight or drug under a car for a good stretch." *And Auf didn't look too good either. Durn his overprotective ways . . .*

"That's too bad," Melvin said.

Ivy nodded. It was. She'd grounded Auf in the house for

a week after that, then been covered up in guilt for punishing him. He was only doing his job too. Deputy Sanders could appreciate that maybe, but she'd never be able to tell him.

"Look, I've got to skedaddle. There's a houseful of hounds back at my place just waiting for their Alpo to come through the door. You know how it can be around feeding time."

"Yeah. We had blueticks growing up, and they'd knock you down for a bone. Can I ask you one more thing?"

"Sure, what is it?"

"When I pulled up, you thought I was Mildred Parson. Are you good friends?"

Ivy swallowed her distaste at the thought. "No, not really."

"Oh, all right then. No matter. It was good to see you again, Miss Cole."

"Wait, don't drive off yet. Why do you ask?"

Melvin seemed to be studying up on the answer. Finally he said, "We just arrested Mildred's husband, Frank, on a Class I felony. Deputy Meeks is on his way to the station with him right now. I reckoned if you were friends with the Parsons, you might want to know about it."

"Sounds serious. What is that?"

"Cruelty to animals. He could get two years or better if convicted, and Doc Hill is champing at the bit to testify against him. That's probably all I should say about it."

Ivy's heart warmed so fast she felt her cheeks flush. She wanted to reach into the patrol car and hug the deputy until his own face turned bright red. Instead, she clamped an iron fist around the joy she felt and said very simply, "How about that? It's always the ones you'd least expect."

"Yes, that always seems to be the case. And now, I better let you get to those dogs."

Ivy had forgotten they were in the midst of a long good-bye. Suddenly, she hated to see it end. "Drop that book by before long, Deputy Sanders, and maybe I'll scrounge us up something to eat for real this time."

"Actually, I believe I owe you a dinner in town. Soon."

"Yes, soon. Good-bye, Deputy." Ivy gave a quick wave as the patrol car pulled away, then she walked on down the street. She had no idea if it was the right direction—it didn't matter. She'd wander around and come upon her van eventually. Right now, though, she was content to stroll along, soaking in the sun, basking in the happiness that Frank Parson was behind bars, and imagining a day sometime not far off when a deputy and a werewolf would share a romantic dinner together.

Chapter 19

Ivy threw off her shoes the minute she walked through the front door. Home. It was good to be home. The day had had too many unexpected twists, and she relished wrapping this cozy blanket of cottage around her. She looked down and noticed her yellow shirt was smudged at the shoulder, no doubt from the assault by that nut a few hours ago. But a shiny new Maytag sitting in her laundry room would take care of that.

Something nudged her knee. Rex was there, impatient he had not been noticed yet. Ivy scooped up the little dog and planted a kiss on his nose.

"That one's for you." She kissed him again. "And that one is for our good fortune."

She was happy. Despite the confrontation with Mildred, the day had taken a turn for the better when Deputy Sanders rolled by in his patrol car. Always there, looking out for her, it seemed. And now she would see him again, to spite herself. She didn't care. Butterflies hadn't danced in her stomach like this since a few crushes in grade school, and the long-lost emotion made her giddy. Thirty-one years old and giddy. Ivy smiled, then planted another kiss on the terrier and set him down. Time to check on the rest of the family and think about opening some cans.

The backyard was lazy. Dogs snoozed at the bottom of the steps and under the overhanging shade tree in the far corner. A tail flipped up here and there, then thumped back into the grass, lifeless.

"I don't believe it." Across the yard, Hansel and Gretel were curled together, the odd retriever-dachshund combination finally coming together in a truce. It was a day for strange partnerships, apparently, and Ivy took it as a sign. The butterflies leaped again.

Ivy scanned the yard for Auf. There he was, away from the other dogs, already on his feet and watching her. When their eyes met, he came to her and Ivy hugged his thick neck. She noticed flecks of gray were forming a circle where a collar might go, and his age quelled the butterfly jubilee. Neither of them was a pup any longer. Auf would be with her for a long time still, his kind were amazingly long-lived, but he was not the warrior of his youth. She felt their roles reversing somewhat: her as the protector and he the charge.

"You'll always be my favorite, Auf," Ivy whispered in his ear.

But the big dog pulled away from her and walked to the fence line. He stared into the woods. Ivy walked to his side.

"I know, Auf. You don't have to tell me. He's out there somewhere, but I'll find him first."

Aufhocker whined and licked Ivy's hand. The woods behind the house looked different now; they were strange, ominous. Carefree romps under moonlight would be made with caution from now on. She would not be ambushed in her own backyard. But he would come looking for her. Just as she, him. It was a cat and mouse game with no mouse, only predators.

"Don't worry. It's going to be okay. They're not all mindless killers. Not all of them. Not all of . . . us." Ivy patted the dog's head and left him, still staring at trees and patiently waiting. The calendar would turn over soon, and her angel would be ready to defend her.

Ivy went back inside. The kitchen, and the dog food, were to the left, but she found herself heading up the stairwell. Everybody was napping anyway; their meal could wait. For now, her bedroom called, the moment with Auf stirring memories that were never far from her, no matter that the event happened more than twenty years ago. The butterflies were dead now, a cold stone taking their place in her stomach.

Ivy's bedroom filled the small upstairs. It had been attic space before she moved in, with plenty of old boxes and mouse droppings to clear out before making the room her own. Now the plank walls were whitewashed and the white iron bed covered by a dusty-rose patch quilt. Wildflowers in plump mason jars decorated the windowsill overlooking the dog lot and forest beyond. On an antique mirrored dresser she salvaged from a yard sale, Ivy'd placed a picture of herself and her mother, taken when they were still living in the mountains of North Carolina. Her father's image was blurred in the background, and she preferred to think of him that way: out of focus, unknown, her father but not a present father at all.

Ivy dropped to her knees in front of the bed and pulled at the braided rug. She wrestled the floorboard out of place and Clifford Hughes's wedding band gleamed from the dark hole. It had been a major mistake, taking that ring and the rest of it, and for what? She had no answer for the compulsive act. She would never be able to return these things to Patricia. Was she thinking the girl would actually want mementos from her husband's demise one day? Whatever smug satisfaction she'd felt stashing these things away had left already, leaving a staggering price to pay in its wake. Now the police were alerted to human involvement and the evidence was right here in this house, her sanctuary. Polluted. And there was nobody to blame but herself. Moon mania. It was the only explanation. She'd get rid of it all soon, or at least find a more original hidey-hole than a loose board in the floor. Under rugs and behind hanging pictures were the first places anybody looked if they had a mind to find something; any B-grade movie could tell a person that.

But that was a worry for another time. Ivy reached past the jewelry and found her journal. It was a comfort in her hand, with its worn cover and the faded crayon pictures

she'd adorned it with as a child. Ivy sat back against the bed
and closed her eyes for a moment. Then she opened the little
notebook, many of the words there were in German. She
turned to the first entry, an account of the last night she ever
had of a childhood and the moment that changed everything.
As Ivy read, she relived the moment all over again, just as
she did every night in her sleep. . . .

*Christmas Eve is quiet now, and it is cold in this closet. I
write in the dark. Boxes, I've pushed against the door. But
they are small boxes. I am hiding in the coats. All the noise—
all the crashing and screaming—has stopped. The only
howling now is the wind. I am afraid to go out, but I am
afraid to stay in. Where are you, Mama! Where are you!*

The pencil scribbled sightless across the page, breaking
lines and slanting into marginal corners. But the little girl
wrote on, finding strength in the words, some control in her
emotions as the fear played itself in lead across the white-
lined page. The journal was a gift from her mother, tucked in
the pocket of her dress when the window exploded inward
and she tumbled out of her chair and in front of the couch.
Whatever came through had not waited to visit the child. It
had gone straight to the kitchen before Ivy even saw what it
was. She scrambled from the floor as screams chased her
into the cramped confines she hoped would hide her. Shoe-
boxes and suitcases piled against the closet door, a pitiful
blockade.

Ivy stopped writing and strained to hear. Nothing but
December wind lapping at the remnants of their holiday
eve. The wait was maddening. *Mama. Mama.* She begged to
hear a voice from the other side telling her to come out,
everything was all right now. How much time had passed?
No chimes from the clock answered her, just the silence of
the wait.

Ivy could stand it no longer. She closed the journal and put
it back in the pocket of her dress. She unstacked the boxes
one by one, then slid the suitcases aside. With a deep breath,
the girl cracked the closet door. The wind snatched the wood

and swung it wide. Little Ivy stood there, in the frame, and stared. Shards of glass from the broken window glittered from the floor in the light of the fireplace's dying embers. Mama's beautiful mantel clock lay still and broken at the base of the fireplace, both hands stuck firmly at twelve. Scattered packages littered the room and ashes whirled about like snow. The fir she and her mother had decorated together leaned cockeyed against the wall behind the couch, ornaments shattered in a mosaic around its trunk.

"Mama?" Ivy's voice hitched in her throat and stuck. The word came out no louder than the curtains fluttering around the ruined window. She walked to the kitchen door and pressed her ear against it. A slick noise came from the other side, like the moist slapping of meat, followed by a soft gurgling. Ivy opened her mouth to call for her mother again, then stopped. She knew suddenly, in the sensitive mind of a young child, that she should not call, should not even breathe, for the sound coming from the kitchen was not natural. She heard no sound from her mother at all.

She could run. Run all the way to Oma and Opa's house, or drag the phone into the closet and call Uncle Stefan to come with his big dogs and the gun. But she couldn't move. She couldn't turn and flee nor hide. She had to know.

Ivy placed her palm flat against the door and pushed softly. It swung an inch, then an inch more. One bright green eye surveyed the interior of the tiny kitchen.

It was there, in the middle of the linoleum floor. An immense bristled back was to the child. Its coat was silver gray, like the full moon itself shining into the room, its light spilling over the sink and shimmering off the hairs of the thing. It hunkered over what could only be Catherine Cole. Ivy could see the familiar slippers protruding from beneath the animal, their fuzzy pink fabric now streaked with red. The creature lapped and tore, its jaws snapping together with each bite. The woman's feet jerked with each rip, then fell still.

Ivy clapped a hand over her mouth and backed away, letting the door close in front of her. But it could not close out what she had just seen, and she wished now she *had* run from this place, had gotten Uncle Stefan's gun herself and come back to finish what this intruder had begun. Rage battled the fear, but it was determination to survive that won and continued moving the child across the room, her wide eyes never leaving the kitchen door. Tears streamed down colorless cheeks, but the scream in her throat lodged there raw. It could come later, again and again and again, but not now. Not now. Her legs moved quicker backward, black patent leather shoes seeking each unseen step carefully, quietly. But not good enough. Her heel struck a mangled package, casting her off balance. She tripped backward, arms pinwheeling to catch the fall and ornaments crunching under her soles. She caught the edge of the couch before hitting the floor and hung there nearly horizontal, straining to stay on her feet and not land squarely in the remains of the Christmas tree.

No sound from the kitchen. Nothing at all. The lapping had stopped. The living room moved in and out of shadow as snow clouds fogged up the moon outside the window. The last of the fire petered out and moonlight staggered across the furniture. Light, then dark. Light, then dark.

Ivy listened, struggling to hear and pull herself upright at the same time. She froze. A sound at last, or her imagination taking over? Ivy's breath drew shallower, and over the thudding of her heart, she was sure of the new noise: the click-click of claws moving stealthily across linoleum.

Ivy righted herself and began backing toward the front door again, caution for her own stealth abandoning her as panic fought to set in. Her spine finally touched the heavy glass doorknob and she started to turn, but a movement across the room stopped her. The kitchen door was slowly opening. Long claws appeared around the door's edge and rested there. A droplet of liquid ran in a jagged black streak to the floor. Ivy did not need light to know the true color of that liquid nor the quality of the heart that had poured it. Her own heart seemed to stop when the door swung all the way open. And there it was, standing impossibly upright and filling the doorway with seven feet of muscle, claws, teeth, and fur.

Ivy could not move, and neither did the beast. They stood across the room, staring at one another. The wolf breathed deeply, taking the child in. It exhaled in a gentle sigh. Orange eyes burned over the long muzzle, and Ivy suddenly felt lost in the light. Her lids were weighted by it, hooding her own eyes to slits. The wolf's breathing sounded rhythmic now, like the rise and fall of ocean tides against a sandy shore, and Ivy swayed. Dreamily, she wondered if this was how the elk or the caribou felt before the jaws clamped around its throat. Surreal calm. At peace. And she didn't care.

The doorknob left the small of Ivy's back. She had some vague idea that her feet were shuffling forward. The wolf stood there, its orange eyes blazing, its fangs dripping the warm red blood of her mother. Waiting for her. Welcoming her.

Ivy walked to the wolf and looked up into the horror that now peered down at her with a face of cruel majestic beauty.

"Fairy tales have been written about you," Ivy whispered. "But I never believed they were true."

The little girl reached up a tiny pale hand and rubbed the fur of the animal's chest. It was coarse and soft at the same time. She ran her hand down the length of the animal's arm, to the elongated hand-claws hanging relaxed by its side. Her fingers curled around the claws one by one, feeling them from fingerlike pad to talon-edged tip.

The wolf hunkered lower, until Ivy could feel its breath on her forehead, could taste its acrid odor on her tongue. She looked up into the fiery eyes, the long snout aging even grayer at the muzzle. It struck her darkly funny that even a creature such as this could succumb to time. Ivy marveled as she saw her hand reach up again and stroke the face just above her. She smiled . . .

. . . and the wolf's lips drew back as well. A ruby droplet fell to splash Ivy's cheek. She blinked twice, three times. She wiped the blood with her hand, smearing it across her porcelain skin. The horror of her mother in the kitchen rushed back to her. Her reddened fingertips shook in front of her face. *"No!"* she screamed.

Ivy turned to run, but a hot razor across her back knocked her to the floor. She tried to crawl away, her elbows digging into the hard floor and the pieces of glass sprinkled over it, but the wolf pounced and straddled her slight form on all fours.

"Please, please . . . *Mommy!*" Ivy cried. She covered her face with her blood-streaked hands.

The wolf pushed its nose into her hair, then the tender flesh of her neck. It moved down her body, to her soft inner thigh. Then it bit.

Ivy and Rex sat huddled together in the corner by Ivy's bed. The journal lay closed at Ivy's feet. She stroked the deep scar high on her left thigh; another zigzagged across the middle of her back. When she'd awoken that fateful night, she was in an ambulance on the way to Cologne. Her father flew in from his business trip in London as soon as he heard the news. William Cole bundled up his daughter and a few belongings—the mantel clock among them—and took them back to New York, the office seat of his computer business, as soon as she was able to fly. He closed his office in Germany immediately afterward and swore he would never travel there again. They never did.

"We never did, Rex," Ivy said, her fingertips trailing over her leg, the raised flesh a Braille reminder of her nightmare. "Not even to see Mama's grave. But I tell you this, little guy, that wolf lived to regret sparing me."

Ivy picked up the journal and placed it back under the rug. The reading had provided the catharsis she was looking for, and the good feelings were returning. She was thankful to have the journal to share with. The therapy of writing had saved her many a time. One day she should burn the journal, she knew. But just like *Lykanthrop,* if discovered, who would believe it anyway?

Chapter 20

Deputy Sanders drove like a maniac. He was at least seven miles over the speed limit, heading south toward Asheville. He'd called Alfred Toomey right after lunch (and right after Miss Cole sauntered away from him down Bloom Street, the promise of a date pumping even more adrenaline into his lead foot). Now he was delivering the book to the retired professor; hopefully he'd be back in Doe Springs before the sheriff and Tee returned from their field trip.

Forty minutes later, Melvin pulled down a shady lane on the northern outskirts of the city. Toomey's house was a restored Victorian, the kind of place where you would expect to see piles of ancient volumes molding in every corner. It crowded in between similar homes, all guarded by giant oaks lining the street.

Melvin rang the doorbell, and Mrs. Toomey, a waddling round woman with a cheerful smile, welcomed him in.

"Alfred is in the study, Deputy Sanders. Can I get you a spot of tea? It's teatime for our guests in the parlor, but you're welcome to some. We're having scones as well."

Melvin wasn't used to such formality. He reached to remove his hat, then remembered he'd left it in the car. He glanced at his feet to make sure he'd not tracked anything inside. "No thank you, ma'am. Your husband didn't tell me you owned a bed-and-breakfast. This is a beautiful house, inside and out." Melvin was disappointed at the sunny interior. He had been picturing something more mysterious, more Sherlock Holmes. The vases of potpourri and pink-papered hallways were not what he'd had in mind.

"I've got plenty to go around if you decide you're hungry after all. I know our visitors would enjoy a policeman's company. It's fascinating, what you do for a living. But if you must go, the study's that way." Mrs. Toomey pointed down the hall, then bustled off to tend to her guests.

The study was open and a waddling round man the spitting image of Mrs. Toomey was already on his feet and coming at Melvin with a cup and plate.

"Deputy Sanders! Come in, have a seat, have some tea, have a scone." Melvin tucked *Lykanthrop* under his arm as Alfred Toomey pushed the plate and teacup into his hands.

"Oh, thank you." Melvin took them and sat on the brown leather couch. A heavy oriental rug covered the marred hardwood floor under his feet, and Toomey's mahogany desk was overrun with books and papers. A faint smell of cigar smoke wafted about the room and bookshelves overflowed from dark paneled walls. Now this was more like it.

"Pardon the mess," Toomey said. He settled in behind his desk. "My shop is in town, but I keep quite an inventory here as well." Toomey shoved a pile of books and papers aside so he and the deputy could converse with an unobstructed view.

"It's more like what I expected, actually."

Professor Toomey rolled his eyes. "Dismal out there, isn't it? It's like falling into a vat of melted ice cream every time I leave this room. It's my last holdout, this study. Alice won't even come in here, and don't think that's an accident on my part. But enough about my personal woes—is that the book?"

"Yes, it is." Melvin set his scone and tea on top of a pile of magazines and set *Lykanthrop* in front of Toomey. The professor slid a pair of wire-rimmed glasses onto his nose and picked up the hefty book. The parchment pages crackled like fire as he leafed through them.

After a few minutes he spoke: "It's German, yes, but an Old World dialect I may have to research. There is no author listed, nor printing house—but then, it's all obviously handwritten anyway. Indeed you are right, Deputy, this book is one of a kind. What you've acquired appears to be a diary or letters, as best I can tell. The entries are first person but by the differing degrees in handwriting, many authors have contributed to it. This is interesting." Toomey had flipped through to the end of the book.

"What is it?"

"The first three quarters of the book are obviously dipped ink."

"Like with a quill from a long time ago."

"Yes. But see here? These later entries are none other than ballpoint. The book is ongoing. The blank pages here in the very back are apparently for more entries. I'm guessing the earliest part of the book could be as old as the seventeenth century, but the later writings are modern. If that's true and the text is not just personal drivel, this book could be historically significant for the time frame it spans." Toomey got more excited as he leafed front to back, middle to front, back to middle—the pages flew as he quickly scanned words, then moved on to other passages.

"If you can tell me the gist of what it says, I'll be on my way."

Abruptly, Toomey slammed the book closed. "Deputy, as a collector of rare books, I am very intrigued by what you have brought me. Even the leather cover is unusual. I have a friend at the university who may be able to help me with the elements of the material and the age of the leather and paper in general. I would like to keep this for a few weeks, if you don't mind."

"I was hoping you could just read it real quick and give it back to me today."

Toomey laughed. "I'm afraid not. It's going to take some time to do this translation."

Melvin debated. His date was dependent on returning this book, and Ivy hadn't been kidding: This thing was more valuable than he'd realized. He wasn't even sure why he cared what it said. What he needed to find out could be discovered easily enough by doing research at the library. Prudy would be more than happy to help him find whatever he was looking for. Friday evening was free—he could return *Lykanthrop* safe and sound, then drive the two of them back to town. Etta's put out a decent all-you-can-eat salad bar on the weekends.

"I don't have weeks to spare, Mr. Toomey. I've borrowed this book from a friend who would not be pleased that it's moved out of my hands. Thank you, but I think I've wasted your time."

Melvin reached for the book but Toomey placed a hand over top of it. "Wait, Deputy Sanders. Give me one week. I think I can do it in that amount of time. Business is slow at my shop and in the B&B—what else do I have to do? You said you borrowed the book from a friend. This friend, I take it, cannot do the translation either. Wouldn't it be a nice surprise to be able to tell him what's actually in his book? I guarantee you, whatever I discover will most likely increase the value of your friend's collection."

Melvin scratched his head. Would Ivy appreciate the gift? Think him thoughtful? It would certainly give them something to talk about. She could compare her society theories, gleaned from the pictures, against the real story. About Friday night, surely he could come up with another excuse to drop by. *Enough pussyfootin' around. Be a man. Just call the woman and ask her out.*

"All right. I guess I could give it up for one week." Melvin had made up his mind.

"Fair enough. I'll call you when it's ready. Now, is there anything else I can help you with? I've got a good selection of nineteenth-century literature on the shelf behind your seat. It makes for fine reading on a dreary night."

"I've sure got enough of those. I don't have a lot of time for recreational reading, though, but there is one more thing you can help me with." Melvin fished out his trusty notebook and turned to the page dated for his and Sheriff Hubbard's first visit to Ivy Cole's. "There is a quote I need translating as well. It's German too, but there shouldn't be anything complicated about it. Here."

Melvin handed the professor his notes. The quote was lifted from Ivy's silver platter, the one personalized by her Uncle Stefan. She'd translated it for him and the sheriff as they stood in her kitchen, the message a sweet declaration from a man who obviously loved and missed his niece. Melvin felt meddlesome, copying the personal script and then turning it over to a stranger. But he couldn't help himself. It was a cop's nature to confirm information and know everything about everybody around him, especially those he had a personal interest in. His father would consider the move strategic. His mother, on the other hand, would see it another way, were she still alive. She might call him distrustful and nosy.

"It was translated for me once before," Melvin explained, "but I didn't get the exact wording down. Something like, 'I love you, I miss you.' I don't know."

Toomey squinted at the handwriting. *"Um elfe kommen die wolfe, um zwolfe bricht das gewölbe."* The professor laughed. "I don't know who translated this for you before, but he obviously didn't know German. Or he was pulling your leg."

"What do you mean?"

"This isn't a valentine, Deputy Sanders. It's a line from a German folk rhyme. It means 'at eleven come the wolves, at twelve the tombs of the dead open.' "

Chapter 21

Sheriff Hubbard and her former husband, Tee, sat once again in the police station, this time a snoring bloodhound by the name of Zeke between them. It had been an exhilarating day. Gloria had forgotten the sizzling energy of Tee and Zeke on a trail. Today had been preliminary work: seeing the attack sites—all four of them—plus the Talbots' sheep farm and the cabin in the woods. Tomorrow Tee and Zeke would strike out on their own. Right now, there was another matter at hand.

"Those footprints were fresh, Glory, no doubt about it. Somebody has been there since your raid," Tee said. The cabin had revealed more than cobwebs when they arrived this afternoon: fresh boot prints around the perimeter and leading inside. "Whoever came back was a big man, or a man with mighty big feet. That was about a size thirteen."

"Could mean absolutely zero, Tee. You weren't here for the mob scene yesterday. Talbot's place will be a draw from now on. Some of the local boys even carried a cot out of the cabin. I could bet money one of them was back out there snooping around and looting for more souvenirs."

"Any of them big enough to have a thirteen foot on 'em?"

"Law Thornton might. He found the cabin, by the way. Showed it to us."

"Which one of your deputies is talking to hunters to-day—is he back yet?"

"I'm right here." Meeks hovered outside the office but came in on cue. "I went down to Brigham's Feed Mill and talked to some people. Hunters use those woods all the time, but nobody knew anything about the cabin. The land is owned by the power company, and Dee Waters over there said loggers may have built the cabin back in the fifties when the land was partially timbered. The main trail we were on yesterday eventually winds out to an old logging road, which, in turn, ends on Route 7."

"We followed the trail out with Zeke today. It does end on Route 7, and it is connected to Lutsky's property through Talbot's farm," Gloria said.

"Where Clifford Hughes was killed."

"Yes." The sheriff sat back in her chair. "Is Sanders still here? I need to know if he talked to Ivy Cole about the wolfhound."

"I'm here, Sheriff." Melvin stepped through the door. He'd barely made it back from Asheville before six o'clock and had headed straight for the sheriff's office only to find the group gathered without him. He hoped he hadn't missed much.

"Good. What do you have for me?"

"Not much, ma'am. I talked with Miss Cole, and the man with the wolfhound has moved up North. The dog is dead, put down after getting hit by a car."

"This Cole woman—she's the trainer you told me about? The one who lives near the Clifford Hughes site with a half dozen dogs?" Tee asked.

"Yes, that's her," Gloria said.

Tee pursed his lips but said nothing else.

Gloria stood up, more to stretch her legs than anything. Today's hike down to Route 7, as thrilling as it may have been, taught her age was harder on people than dogs. Zeke clipped along like a puppy, while his two human partners lagged behind. Now sore knees were one more thorn to irritate an already festering aggravation.

"I'm sorry I don't have more to report on the wolfhound, Sheriff."

"Doesn't much matter, Sanders. We've got Zeke now."

They all looked at the sleeping hound by Tee's feet. The dog farted loudly, then resumed his steady snore.

"Sheriff, here are the file duplicates you asked for." Delores, the station's main administrative assistant when she wasn't playing baby-sitter to her eight grandchildren, squeezed through the men filling up Gloria's office. She laid the stack on her desk. "My shift's ending and I'm going home, if you don't need me anymore."

"I'll see you tomorrow. Thank you." Gloria turned to Tee. "For you. Happy reading. It's after six already—you've had a real long day. I suggest you go get acquainted with your new headquarters and these files. If Musket's place is too uncomfortable, Sanders or Meeks might put you up for a while."

The deputies said nothing, and Tee held back the obvious reply: *I could come stay at your place, Glory.* But the situation between them was prickly enough. Instead, he said, "I've slept in worse places. But thanks for thinking of me."

Tee took the bundle under his arm, then nudged Zeke awake. His eyes fell to Deputy Sanders's feet.

"What size is your hoof, son?" Tee said.

Melvin looked down at the toes of his black boots. "They're twelve and a half, sir. Sometimes thirteen, depending on the shoe."

"Well, now we know what we're shooting for." Tee eyed Sanders up and down. Zeke sprang to life and made for the door. Tee followed him. "Good night, all." He walked out, then poked his head back in. "Unless, Glory, you'd like to get a bite before calling it a day. I'm half starved after that marathon Zeke made us run today."

Gloria's first impulse was to say no, but truth was, she

was starving too. Aching and starving. She could go home and sit in miserable hungry silence while Chester licked himself at the foot of the couch, or she could go down to the diner and chat with Tee about things other than the grim. She really did want to hear about fly-fishing in Montana and the ranch out there. "I could use some dinner. Sanders, Meeks, I'll see you bright and early in the morning."

Meeks glared at Tee's back as he and the sheriff left the station.

"You don't like Tee much, do you, John?" Melvin said.

Deputy Meeks never saw fit to pretend. "I don't trust him is all. He broke her heart once before, and there they go off together anyway. She doesn't need that kind of distraction right now."

"You forget what's going with them. If I know the sheriff, they'll spend all evening nose-deep in those files. Not much fun in that." Melvin clapped Meeks on the back. "I'm going to make my rounds. See you in the morrow."

"Yeah, tomorrow," Meeks said. He glanced at the calendar on the wall as Deputy Sanders walked out.

Melvin was at the library again. He walked up the cement sidewalk and stopped cold while reaching for the metal handle on the glass door. A cardboard poster was taped at chin level, its borders decorated with Magic Marker drawings of snarling wolfmen and yellow moons. The title of the poster was in large block letters: Werewolf Survival Tips.

"Good Lord." Melvin opened the door and went inside.

Prudy Township raised her eyebrows when he passed the circulation desk. Behind her, spitting and clacking, was the window air conditioner, sadly losing its battle against the evening humidity. "Back so soon, Deputy?"

"Passing through in a hurry, ma'am."

"Need any help?"

"Maybe. Or not. I don't know yet."

"You let me know." Prudy went back to whatever it was librarians did at the circulation desk. Melvin was glad she was past the mood for flirting.

Melvin walked among the rows and rows of books, feeling the warmth of worn spines beckoning to be rescued from their dusty shelves. He scanned the titles, recalling a few of his own adventurous turns with Huck Finn and Captain Nemo as a kid, before adulthood arrived to steal any time he might put aside for enjoying fantastical journeys across printed pages. Maybe he should have taken the professor up on that offer for nineteenth-century literature. That would certainly impress Miss Cole. Ivy. He needed to get in the habit of the first name. Maybe she would do the same.

Fifteen minutes later, Melvin was back at the circulation desk. Prudy Township looked too smug for Melvin's taste as she stamped his brand-new library card for *Werewolves, Vampires, and Modern Folklore Revealed; Shapeshifters and Signs of the Paranormal;* and *Serial Killers Throughout History: A Look at Violent Psychoses.*

Books tucked under his arm, Melvin left the library and walked toward Etta's Diner for a sandwich. He stopped in front of the picture window. Seated inside were the sheriff and Tee. They were laughing, the files sitting untouched in an extra chair. Melvin shook his head. Poor Meeks, missing out on love. Melvin hoped his buddy didn't drive by and see them in there, having an enjoyable evening after all. On the other hand, good for the sheriff. She needed a little bit of joy in her life right now.

Melvin decided to forego the sandwich and go back to his car. Let the two exes have an evening alone. Tomorrow they'd be kicked into high gear again, and this relaxed moment might be their last. He climbed in his vehicle and was startled when a voice said hello. Ivy Cole sat in the passenger seat.

"Miss Cole! You shouldn't scare a police officer like that. Now who's stalking who?" Melvin threw the books in the backseat before Ivy could see the titles. One smug look today was enough. And if the sheriff found out he'd left his cruiser unlocked and unattended, he'd be dealing with a whole lot worse. *Focus, man!*

"You're quite the bookworm lately, Deputy. Anything you might recommend?"

"Police books. About as interesting as stereo instructions. What are you doing here?"

Ivy didn't answer right away, and Melvin thought she might be . . . blushing?

"Okay, here goes. I've thought of all kinds of excuses to be sitting here, but I'm going to jump right in with the honest truth." Ivy took a deep breath. "I was thinking about when I saw you earlier, about *soon* and all that. And then I thought, what does 'soon' really mean anyway? And then I was thinking, I don't have anything to do this weekend, is that soon or too soon or—"

"Ivy, would you like to go get something to eat while you figure out how to ask me on a date?"

A shy smile broke through the pink in Ivy's cheeks. They both stared out the windshield for a moment. Melvin could smell the woman's hair, her skin, even her breath from where he sat. She smelled like warm honey.

"I'd like that," Ivy said. "Etta's is right over there."

"Let's go to that barbeque place on 22. I hear it's good."

As Melvin pulled away from the curb, Gloria and Tee emerged from the diner.

"Isn't that your deputy?" Tee pointed to the police car rolling away from them.

Gloria squinted in the setting sun. "Yes, that's Sanders."

"Who's the woman?"

"It looks like the dog trainer, Ivy Cole."

"Where do you s'pose they're heading off to?"

"That is a very good question." Gloria watched the car until it was out of sight.

Chapter 22

Ivy and Melvin sat across from one another in a corner booth. Peanut shells littered the floor around them, and Hank Williams Jr. belted out "A Country Boy Can Survive" on the jukebox.

"Here you go—two of Polly's Pulled Pork Platters with extra hushpuppies for the lady, and I'll be right back with some more sweet tea." The waitress set the paper plates down and hurried off for the refills.

"You going to eat all that?" Melvin doubted even he could finish what was piled on Ivy's plate.

"I can eat all this and half of yours. I have an astounding appetite."

"I'll believe it when I see it." Melvin unwrapped his plasticware and tucked the napkin into his shirt. "I knew you'd love this place. It's all class," he said. He raised his foam cup of tea.

"You really know how to court a girl. Cheers, Deputy." Ivy laughed and touched her cup to his. They took long drinks while searching for the next thing to say. Melvin found words first.

"You know, *Ivy,* since we're on a first-name basis now, you might think about calling me Melvin."

Ivy cocked her head to the side, her second hushpuppy rapidly disappearing while she talked. "It's hard to do that."

"And why's that? Don't tell me my authority intimidates you." Melvin tried to keep a straight face as he said it.

"It's not that, although your position is certainly awe-inspiring."

"Okay, that sounded like a jab. I may have to pull out my notebook again if you don't cooperate."

"Oh no, anything but that."

"Seriously, why can't you call me Melvin?"

Ivy downed a forkful of barbeque. She chewed thoughtfully, then answered him. "It doesn't suit you. You look like a Jake or Jack or Luke. Melvin sounds too nerdy."

"I'll let you in on a secret." Melvin leaned in closer. "I'm really a nerd in disguise. This whole tough cop thing is my cover."

"That's all right, many people wear two faces from time to time."

"That they do. I'll tell you another secret: Melvin is my middle name. My first name is much worse."

"I find that hard to believe."

"Well, believe it. Are you ready? Bartholomew. I am, officially, Bartholomew Melvin Sanders, named for my great-grandfather. At your service."

"Bart Sanders—now that fits you!"

Melvin shrugged. "Tell me about you, Ivy. All I know is you train dogs and have a cute house."

The waitress reappeared with the refills and plopped the check down by Melvin's plate. "Y'all want any dessert, just holler. I'll be over there mopping up."

"I think they're wanting to close. Maybe we should leave," Ivy said as the waitress walked away.

"No ducking the question. I come here all the time and don't worry—if they want us out, they have no problem saying so."

Ivy rattled ice in her cup and considered Melvin's original question. She was far better at listening than talking. She liked hearing about other people's lives, their hopes and dreams. Nothing thrilled her more than going through a family's albums and getting a glimpse of what a normal life might be like. But her own life? "There's not much to know about me. My mother was a German immigrant; my father was a businessman from North Carolina. Mama died when I was young, and Dad raised me in New York. Actually, a nanny raised me. My father was away a lot. I grew up, got a career, moved around too much, then settled here in Doe Springs."

"I think there's plenty to know about you, Ivy Cole. Interesting lifestyle you've had."

"In my twenties I thought so too. I felt like a gypsy, what with me and Auf flitting around the country doing whatever we wanted. Sometimes I stayed in places long enough to get a training business going, but then I'd get restless and move on. When I hit thirty, I started to feel worn out. There's something about that age that makes you want to put some roots down, know what I mean?"

Melvin nodded. He felt that way when he came to Doe Springs too. Melvin had not known restlessness in the same way Ivy had, but there had been anxiousness to him after leaving the police academy. Anxious to build a life. Anxious to establish himself. He'd quelled all that anxiety by jumping right into a job in Doe Springs and a mortgage soon after.

"Where's the longest you ever stayed?" Melvin asked.

"New Orleans. I loved that town. I spent nearly two years there."

"Why New Orleans? I've heard it's on the seedy side."

"There's that part of it, sure, but there is a feeling that's hard to explain, being down on the bayou. It's a deeply mysterious place, Melvin, not so unlike the mountains in that respect. There were things in New Orleans the likes of even I'd never seen before, and I've seen some things, Deputy. I've seen some things."

Ivy stared into her coleslaw a moment too long, but before Melvin had chance to explore her last comment further, Ivy leaped forward in geography and the conversation. More brightly, she continued, "But I've also lived out West in South Dakota, Oregon, Arizona—you name it. They were all wonderful. Every place has something special about it. But once I explored every nook and cranny of a community, I felt like I'd wrung the specialness out of it. Then it would be time to move on to the next location."

"After all that, how did you find our hole in the wall? And I say that lovingly."

"You wouldn't believe me if I told you."

"Try me. I'm gullible."

"I was living in Los Angeles when the urge hit me to move again. L.A. was not for me anyway. Too big and busy, plus I was having trouble with neighbors over my dogs. So

I took out a map, closed my eyes, and set my finger down. It landed on—"

"Doe Springs?"

"No. Cuba. Right then I decided that was no way for a mature young woman of thirty to make decisions for her future. And it occurred to me that flying by the seat of my pants every day might really have been a way of running away from things."

"What things?"

"Lost family. Lost friends. I left my father's Manhattan apartment at eighteen and broke all contact with that side of the family. I was striking out on my own then, braving the world, so to speak. It wasn't nearly as fun as I thought it would be. At thirty years old it hit me: I was lonely and I wanted to go home."

"Back to New York?"

"Heaven's no. That wasn't home. I'm talking about North Carolina. Here. The mountains. My hometown is only a couple hours from here, but I didn't want to go back there because that's where all Daddy's people are. But my stepmother's sister and I have always been close, and she lives in Doe Springs. I visited here just a few times when I was growing up, but I remembered how wonderful it was. So I packed up Auf and a few more dogs I'd acquired along the way, and here we are."

"Who is your aunt in Doe Springs?"

"The Widow Pritchard, do you know her? Her sister, Una, was my nanny at first, but later she upgraded her position to stepmother."

Melvin didn't need to be a cop to hear the disgust in her voice. "Wicked stepmother?"

"You have no idea."

Melvin got the message to steer clear of it. There would be no repeating of their first date, where the conversation had ventured into sour territory. He decided to open a different can of worms. "You said you broke ties with your father's family, why's that?"

"They're all crazy. Is that a good enough reason?"

"Not really. It's the South. Down here we wear crazy like a badge of honor."

"Fair enough. It was because of *her*, mostly. Una. You see, the Coles didn't like Mama. They couldn't cotton to Daddy hooking up with a foreigner. That was almost as bad as if he'd married a Yankee—it was hard enough on them when he showed some talent in computers and moved to New York. The Coles were into textiles, which, as you know, was a successful industry here for the longest time, and Grand-daddy Cole expected his son to follow the same footsteps. Good thing he didn't, since the industry's been bottoming out, but I'm wandering off the subject. Long story short, they were so happy when Dad married Una, I felt insulted, like they were glad Mama was gone. With all their money, not one of them flew to Germany for her funeral."

The new can of worms had landed Melvin back in the same ole pot. He might as well stir it a little and get to know Ivy as well as he could. Her past was fascinating to him, a man who'd grown up in the Appalachians over two states and hadn't ventured much outside the links of that mountain chain. "What did your mother die of?"

"What's that?" Ivy's coleslaw was midway to her mouth, suspended by the question.

"If it's too personal, I'm sorry. I shouldn't have asked. But I lost my mother and father a few years back, and I know how hard it can be."

"I'm sorry too, for you. Yes, it can be very hard. Thank you."

"What about your father, do you ever see him?"

Ivy sighed and set her fork down. "No. I'm afraid I ate him."

"Excuse me?"

"I said I hate him. Look, Melvin, here we were having a great time, but somehow we landed in this depressing hole. Death and controversy don't make good date material, let's change the subject."

Melvin took the last bite of his barbeque and wiped his mouth with the napkin in his shirt. "Here, here. But I have to tell you, yours is quite a story. Nannies, traveling, family businesses—why am I getting the feeling I'm out with a rich society girl?"

"Humph. I'm not rich, I'm comfortable. If I were rich, I'd have a brand-new van, twenty times as many dogs, and a cottage for every one of them. And if you call digging up crawdads out of the creek and walking barefoot on dirt roads activities of a society girl, then guilty as charged."

"Two of my favorite pastimes. I had no idea we have so much in common."

"How about that?" A slow, lazy smile spread across Ivy's face. Her stomach was full and she felt suddenly, contentedly sleepy. Normally overly alert to everything around her, being in the deputy's presence lowered her guard. She'd talked too much, revealed way too much, but she felt secure, as alien an emotion as the tingling she'd felt earlier while thinking about him. "I'm exhausted talking about myself, Melvin, and the waitress is giving us the evil eye. We should take the cue and go home. But I've had a real nice time. And look, I finished every last bite on my plate."

Chapter 23

Melvin settled back in his brown leather recliner, the satisfaction of a perfect evening enveloping him. He and Ivy had finally managed to spend time together without jabs or barbs or unintended flubs on his part. He would recount their conversation again and again tonight in bed, replacing the familiar ceiling tiles he counted each night with the curve of her face as he tried to force sleep.

But that would be later. Adrenaline had buoyed him out of

exhaustion, and he found the hours just before midnight a comfortable time to study.

A stack of books rested beside the recliner, the latest three acquired this afternoon at the library. Melvin took the top book off the stack and stared at the glossy cover: *Werewolves, Vampires, and Modern Folklore Revealed.* He opened the book and dove in.

At half past midnight, Melvin's newest notebook—a three-hundred-page spiral-bound monster—lay open on his lap and his once neatly stacked books were scattered about the feet of the recliner. His hand ached. Writer's cramp. It was not a condition he'd have feared for himself ordinarily, but several nights of this in a row were turning his right hand into a claw.

Melvin hooked his pen in the top of the notebook binding and massaged his fingers. It was quite an education he was getting, about the werewolf myth and its parallels to criminal behavior throughout history. He was surprised to learn that werewolfry was not always a legend or tall-tale told to keep errant children in line. The most learned and intellectual of the Middle Ages wholeheartedly believed that the devil walked among man as wolf, a crime against God and nature. The poor and ignorant who could not defend themselves in tribunal courts; the sick, such as epileptics; the inexplicably afflicted, such as those with Down's syndrome or autism; or simply the schizophrenic and insane met horrible, torturous fates at the hands of the religious Inquisitors, who were bent on punishing and executing the accused for their villainy.

But there were true criminals—if not werewolves—among them. Names and dates leaped off pages and into Melvin's notebook as quickly as he could capture them.

Paris, 1598: A seemingly simple tailor burned as a werewolf for the fatal torturing of children, after which he powdered and dressed their bodies.

Nineteen-eighteen to 1924, Fritz Haarmann, dubbed the "Hanover Vampire": Butcher shop owner and sadistic cannibal, he attacked his victims with such viciousness he would nearly sever their heads from their bodies using nothing but his own teeth. Remains of the dead he ground into steaks and sausages to sell in his shop.

September 1603: Another French case, this involving Jean Grenier, a thirteen-year-old boy. . . .

Melvin started to glaze over the account of the child, expecting him to be another tragic victim of a serial killer from centuries ago, until this quote from Grenier drew him back to the page: "I have killed dogs and drunk their blood." Melvin read closer, this account of a lost young soul who confessed to killing not only dogs but also people under the guise of a werewolf. The Lord of the Forest, he claimed, provided him with a wolf skin and magic salve, which effected his transformation whenever he chose. The son of a poor laborer, this bedraggled simpleton was so obviously mentally deranged that even the courts of the Inquisition showed mercy and sent him to live at a Franciscan friary in Bordeaux. But even there, among the most holy, the boy continued to run about on all fours and profess his cravings for human flesh until his death at age twenty.

Melvin rubbed his tired eyes and pictured the boy, a boy whose own personal reality was not that of a human but of a wolf. The child didn't just act it out. He *believed* it.

Melvin flipped over to the next chapter and continued to read. In time, he discovered, the Inquisition, namely the church, relinquished its hold on werewolfism, and the myth-turned-theological fact began to turn to the realm of the scientific. Lycanthropy was finally accepted as a pathological condition in which the patient dealt not with pacts with Satan but rather with bouts of delirium and melancholia, their symptoms suspiciously wolflike. There was no werewolf, these scholars said, and the true victims were the afflicted themselves.

"The true victims were the afflicted themselves." Melvin repeated the line, then closed the book on it. He eyed all the others strewn around his chair, hundreds of their pages flagged with sticky notes and paper clips. They looked used up, and he felt he had something in common with the bound volumes. He was feeling pretty used up himself lately. But his notebook was nearly full of information—or a waste of time, who knew. At any rate, he wasn't much tired, but yawns were catching him about every four pages he read, so maybe his body was trying to tell him something after all. Melvin glanced at his watch. One-twenty-seven a.m. It was as good a time for bed as any.

A few minutes later the deputy was prone underneath his comforter in the bedroom, staring at his ceiling overhead. But instead of the face of a particular lady filling the darkness behind his slitted lids, ideas and speculations formed and parted, swirled and split like spectral images looking for cohesion. Finally, a semblance presented itself and Melvin saw his theory take shape just before a restless sleep tried to claim him: A lone figure stood silhouetted within a vast forest, a four-legged wolfen beast crouching beside him.

Melvin sat up in bed, wide awake. It was far-fetched, but Doe Springs was steeped in far-fetchedness right now, what with all the ghost stories that were touring the town. The sheriff might just go for it. He'd think on this idea a little more.

Sleep was well past him again. Melvin pulled on jogging shorts and tennis shoes for a run.

Chapter 24

His footsteps barely registered on the dark wooded path. For a large man, he had accomplished stealth through the monthly teachings of the moon. This night, his teacher hid behind a bevy of tumbling storm clouds. What little light the crescent afforded through each brief break in the gray shroud made no matter to the man. He knew this path all too well.

The man moved in long strides toward his destination. This would be his last trip to the cabin. The town sheriff was watching it too closely, and the new interloper with the ugly dog presented an even bigger problem.

The cabin sank into the side of the mountain like an aged boulder. Pines swayed over top of it, their branches scritch-scratching the rusted tin roof. So obscure and remote, it had been the perfect hideaway for his full-moon transmogrifica-tions. Now he had precious little time to discover a new place before the full moon showed her mellow face again.

The man pushed open the cabin door. The doorknob was gone, taken by the sheriff's deputy for fingerprints. Another thing from the cabin had been removed as well: the cot, where he sweated and writhed during the painful morph into a creature he had come to worship almost as a separate entity.

But they had missed the most important thing of all. He had come back to complete this task before, but the baying of the interloper's hound had alerted him to the policemen's approach. In his haste to escape, he had not covered his tracks—a sloppy, irreversible mistake. He was making too many of those. Tonight there would be no mistakes.

The man stood in the center of the dark room. An owl screeched forlornly from somewhere outside, and he longed to howl a lonely cry of his own in response. The forest at three a.m. might frighten a lesser man, but he knew—as the forest knew—that his was the most terrifying presence among them. He laughed unexpectedly at the thought, but the mirthless sound in the cabin was as dry as the bones be-neath his feet.

The man knelt and clawed at the floorboards. He pried a section loose and stared with a mixture of sadness and true love at the sight within. A small skeleton stared up from the hole, the skull's empty sockets accusing him no more.

She had been his first and only human so far, just a little girl from another town. He had driven away, out into the country that night, to complete the transformation and avoid any human contact. Since first acquiring the monthly gift, he had taken great pains to isolate the creature to accomplish the least harm. In the woods, as the wolf, he hunted deer, rabbits, whatever flesh-and-blood animal he came upon to render and devour. The hunger was never satisfied, but the desire for murderous violence at least had an outlet.

Then that one night, that one fateful night, he came upon her. She was only six, the girl Annie. She had wandered away from her family, foolishly and unknowingly camping in his forest. Mother and father soundly sleeping, the girl left the tent to find the privacy to pee.

The wolf, so painfully hungry, smelled the warm scent she left in the dirt before she had even finished. The fox in his teeth fell to the ground as the new scent pulled his head into the girl's direction.

He saw her clearly through the limbs and leaves he hid among to watch—perfect, she was, shining white like a pearl in contrast to the night-blackened swells of rhododendron she'd chosen to squat among. She rose, business accomplished, and turned circles, not knowing which way led back to safety. In a moment, she would scream for Mommy and Daddy, and he could not let that happen. Oh no indeed.

The wolf lunged at the child's back, knocking the air from her lungs. He ripped out the soft throat, tearing the scream away before she could draw in the breath to emit it. The blood was sugar on his tongue. He slashed with his claws, across her chest, her belly, her legs. Blood sprayed all around him like a fountain mist and he lapped the droplets in midair. The agony in his stomach subsided as he gobbled flesh from small bones. . . .

The cabin closed around the man once more. Shaking hands stilled themselves on bent knees, and a bead of saliva resting on parted lips broke to run down his quivering chin. Many times had he hung his head while tears dropped freely on the girl's mangled remains. She was the only and the last, he'd sworn to himself when daylight had ascended and left him with the evidence of his crime. He'd held true to his own word for so long now, until coming here, to Doe Springs, when the discovery that another wolf hunted among them swung the doors of a lightened conscience wide. He was free, and this memory of his cruel deed suddenly less haunting. The small skeleton he spirited from one location to the next was no longer a guilty torment of self-punishment.

It had, in fact, become a fantasy of sorts, a pornographic dream to relish and despise at once. *She was a child, just a child, and yet, blood knows no distinction.*

"God help me." The man wiped his eyes, then he laughed again. The deep-throated sound filled the cabin and echoed louder into the surrounding darkness outside. The owl cried once more, then took flight from its branch in the pine over-head.

The man gingerly lifted the bones from their hiding place and tucked them into a burlap sack. Then he scooted away through the night, the reminder of his atrocities secure at his side as the rain finally fell.

Part Three

"The creature threw back its head and a wolfen cry,
absent from the Blue Ridge for a century,
filled up the mountains and the hollows."

Chapter 25

Sheriff Hubbard sat on her deck, the weathered wicker chair imprinting an unflattering pattern across the backs of her thighs. In an uncharacteristically light moment, she'd thrown on shorts instead of jeans and come outside to savor her morning coffee. Work had traveled outside with her and lay spread across the wooden patio table, but for the moment, the rising sun was barely arcing above the tree-ruffled hill across from her, and she was determined to enjoy it. Chester, too, was delighting in the morning. He charged through the mist still floating above dew-wet grass, birds and squirrels scattering ahead of him.

Gloria watched the Labrador with a tinge of envy. How simple and sweet life could be. How wonderful to have a whole day to romp and explore, or do nothing at all. A picnic by the river—that would be nice on a day like this. Maybe someone would join her. Maybe . . . maybe Tee, perhaps, and they could laugh and talk about old times, just like they had at the diner. And there had been some very good times in their past: hiking in the Smokies, rafting on the Dan River, exploring lighthouses at the Outer Banks where they'd honeymooned for three whole days before having to return to work. There had not been much time off together, but they made the most of every moment they'd had.

And then they were divorced, and it was all over.

The daydream dissipated like the mist around Chester's busy legs. The sun's warmth suddenly felt stifling, and it lit up the grisly pictures on the table too brightly. Gloria poured the rest of her coffee over the side of the deck and gathered up the photographs. She walked inside and threw the pile on the kitchen counter. There would be no picnics for her or anybody else till the Devil of Doe Springs matter was resolved.

Special times with Tee would most likely remain a memory. He and Zeke worked alone, and he'd made it perfectly clear after the initial tour of Doe Springs that that was the way he wanted it. After this was all over with, he'd be back on a plane for Montana, and she'd be here in North Carolina, shouldering the single life like a real trooper. Or sheriff.

Gloria poured another cup of coffee and leaned against the sink. She would go through the photographs before donning her uniform and driving to the office. Tee had his own copies now and every day they compared notes on what they saw. Each morning she studied the pictures one by one, trying to focus on the smallest details as if seeing them for the first time. Bone chips and tissues and splattered bits of who-knew-what were embedded in the grains of the photos and permanently embedded in the mind of the sheriff. Four human victims, dozens of destroyed livestock, hundreds of pieces recovered, many more apparently devoured.

The photos at the peak of the Kodak mountain showed the most wear. Gloria's love of animals was unquestioned—Chester, her only child, was well known in town and out—but it was the people who were her top priority. She held their photographs like a fan in front of her, four pictures of when they were whole and alive.

Manny Wilson: twenty-one years old, the youngest victim, a thief and delinquent. Dub Dawson: former school janitor, acquitted child molester last jailed for multiple DWIs. Maddy-Bell Lindsay: horse breeder, the county shut her down and removed twelve starving Arabians and two dead foals. Clifford Hughes: deliveryman, wife beater.

Not a good apple in the bunch. All killed over a full moon. All mauled and mutilated by the same animal or pack of animals. No clues, no tracks. No sign of human involvement, until Hughes. Two eyewitness accounts to a wolf attack on a dog, a wolf that, according to an elderly sheep farmer, could stand upright. And unidentified fur at a logger's cabin.

"A vigilante mystery," Gloria said to the frozen images.

Her deputy Melvin Sanders had an interesting theory. He'd finally cornered her with his ideas the same morning she'd planned to interrogate him about his rendezvous with Ivy Cole. Sanders came into the sheriff's office toting library books and his *(dreaded)* notebook—an even bigger one. He'd closed the door and pulled a chair up so close to her desk she could make out the tops of his knees.

"Sheriff, I have some thoughts about what's going on," Sanders had said.

Gloria eyed the books, then crossed her hands in front of her. "Let's hear it."

"I've been doing some research," her deputy began, as he spread out the books and opened his notes to the first page. "Do you remember what that Native American man from the reservation said?"

Gloria nodded.

"Okay, I think he was actually on to something. Look at this."

"Hold it right there, Sanders. You think we have a werewolf running amok in Doe Springs," the sheriff deadpanned.

"Yes, kind of. Let me show you what I've found." Sanders cited his notes. " 'People throughout history have believed themselves to be werewolves or taken on a close identity with wolves.' " He looked up at the sheriff. "That's the crux of what I'm getting at. I've found out that what's happening here may not be so unusual after all."

"Okay, I'm listening." Gloria's fingers began the familiar drumroll, a cue for Sanders to get on with it.

"There was a well-known case in France about a man named Gilles Garnier. Around 1572 or '73 he was said to have mutilated children with his hands and teeth and was allegedly strong enough to have pulled a victim's leg clean off his body. He also ate the children's flesh, and fifty locals testified they had seen Gilles in action. The most interesting part of this, Sheriff, is he confessed to the court that he committed the murders as a wolf, a werewolf, a *loup-garou*. This kind of thing—blaming werewolves for human acts of bestiality—was common in the Middle Ages."

"Mass hysteria?"

"Most likely. I mean, a normal man wouldn't be capable

of such things, that's how they would see it back then. It had
to be the work of something supernaturally evil. People were
predisposed to seeing what played into their fantasies."

"Like the Talbots?"

"Yeah, I think so. I found a lot of stuff like this at the library. In 1589, Peter Stumpf, or Stubbe, of Cologne was tortured and executed as a werewolf. The Gandillon family—a
whole family, mind you—were burned as werewolves in
1598. Around 1640, an entire city in Germany, Greifswald,
was said to be overrun with the critters. There were so many
accounts of werewolfism throughout eighteenth-century Ireland, it was nicknamed 'the Wolfland' in England." Melvin
flipped pages almost quicker than he could read them.
"Moving up in history to the early 1900s, a man named Al-
bert Fish killed and ate between eight and fifteen children,
and that happened here in America—D.C. to be exact. He
was executed in 1935. California's Harry Gordon used a
straight razor to do the work of claws, slashing women to
ribbons. The media called him The Werewolf of San Fran-
cisco and the nickname stuck. Serial killer David Berkowitz
claimed a neighbor's big black dog told him to commit murders, and even Hitler, who referred to himself as Father Wolf,
was rumored to have such rages he would drop down and
chew the carpet. It goes on and on—"

"That's what I'm afraid of. Let's cut to the chase here.
We've got werewolf sightings, cannibalism, serial killers,
and a Nazi. I want to hear your theory, not a history lesson."

"I'm getting to that, Sheriff. Just bear with me a little
longer."

Gloria had little patience with drawn-out explanations—
she was a get-to-the-meat-of-it-in-a-hurry kind of officer.
But her deputy had apparently spent hours putting together
this idea. He would want his research on the table and his
reasoning thoroughly explained before announcing what she
was waiting to hear.

Undaunted, Sanders continued to flip and read. " 'Scien-
tists and doctors have studied the werewolf phenomenon for
years. As early as the fifteen and sixteen hundreds, lycanthropy was used to describe violent forms of insanity and

depression, but the afflicted were mistakenly identified by commoners as werewolves. Between 1520 and 1630, thirty thousand people were persecuted as werewolves in Europe.' " He looked up from the notes. "And executed, of course. You know, burned, beheaded, buried alive, and so forth." Sanders's eyes went back to the page. " 'A recent theory by a professor at the University of Maryland claims peasants ate bad rye bread, which was contaminated by a fungus that acted like a drug.' Instead of mentally ill patients or real-life werewolves, Sheriff Hubbard, the professor believes these people were delusional because of drugs."

Sanders closed the notebook at last and leaned back in his chair. The only sound was Gloria's fingers lightly tapping the scarred surface of her desk. The deputy had a point and they were close to it, she was sure. Eventually, he'd spring it on her. She could wait. Da-da-da-*da*.

"I think, Sheriff, there is somebody out there who truly believes, whether through insanity or drugs, that he is a werewolf. I believe he may be wearing a suit of some kind, fashioned like a wolf suit. I think this person has an animal he believes to be his familiar, and what damage he cannot inflict himself, this animal can. It's highly trained and vicious, probably hidden away somewhere. I doubt a dog like this would be taking walks with its owner in the park."

Gloria willed her fingers to stop. Sanders's ideas were not groundbreaking; she and Tee had had similar discussions. But the werewolf suit–insanity link was very intriguing. They had considered a canine hybrid, considered an intelligent person running the show, but they had not entertained the idea that this person might really believe he was a shapeshifter.

"We've found no human bite marks on the corpses," Gloria said finally.

"Maybe he uses something else instead of his own teeth. Maybe he just rips with his hands once the dog disables and maims the victim."

"A joint effort? Dog and man working side by side?" Gloria remembered something Ivy Cole had told Sanders during his quest for the wolfhound information, something about wolves and man helping one another through the ages.

"Yes, I believe so," Sanders said.

And that had been the extent of their meeting. But Gloria had not discounted what Sanders was telling her. In fact, she'd rolled the ideas past Tee as well. Sanders's hypothesis, as bizarre as it sounded, actually made some sense. A lunatic running around in a wolf suit was no more bizarre than some of the antics of the serial killers Sanders continued to cite that day, Dahmer among them.

Anything is possible in this crazy world, the sheriff thought to herself. Gloria put the photographs of the victims down and cupped both hands around her coffee mug. She wished she had a more satisfying vice. Was she too old to take up smoking and not look ridiculous? Probably. Drinking was out of the question. Her father had been an alcoholic, and Town Drunk was not a title she aspired to. She preferred Town Sheriff, even though events in her life tested that aspiration time and again.

She sighed and went back to work in her head, vices dismissed and the coffee tasteless on her tongue. She gathered the pictures to stuff back in their envelope, but one glossy eight-by-ten slipped to the floor. Gloria stooped to pick it up. The pig's face, what was left of it, stared up at Gloria through one perfect, untouched eye.

"What did you see, little piggy? What did you see?" Gloria squinted at the photo. Not at the animal's good eye, but the empty socket beside it. Actually, through it to the ground behind the skull. Glinting up through the gouged mass of tissue appeared to be a metallic object.

Gloria leaned over the sink and opened the window shades. Harsh sunlight poured in, and she tilted the photograph out of the glare. The hole in the pig's eye bored out the back of his head. The object looked to be wedged on the bottom rim of the hole.

Gloria picked up the phone, picnics and lazy Saturdays forgotten.

"Tee, meet me at Dennis Largen's farm. Bring Zeke. We missed something, and with any luck, it's still there."

Gloria's next call was to round up her overworked deputies. Meeks was on his way. Deputy Sanders—MIA. It was his day off (she gave her men one day a week, despite her own seven-day-a-week work schedule). Nevertheless, even on days off they were to be immediately available. She left a message at Sanders's home and at the office, in case he called in. Nasty little pinpricks of anger started a stinging burn under the collar of her shirt. She had let the deputy off the hook one time already. When he came in with the werewolf research, she decided to let the interrogation of why Ivy Cole was in his patrol car slide. As it stood, there was really no reason for Sanders not to see the dog trainer. But it was a poor time to strike up a relationship, and patrol cars were not for cruising dates.

Gloria's intuition—not as a sheriff, but as a woman—told her exactly where Sanders was right now, and who with. *Hell*, she thought without much humor, *they're probably on a picnic*.

Chapter 26

Melvin spread the blanket alongside the creek while Ivy carried the picnic basket from his truck. He found this spot some time ago while helping some folks at the nearby campground search for their lost cat. The cat came back on its own, but Melvin never forgot the beauty of the isolated meadow, nor the near-grown-over dirt road that led to it. Summer had arrived, bringing with it patches of wildflowers strewn about the field in erratic patterns like flecks of paint shaken from an artist's brush. The creek he'd settled by murmured quietly over water-smoothed stones—maybe later he'd test Ivy's seriousness about flipping rocks for crawdads. Behind them and all around, rolling hills almost too gentle to be considered mountains cradled them in.

Ivy plopped down beside Melvin, the heavy picnic basket draped over one arm and her flip-flops lying topsy-turvy in the grass. While she relaxed in denim cutoffs and a white tank, Melvin felt formal in his creased khakis and blue button-down shirt. When he'd arrived to pick up Ivy an hour before, she asked if he'd like a dinner jacket to go with his picnic attire.

"We have enough here to feed the whole town, Melvin. You took my appetite seriously, didn't you?" Ivy began unpacking fried chicken, macaroni salad, Watergate salad, coleslaw, two different kinds of pie, and a bundle of biscuits. Melvin popped the tabs on two Yoo-hoos and propped one in the crease of blanket by Ivy's side.

"I take picnicking very seriously. In fact, I come from a long line of picnickers," he said.

"I can tell. Only someone with that kind of experience could come up with a spot as wonderful as this. I thought I'd been all over Jack's property, but I've never seen this place."

"That solves a mystery—I didn't know where the heck we were."

"I bet we could walk to my house from here." Ivy pointed to the hills behind them.

"I'll pass on the overland route. I prefer to drive ten miles out of my way, thank you."

Ivy took a sip of Yoo-hoo and put a hearty chicken leg on her plate. Fishing about in the picnic basket for napkins, she grasped a bottle of wine instead. It was peach, and chilled. "You pulled out all the stops today, Melvin. I am mightily impressed."

"Get ready for some first-class seduction, Miss Ivy Cole. I'm a regular Casanova." Melvin wiggled his eyebrows, and Ivy laughed.

The two piled their plates high and listened to the brook serenade their meal. They ate in silence, basking in each other's company, the warmth of noontime, the peacefulness of the Blue Ridge. A shadow passed over them briefly, a hawk. Ivy watched the graceful animal, sailing free through the gold of the sun. She set her empty plate aside, and

Melvin poured wine in clear cups. Small chunks of icy peach floated in the clear liquid.

"This is delicious, Melvin."

"You can thank my mama. She taught me how to make it. I've been waiting for a special occasion to try it out. Wine making runs in my blood."

"Oh? Did your family own a vineyard?"

"No, but my great-grandfather ran 'shine in the West Virginia hills. His still was legendary, from what I understand."

"As a lawman, you must be very proud."

"I even put it on my resume."

"Well, I'm not just talking about the perfect wine. I'm talking about everything, this whole day." Ivy leaned back on her elbows and sighed blissfully. Melvin leaned on an elbow beside her.

"I'm glad I did something right. It's not easy, planning the ideal picnic on the fly. I usually need a couple weeks to pull something like this off. Ordering up the weather was a real pain in the neck, but I managed to come through."

"That you did. I don't know whether to get up and run through this field in my bare feet, or fall asleep right here in the grass. What's your vote?"

"Oh, I dunno. I feel kind of shiftless myself. A meal like we just had needs to be slept off, in my opinion."

Ivy lay completely back and continued watching the hawk. Melvin followed her gaze to the blue sky.

"What do you see up there, Melvin?"

The deputy watched puffy cumulus clouds blow slowly above them. The lone mass passed over the sun momentarily, and the hawk stood out like a black speck on white linen. "I see probably one of the prettiest Saturdays on the calendar. What do you see?"

Ivy put her hands behind her head. Her stomach was too full, her eyelids too heavy. With a sleepy drawl, she said, "I see the moon."

Melvin scanned the sky. "Looks like the sun and a couple of newcomer clouds to me."

"It will be visible right about there after sundown." Ivy

held her finger out toward the sky, as if placing it on a minis-cule dot just beyond where the hawk was flying. "It's there, just waiting for the daylight to vanish and let it shine. That hawk is sailing toward it, a moth to a flame."

" 'The man who has seen the rising moon break out of the clouds at midnight has been present like an archangel at the creation of light and of the world.' "

Ivy propped back up on her elbow. "That wouldn't be Ralph Waldo Emerson you're quoting, would it?"

"Shoot, you've heard of him? I was hoping I could pass that one off as my own."

"You are full of surprises, Deputy." She said it with a smile, but Melvin heard something else in her voice, a note that stole the compliment away. It was sadness.

"I take it back," Melvin said softly.

"What's that?" Ivy closed her eyes, finally succumbing to the lull of humming bees and gurgling water. The clouds had brought a breeze to complete the idyllic moment.

"What I said I see. I'd like to change my answer."

"Go ahead."

"I see the most beautiful woman in Doe Springs." Melvin brushed a strand of hair from her cheek. The warmth of her skin lingered on his fingertips.

Ivy opened one eye to peer at the deputy. "Only Doe Springs? Not the world?"

"I didn't want to be too over the top for my first compliment."

"Flattery will get you everywhere, Melvin. What else?" Ivy opened both eyes and looked up into Melvin's face, mar-veling that such a rugged exterior could house such a gentle, humble man.

"What else? Uh, well, you're smart—" Melvin stumbled.

"Relax, Casanova. I'm kidding."

"Whew. I hadn't rehearsed any extra lines. That was my one big one. Did it work?"

"You tell me." Ivy leaned toward the deputy, her face tilted upward to his. He cupped her chin in his palm and leaned down to meet her. Overhead, the hawk circled in silence.

Chapter 27

Gloria's Jeep bounced and jolted down the cow path that would eventually widen out to the homestead known as the Largen Place. In reality, it was a sad backwoods number, erected from part mud-daubed log cabin, part trailer attached as a room addition back in '72 (how Dennis got *that* thing in here remained one of the unsolved mysteries of the world). The Cherokee took the rutted tractor-traveled road in stride, but its paint job would be worse for the wear. Branches scraped every side of the vehicle as it squeezed its way toward its destination. Lost in the sheriff's rearview was Tee, back there somewhere battling it out with Musket's borrowed Ford and some reluctant four-wheel drive.

The woods keyholed at last, the narrow road exiting into a cleared parcel of property encircled by a shrine of trees that formed a formidable perimeter around Largen's farm. There wasn't much to it. The house/trailer was backed by gray, weathered-out sheds that would come down on their own in a year or two. Plank fence topped with barbed wire formed pens that once held twenty-plus pigs. Now a few chickens pecked around in the mud lots, and a goat with two kids stood watch from the top of an abandoned Buick. A scraggly patch of grass grew from a hole in the rusted-out hood, and the goats snipped at the blades and chewed without much interest as the sheriff pulled in the front yard and parked.

The Largens had built a porch onto the trailer side of the house. Gloria, with more than a little care, navigated the stacked cement blocks that led up to the aluminum front door. She banged on it. Nobody answered. She cupped her hands and peered through the Kleenex-box-sized window on the door. An orange couch strewn with laundry and empty Beanee Weenee cans was all she could make out.

"Dennis! I know you're in there. I see your four-wheeler beside the house. Come on out!"

A thud from inside, then quiet again.

"I mean it, Dennis. Don't make me have to come in and get you!"

"Go away!" The voice was muffled, calling from a back room she couldn't see.

"Do you know who this is?"

"I don't give a pig's knuckle on a cheese cracker who it is. Get the hell off my property or I'm coming out with both barrels blazing!"

"This is the sheriff speaking, Dennis. I'm not going to warn you again."

The door ripped inward and a Goliath of a man filled its place, all belly and beard and shotgun, aimed at the ground. "Well why didn't you say so, Sheriff!" A big grin split the hair on his face and the shotgun flew through the air to the couch. "If I'd a knowed it was you, I'd come on out the first time. How you been?" Dennis grabbed Gloria in a bear hug and squeezed her till she coughed. Behind them, Tee's truck coughed as well, and died.

"You bringing me some company?" Dennis still held the sheriff, and she peeled him off one arm at a time. The man had declared undying loyalty to her a few years back when she let him off light on a distilling charge. What Dennis didn't know—and she'd never tell him—was he'd managed to brew up nothing better than obnoxiously bad vinegar, and there was no law against that. But the fear of her changing her mind about jailing him kept his 'shining efforts on a leash and put his focus back on pig farming. At least, until last January. But there'd be no time to search for alternative incomes on the Largen place today.

Tee unloaded himself from the pickup and his dog fell out behind him. He came toward the couple on the porch with his hand out. "I'm Tee and this here is Zeke. Nice to see you."

Dennis looked at Gloria and she could tell he was thinking about his shotgun again. "It's okay, Dennis. Tee's my ex-husband."

"Well I'll be! If it ain't *the* Tee Hubbard!" Dennis jumped off the porch and swallowed Tee's hand in his own. He pumped the tracker's arm up and down like jacking up water from an unprimed well. "Pleased to meet you, just pleased as rain to meet you. So you're the one married to our little sheriff here. Montana's a long way from North Carolina, got to mind you, but welcome to the homestead. I got some beer in the cooler and a mess of fresh squirrel curing on a clothesline out back; pull up a stump and we'll swap some tales while I fry us up a couple."

"Dennis, we're not here to socialize. We're on duty, and my deputy should be showing up any time," Gloria said.

"Working, are you? Must have something to do with my pigs then." Dennis's sunny smile suddenly went all to hangdog. He sat down on the edge of his porch and planted two meaty hands on his knees. "It's been hard, Sheriff. Mighty hard. Those hogs were my livelihood. The Mrs. ran off in April because of it. That, and the fact she was scared out of her wits. Wouldn't leave the house, quit working in the yard. I had to take up all the chores, inside and out."

Tee looked around but Gloria's glare held his tongue for him. Dennis continued. "Now alls I got are some chickens and a few goats. Couldn't interest you in a goat, could I, Tee? I'll send one back with you today for just twenty-five dollars. Hell, make it twenty. You can pick out whichever one you want. They'll keep your yard eat down to nothing. You won't have to mow another day in your life."

"Dennis, we need to take another look around your pig lots, if that's all right." Gloria interrupted the sales pitch.

"Oh, sure. Have the run of the place. What 'er you looking for? I'd like to help out."

"Maybe you *can* help us. We're looking for this." Gloria held up the picture of the farmer's brutalized pig.

Dennis scratched his head. "Glad I got my lunch down a'ready. Um, I don't rightly see what you're talking about, Sheriff. That pig's long gone, along with all the rest of what I could scrape up."

Tee was staring at the photograph too. "There. I see it. A metallic object in the corner of the eye. Is that . . . gold?"

Gloria nodded. "Dennis, do you remember seeing any metal around the animals' remains when you moved them?"

"Nah, Sheriff. I mean, I wasn't really looking, if you know what I mean."

"What did you do with the carcasses?"

Dennis scratched his head again and looked off through the trees beyond the pig lots.

"Buried?" Tee said.

"Not exactly."

"You just piled them up out there somewhere, didn't you?" Gloria didn't expect much different, although she'd told him to sanitarily dispose of everything on that cold day back in the winter, when they'd all stood in front of Dennis's lots, shoulder to shoulder with the fingers of January's bitter wind poking into the necks of their jackets and freezing their skin. But she had already turned numb that day, before feeling winter's personal touch. The hogs' disemboweled, dismembered bodies squished into the snow turned her blood to ice. It had not been a clean kill site, like that of the humans, when so much was eaten and so little left to recover. Here the violence had rampaged from one animal to the next, ripping wastefully before taking the next life.

"Dang it, Sheriff," Dennis said, drawing the sheriff's attention back to the present, "I didn't have time to go burying a whole bunch of dead hogs. The ground was all froze up anyways. I figured the wild animals could take care of all that without me breaking my back too."

"And what if you drew the thing that ate them right back here, what about that?"

"Yeah, that's just what the Mrs. had to say about it."

"On top of that, you live near the river, a natural water source. Carcasses can be a very bad contaminant."

"I didn't put them anywheres near no water, I got better sense than that. You ain't going to give me a ticket for it, are you, Sheriff? I ain't got a pot to piss in as it is—"

"Relax, Dennis. Under the circumstances, I'm glad the bodies are still here. We're going to need to see that area and your pig lots. You can help us out the most by staying in the house."

Dennis frowned, disappointed. "I won't be in the way."

"That's right. Because you're going to be in the house." Gloria noticed a man walking up behind their parked vehicles. "Here comes Meeks."

The deputy stood beside the group, winded. "I got here as fast as I could."

"Where's your car?"

"Stuck in a ditch a half mile back. I had to walk the rest the way in. Spring rain wash you out or what, Dennis? It wasn't this bad back in January."

"Ah, the whole place went all to hell when that thing came through here. Any leads on the werewolf, Sheriff? That's what got my pigs, ain't it? That's why you're here, ain't it—the werewolf?"

Gloria stared at the man hard before answering. Meeks couldn't suppress an eye roll before looking away. Tee watched his ex-wife, amused.

"It's not a werewolf, Dennis," Gloria said, her tone as flat as the tires on the rusted-out Buick.

"Alls I'm saying is if it quacks like a duck . . . " Dennis waited for the sheriff to own up to it, but she continued to stare at him, unblinking. "I mean, I ain't no fancy detective but come on, Sheriff Hubbard, everybody knows what's going on around here. You don't have to hide it. It'd be better if it came on out in the open instead of having folks whispering about it over their fences."

"Go inside, Dennis. We won't be long."

"Whatever you say, Sheriff. But I hope you catch it alive, at least. There's a whole bunch of us would line up and pay good money to take some shots at it. Tee, Meeks." Dennis Largen nodded at the police officers and retreated into his trailer. Gloria saw the man reappear in front of the window facing the pig lots. He'd be watching, and there was nothing she could do about that.

"What's going on, Sheriff?" Meeks took the picture Gloria held out to him.

"Look in the corner of the eye. That's what we're after."

The deputy squinted at the speck in the photo. "Any idea what it is?"

"None." Gloria strode to the back of her Jeep and pulled out two metal detectors. "But whatever it is, it's still here. I've got a feeling about that." She handed Tee one detector and Meeks the other. "Me and Meeks will start with the mud lots over here, and you and Zeke can head for the pig pile in the woods. Can Zeke find metal?"

"Zeke can sniff out anything. But I'll use this too. No point having idle hands." Tee hefted the detector and went to work.

Gloria watched him walk away.

"Does he know where he's going?" Meeks asked.

"Tee always knows where he's going. Come on."

Forty-five minutes passed, but Gloria continued scraping through the earth, unmindful of her bleeding nails or the mud and manure plastered to the knees of her pants. Meeks was nearby, sweeping the metal detector left and right, going over the same ground they'd covered twice already. The chickens scattered when they'd first come into the pig lots, but the goats had become a-whole-nother issue altogether. Seven more had shown up to join the original group on the Buick, and they'd all made their way over to the pens to become a general nuisance. Meeks had shooed them a half dozen times, while the sheriff remained bent over the ground in some kind of hypnotic digging frenzy.

"Sheriff?" Meeks stood over the woman crouched in the dirt. She didn't respond, just continued raking, turning, overturning. . . .

Meeks knelt beside her, the metal detector lying quiet by his side.

"Sheriff Hubbard? Sheriff? Gloria!"

The woman's head snapped to the side. "What, Deputy?" She wiped her face, leaving a brown smear across one cheek. Her hair hung in moist tendrils around her face, and Meeks curbed the urge to brush them back behind her ears or smooth the loose pieces under the rubber band that held her customary ponytail. She looked older today, worn. He wished he could take her stress away, make it all better, but there was nothing he could do.

"We're not having any luck, Sheriff. I've gone in circles with this gadget and found nothing, not even loose change."

"Then spread out! Go outside the lots. We'll start making our way into the woods, heading in Tee's direction."

"It's not here, Sheriff. I think there's no reason to keep on—"

"No reason? Do you know what's almost on us again, Deputy?"

Meeks didn't answer. He wasn't sure she meant for him to.

"The full moon, Meeks, and there is some lunatic out there well aware of the fact. We're racing against the calendar, and if we don't find something—anything—to help us catch this thing, I may have to face another family to tell them their son or daughter or who-the-hell-ever won't be coming home."

Meeks remained quiet, staring at the woman with filth smeared across her face and hands and clothes. He'd never seen the sheriff like this before: desperate, frantic. He didn't like it. This was not his Gloria, confident and strong.

"Meeks, I'm sorry. I didn't mean to—"

Zeke's baying cut her off. The deputy and sheriff leaped to their feet, conversation forgotten.

"He's found something. Come on." The sheriff took off toward the noise, Meeks behind her.

They found Tee at the foot of a ravine. Thick tree roots wormed out of the earth along the steep sides of it, and the officers used them as steps to make their way to the bottom. They were in a trash dump, surrounded by cracked rubber tires and twisted-up car parts. Broken bags of rotting garbage lay belly up, their contents exploded out when they were tossed over the side of the gully. In the middle of it all stood Tee and Zeke, ankle deep in bones.

"What have you got, Tee? We heard Zeke," Gloria said, making her way through the refuse toward him. A black snake slithered across her path to disappear underneath a discarded refrigerator, and she kicked a tin can after it. She should ticket Dennis after all for illegal dumping—the four-wheeler tracks they'd followed here from his place was evidence enough—but that would be a matter for a lesser day. She paused to see if anything else would dart around her feet before finally stepping into the pile of bones with her ex and his dog. Dried marrow snapped like branches under her shoes. She slid a skull aside to get purchase on the ground.

Tee held a paper bag in one gloved hand. Zeke sat quietly, his droopy eyes and slack jowls belying the excited barking of only minutes ago.

"It looks like a gold cap," Tee said, handing Gloria the paper sack and pulling off his gloves. "We found it right here, wedged in this socket just like in the picture. Can you believe the luck?" Tee nudged a cracked pig skull with his cowboy boot. One side of the skull was completely crushed, but the other side was smooth and perfect. It reminded Gloria of the way tornadoes could pass through a town, obliterating one side of a street but leaving the other untouched.

"A gold cap. What do you mean—from a tooth?" Meeks asked. He stood on the outskirts of the bone pile.

"Yup. A human tooth."

Gloria peered into the bag at the bit of metal. It was dull-looking and chipped. Tee might be wrong. It could be nothing, just a bit of scrap. But what would it be doing stuck in a pig's eye, so deeply embedded that it remained there even after all these months? On the other hand, what if it did belong to a person? Even stranger. *Man and wolf working together.*

"How do we know this is even what we're looking for?" Meeks said, now standing over Gloria's shoulder to see into the bag for himself. "That doesn't look like anything to me."

"It's a gold cap for a tooth, and it's been stuck in this bone since the animal was killed last winter." Tee stuffed the latex gloves in his jeans and pulled down the brim of his cowboy hat. Gloria knew what that meant. Discussion over, time to move on. He always looked ready to step onto a horse and ride away after adjusting his hat like that. In a minute he'd be scaling the incline with Zeke, the rest of his group rushing to keep up.

"We'll get a DNA sample on this," Gloria said. She

started to hand the bag to Meeks, then put it in her pocket instead. Meeks dropped his outstretched hand.

"Should we continue looking, just in case?" Gloria threw it out there, but she already knew Tee's answer.

"It's what we're after, Glory. I say we take the rest of the afternoon to pore through all the pictures again. There could be something else you missed."

Gloria drove to the police station. A tow truck was going back up to Dennis's to yank her deputy out of the ditch and haul Musket's pickup to the garage, but none of those things were of concern to her right at this moment. What was hot on her mind now was the piece of yellow metal secure in her pocket, and Tee's last comment ringing in her ears. *There could be something else you missed.*

Chapter 28

" 'Since the very earliest accounts of werewolves, those who would seek to explain the onset of such frightening behavior have stated with authority that it is the light of the full moon that serves as the catalyst for the transformation of human into wolf. The ancient Greeks and Romans associated the moon with the underworld and those human and inhuman entities who used the night to work their dark magic. Witches, werewolves, and other shapeshifters received great power from the moon—and just as the moon changed its shape throughout the month, so could these servants of the underworld transform their shapes into bats, wolves, dogs, rats, or any creature they so chose.' "

Bonnie Hill, Doc Hill's seventeen-year-old daughter, shone the flashlight underneath her chin, the light distorting her face into a ghoul's. She repeated the last line from the book on the ground in front of her: "transform their shapes into bats, wolves, dogs, rats, or any creature they so chose."

"I'd want to be . . . a lion. Grrrrr." Clara, Bonnie's best friend seated on the other side of the campfire, curved her fingers into claws and dug into her boyfriend Randall's sides. Randall fought back, tickling Clara until she screamed surrender.

"This is stupid." Darryl, who wanted to be more than a friend to Bonnie, muttered under his breath. He watched the others with a frown on his face.

"What's that, Darryl?" Bonnie looked up from her book.

He wished he hadn't said it aloud, but somebody had to. They'd been sitting here for better than an hour decked out in garlic and listening to Bonnie go on and on about were-wolves, warlocks, and the like. This was not what he'd had in mind for their first date. Okay, maybe Bonnie didn't think it was a date, but it could be, if he could get her out of these woods and somewhere less lame, like cruising Main Street where all his other buddies were tonight.

Darryl pulled the garlic necklace over his head, fashioned by Bonnie and Clara that afternoon. They'd used Mrs. Hill's knitting yarn and whole cloves bought from the Pig and Poke to make the silly things for their big night under the full moon. Randall, egging the situation on, had brought along a supply of miniature crosses with plastic Jesuses tacked to them. He swiped them from his father's church basement. Randall's dad was a Baptist minister—his son might be in for a good hide-tanning if the theft ever came to light.

Bonnie laid the flashlight in front of her crossed ankles. The campfire's flames illuminated enough of her three friends' faces to tell that two of them were having a good time; the other, decidedly, was not. "Stupid, huh? How else do you explain what's happening in Doe Springs? I've never seen a clearer-cut case of werewolfism in all my life."

"In all your life? And just how many werewolves have you come across in your wide travels from one end of the county to the other?"

"For your information, smarty pants, zero. But that's all going to change tonight. Look what I brought." Bonnie opened the backpack by her side and pulled out Doc Hill's 35 mm Canon. "We'll see who's laughing after I go into town with this."

"Oh brother." Darryl shook his head. "I haven't even seen a raccoon since we got here, and you think a werewolf is going to run by? What are we supposed to do if it does? 'Uh, excuse me, Mr. Werewolf, can you stop and pose for this picture for a minute? Maybe I can get a shot of you eating our friend Randall over here. Thanks.' "

"I brought it _in case_ we see something," Bonnie shot back. "We're having a little fun is all, Darryl. Don't get so serious about everything. Now, listen to this." The girl picked up the flashlight and turned to another section in the book, one that she had bookmarked with a fuzzy pink feather. "Ways to become a werewolf. Number one: Wear a magic girdle or belt made from the flesh of a human or a rabid wolf."

"That's gross." Clara wrinkled her nose and the girls giggled.

"Number two: Conjure up the dark forces and ask for the power of transformation. Ooh, that sounds like fun. Number three: Drink water collected in the pawprint of a wolf. Really gross."

"Really bogus." Darryl said the words in the midst of a fake cough behind his fist, but Bonnie slammed the book shut, breaking her pink feather in half.

"If I'd known you were going to be such a stick in the mud, Darryl, I wouldn't have let Randall bring you along."

That hurt a little bit. Darryl shut up, his necklace lying in a garlic puddle by his tennis shoes. It didn't last long. "Maybe we _should_ be serious. Real people have died."

The teenagers were all quiet at that. The fire crackled, and tiny sparks floated upward to drift away into the dark branches above them. The campground was deserted, closed down last summer when its owner disappeared. Speculation was he'd run off with a waitress from Pine Knot. The kids had left their car parked on one side of the entrance blockade and hiked down to the first available campsite a couple hundred feet away. Now they huddled in their private circle, a full moon overhead and a black forest wrapping around

them. The familiar night sounds of scuttling through underbrush and twigs breaking suddenly took on a different tone.
Something screeched overhead, and the group jumped.

"It's just an owl. I hear them in our barn all the time."
Randall attempted a laugh, but his voice cracked and hit a
preadolescent high note that emulated the screech.

"Yeah, we get a lot of those around our place too. Just an
owl," Darryl said.

Clara rubbed the edges of the cross Randall had given her.
"Truthfully, guys," she said finally, her soft words barely
making it over the wavering fire, "it can't be a regular wolf,
can it? They would have found it by now. Or shot it by now.
Or something."

"Maybe we should have brought some silver. Suddenly
this garlic don't feel so good. Does anybody know if garlic
works on werewolves? I thought that was for vampires,"
Randall said.

Bonnie leaned in closer to the fire, feeling her own garlic
pendulum swing against her chest. Flickering light cast
about her young skin, coloring it in reds and yellows. "I hear
them," she said.

"You hear what?" Clara's eyes darted around.

"In Dad's waiting room. The whisperings. The nervous
looks, like people are afraid to even sit unless their backs are
against the wall. Last week Margie Talbot brought their dog
Baxter in for a checkup. She doesn't look like the same
woman. Her hair's gone completely white. I heard her talking
to Daddy—she wanted to make sure Baxter wasn't tainted
somehow by what came upon their place. She said he'd been
acting real strange, and they wanted Daddy's opinion about
putting him down."

"Did Dr. Hill do it?" Clara asked.

"No. He told Margie to go home. But she said Baxter's no
good as a sheepdog anymore. Won't go anywhere near the
pasture, just wants to hang in the house all the time, and he
whines and cries all night long. She said they're going crazy
from it. I think they might sell out and move."

"Angus Shepherd put his farm up too. My dad listed it last
week," Darryl said. "Angus told him if it doesn't sell before

winter rolls back around, it can go to auction for all he cares. I think he left already and the farm's sitting there empty."

"I didn't think you could pry those old timers off their property with a stick," Clara said.

"They don't want to go, but with their livestock all getting killed, what else is there for them? Every one of Angus's cows got eat up. You talking about your dads . . . imagine what it's like at my house. Sunday school's been the most interesting I can ever remember." Randall was actually enjoying Sunday school for a change, but his parents were aggravated to know it took paranormal rumors to get the classroom buzzing. Talk of werewolves had accomplished what ninety-year-old blue-haired Sunday school teachers couldn't: The kids were picking up their Bibles with a passion.

"I knew I liked you for a reason, Randall. Always looking on the bright side." Clara took his hand, but her other clutched the miniature Jesus to the point her fingers were white-knuckled and the Savior was coming untacked.

Bonnie picked up the book again but didn't open it this time. "I think we've had enough of this tonight. I think we've had enough of all of this period." She stuffed the thick paperback into her backpack.

"Where did you get that book anyway?" Darryl asked.

"The library. Mrs. Township says I was lucky to find it. Even the police are checking out this stuff," Bonnie answered. "I saw Deputy Sanders walk out of there with a whole stack under his arm. I think the police know something they're not telling."

"There's sure something you're not telling," Clara giggled, the girly side of her overriding a creeping uneasiness.

"What are you talking about?"

"I remember that day we went out to the Talbots' and you started drooling when you saw Deputy Sanders. What were you doing at the town library—following him? The high school has a library and you don't go in there unless you're forced to for a class."

Darryl's frown was back. "What is he, about forty?"

"He's in his twenties and I'm not that far behind," Bonnie said. "When you think about it, we're almost the same age."

"You've got to be kidding me. That's who you've got the secret crush on? Deputy Dawg of Doe Springs? Get real!"

"I do not have a crush on him, but so what if I did? At least he's not a big jerk like some people I know."

"Or a brat, like some people I know."

"I'm not being a brat."

"You are too." Darryl was losing this girl by the second, but he didn't care. She'd never like him anyway, not when his competition was old men on the police force.

"You're just like your father, Darryl. A big, fat, pushy jerk." *Only better looking,* but she didn't say it.

"Don't ever call me like my father, Bonnie."

The arguing drowned out everything: the screeching owl, the campfire, the concern over murderous werewolves. Randall shook his hand loose from Clara's and scooted out of the firelight. He'd wait for the storm to clear in the peaceful shadows. Behind him, something clicked, as subtle as an acorn falling from a tree onto a rock. Then something hit the back of his neck. He slapped it with his hand and saw it was, indeed, an acorn.

Randall got up and walked a few feet away, leaving Clara to play mediator between the two lovebirds. It was inevitable: Two people who jabbed each other that much would be going steady before the week was out. But Randall would razz Darryl about that later. Right now he wanted to know who was throwing acorns at the campfire.

Randall walked farther away from the campfire and into the trees. The packed ground of the campsite was hard, but the forest was taking it back over. New underbrush was growing in, encroaching on the formerly manicured sites lining the side of the dirt path they'd hiked in on. Prickly and nearly waist high, it stopped Randall from going any farther. He stood on tiptoe and peered over the vines and taller bushes, but could only see nighttime on the other side. But he heard . . . what? A whoosh of air, then the wheezing of it drawing back in. Something was breathing on the other side of the brush.

The boy returned slowly to the heels of his feet. It was the only movement he could manage. He was trapped in place, his fear spiking him into the ground as securely as the rooted trees surrounding him. The wheezing rose and fell. Randall's own breath started to match cadence, then he realized that wasn't true at all—he'd stopped breathing altogether. The moist intake only a few feet away held a rattle, and a picture filled Randall's head. It was his grandfather standing on the other side of the bushes, come back from the grave. Worm-filled sockets stared at the boy and dirt-caked fingers held the oxygen mask over his rotted mouth. Emphysema had claimed the man, and nightmares claimed his grandson for months after his long-suffering death. But here it was again, and worse: the boy's nightmare in the flesh.

A branch snapped, and Randall was released. He turned, and with control that surprised even him, walked back to his friends.

Bonnie and Darryl were still at it, but he moved in between them. "Get up right now and start walking to the car."

"You know what, Randall? You can never invite any of your lame-brained friends to go anywhere with us ever again, I mean it."

"Bonnie, shut up and get your backpack. We've got to leave now."

Clara stood up and the others joined her. "What's wrong, Randall?"

"Nobody freak out, but there's something over there watching us."

"What? Where?" Clara whipped around toward the brush, but Randall grabbed her arm.

"I said don't freak out. If we move real slow, we'll be all right. It's just watching us right now."

"What did you see?" Darryl said.

"I didn't see anything. I heard it. It's in the brush, and it sounded big."

Darryl grunted. "Yeah, right."

"I'm not messing around, man. I heard what I heard. Let's go."

Darryl read his friend's face. It was the same expression he wore when he came to school and told his buddies that his father was pulling him off the baseball team because it took too much time away from his Bible studies. He wasn't kidding then, as incredulous as the team was to be losing their best player. And he wasn't kidding now.

"Yeah, Randall, you heard what you heard. Let's go."

Darryl bent to pick up Bonnie's flashlight for her, but she snatched it out from under his hand. "Here. You can carry the backpack." She thrust it at him. "Wait a minute." Bonnie fished around inside and pulled out the plastic Jesus. "Not a word."

"I wasn't going to say anything." Darryl was rethinking the garlic too. He wished he'd put the necklace back on, but now it lay charred on the edge of the fire. He glanced up the dirt path, trying to see the silhouette of his car. It seemed like miles, not yards, away.

"Shhh! Did you hear that?" Clara hung on Randall's arm, pulling him lopsided. His shirt was nearly off the shoulder she was holding it so tight.

The group strained to hear, but only the fire spoke to them.

"All you heard was the fire crackling or a squirrel running around," Darryl said. "Let's get out of here. We're going to be jumping at our own shadows if we keep this up. Nice job, Bonnie, for this brilliant idea. Remind me to never let you pick our dates again."

For once Bonnie had nothing to say. First of all, the boy wanted to take her out on another date. She didn't even know this was a date. Bonnie warmed at the idea, despite what a jerk he was. Secondly, Darryl was right—this had been a stupid idea. And Clara was right as well, because Bonnie heard something moving in the trees too. Twigs snapping, cracking, giving to something's weight. Whatever it was could be slowly moving through the brushy barrier, and they couldn't even see it. But Bonnie didn't want to shine the light that way. She didn't want to see it. It was nothing, as long as she couldn't see it.

The huddling group crab-walked toward the car, too nervous to totally turn their backs on the direction of their campfire. All around, the night seemed impossibly quiet. Even the owl had abandoned them.

A crash in the forest off to the right. The teenagers

grabbed each other and froze. They waited, but silence veiled the woods once more.

"What was that?" Clara trembled against Randall's chest, but he couldn't tell if it was really her or his own thudding heart shaking his body.

"Maybe a tree fell," Randall said.

"That's probably all it was. Keep going; we're almost to the car," Darryl ordered.

"Do you smell something? Does anybody else smell something?" Clara was talking too loud. Bonnie wondered if she should smack her. Isn't that what people did when somebody got hysterical? Knock sense back into them?

"Don't worry about it. Walk!" Darryl continued toward the vehicle, Clara, Bonnie, and Randall crowded around his back. Bonnie shone the flashlight around his side, its hazy light leading the way.

The old Volvo, a hand-me-down from Darryl's father, was not a cool high schooler's car. Darryl had pouted when he did not get the Mustang convertible of his dreams. Now he said a thank-you under his breath for his father's concern about safety over teenage image. The car was a tank, and that was a comfort. They could run down whatever lumbered out of the forest, if it came to that.

The metal of the door handle felt reassuring under Darryl's hand. He lifted the latch, but the door didn't budge.

"Give me the keys, Randall." Darryl reached out his hand.

"I gave them to you already."

Yes, he did. Darryl remembered Randall setting the keys by his knee at the fire, just before Bonnie pulled out that dumb book and scared the crap out of them all.

Darryl patted his jeans pockets, front and back. He checked his shirt pocket. He checked the jeans pockets again.

"What's wrong? Open the doors." Clara grabbed the latch on the passenger side and started yanking. It clacked like a relentless tap dancer but didn't open.

"Stop it, Clara. Be quiet," Bonnie hissed. The clacking stopped.

"Check your pockets, Randall," Darryl said.

"Dang it, Darryl, I gave you the keys."

"I know! But check again anyway."

Randall patted himself down. He shook his head.

"That's just great. This is like a bad movie. The monster's in the woods, and the four idiot teenagers have locked themselves out of the car. Now what?" Clara was close to tears. This was not how the evening was meant to go. They were supposed to tell a few ghost stories and roast marshmallows—a harmless thrill to brag to their friends about when school started up again: how they braved the Doe Spring woods on a full moon, just the four of them. But *nooooo*, that wasn't how this was going down at all. Come morning, she and Bonnie would *not* be friends.

Darryl looked toward the campfire. It had burned to embers. Its light no longer reached across the campsite. Whatever was watching them could be standing on the outskirts of the light right now, waiting. But the keys were most likely still there, right where his knee had rested in the dirt, touching Bonnie's knee. No wonder he didn't pay attention when Randall gave him the keys. "Everybody stay here. I'll go back over there and look for them."

"I'll help you," Bonnie said. "This is all my fault anyway."

"No, stay here," Clara said. "We can break the window and hot-wire the car. Let's just leave, please."

"I'm with Clara. Forget the keys," Randall said.

"Look, I don't know what you heard over there, Randall, but guys, come on, we're getting all worked up because of a library book and Talbot's newspaper article. Get a grip, there is nothing out here but us. I'm not breaking the window on my car. Dad would kill me. Plus not one of us can hot-wire anything. So would you all relax?" Darryl dropped the backpack and took Bonnie's flashlight, which she gave up willingly this time. He aimed the light in front of them. A soft hand slipped into his, and he suddenly felt very brave. Randall and Clara clasped hands as well and hung back as their friends walked away.

Bonnie and Darryl moved quicker this time. Caution would give way to panic soon if they didn't find those keys.

The woods felt closer than before, as if the night were swallowing them. Darryl swept the ground with the light as they walked to the fire, just in case he'd dropped the keys on the way back to the car.

"I'm sorry, Darryl," Bonnie said beside him.

"For what?"

"For bringing us to the campground."

"I drove the car. I could have gone the other way."

"Why didn't you?"

"Because you asked me to drive us out here."

The fire was almost completely out when they got to it. Weird shapes danced helter-skelter around its edges. Their own shadows stretched and contorted in front of them.

"I don't see them," Bonnie said. "We're going to have to dig around. Maybe they accidentally got kicked into the fire when we got up to leave."

Darryl nudged a blackened log aside. Final sparks flew out of the ashes. The fire went dead. "Here they are—I found them!" Bonnie said, jangling the keys in triumph.

And then they heard it.

Darryl jerked the flashlight up, into two wide reflective eyes on the edge of the campsite, unblinking, unmoving. Bonnie's gasp raked inward and spittle choked her own scream. She coughed before sputtering words: "It's a deer. A freakin' deer!"

The teenagers were hugging each other, not realizing they'd gone into a comic embrace before the "monster" revealed itself. Embarrassed, Bonnie was the first to let go. Darryl kept the light on the animal, but it continued to stand its ground.

"Something's not right, Bonnie. Why's it not running off?"

Darryl hunkered down and crept closer to the deer. Its breath whistled in and out, and the boy saw bubbles form and pop around its mouth and nostrils. They were red.

"Oh my God . . . " Darryl said.

"What is it, Darryl? What do you see?"

"Get out of here, Bonnie. Turn around and run."

"What is it? Tell me!"

Darryl didn't need to answer. The deer hobbled forward,

a pitiful bleating escaping through the red bubbles. It wob-
bled unnaturally, like a stiff, broken puppet on tangled strings.
Its hindquarters sloped awkwardly and Bonnie saw what Darryl did not want her to. The left hind leg was gone. A knobby
chunk of bone jutted below the animal's flank and sinewy
strings trailed out from it. The deer hopped forward again,
then collapsed.

Bonnie and Darryl stared at the animal with their mouths
open, just as the screams from the car began.

Chapter 29

Sheriff Hubbard's fingers played across the top of her steering
wheel like tapping piano keys. The clock stuck on the dashboard glowed a digital eleven-fifty-seven p.m., and it was hot
in the car. Gloria rolled all four windows down, but that allowed the mosquitoes in. She wasn't sure which was worse:
the muggy air or the bugs. Outside the Jeep the night was cool.
All mountain nights were cool, but officers' uniforms were not.

No matter. She was probably the most comfortable of the
lot right now. Tee was patrolling the north county, limping
along in the patched-together pickup with Zeke riding shotgun, while Deputy Sanders kept downtown's streets occu-
pied, sometimes in his cruiser, sometimes on foot. Deputy
Meeks volunteered for the most dangerous—or most boring—assignment of all. He was currently camped out near
the logger's cabin. How exactly, Gloria wasn't sure. For one
laughable moment, she saw her serious-minded deputy
straddling a tree limb with his walkie in one hand and binoc-
ulars trained on the cabin in the other.

The sheriff yawned and stepped out of the Jeep to de-
cramp. She herself was on the back side of Jack Lutsky's

property, and Ivy Cole's house was visible across a strip of newly harrowed field. The tree line picked up pretty quickly, though, affording the sheriff only a sliver of view. She could work with it. Making do was part of the job. The full moon helped—it was particularly clear tonight. Stars spiraled out from the moon into vivid constellations. The Blue Ridge swelled underneath them in what seemed like only an arm's length away. Gloria pictured herself standing atop the tallest rise and reaching up to touch the stellar sky. It was a wistful thought that almost made her smile: stargazing from a mountaintop by the light of the moon.

But Gloria was watching a different light, the one that had been on in Ivy Cole's upstairs since the sheriff parked on the edge of the field four hours ago. The trainer's back-yard was vacant; all the dogs must be inside. Ivy's van sat in the driveway.

"Sheriff Hubbard, Tee here; do you copy?" the radio in the Cherokee crackled. Gloria got back in the Jeep. Her legs and back didn't feel much better, but the chilled air had revived her.

"I'm here, Tee."

"All's quiet on this end. How are things in your part of the county?"

"Sound asleep since nine in most houses I've passed. Looks like the farmers truly are early to bed."

"Do you want me to work my way your direction?"

"Yes and no. Keep driving around. At least if folks see us out and about, it might provide some peace of mind. That is, if anybody's still up but us."

"What's your location?"

"I'm at Lutsky's."

"Near where Hughes was killed? You thinking something will happen down that way again?"

"You never know."

The radio cracked and whistled, then Tee's voice came through again. "How are you holding up, Glory?"

"Fine. Nothing that a good cup of coffee couldn't cure. How 'bout you?"

"I don't mean tonight. I mean overall."

"Lord, save me now. Tee Hubbard wants to talk about feelings. I'm on a stakeout, Tee. It's not the time or the place."

"You give me the same excuses no matter when or where we are. What happened between us—that was a long time ago, Glory. I worry you're too bent on tilling up old sour ground with this case. There are some things you need to leave buried. We can't catch them all."

"Is that your fancy roundabout way of saying I'm living in the past?"

"I don't do fancy or roundabout. I thought it was clear enough. Are you?"

"No, Tee, I'm not. And no, we can't catch them all; that's Police Training 101. But I will catch this one. I'll see you in the morning. Holler if anything interesting happens. And let's pray it doesn't. Over and out." Gloria clicked off the radio before Tee could respond. What she wanted to say to him was exactly what she knew she shouldn't. They'd failed a little girl, they'd failed a marriage, they'd failed as cops, bottom line. There was nothing else to say, not that he'd been tearing up any phone lines over the years to do any different. She certainly never talked about it with anyone else. People didn't want to see their sheriff as fallible or insecure or suffering from being a normal human being with all its imperfections and doubts. Sheriffs were pillars of strength, and women especially could not show a weak spot in the seams.

But damn him, he knew her too well, and tonight it made her angry. She didn't want this deepest part of herself delved into—the part that relived the hysterical parents and the remote campground and the bloody mountain laurels that had caught the splash of a child laid open and carted away. Every day it walked with her, rode with her, slept with her while her mind turned the pieces, trying to find one little clue, trying to discover that one piece of the puzzle, *the one thing she missed,* that could have brought a kidnapper *(killer)* to justice.

Gloria reached into her wallet and pulled out a wrinkled

photograph, not very old but faded from so much handling. A happy pigtailed child stared up from the picture. Annie.

Gloria put her head down on the steering wheel, and cried.

Chapter 30

The deer lay unmoving, its raspy breathing finally eased to nothingness, but the screams coming from the direction of the car were even more frightening. Darryl shone the flashlight back up the path, but the car and his friends were too far away. The light petered out into darkness.

"That was Clara screaming," Bonnie said. "Darryl, what's happening?" She looked into the boy's face but saw only her fearful reflection.

"Clara, Randall—what's going on?" Darryl called.

No answer.

"We have to go up there, Darryl." Bonnie took off her garlic necklace and put it around the boy's neck. Then she held Randall's stolen cross in front of her. They clasped hands again, armed with only the flashlight and plastic Jesus. The teenagers crept along, dreading every step, afraid of what lay behind them, afraid of what might leap out at them up ahead.

"I see them," Darryl said finally. "They're on top of the Volvo." Two thoughts hit him simultaneously: *Dad will have my hide if they dent the roof,* followed by *I can't believe I'm thinking of that at a time like this.*

"There's something up here!" Randall's voice was nearly unrecognizable. Darryl wasn't even sure it was Randall. It could have been Clara. The beam of the flashlight was still too short to reach them, but the moon spotlighted the car well enough. The teenagers were balled together in a knot. Clara held something in her fist, something he could barely make out—Jesus had been replaced by a marshmallow poker.

Randall was yelling again. "It crossed the path behind us and took off into the trees. It was huge, Darryl. We don't see it now. Hightail it, guys. Dammit, run!"

Darryl squeezed Bonnie's hand, and they did run. The panic Darryl had hoped to avoid nipped at their flying heels. Herky-jerky light zinged off leaves, old fire pits, an abandoned Dumpster, as the twosome fled the rest of the distance. The flashlight bounced to the ground, but they left it and ran even faster. The gap narrowed between them and the car; they were only twenty feet away.

The black figure leapt into the path of the teenagers. Behind it, Randall and Clara screamed again.

Darryl and Bonnie slid to a stop, paralyzed. They couldn't believe it, could barely grasp what they saw. Before them crouched the Devil of Doe Springs. Lips pulled back from impossibly long fangs. The nose wrinkled upward, snarling the entire muzzle of the black and silver face and exposing even more teeth. Slowly, unbelievably, the animal stood upright. It towered in front of them.

"This can't be real. This can't be real," Bonnie whimpered. A tear wound its way down her cheek.

The creature threw back its head and a wolfen cry, absent from the Blue Ridge for a century, filled up the mountains and the hollows. The sound was mournful, *mourning for us,* Bonnie thought. It vibrated through her body, through her skin, through her bones. Tones and inflections, like the language of a primitive music, seemed to speak to her. *How sad it is, look how lonely and pitiful and beautiful, oh that sound, like a wild lullaby . . .*

Bonnie's hand slid from Darryl's. It was too heavy to hold up any longer. All her limbs felt so heavy, the run to the car had been so long, the fear pushing them had been so unnecessary. Sleep. Sleep was the answer. Sleep to the tune of the howling moon. Bonnie's knees buckled and she fell to the ground.

"Bonnie, what is wrong with you? Get up."

"I don't know if I can," Bonnie said in a sighing voice.

The girl's sudden collapse snapped Darryl to action. He snatched the holy trinket she still clutched and stuck it in front of them. Darryl's voice shook as bad as his hands, but the words were clear enough. "This is the Lord Jesus Christ right here. So you go on and leave us alone." He thrust the cross forward for emphasis.

"It's no use, Darryl," Bonnie said. "Randall was right. All this stuff is for vampires. It's all no use. . . . "

The wolf didn't move. It watched as Darryl slowly reached down and grasped Bonnie's arm with his free hand, hauling her to her feet. Darryl took a step backward, pulling Bonnie with him. At the same motion, the wolf fell to all fours. It took a step toward the young couple, then the great hindquarters bunched, ready to spring.

A round of garlic rocketed from the Volvo and struck the wolf's back. "Over here, you big dumb werewolf!" Randall hadn't been all-star pitcher on his baseball team for nothing. The wolf's head whipped around. Randall wound up and let loose another clove, hitting the animal square between the orange eyes. They flashed like high beams at the impact, and the wolf roared.

"Go, Bonnie. Go!" Darryl spun around, nearly yanking Bonnie down. They stumbled together, then regained their feet and flew. The teeth Darryl expected in his back never came.

"Look out! Look out!" Clara shrieked. She pointed the metal skewer down the dirt road.

Something was running toward them. It galloped past the Volvo and headed straight for Darryl and Bonnie. The black wolf watched the other approach. It raised its nose to the wind, breathing in the new emerging scent. Then it lowered itself and braced all four legs, the hackles along its back raising a coarse black ridgeline from neck to tail.

The second wolf emerged into the moonlight. The light reflected off the silver-white fur, giving the animal opalescence, like mother-of-pearl. Dark lids ringed the orange of its eyes, and claws thicker than a bear's plowed through the earth to get to its kind. The silver wolf rose up on powerful

haunches and the black wolf rose upright once more to meet
it. Then the silver bounded into the black, knocking them
both to the dirt. Snarling and slashing, the two animals scrambled on the ground in a frenzied mass. Fangs flashed and
skin tore as they attacked each other. Blood flecked across
pristine white fur in a spray; a flap of skin hung from a
wound on the black wolf's shoulder.

The wolves broke apart and circled one another on all
fours. Orange eyes fixed on orange eyes, two of a kind but not
the same at all. The black wolf lunged first this time, but the
silver was ready. It sidestepped, then grabbed the other animal by the throat. The silver pinned it to the ground, the arteries of the other's neck thumping against its tongue. The
black paddled its feet against the stronger adversary. A whine
of submission escaped past the four-inch canines holding it
down. The black's ears flattened against its skull, and its tail
wound between its legs to tuck against its belly.

The silver-white wolf squeezed, feeling blood seeping
into its mouth. It was bitter, the taste of old blood. Not from
this wolf, relatively new to the ancient fold, but from the ancestors' blood that coursed through its violent veins.

The silver's jaws went slack and it backed away. The black
wolf scrambled to its feet. Blood poured from the tear in its
shoulder and from the punctures in its neck. Saliva and dirt
matted the shiny coat across the broad back. It looked at the
silver-white wolf one last time, then bounded into the forest.

The silver-white wolf shook itself, flinging blood droplets
from a gash in its flank. Bonnie and Darryl stared down at
the animal from the top of a not-nearly-tall-enough tree. The
wolf walked to the base of the trunk and sniffed. It looked up
at the teenagers, satisfied. The girl was safe, unharmed. The
wolf sniffed the air once more—the danger had passed. The
black was gone. For now.

The white wolf bounded into the dark of the forest and
then, she too, was gone.

At five-fifty-three a.m., a small ghostly figure limped out of
the woods. Her white-blond hair glowed like the moon itself,

but her faltering movements indicated something was very wrong.

Aufhocker nosed open the back door and met his mistress at the edge of the fence. She leaned heavily on the shepherd as she staggered up the steps into the house.

Sheriff Hubbard's had not been the only eyes on Ivy Cole's house this night. An old Ford pickup was parked hidden down the road from the sheriff's car. Tee was there to watch over Glory as much as anything else. She was a good cop and a strong woman, but Tee couldn't let go of his old-fashioned notion of looking after the ones he loved. When her car pulled away at five-forty-five a.m., he decided to stick out the vigil long enough to see her almost back to the station. God forbid Glory accidentally discover him in her neck of the woods when he was supposed to be patrolling elsewhere. And now he was glad he stuck around. Peculiar, seeing the little lady limp out of the woods, greeted by a big black dog. Mighty peculiar.

And parked just down the road from the pickup, pulled off behind a thorny tangle of wild blackberry, sat a deputy in his patrol car. He watched the woman come out of the woods and go into her house.

"You saw too, didn't you, Tee?" the deputy said to himself. This could be bad. This could be very bad, indeed. Tee and the ugly dog would have to go.

Chapter 31

A spattering of rain hit Gloria's window, sliding down in slow silver veins like tears against the glass. The sheriff was at her desk again, holding an empty coffee cup of which she'd sadly had no time to fill. She'd left Lutsky's property when the sun promised to take the moon's seat in the sky, but a thunderhead had rolled up instead. The rain and eight ranting parents, led by four raving teenagers, had greeted her the minute she walked through the station doors. Delores had thrown up both hands in relief when Gloria strode in, then, in an act of sublime cowardice, waved the throng straight to Gloria's office before she'd had one brief moment to fortify herself with the brown liquid she craved. She clung to her cup now, as if it would magically fill and make all this ruckus go away. A dozen people were talking at once, and the chatter blended into a drone of complete nonsense.

"Everyone must calm down," Gloria said. The din rolled over her, and she banged her coffee mug on the desk. *"Quiet!"*

The curtain fell on the noise abruptly, and the parents looked around to see who would speak first. Darryl's father, Peter Burnett, opened his mouth, but Betty Hill beat him to it.

"We thought they were at the movies. They could have all been killed!" Bonnie's mother wrung her hands like old dishrags. Doc Hill placed an arm around his wife; the other hand rested on his daughter's shoulder.

"We know this is all very difficult to believe, Sheriff," Doc Hill said, "but our Bonnie wouldn't lie about something like this. There were wolves at Daddy Badger's Campground—two of them—and they tried to attack our children."

"Werewolves, Daddy, not wolves. They were gigantic,

and they walked on their hind legs." Bonnie looked up at her father, wide brown eyes begging him to believe her. Doc patted her shoulder.

Mr. Burnett could hold back no longer. He nudged around Doc to the front of Gloria's desk.

"Look, I don't know what they saw. Doc, with all due respect, these are good kids, each and every one, and I know they wouldn't intentionally lie. But Darryl tells me they were reading this when the alleged sighting occurred." Peter Burnett, who was a part-time tax attorney when he wasn't selling houses, tossed Bonnie's library book on the table. A long-snouted, heavily fanged Hollywood wolfman snarled from the cover. "Here's the evidence."

"Evidence of what, Peter, that our children are literate?" Betty snapped. Randall's and Clara's folks were quiet, but Gloria saw the minister mouth "poppycock" and point to the Hills.

Darryl turned an angry face to his father. "We didn't imagine this, Dad. Those things were real. They were only a few feet away from us."

"And yet, you managed to escape. Two . . . werewolves? . . . were feet away from you, yet here you sit."

"Don't sound so disappointed, Dad."

Burnett threw up his hands. "I'm just saying I think some imaginations got away last night. The full moon, this book. And how can you explain this?" He held up Doc's Canon. "Not a single photograph from any of you."

Doc snatched his camera. "I doubt there's much time to practice photography when you're running for your life. Why are you here, Peter, if you don't believe any of it?"

"I'm trying to provide a rational voice. They saw something, sure. But it was probably a couple of lost dogs gave them a scare."

"How do you explain the deer?" Clara's mother piped up.

"An injured deer does not mean we have werewolves in Daddy Badger's Campground." Reverend Leowald entered the conversation, finally deciding on his stand.

"It saved us," Bonnie said.

Everyone turned to Bonnie.

"That's how we survived," she continued. "The black

wolf would have killed us all. But then, the white one—it attacked the first and we were able to get away."

"Like two wolves fighting over a territory?" Gloria asked.

Bonnie shook her head no. "I don't know how I know, but the second wolf came to save us. The way it looked at me after it scared the black wolf away . . . I sense it somehow. The white one never meant to hurt us."

"Oh, brother. The white knight scared the black knight away, good versus evil. Classic." Peter Burnett walked to the farthest corner of the office and crossed his arms. Mrs. Burnett stood beside him, looking like she had something, anything, better to do.

Gloria pressed her intercom. "Deputy Sanders, Deputy Meeks, come in here, please."

To the parents she said, "With your permission, I'd like to take these kids back out to the campground."

Sanders crowded into the office and stood elbow to elbow with the others. "Yes, Sheriff?"

"We're taking a ride down to Daddy Badger's. There's been a significant wolf sighting last night. Excuse me— wolves."

"Wolves in the campground? Were you kids there? That campground's closed."

Gloria eyed the teens. "Yes it is, but we'll talk about trespassing later. Where's Meeks?"

Sanders walked to the sheriff's desk. "Um, he called in sick, Sheriff. Thinks he caught something nasty while hanging out in the woods last night."

Gloria sighed. "Well, is Tee in yet?"

"No."

Gloria drummed on the edge of her coffee mug for a moment.

This is exactly the time she needed Zeke. *Dammit, Tee.*

"All right. We'll head to the campground and I'll call Tee to meet us there."

The sheriff drove toward the barricade at the entrance to Daddy Badger's Campground. High weeds tickled the underside of her vehicle on the unkempt dirt road, and she watched the rearview to make sure nobody got stuck. Burnett's Mercedes (the only Mercedes in Doe Springs) might have a hard time out here, but no such luck. It tagged doggedly behind Sanders's car with hardly any trouble at all.

Gloria noted the fresh tire tracks from the kids' vehicle in the mud, but by the zigzagging ruts in the ground, she could tell they were not the only visitors to frequent the deserted camp. *A campground—another mountain campground—deserted, children attacked in the night, screaming parents . . .*

A rivulet of sweat dripped from under the sheriff's hat and across the ridge of her brow. She blinked it away, annoyed, but then a sudden tightness beneath her breastbone stole her breath. She gasped for air but her lungs felt too shrunken to draw the oxygen in. Dizziness drove the car to the shoulder. She paused there, holding her chest. *Please, God, don't give me a heart attack yet, wait till my job is done.* Gloria forced her breathing into a slow and even rhythm. The constriction began to ease and the blood rushing through her ears was replaced by a dull rapping. It was not in her head after all. A knuckle tapped her window.

"You all right, Sheriff? I almost rear-ended you." Sanders's face filled up the glass as he peered in at her.

"I'm fine. I'm just in bad need of some caffeine. Give me a minute." The spell was over with so quick, she wondered if she'd imagined it. It was stress, sure as shootin'. The similarities between her past and present had caught up with her in one climactic moment. But she could talk parallel universes and unfair coincidences with Tee later. (The physical episode, she'd choose not to mention.) The thought pushed her to try the tracker one more time. She'd already called twice on the way over. Still no answer. Gloria made a mental note to ride by his house on the way back. A pang of guilt hit her as hard as the panic attack: *I should have let him stay with me.* The sheriff wearily pushed the thought away. The parents were already out of their cars and on the move. Exhausted as she was, she had to focus on the task at hand. The present, not the past, as Tee might say. Although sometimes answers could be found by looking over one's shoulder.

She'd explore that idea more with him later too. *Where the hell was he today?*

Gloria stepped from the Cherokee and joined Sanders. The rain had stopped but a cheerless drizzle weighted clothing on skin. Fog was rolling in with it, and no doubt there would be traffic calls from tourists ditched alongside the Blue Ridge Parkway before too long. Hopefully, she would be finished up here before then, now that she was one deputy, detective, and dog short.

Darryl walked up to the officers, his drawn, pallid face disappearing into the gray-washed weather. "This way," he said.

The ashes of the previous night lay in damp clumps in the fire pit. Tennis shoe prints ran all around it and led up and down to the dirt road behind them. Darryl was joined by his three friends, all taking center stage to the audience of adults. Randall pointed to the brushy wall at the rear of the campsite. Honeysuckle creepers made up most of the viney web, but they were broken and crushed where something had plowed through the middle of them. "That's where I heard the breathing," Randall said. Bonnie added: "And it must have been the deer. We saw it right there," she waved her hand from honeysuckle to fire edge, "and then it fell right here."

Everyone looked to the spot where supposedly a mangled deer faltered and died.

"Not a speck of blood." Peter Burnett leaned over the ground to get a better look. "Not one speck."

"Please stand back, sir." Sanders pulled the man away, his fingers sinking slightly into the meaty shoulder. Burnett shrugged the deputy's hand off and moved out of his reach.

"Over here's about where we were when the first were-wolf came out of the woods." Darryl stood halfway back up to the road. "My car was parked where the sheriff's is."

"And we were on top of it. We could see everything," Clara said.

"Pretty dark out here, though, with your fire out?" Gloria said. Sanders already had his notebook in hand and was scribbling away. The pen paused a moment, waiting for Clara's answer. Randall jumped in: "It was dark," he said, "but the moon was on us. A lot of light came into the clearing. In the trees, that's where we couldn't see. The werewolf could have been watching us for a long time and we wouldn't have known. The second werewolf came down the road from the other direction, not the way we came in."

Gloria took her deputy's notebook and pen. She scribbled her own note in handwriting Sanders could barely read: *Daddy Badger's adjoins power company and Lutsky property???—double-check map in office.* The sheriff shoved the paper back in his hands and turned to Darryl again.

"The wolves were how far away from you?" the sheriff asked.

"The black wolf was right in front of us," Bonnie said, joining Darryl. "We could almost touch it."

Gloria walked to the teenagers, and the knot of parents followed. Sanders stayed between the sheriff and the group. The sheriff squatted and examined the ground. "You ran to that tree over there, yes?" More shoe prints marking wide strides in the rain-damp earth told the obvious, but she had to ask anyway.

"Yeah, that's the one," Darryl said.

Sanders knelt by the sheriff. They looked at one another, then slowly stood. The deputy closed his notebook and put it in his pocket. Gloria rubbed the black circles under her eyes, and sighed.

The parents gathered around, now that the deputy blockade had moved.

"You see we're telling the truth now, right?" Darryl said. "You see our tracks all over the place, exactly as we said it. The deer is gone, sure, but one of the wolves must have dragged it off after we left."

Gloria nodded. "Well, son, here's the problem, I see *your* tracks—"

"That proves it then!" Randall and Clara said in unison.

"That doesn't prove anything!" Burnett's high-strung voice practically squeaked. "Where are the deer tracks? Where are the wolf tracks? This place is trampled like a herd of Nike'd buffalo ran over it, but there are no animal prints anywhere!"

"Mr. Burnett, if you don't relax, my deputy is going to escort you to your vehicle," Gloria said. Sanders loomed over the chubby little man to emphasize the sheriff's point.

"The wolf tracks? They should be all over the place. There should be a set following us to the tree." Darryl ran up and down the path, then over to the hemlock. Tennis shoes tore up the moss at its trunk, but that was all. The light rain had barely stirred the teenagers' footprints, yet the animal tracks seemed to have been washed completely away.

"I don't get it. Those things would have weighed five times what I do. Their pawprints should be clearer than anybody's." Darryl continued to circle the tree, and the other teenagers joined him. They bent double, searching the ground for anything that would back up their story.

Peter Burnett snorted loudly and walked to the car, his wife striding behind him. The other parents looked uncertain; then Reverend Leowald shook his head and walked after the Burnetts. Mrs. Leowald and Clara's parents took up the path too.

Doc Hill watched them go. "Good riddance," he said. "What do you make of it, Sheriff? It'd gall me something awful to think Burnett could be right."

"Could he be? Overactive imaginations got the best of the kids?"

Doc thought a minute. "No. Sheriff, I know my daughter. She saw something last night and it shook her up pretty bad. Something happened here, whether we're able to explain it or not."

Gloria put her hand lightly on the good vet's arm. "I admire your faith in Bonnie, Doc. Let's get out of the rain."

At the top of the road, Peter Burnett held the Mercedes door open for his son. Darryl climbed into the backseat and stared straight ahead. Burnett looked down the line of cars to the sheriff's, where she had one leg already in the door. "Thanks for the wasted morning, Sheriff Hubbard," he called. "Hope you have a good rest of the day."

Chapter 32

While Sheriff Hubbard turned her car toward Musket Dobbins's rental house, Deputy Sanders headed the opposite direction. In fifteen minutes (sooner, had the thick fog not rolled in) the patrol car parked in front of the now-familiar cottage. Rex stood sentinel in the front yard, all fifteen inches of him at attention with his snout pushed through the picket fence and his tail straight up in the air.

Melvin approached the gate, barely noticing the little dog waiting to attack his shin. Rex's furry bottom dropped low like a cat's and his front paws patted a pink tea rose flat as he tensed for the spring any second now. Chocolate-drop eyes followed Melvin's hand to the gate latch.

The deputy stepped onto the first cobblestone when something brushed his pant leg, followed by a tug and a rip. "Hey!" Melvin jumped back, but his assailant remained attached.

"Rex! For heaven's sake." Ivy limped onto the front porch. Rex released the deputy's uniform and pranced to his mistress, a swatch of brown hanging from his teeth. Ivy grabbed the torn fabric and shooed the terrier into the house. Melvin saw the dog's front paws appear as he jumped up to watch them through the screen door.

"Melvin, I don't know what to say. I am so sorry about that." Ivy was humored and horrified at the same time. Her dog had attacked an officer of the law right here in the front yard and was obviously very proud of himself to have done so. Ivy aimed an embarrassed smile and a shrug Melvin's way. "My dogs have been jumpy lately. I can sew that up for you real quick, if you've got a minute." Ivy handed the deputy the material. He held the patch over the new hole in his pants, then stuffed the fabric in his pocket.

"That's either a new ploy to keep me around longer or to get yourself arrested. Which way were you playing it?" he said.

"I don't look good in stripes—take that how you will. Why didn't you tell me you were coming? I'd have made us some lunch. Sit a spell to wait out the fog?"

Ivy winced as she lowered herself onto the porch swing and patted the seat beside her. Melvin didn't join her, choosing instead to stand. He seemed all business today, but the black band of sock and white leg shining through his pant leg diminished the intimidating stance.

"You look terrible," Melvin said.

Ivy laughed. "All roses and compliments to begin with, but give a man what he wants and look what happens."

Melvin didn't even break a smile. "Seriously, what's wrong with you? You're sitting stiff as a sun-dried shirt and I saw you limping."

"That's what happens when you get my age." Ivy waited for the deputy's snappy comeback, but he refused to play. "Oh, all right. I think I pulled my lower back and hip working with a dog yesterday. Unruly St. Bernard almost jerked me off my feet."

"You need to be more careful, Ivy."

The deputy's tone sobered her. "Maybe a better question, Melvin, is what's wrong with you? You're all out of sorts about something."

"A bunch of kids say they came face-to-face with the Devil of Doe Springs last night, only they claim there are two of the things. It happened at Daddy Badger's."

Ivy was all wide-eyed concern. "Was anybody hurt?"

"No. Amazingly enough, they walked away without a scratch."

"Sounds like somebody's got a big imagination then. Besides, two of them? I thought there was only one."

"Seems we've got Devils coming out of the woodwork now, all colors and sizes. The kids may have been confused about what they saw, or lying, but I don't much think so. Point is, the campground."

"What about it?"

"It's near where we picnicked."

"Oh, I get it. Which is near here. It's a small community, Deputy. Everything is near everything else. Daddy Badger's is also near town, near the river, near the Parkway, near you. . . ."

Melvin leaned over Ivy. She hoped to feel his lips on the top of her head, but only his breath caressed her. He abruptly pulled away.

"Just be careful," he said.

When the deputy was gone, Rex nosed the screen door open and nuzzled Ivy's leg. The dog looked after the patrol car disappearing over the hill. Ivy scratched the mutt's head.

"Yes, I agree, Rex. That was strange." The deputy's coldness masked in concern chilled her worse than the fog. So unlike their last day together. What had changed? Ivy suddenly wished she had asked for *Lykanthrop*'s return, if nothing other than to feel the comfort of having the book close to her again.

Ivy watched the last glimpse of the patrol car's red taillights sink out of sight, unmindful the orange behind her green eyes blazed.

Dear Journal,

His blood was in me. I took it, tasted it, relished it. But it told me his story plain enough, and now I know. He is the Werewolf Absolute. Not of a pure Wolf lineage like mine, whose ancestors ran in packs and loved one another and taught mankind the ways of nature. Rather, his heritage is more human, more vicious and hostile and irrational in its desire to kill. There is no purpose to it but his own gain. While my creators finally shied from man, retreating farther into the wilderness to escape, his pursued them for nothing better than the silk of their pelts and the quest to quell fear. But those men had nothing to fear. Then.

In my heart, I am wolf forced to wear the human. He is human forced into the guise of the wolf. It is what breeds the most dangerous wolves—this irony of becoming part of what one hates most.

I pitied him.

I cleaned up his mess and removed all of his sloppy evidences. I let him go, and have endangered my extended pack in doing so. Bonnie is safe for now, but what of the others I love?

Chapter 33

The trailer park was quiet in the fog. Aluminum homes lined up like shotgun houses along the cracked pavement of the drive. The blacktop finally petered out, crumbling at the end of the trailer park entrance and giving way to gravel. Tee's rental house, a single-wide tottering on cinder block supports, was at the very end of this road. Slightly warped in the middle, the twenty-year-old brown-and-white Oakwood seemed to be frowning at whomever approached it.

There were not many rentals in Doe Springs, but the sheriff was ashamed of herself. Terence Hubbard came all the way from Montana to help her and this was the best she could do. She was not passive aggressive by nature, but Tee must have surely seen this as a slight. *No whining,* she could hear him saying to recruits in that low-toned "you better listen to me" way of his. He lived by his own words and she'd never hear a complaint out of him, but she didn't need to. She would fix this. As soon as Gloria found her ex-husband, he was coming home with her. At least for a little while.

Musket's Ford was parked in the yard, and Gloria pulled up beside it. Tee was home. A bad feeling wiggled around in her stomach. He would have called in or answered his phone if something were not wrong. Gloria touched her chest, the tightness from this morning gone but the phantom pain of memory still lingering. She had heard of loved ones feeling other loved ones' pain even when miles and miles apart. Tee was only in his forties, but men that young were having heart attacks every day.

Gloria knocked on the door. Surprisingly, it swung open. "Tee? Zeke? Anybody home?" Gloria stood in the doorway not sure what to do. The truck was here, the door was unlocked, but no sign of Zeke, who should have been all over her by now.

The living room, barely fourteen feet across, was threadbare but tidy, exceptionally so. Tee's military past could never escape him. Everything had its place and was in it. It had been a bone of contention between them as a married couple: The sheriff liked comfortable clutter.

Gloria walked through the living room and down the cramped hallway. Two closed doors lay to the left and another at the end of the hall facing her. She braced herself outside the first door, hoping not to see the man she had once loved *(always loved)* sprawled across a bed, his hand bent in a claw clutching at his chest·and Zeke moping by his side. Gloria turned the knob. It *was* Tee's bedroom, unmistakable with its tautly drawn coverlet worthy of a good quarter bounce, but it was empty. Gloria let out a sigh and moved to the second door. A spare bedroom. She opened the last door to what could only be the bath.

Something wasn't right. Gloria walked to the bathroom counter and ran her hand over the yellowing, chipped laminate. The countertop was bare. She opened the cabinets underneath. A lone roll of toilet paper bounced onto the linoleum. Nothing else lay under the sink but pipes.

Gloria went back to Tee's bedroom and opened the closet. Wire hangers rattled as she pushed them to the side. Tee's clothes were gone.

"Sheriff Hubbard! That you?" someone called. Gloria emerged to see the landlord, Musket Dobbins, standing in the living room with an envelope in one hand and a pork-and-beans can in the other. Musket spit a wad of tobacco into the tin cup as Gloria approached. "I do believe he left this old house in better shape than when he found it, Sheriff."

"Musket, what's going on? Where is Tee?"

A brown string of tobacco juice meandered down Musket's chin. He wiped it on his shirt sleeve before answering. "Well now, I don't rightly know where Mr. Hubbard might be this minute. He checked out."

"Checked out? When?"

"This morning sometime, I reckon. Left his keys in my mailbox, for the truck too. I thought you might be here looking for your deposit." Musket held out the envelope.

Gloria took it and looked inside. It was fifty dollars. "There was no note with the keys?"

"Nope."

"Did you see Mr. Hubbard come in last night? Zeke would have been with him."

"Zeke? That's a fine dog. Quiet and housebroke. Didn't have no trouble with that dog in here."

"But did you see them last night?"

Musket scratched the thinning hair on his head. "Naw, can't say I did see 'em, but now truthfully, Sheriff, can't say that I didn't. People come and go as they please around here and long's they ain't troublemakers, I don't much pay 'em any mind."

Gloria brushed past Musket to her car. He followed her outside. "How's the werewolf hunt coming, Sheriff?"

"Oh for Christ's sake." Gloria climbed into her Jeep.

"You tell Mr. Hubbard to come on back any time he like, Sheriff. And that old hound dog too!"

Musket waved at the sheriff's car, fading away as if eaten up by the thickening fog.

Chapter 34

Deputy Sanders threw his hat on the couch and went straight to the bedroom to change pants. He only had one other pair for his uniform. Being attacked by a terrier after the curious morning at Daddy Badger's was proof positive that this was cranking up to be a *lovely* day. He needed to beat it back to the station, but on top of everything else, his insides churned in an unfriendly fashion. Meeks crossed his mind briefly, and the sheriff wasn't looking too good either. Seeing her slumped over the steering wheel had scared him more than he let on. And then there was Ivy, crippled. They were all going to the dogs.

I can't get sick. Not now. I need a drink.

A new pair of pants and an empty milk carton later, Melvin's stomach settled. He reseated his cap, then noticed the blinking light on the answering machine. Melvin pressed play.

"Hello . . . er . . . Deputy Sanders? This is Professor Toomey in Asheville. I've got your book translated. I don't want to get into details over the phone, but to say the book is unusual is an understatement. I'll be in my shop all day tomorrow if you want to drop in. Good-bye."

Melvin stared at the machine. "It's about time." Toomey'd had the book well beyond their agreed upon deadline. The deputy was thankful Ivy had never asked for it. Once they were officially dating, she seemed to have forgotten he'd borrowed one of her most valuable possessions.

But a pickup tomorrow was iffy. Melvin would be stuck in Doe Springs if Meeks was still out. Plus, he had an appointment to take care of: one with the Widow Pritchard. It was to be a busy next few days, working shorthanded till Meeks came back, plus juggling the investigation with the sheriff and gathering information for his own on the side. A visit to evaluate how Meeks was making out seemed in order. Melvin figured he'd be neighborly and pick up some cough drops for his fellow lawman on the way over, and some Pepto-Bismol for himself.

Melvin stood outside the modest brick ranch with the light rain pelting his head. The brim of his hat formed a gutter that spilled droplets in an annoying pit-pat, pit-pat onto his shoulders. If the sun ever beat through the clouds, a muggy afternoon would be in order; but that was preferable to a day floundering blindly about in the mist. Melvin hated going to Meeks's house under normal circumstances, and under dreary circumstances, it was worse. The house was not out of the way (only seven miles as the crow flies) nor was it unkempt. The bottom line was the other deputy's style of decorating—it gave Melvin the creeps. He wouldn't stay long if he could help it.

Melvin rang the doorbell a second time, then regretted it. Meeks was probably in bed and might not appreciate being flushed out of it. Melvin turned to leave when he heard the deadbolt turn over.

Deputy Jonathan Meeks opened the door, a bathrobe tied tightly at his waist and a hot towel wrapped around his neck. His normally tanned skin had an off-color sheen to it, like old mustard.

"You look like hell," Melvin said. He held out the cough drops.

"Thanks," Meeks managed to croak. He clutched the towel tighter around his throat. "What are you doing here?"

"I came by to check on you, but you look as bad as you sounded on the phone. What did the doctor say?"

"Something akin to the flu with a dose of laryngitis thrown in. I'd let you inside, but it's probably not a good idea."

"Yeah. Sheriff doesn't need us both out." Melvin had hoped Meeks suffered from a twenty-four-hour bug, but this looked like something of a long haul.

"I might be back in tomorrow or after," Meeks said.

"I seriously doubt that. Don't worry about it—take the time you need. You did miss some excitement this morning, though." Melvin gave Meeks the short version.

"Wouldn't you know it? My one day out and something interesting happens. What did the sheriff think of it? Better yet, what did our celebrity cowboy think?"

"Dunno. Tee didn't show up. He might've been on to something else this morning. Sheriff's gone to find him."

Melvin thought he saw a shift in the set of Meeks's mouth. The man looked almost happy for a moment. "I bet that got the sheriff all bent out of shape." He sounded hopeful. "Anyway, those kids will think twice before breaking the law again. Miserable little trespassers. They shouldn't have been let out of the house last night to begin with. Parents should know better, especially Doc."

"Yeah, go figure." Melvin squinted up at the invisible sky, opaque behind its curtain of gray. It was awkward, standing in the soggy yard and talking to Meeks in his bathrobe. But at least he didn't have to go inside and sit with the dead. "So you didn't see anything at the cabin last night?"

Meeks shook his head, then quickly adjusted the towel. "Nothing up there but me and the mosquitoes. And a virus, apparently."

"Let me know if you need anything. I can cook a mean chicken soup."

"I got it covered." Meeks held up a take-out flyer from Etta's. Etta's didn't deliver, but Lynette didn't mind running out a sandwich every now and then. "I was just getting ready to order, but I doubt I can keep anything down anyway, made to order by Etta or otherwise."

"I'll let you get back to it. I'll tell the sheriff you're still alive." Melvin slapped the ill man on the shoulder before turning away.

Meeks shut the door softly behind him. His six-foot frame doubled over, the pain from Sanders's innocent clap nearly bringing tears to his eyes. The towel toppled to the floor;

Meeks let the cough drops and take-out flyer fall after it. Purple stripes ringed his exposed neck, and a row of blood-clotted indentions were only now starting to close. His whole neck throbbed—even the pressure of the terry cloth had been excruciating.

Meeks straightened and braced against the wall as a new round of cramps bunched his muscular back into a rigid swell of knots. He gritted his teeth until the cramping loosened enough for him to move. As he pushed off the wall, he felt the weight of eyes upon him. Across the room, the buffalo head above the fireplace was leering at his aching torso.

"Go ahead. Laugh it up." Meeks took a deep breath, gathering his strength. From all around the living room, judgmental eyes fixed on the deputy. They were his menagerie accumulated when he was merely human. A stuffed fox climbed a log by the recliner. A rare white bobcat clawed the air by an end table. Elk, deer, and wild boar heads glared from their crowded position on the wall above the television, and smaller furry bodies crouched nose-to-tail down the hall. Stuffed, lifeless animals crept and clawed and hung everywhere. They were Meeks's constant companions. He'd employed rifles, shotguns, and even bows and arrows on his hunting trips across the U.S. to acquire them. But nothing compared to the last kill he made, before the gift was bestowed upon him those short years ago and a manmade weapon was no longer necessary. His masterpiece, in the place of honor by the bed. Meeks shuffled that way.

Meeks's bedroom was simple and small. Too small. When he'd moved into the house shortly after Gloria Hubbard took him on, the first task in order was knocking out the wall between the house's only two bedrooms. He needed space, lots of it, for his most prized souvenirs. There were seven of them, each in different poses. The taxidermist had followed Meeks's instructions to the letter: Make them look as ferocious as you can. Hackles raised and lips eternally snarling, the pack of gray wolves circled Meeks's bed.

In reality, when he'd gone on the hunting trip, there had been nothing ferocious about the animals as they fled beneath the shadow of the helicopter. Exhausted, the wolves finally slowed, their efforts to escape quickly worn down by the deep snow and the relentless pursuit of the machine. Meeks picked them off easily with his Winchester as the pilot guided the hunter as close to the ground as he dared. One after the other, the wolves' magnificent coats were splattered with red as their bodies slid to a halt in the crystallized landscape. When the helicopter landed, the entire pack was dead.

Meeks had crunched through the snow and knelt by the alpha female. Ninety pounds, lean and shaggy, Meeks was surprised that life still beat in her desperate heart. She looked at him, and Jonathan Meeks felt in that instance there was awareness in the amber eyes. The moment became stilled. Gently whirling snow and wind and the beat of slowing chopper blades faded into the silence of the tundra, as Meeks felt for the first time a connection of one being on this earth with another. The rush of a thousand years passed through him as he recognized the depth of knowledge within the dimming wolf. She was the wilderness, the heart of wild. She had been man's greatest friend, and his most feared enemy. The mountains and the rivers and the paths of the forest were the rhythm of her heartbeat, and the freedom of the pack, her very breath.

Within that moment, Jonathan Meeks did not feel the communal call of mankind and its superficial superiority. He felt instead a realization of his place in the universe, a speck in time tied to life and death and the miracle of survival. *She* was the survivor, the observer, the teacher, the warrior. And it made him feel small.

The wolf's paw softly paddled the ground, grazing his boot, and her tail thudded once against the snow. Over the crest of the ridge, Meeks heard a short howling. Three wobbly heads poked above the ridge line, pups of barely four weeks old. The female howled in return, her body shuddering as it struggled to overcome the wound that had torn away her side. Meeks shouldered his rifle and put the life out of her eyes forever. Then he forged over the hill. Three more shots cracked the silence across the Alaskan landscape.

The puppies were not in the bedroom with the rest of the pack. Small and scraggly, Meeks saw no point in spending money on them. Over the years he'd come to think maybe he'd wasted his money on all of them. In researching his new power, Meeks discovered he shared little with the wolves he thought he might emulate. Their behavior was not his, their ways were not his. He found them to be, perhaps, too civilized, too emotional, too weak in that their desire to hunt was based on subsistence rather than an innate thirst for blood like he had once believed.

In disgust, he turned away from the wolf and embraced werewolf lore. There he found kindred spirits. The guilt for desiring murder was absolved. The thought of taking human life was now becoming no different than squelching out the animal vermin he'd hunted before. But it was, decidedly, more of a challenge. There had been plenty of misses in his hunts this past year, and he'd returned to animals for the thrill of the sport and, simply, to feed his stomach.

Last night, the acquisition of four young trophies, as sure a bet as picking off Angus's slow-witted cattle, was botched again. His most precious prize of all was lonely in her resting place underneath the bed. At night he would remove her skull from its somber burlap grave and place it beside him on the pillow. It should be dangerous to have her here, but the sheriff and Sanders still stumbled about in the dark, when the answer had been given to them time and again. He could stash a dozen bone-filled sacks about this house and never worry. The cabin had been another mistake. He never should have strayed from home.

Meeks slipped off the robe and settled naked onto the edge of the bed. The bands of muscle in his tight stomach and broad chest rose and fell with each deep breath as he settled in for what could be mere hours or even days—there was no way to know for sure how long the process would take. He rested his hand on the head of the alpha female for comfort, the wisdom in her eyes now dumbed by glass stones. She could watch as he watched, for mounted on the wall across from Meeks was a gilded mirror. He'd purchased the gaudy, bulky thing at an auction for one entire month's pay. The mirror had seen the transformation time and again, but to-day's act was a first. Meeks studied his reflection with the wonder of a child. He had never been hurt like this before, and seeing the mending take place was incredible. Wouldn't Sanders have gotten a kick out of this, if he'd invited the man in? Had it been a full moon, maybe Meeks would have.

The deputy winced as the threads in his shoulder continued to knit. Last night, as he'd climbed back into the patrol car a man again, he'd not realized how badly he'd been injured, his strength still buoyed by moonlight and adrenaline. In fact, he thought he might have left the campground the better of the two, despite the battle's embarrassing end.

But as the moon grew farther distant, swallowed by the increasing daylight, the pain worsened until he feared he'd need the hospital after all. Then, abruptly—thankfully—the crescendo of upword spiraling agony began to backslide into something bearable. His body burned, itched, and ached simultaneously while the skin repaired itself, his strength returning with each passing hour. The loose flap was already mostly intact, but his neck was still completely unexplainable to anyone who might ask. Nevertheless, Meeks hoped he could keep his word to Sanders by returning to work in a timely manner. Sick days were limited on the force, and the sheriff would be in a pickle with just one deputy available. Sanders was great on the job, but Meeks felt a special pride in knowing it was in the more experienced of the two that Sheriff Hubbard felt the most confidence.

Ah, his sweet Gloria. She had no idea he followed her all the way from Montgomery County, home to the Uwharrie National Forest and little Annie's last campout. That he'd waited and waited for an opening in her department, when fate finally handed him the job. But closeness had eluded them, for as soon as he arrived, fate handed the deputy another possibility: that of a true mate, one of his own kind. It had to be fate—he did not believe in blind luck. For another wolf to be in Doe Springs was too good to be mere coincidence. Tee Hubbard's arrival sealed what he thought karma was trying to tell him all along: The sheriff was not for him, the other most certainly was.

Meeks's mind wandered to last night, and he regretted his serious injuries just for the fact he could be on the road to-day, stalking the she-wolf by car. She would be injured too, this woman who favored the moon with her fire orange eyes and milk-white hair.

Meeks groaned as the musky scent of her filled his senses from memory. He closed his eyes and relived the moment she stepped into the clearing. He could tell immediately by her size and power that she had received the gift much longer ago than he. She could have killed him, but he was spared. Favored by the white wolf, perhaps. Yes, favored. Meeks opened his eyes and smiled at his reflection, the bruises collaring his throat—marks from her vicious teeth—not quite as vivid as before.

"When I am well, you will see me again. I promise you that." Meeks's fingernails dug into the fur of the gray wolf beside him until a tuft ripped loose and drifted to the floor. He closed his eyes again and patiently waited for the mending to end.

Chapter 35

Gloria pulled into her parking space in front of the Doe Springs Sheriff's Office and got out. It was one of the rare times she'd gotten to use her own spot since Tee's arrival. He'd made it a point to pull that ragtag pickup right up to the front door every single day since he got here just to pick at her. It annoyed her from the get-go, but she wouldn't give him the satisfaction of saying so. Right now, annoyed was the last of what she felt. Seeing the pickup in her parking space instead of abandoned in front of Musket's trailer would have been a big relief.

Gloria entered the station and went straight to her cluttered desk. She checked her phone, then flipped through loose papers and sticky notes, hoping to find a message from Tee. Only an emergency would pull him away from a major investigation without clearing it with her first.

A light knock on the door halted the search.

"Come in, Shirley. I was about to visit you. Has Tee been in today?"

"Yes, ma'am. Of sorts." Shirley held a note; Gloria could see Tee's name at the bottom of it. "This is for you. It came—"

Gloria snatched the piece of paper and read:

Glory,
  Hey, kiddo—Hate to leave you high and dry like this, but I'm on to something. I'll give you the details when I see you.

Tee

"Me and Delores thought that was kind of sweet, him calling you kiddo." Shirley, a mother of two twenty-year-old daughters, giggled like a schoolgirl.

Gloria wasn't as enamored. "This is from Tee? When?"

"From this morning. But I knew you had your hands full with all those parents stirred up in your office. It was like somebody took a can of gerbils and shook it real hard, then set them loose in the middle of our police station. I never heard such crazy talk before. Me and Delores felt guilty herding them into your office like that, but they were raising such a fit out here it was a relief to be rid of them. Did all that work out all right, Sheriff?"

"Shirley, about the note."

"I didn't want to bother you was what I was trying to get at. Then you took off before I remembered I even had the blamed thing. Is it very important?"

"This is your handwriting."

Shirley cocked her head. "Of course. Delores took the phone call, but she told me what Mr. Hubbard said. I wrote it down exactly. Delores broke her right finger playing ball with her grandson last Wednesday, so she can't write a thing, poor dear. I told her she shouldn't be answering the phone if she can't take a message, but . . . " Shirley let the sentence trail with a shrug of her shoulders. "Is everything all right, Sheriff? You look peaked. Can I get you a cup of coffee?"

Gloria rubbed her temple. It was the first question she'd felt like answering all day. "You know what, Shirley? I would love a cup of your coffee. Thank you."

"Coming right up." Shirley left the sheriff alone with Tee's message. Gloria sank in her chair, fatigue and concern canceling each other out. Shirley entered with an apologetic smile and empty hands. "I'm sorry, Sheriff," she said. "The pot's empty and looks like we're out of filters."

The day was becoming unbearable.

Chapter 36

Alfred Toomey piddled in his shop. It was one of his favorite pastimes. While other people worked jobs, Toomey worked a passion—books. He couldn't get enough of them. Mrs. Toomey, on the other hand, had had quite enough of them. Alfred's study was overflowing into the rest of the house, and musty bound covers from other centuries did not sit well with the potpourri and rose-scented sachets of an updated Victorian bed-and-breakfast. "Allergies, Alfred," Alice told him. "We can't have our guests sniffing up dust from your old smelly collections." Which made little difference anyway, if business did not soon pick up in at least one of their livelihoods. Nevertheless, here he was on a dreary foggy day, made perfect for reading or studying, trying instead to find a hole in which to stuff eighty-seven more books.

Toomey pulled hardcover after hardcover out of the boxes he'd carted in from the van, wondering where on earth in his overcrowded shop he would put them. After much cramming and pushing and panting and cursing, the shelves still refused to give way, and Toomey succumbed to what he really wanted to do in the first place: reread the Doe Springs deputy's book. He'd brought it in first, gingerly wrapped in plastic to protect the cover from the weather. It rested on his desk in the back of the closet-sized store as a reminder that Sanders might be stopping by the following day to retrieve it. But truthfully, Toomey hated to see it go. He'd been right: The book was valuable. What a waste to see it go back to a private owner. A book like this needed to be shared, discussed, analyzed by a panel, put before scholars for cultural study. Not stuck on a shelf to meet the fate of all his other books—forgotten.

Toomey settled behind his desk, much the way a satisfied hen lowers onto her nest of eggs. The soft leather cushion of the wing chair welcomed him. It was molded in the shape of the professor's familiar seat, testimony to the impossible hours he spent there poring over words from another time.

Lykanthrop lay before him, the word itself blurry through the drizzle-dappled plastic. Toomey unwrapped the book, made even fatter by the pages and pages of notes he'd inserted with each completed interpretive effort. The volume had revealed many secrets, starting with the assessment of its leather cover. What Toomey had discovered would be of great interest to the deputy and to the owner. The cover's leather was human. Three-hundred-year-old cured European, to be exact. Male or female, however, was undetermined. Toomey was disappointed not to know; he felt great significance could often lie in the smallest of details.

In unraveling the words scrawled in a dozen different dialects, he'd also found the pages held different languages, German only one among them. After working on the cover, Dr. Schlesinger from the university jumped in to help with the additional language translation. So excited was he to aid his retired old friend on this project, he came to the house every night, where they holed up in Alfred's study, smoking cigars and arguing over syntax sometimes till two in the morning.

The entire "story" they revealed was entirely in the format Alfred had already determined: letters, diary entries, accounts of what each writer claimed to be his own personal experience. Those experiences were a record, passed down through generations of a particular family—not one of a typical genetic lineage, but a cult family of what Schlesinger and Toomey could only call sociopaths. They were an exclusive group, bound in their religion of lycanthropy. Paragraph after paragraph described rites of passage under the full moon, young men and women brought into the fold based on their worthiness, their memberships sealed by first kills. The most powerful in the order commanded ownership of the book. It was a bible, a bible of the lycanthrope.

Schlesinger had gone straight to the university archives to research cult activity in Europe and werewolf legends. He came back, an animated character thrilling to share trivia dating back to the ancient Greeks and Romans, a time when werewolfism was rampant. "The church of the Middle Ages too, had done its fair share of enforcing belief in shapeshifters," Toomey's colleague said, standing behind a mound of books like it was his podium at the school. He preached to Toomey as if two hundred students sat before him, pencils ready. "To deny werewolves existed in 1270 was an act of heresy. Later, the Inquisition upheld an entire economy based on the heads of witches and werewolves. Torturers, executioners, and all involved in the persecution of the accused needed to eat too. To not have sorcery in their midst was bad for business, not to mention peasants may have gotten unruly if the fear of the church's wrath were not there to keep them in check. At least, so thinketh the church, eh?"

Ancient European histories and mythologies cited numerous "wolf peoples" for consideration as the source of *Lykanthrop*'s cult, but Schlesinger narrowed it down to three candidates: the Viking Berserkers, fierce, maniacal warriors who donned the skins of bears and wolves when going into battle; the Neurians, a hunting clan that once lived in the region of west Russia and, for a few days each year, could allegedly change into wolves; and the wolf cult *Hirpi Sorani* near Rome, a group that donned the skins of wolves while they danced and walked through fire carrying the viscera of sacrificed animals.

But all of it was conjecture. The book was frustratingly silent in context of its true origins and originator. Toomey and Schlesinger moved beyond that, hunting for clues in the information that was provided. Most interesting to note, the final entry of *Lykanthrop* was fairly recent—dated 1984 and signed by a person identified only by one initial: U. Disappointingly, none of the entries were signed by anymore than that or sometimes just a symbol. The manuscript mostly rambled through detailed feats of shapeshifting itself—an individual experience that brought some orgasmic pleasure, others intense howling pain, and still others little more sensation than a discomforting ache of the joints. (Toomey and Schlesinger hypothesized psychoactive mushrooms may have played a part in the earliest shapeshifting accounts, opium and street narcotics in the later ones.) A few entries outlined in grisly revelation the passage into the order by the first kill. Toomey now understood the policeman's interest in this volume. The illustrations and text on those pages closely resembled the current accounts of the deaths in Doe Springs, not to mention it held record of murders by a cult that, if indeed real, were as recent as twenty years ago.

Toomey flipped to the end of the book, where several blank pages awaited fresh descriptions from a new member to the lycanthrope family. He stopped on the mysterious U and reread the brief account of entry into the macabre:

I shivered in the blood in the cold December wind. Little do I recall of the act itself, only the taste of sweet flesh and warmth on my lips as I devoured it. I smelled her fear and drank it to satisfy the thirst I felt to fulfill my place in this order. I chose the victim well, but regret her child. . . . O goddess of the Moon, forgive my jealous heart.

"Psychotic episodes, cannibalism," Toomey mumbled. The professor traced the carefully inked words, wondering about the person who put them there. The neat pen and poetic flow spoke of the effeminate. The victim too, a woman. Toomey pondered the jealousy that prompted the loss of this poor soul's life, and what of the child mentioned? He could only assume it met the fate of its mother on some full-mooned winter's night.

As Toomey's eyes pored over the left-hand page, he subconsciously stroked the page on the right. The parchment was cool under his touch, comforting, smooth. . . .

No, not smooth. Toomey squinted at the paper beneath his right hand. Dimples pocked the paper and were connected by slight furrows plowed by the point of a writing instrument. Toomey ran his hand along the inside binding. A smile rippled across the retired professor's face as his fingers found the unmistakable remnants of raggedly torn pages.

There was another entry. Toomey scrabbled through his desk drawer looking for a lead pencil or one of the crayons he kept handy for entertaining rowdy children who came into the store. The impressions in the book were faint, but a rubbing might reveal enough to piece the words together. By what he could see, or mostly feel, the missing entry covered the entire page.

Toomey suppressed an "Aha!" as his fingernails sunk into the edge of a crayon wedged into the very back of his drawer. He seized the gray Crayola and ripped its paper away. Placing the crayon over the book page, Toomey thought nothing of how irate the deputy might become at his soiling the paper. He lightly rubbed until words appeared through the colored wax like the image of a developing photograph. The crayon swished faster as letters revealed themselves. It was English!

Professor Toomey strangled the neck of his desk lamp as he yanked it over the page. The message was barely, nearly, impossibly, almost there. He widened his eyes, then squinted, seeking the best view to pull out words from the invisible paragraphs and string them together into sentences. He scanned top to bottom, when his eye snagged on something with perfect clarity—the first full set of initials in the entire book: I.V.

It wasn't much, but it was something—a new jumping-off point for more research if Sanders would allow him another week of study. *If*. That phone call would be forthcoming, then he'd be on the phone to Dr. Schlesinger. They could make more of the rubbings at the university. There were sophisticated ways beyond Crayola's capacity to pull embedded text from old parchment pages.

The bell over the shop door jingled, startling the professor. Irritation flared in his forehead, turning it bright pink. Alice had followed him, no doubt, her Jetta lopsided with the weight of too much cargo. Toomey pictured more of his books spilling out the open windows of the compact car and sprinkling like breadcrumbs down the highway. He reluctantly left his newest discovery and went out into the shop. It wasn't Alice after all, but a lovely blond lady underneath the bell. She stood partially obscured by a shelf of medical encyclopedias, circa 1925.

"I'm sorry, Miss, the shop is closed today," Toomey said, walking around to see her fully. The woman wore a simple yellow cotton dress and leather sandals. The tops of her feet were damp from the rain. Beside the woman, sitting at attention and unleashed, was a giant black shepherd.

"Madam! We certainly do not allow dogs in this shop. This is a rare books store."

"I realize that, Professor Toomey, and that is why I am here."

"Do I know you, Miss? Were you one of my students?"

The woman smiled, and Toomey could not describe it. The room seemed to brighten the color of her dress. "No, I'm afraid not. Actually, Deputy Melvin Sanders sent me to get the book. I assume you know the one I mean?"

Toomey eyed the dog one more time, but he seemed well mannered enough. What was he hurting, really, just sitting there like that? "Yes, the book. *Lykanthrop*. You say Deputy Sanders sent you?"

"Yes."

Toomey had hoped for elaboration, a longer answer to springboard more conversation and give excuse for looking.

into that winsome smile, those sparkling eyes. . . . But the book, he couldn't hand it over to just anyone.

"I'm sorry. I can't hand Deputy Sanders's book over to just anyone. Rare books are valuable property. I'm sure you understand."

"I do, certainly, and I appreciate your thoughtfulness. But I assure you, Melvin will not mind my taking the book."

The professor couldn't hide his disappointment. He'd hoped to gain at least another week *(maybe two, that wouldn't be unreasonable, would it?)* for his studies of *Lykanthrop,* but it looked as if it were all coming to an end right now. He sighed. "All right, then. Let me have your name and I'll call the deputy to confirm the pickup. Forgive the formality."

The woman took a step toward Toomey, and the dog rose to its feet. It stayed close to her side, ears up, expectant. "That won't be necessary, Mr. Toomey. You see, I am the owner of *Lykanthrop.* Surely Deputy Sanders mentioned me."

Toomey brightened. He could not believe his good fortune. "He never told me who owned it, only that it was a friend. I have to say, that it is one of the most intriguing books I've ever encountered. I'm assuming you are not aware of the translations?"

"No, I'm afraid not. I purchased the book at an estate auction years ago. I never took the time to have it translated. I just knew it was old and beautifully illustrated. Anyway, when the librarian in Doe Springs told me Melvin sent it to you, I was delighted. I don't know why he thought it should be kept secret from me."

"I got the impression it is a surprise for you. And, I must say, what a surprise it is."

"You've translated the entire text then?"

"Yes, yes. It took me weeks to properly identify all the dialects. The language is from mostly Germanic tribes all over Europe, but there is also Irish, Dutch, French, Italian, Scotch, Hungarian, Russian. . . . And then, this afternoon, I discovered a hidden entry by doing a rubbing. With your permission, and the deputy's clearance, I'd like to work on the book for at least another week or two. Let me have your name—I can make one quick phone call to Deputy Sanders, then we can sit down and go over the book and illustrations in detail. In fact, I would love to discuss what I've found with both of you." In fact, Toomey would like to discuss the book with whomever would listen, but he needed the deputy's permission beforehand. What if it did have some bearing on the Doe Springs case?

"Mr. Toomey, have you spoken of this book with anyone else?"

Toomey sized up the question. It was baited, he could tell, and only a negative was the positive answer. Deputy Sanders wanted the book kept private, and this woman, owner or not, apparently did too. So there really was only one thing he could say for the time being. "Of course not. I'm the only person in the region who could decipher this literature. But I can see why the police in Doe Springs would be interested."

"And why is that, Mr. Toomey?" The woman's smile was suddenly gone, disappeared behind the clouds of a sorrow-tinged sigh. The room dimmed again and the old books surrounding them looked even older than before.

"The killings in *Lykanthrop*—what's described is very much like what is happening in . . . " Toomey stopped talking. The woman had moved even closer, had glided toward him when his mind was buried in the story of her book. The shepherd was on its feet and within touching distance, head lowered and muzzle quivering slightly. Toomey took a step backward.

"I have quite a bit more shelving to do, Miss. You're welcome to come back tomorrow and pick up your book. It's not here at the moment, but I'll be sure to bring it with me in the morning, after I speak with Deputy Sanders, of course."

The woman stared at him blandly and Toomey felt an odd stirring in his stomach. The uneasiness prickled his skin and raised the hairs along the back of his neck. The dog seemed to sense the change in the atmosphere, for its quivering muzzle broke into a full-blown growl, one of which the woman seemed in no hurry to quiet.

"Certainly, Professor. I'll speak with the deputy as well, and I'll be sure to let him know how conscientious you were in protecting *my* property."

Abruptly, the woman turned, her blond hair fanning out behind her. Toomey noticed a falter in her stride. She limped into the fog, the shepherd hugging her side.

Toomey went to the telephone by the cash register to call Deputy Sanders in Doe Springs. It occurred to him the woman never did give her name; a description for the deputy would have to do. Receiver to his ear and back to the storefront, Toomey did not hear the click of the shop door reopen nor the chime of its bell. He turned at the steps coming toward him. "I'm sorry, we're closed. Oh, it's you. . . ."

Chapter 37

Meeks was not back at work, Deputy Sanders was trapped in Doe Springs, and the sheriff had been particularly snippy since Tee walked off the case. They seemed none the closer to catching their—whatever it was—than before, and the criminal lab, backed up for weeks, still had the mystery fur and alleged tooth cap. To make matters worse, Ivy left a message on his machine last night demanding her book back, but there was a new development involving *Lykanthrop* and Professor Toomey. And he didn't know how to break it to the woman.

Melvin sat on his worn-leather couch, clutching his Pepto-Bismol and wondering where he'd gone wrong. There had been a plan to his life, going all the way back to the first cops and robbers games of kid-dom and that first shared Hershey bar with Maggie Sue Tenner in kindergarten. This stress was not what he'd counted on. Chasing regular bad guys, that was what he trained for at the police academy, not hiking around in the forest chasing creepy-crawly things that shared more with ghosts than flesh-and-blood assailants.

And his personal life was upside down and bass-ackwards, as his daddy would say it. The sweet, simple country girl he dreamed he would settle down with and take care of for life had been replaced by an independent woman who made him feel like a nervous schoolboy with a crush.

Melvin took a satisfying swig of the pink stuff and mulled it over. There was nothing to be done about it, really. Nothing a'tall. He'd have to face the thing in the forest eventually—it couldn't elude them forever—but he dreaded facing Ivy Cole right now worst of all. How *could* he face her? She'd left messages at the station and his house, yet he hadn't returned a single call. And when she finally cornered him—he couldn't elude her forever either—what would she think of him when he confessed her book may be gone for good?

The phone rang at that thought, and dread whiplashed in the pit of his stomach. The black rotary phone jangled twice more before he put down the pink bottle of security and picked up what could only amount to bad.

"Hello?"

"Hello, Deputy. Forget to check your caller I.D.?"

"Hello, Ivy. I was just thinking about you."

"Next time don't think. Call. Where have you been? I couldn't get you at the station or your house yesterday."

He wished he had a good excuse, like laid up in the hospital with a degenerative disease. But he gave her the only believable thing he had. "Working. A lot. Yesterday was a busy day—I had to go buy new pants."

She didn't laugh at his joke. There was no response at all, save the crackle on the line of his old-fashioned telephone. She was a million miles away from him in the tone of that silence alone.

"Ivy, there's something I have to tell you."

"I already know. I train Prudy Township's Pekinese, and when I called to cancel her appointment yesterday because of my injury, guess what—she's quite the talker on the phone. Told me all about your rare book and the Asheville professor."

Ivy paused to let the words sink in. Melvin answered her

with silence of his own. She continued: "I don't understand why you felt the need to sneak my book off without my permission, Deputy, but I'm willing to forget about it for the sake of our friendship. I was really mad last night, but I'll get over it. Now I just want my book back. Today."

"I don't have it." Melvin blurted. His stomach roiled, and in his head, mathematical figures swirled in increasingly larger combinations. How much would a book like that cost? His bank account was modest, but maybe he could sell a kidney.

"Then go get it." Silence answered the command. "Hello? Melvin, are you there?"

Melvin sighed. "Yes. Pardon my distraction; I was figuring up a payment plan."

"What are you talking about?"

The frost-edged panic in her voice sank Melvin deeper into his sofa. "I'm sorry, Ivy. Prudy was right—I did take *Lykanthrop* to a retired professor in Asheville. He was only supposed to keep it a week, but he kept needing more time to work on it. Finally today I was to go get it, but I got a bulletin this morning at work. Toomey is missing and so is a bunch of valuable inventory. Yours was part of it. The Asheville police didn't find your book in his shop or the house. Turns out Toomey had a lot of debt. They think that could be the reason he took off."

"That doesn't make any sense. He stole his own books to pawn somewhere, plus mine?"

"It's not his stuff that's missing. He took books belonging to the university where he used to teach. Toomey does preservation work for the school's museum, and these books were apparently worth a lot of money. Long story short, Toomey is gone for the time being, and I feel like a heel. I know they'll find your book, Ivy. I'm sure they will."

Melvin could hear the woman's steady breathing. He tried again. "I'm so sorry, Ivy. I know that book was special to you."

"You have no idea how special it was."

"I'll pay you for it. Name your price."

"That's all well and good, Deputy, but I can't do that. The

book was beyond money. It was priceless. You promised you wouldn't let it out of your sight."

Melvin grabbed the Pepto-Bismol again and turned the bottle up, but it was empty. He fished a roll of Tums out of his pocket. "I can't apologize enough."

"You're right, you can't. You are lucky I like you so much, Deputy Sanders. Good-bye."

Melvin hung up the phone and fell sideways onto the soft-grained cushions. He chewed the rest of the Tums. Deputy Sanders, she'd called him. The relationship was re-treating backward quicker than he could chase after it.

The grandfather clock in the living room corner chimed, and Melvin abruptly sat up. He would have to ferret out time to worry about all this later. He was back on the job, and right now he had a date with the elderly Widow Pritchard.

Chapter 38

The Widow Pritchard knelt in her flower garden alongside the front of the house, the loam a moist cushion to her aged knees. She worked the dirt with a small shovel in her capable hands, turning and rolling it around the base of a newly planted hydrangea. It felt good to the widow, the planting. She savored the flowers themselves, but even the soil brought a tangible satisfaction that boosted her spirits on melancholy days. How could it not? The smell of the earth was a good smell; life started and ended here, in the dirt, in the fertile soil. Working the garden kept her eighty-seven years young.

Ava sang as she toiled, but the happiness warbled to a close when she heard the unmistakable roar of a police car coming down the road toward her home.

"Lord, Lord, but you are prompt, young deputy." Ava rose to her feet and brushed the dirt from her faded denim overalls. She tossed the spade on the ground beside her hoe and rake. Two more hydrangeas rested in black plastic pots. She'd get to them directly. Business was afoot; she'd best take care of it. Ivy had warned her the deputy might come to call one day, and sure as a bad bet, here he was.

The car sidled to a stop in the crushed gravel drive. Ava pushed the brim of her straw hat over the knob of her bun as Deputy Sanders walked toward her. The closer he got, the farther up she tilted the hat to see him.

"Afternoon, Mrs. Pritchard. I hope I'm not bothering you."

The shadow halo of the hat brim hid most of the widow's face, but there was a disapproving set to her pursed lips. Deputy Sanders snatched off his own hat and held it to his chest, eliciting a smile at last from his host.

"You are everything I expected, young man, and about a foot extra. Come inside. I've some sun tea chilling in the icebox."

The deputy followed Widow Pritchard up her porch steps. His head cleared the ceiling of the porch by a good foot, a testament to the magnitude of the old place. It was always the first thing he noticed about houses—their scale—and this one fit him. Mirrors would soar above sinks, he imagined, and doorjambs would accommodate even bigger men than he. The widow led the deputy through two sitting rooms and down a long hallway, a dainty lilliputian wending through the mouse holes of giants with her own colossal guest in tow.

They arrived at the sunroom, and the smell of old-timey roses and ginger spice enveloped the odd couple. Ava waved to a round patio table and a couple of comfortable-looking chairs. "Have a seat, Deputy Sanders," Ava said. She disappeared down the hall again and came back with a tray of frosted Mason jar glasses and a crystal vase of tea.

"The pitcher's fancy for company, sugar, but there's nothing like sipping on sun tea from a frosted Mason jar. I could break out the good glasses, but take my word for it."

"I'm a paper cup man myself, ma'am, so jars are a step up. Thank you." Ice cubes rattled as Melvin took a long drink, the sound pure summertime to his ears.

Ava plopped into a padded wicker chair across from Melvin and poured herself a hearty glassful of the russet liquid. It was good, as she knew it would be. Jeb had loved a big jar of sweet iced tea after working in the garden, and he swore Ava's must be concocted from old Southern magic. But no point getting nostalgic over tea. Jeb was gone, God rest his dear soul, and a Doe Springs deputy was in her sunroom at the moment. Amenities attended to, Ava didn't waste time getting to the facts. "State your business, sugar. Time is short when you're eighty-seven."

"Yes, ma'am," Melvin set the near-empty tea glass down. "I'm a little uncomfortable asking you about this."

"You've got my attention. It's not every day I get to discuss uncomfortable matters with handsome young men."

"Um, yes, ma'am. It's about a mutual friend of ours."

Ava laughed. "That could be the whole town." She could make it easy on the deputy, save him all his polite beating-around-the-bush effort. She knew good and well why he was here. He wanted information about his girlfriend. Ava was too old to play high school games, but affairs of the heart could make an amusing pastime for whiling away an afternoon. Let him come out with his meddlesome questions in his own time. Old or not, a handsome young man in her parlor was never a bad thing and certainly not an often one. She might as well enjoy the company along with the tea. The still-potted hydrangeas weren't going anywhere quick.

"I suppose we would have a lot of mutual friends. You've lived here a long time," Melvin said.

"My whole life. Raised in this house, in fact. Now, who is this mystery person? You've piqued an old gal's interest and I'd like to find out why the Doe Springs police want my help."

"I'm doing a routine background check on people who live in the vicinity of the Clifford Hughes attack site. He was killed near Miss Ivy Cole's home and I know you're related. It's no big deal; I just need some general information about her, and you being kin, I figured you knew her better than anybody."

"I get the feeling you might know a lot about Miss Cole already. Why don't you ask her whatever it is you need to know?"

"I'll do that too, but background checks are more thorough with outside perspective. It's for my boss," Melvin added, as if that would finally convince her.

"That must be very time-consuming, knocking on other people's doors instead of going straight to the horse's mouth. I doubt there's anything I can tell you about Ivy she hasn't told you herself."

"What do you mean?"

"Ah, sugar, I didn't just fall off the turnip truck. Ivy's mentioned you a time or two. I know you see each other, so you can drop the cop routine and shoot straight. Go ahead and ask me what you really want to know."

Red blossomed above Melvin's shirt collar like the emergence of one of Ava's creeping roses. He didn't know what to say. His notebook rested blankly inside his shirt pocket, and that was where it would most likely remain. Without the cover of police work, he was lost. Melvin was not prepared to sit down for a real heart-to-heart about his love life with a lady who reminded him of his beloved grandmother.

"Now don't go getting all embarrassed," Ava said. "It's touching you want to know more about my girl, albeit your tactics are a little on the sneaky side. But I'll overlook it. She's tight-lipped, that one. But I can tell you got a taste for her."

Melvin cleared his throat and forged ahead onto the direct path Ava had laid before him. "I do care about her. And I worry about her because of it."

"Oh? Is Ivy in trouble of some kind?" Ava shifted forward in her seat, the sudden intensity of her gaze unsettling to the officer.

"No, no. I mean, I worry about her because she's over there by herself with nobody to look after her."

"And you want to be that somebody."

"I would certainly like to get to know Ivy better, to see if I could be that somebody someday. But she puts up a wall when it comes to her personal life." It was true. After their first date at the barbeque shack, she'd been tight-lipped ever since. She had a talent for diverting conversation back on him and as far away from herself as possible.

"What do you want to know?" Ava crossed her hands in her lap.

"How her mother died. How your sister Una went from being the nanny in Germany to the stepmother in New York."

Ava's eyes widened. "Ivy told you about that? She talked about her mother and Una?"

"Some."

Not enough, Ava knew, or Deputy Sanders would not be here. But what was Ivy thinking to bring up any of it? She must truly be in love this time, and it was making her foolish. Ava tried to keep a pleasant expression, but she was sure the astute deputy had picked up on her displeasure right away. The false story she was prepared to relate would sound to Sanders every bit as made up as it really was. She'd have to reveal small truths so as not to contradict anything Ivy had said. *Wait till I talk to that girl again.* . . . . Suddenly the afternoon was short and company had been here too long already. Handsome had lost its appeal, and the hydrangeas were wilting without her.

"So you want to hear about Una. What a pistol." Ava shook her head. "Like I told you before, I've lived here my whole life. Una didn't. While our family took an occasional vacation here and there, Una went on entire adventures. Determined to see the world, she was, and there wasn't a happier day in her life than when she finally made it out of North Carolina, all the way across the ocean to Europe. She traveled around, doing this job or that job. And that's how she met the Coles in Germany."

"Did Mrs. Cole employ Una as the nanny while they lived over there?"

"Una never worked for Catherine."

"So she was employed by Mr. Cole? Or were they acquaintances until the need for some parenting help came up?"

"I don't know." Ava finished off her drink and set the

Mason jar down a little too firmly. "I mean, I'm not sure how she met William. Una just called me one day out of the blue and said she'd found a job as a nanny that was relocating her back to the States."

"And she never told you how that all came about?"

"Una was the baby out of six children. I wasn't her closest confidante of the brood. But I can tell you this: Una loved Ivy like she was her own. Doted on the child. All in all, I'm not surprised Una became a nanny—she couldn't have children and she'd always wanted one. Ivy was a blessing to her."

Melvin itched to pull out his notebook. This was not the wicked stepmother impression Ivy had given him. Quite the opposite. "Mrs. Pritchard, were Una and William Cole having an affair before Mrs. Cole died?"

The question was a smack in the face. This was not the kind of inquiry Ava had expected from the officer. She'd been prepared to lay bare Ivy's likes and dislikes, interests and hobbies, and maybe some funny stories from her childhood. If Deputy Sanders wanted to know Ivy better, the widow saw no harm in it. But this was different entirely. He was mucking around in a quagmire that could suck them all down with it.

"If you're wanting to know Ivy and get on her good side, you might think twice about going there, Deputy Sanders. The question itself is an insult, and insults don't land prospective boyfriends in good graces. It usually lands them square on their derrieres."

"Yes, ma'am. I apologize for being insulting. But were they?"

Ava slowly took off her diamond-rimmed specs to stare at the deputy directly. He swore her eyes were clearer without them. "You're treading into real personal territory, sugar. Families don't air their underwear on the clothesline by the front of the house. That's saved for the back door. I've told you all I will about my sister. It's disloyal, dredging up bygone events, and inappropriate on your part to be asking about them.

"You'll have to ask Ivy the rest of your questions. To give

you any more information to use against her in your personal relationship, I won't do it. Frankly, if I were you, I'd take an old woman's advice: Rummaging through the past is hurtful to Ivy—you need to let all this go and deal with the present. I believe you've got a killer to catch."

"Yes, I do. Two killers, possibly, and they're running around in the woods near Ivy's house. But you are right, that has nothing to do with any of this. I didn't mean to offend you or make you think I'm doing something underhanded behind Ivy's back."

The widow's stern facade splintered abruptly, making her look harsh and vulnerable at the same time. "Two of them? There is another . . . ?" The obvious dawned on Ava, something she had not considered before. She had assumed there really was nothing on their mountaintop besides a wild thing attacking other animals at random. As much as Ava hated the thoughts of those maulings, Mother Nature had provided a cover for Ivy through a rogue villain of her own design. Talbot's sighting, she thought, was fueled by an overactive imagination projected onto a black bear. Ivy had never alluded to any different. Why hadn't she said anything? To protect her aunt from worry, no doubt. That would be just like her.

Ava sighed as the realization sank in. Werewolves were running amok in Doe Springs—an interesting development—and here this kid sat, grilling her on things best long forgotten. The widow put the pieces of her crumpled composure back together and effected a twisted smile aimed at the deputy. She hoped it looked remotely genuine.

"Ridiculous. If there were a whole bunch of these crazed animals on the loose, more than one half-blind old man would have seen them by now."

"Well, in fact, he's not the only—"

"Oh my goodness, look what time it is," Ava interrupted. She didn't want to hear anymore. She needed to be alone and sort through all this without a bird dog lawman watching every twitch of her brow or pupil dilation. Analytical types made her nervous and that was not an emotion to which she was accustomed. "I hate to rush you off, but the day's fading away and I've got more pots to tend." Ava started gathering up Mason jars and putting them back on the tray. The tea pitcher was clear again, its contents steadily drained through the course of conversation.

Deputy Sanders didn't budge. He sat there solid as an oak stump and tapped his knuckles absentmindedly on the table. "Mrs. Pritchard, there's just one more thing."

Ava was on her feet, ready to shoo the deputy the moment he stood. "Yes?"

"Where are your sister and William Cole today?"

"Good day, Deputy," Ava said too sweetly, the last word catching over the hard lump of irritation in her throat.

The Widow Pritchard watched Deputy Sanders through the lacy curtains in her living room. Satisfied he was gone, she turned to a framed photograph of her late husband on the wall beside the window. He looked more austere than he really was in that picture, but it was taken in the day when a smile looked out of place in a black-and-white portrait.

Ava carried the frame to her velvet settee and held it for a time. Had Jeb been here, he would have told the policeman everything. Not for Ivy's sake, but for the sake of others she might take. Ivy had been a conflicting presence in their life. Jeb despised the wolf, while Ava had embraced it. She took the portrait down and gingerly lifted the back away. Inside, carefully folded and pressed into fine creases, was a newspaper clipping. Ava unfolded the article, its headline declaring "Missing software magnate and wife presumed dead, daughter inherits estate." Underneath the article was another piece of paper, aged to the color of Ava's sun tea and marked by the swirly script of a young girl on the verge of womanhood.

The girl, I.V., had written the entry in English—a silly thing to do—but Ava understood the teenager's thinking. It was her signed confession, chronicling tremendous guilt for the acts she committed against those who wronged her but had loved her, just the same.

Ava found the book in her sister's belongings when she

flew to New York to collect them. The book rightfully belonged to the girl by tradition, so Ava left it in the Manhattan apartment, minus the page that could send her away. The page was precious to Ava for another reason. It held the last account of her sister alive, and the final account of her death.

"The price you paid for love was great, dear Una. It ended the way you feared it would. I've protected her, like you asked me to, but she's in trouble again. I think she's in real trouble. What should I do?" Ava stroked the parchment as if by mere touch she could feel the spirit of her sister underneath her fingertips. But there was nothing. No answer whispered from the faded ink, no sounds stirred in the vacant old house.

Ava grasped the paper with both hands, and it gave way like the shuddering of a soul's last breath with each downward rip. The widow carried the torn pieces to the kitchen sink. She watched their edges turn black, then to ash as they burned.

Chapter 39

The Widow Pritchard was not the only one with a secret stash. The gym bag in the trunk of Melvin's cruiser was filled with prior knowledge. He was armed well to press the widow on sticky subjects she wrinkled up her nose at, but he was hoping she would volunteer something on her own, something new and insightful that the newspaper clippings from Europe, New York, New Orleans, and South Dakota hadn't told him. The background check Melvin mentioned to Ava was not a lie. But perhaps omission of information was. Not to the widow, but to the sheriff. Melvin's curiosity about his secretive girlfriend had uncovered unsettling

things, things he'd kept to himself and now carried like a
weight heavier than the stack of informative burdens accu-
mulating in his gym bag. He pondered these things as he
drove away from the widow and her guarded interview, her
elegant Victorian shrinking to a small speck in his
rearview.

The search had begun quite by accident back in the Doe
Springs library, a place where, much to the delight of the librarian, Melvin seemed to be finding himself more and
more. After sharing his theories about the Devil of Doe
Springs with the sheriff (and citing all his reading based on
criminal psychoses), she'd seemed none too enthralled with
any of his ideas, and this day he was returning a new round
of library books. The sheriff's lack of response at their
meeting had not disheartened him any. She was like that.
Gloria Hubbard was not excitable. She'd take what he'd
given her and stew on it in private. But he'd continued reading anyway, checking out new volumes on a weekly basis,
searching through legends and theories from minds greater
than his.

Melvin dropped the books through the return slot and
walked quickly away from Mrs. Township, intent on blowing the last half hour of his lunch break in peace. Melvin
scanned the shelves for anything else of interest. His eye fell
on the dusty monolithic monitor by the reference section.
Boredom and a weariness of all things evil, Melvin huddled
in the corner cubicle on the library's only Internet accessible
computer and typed in something he'd given little thought to
in a long time—baseball. He'd played as a kid, always just
for fun, but it was the one thing he and his dad had loved to
do together: tossing the ball across the front yard at the end
of his workday. The passion stuck, perhaps out of nostalgia
or merely the chromosome factor of being born male, but
there was something comforting, right at this moment, about
thinking of nothing other than America's game.

After catching up on the scores, Melvin's idle fingers,
guilty for allowing downtime to personal amusement, found
a mind of their own and typed in "animal mauling." He received nearly six hundred hits, mostly pertaining to dog

bites, exotic pet attacks, activists blaming people for such attacks, counteractivists claiming people who blame other people for animal attacks ought to be shot. At the bottom of the ninth page, a caption drew the deputy's attention: "Wilderness Guide Mauled in SD." Ivy had lived in South Dakota; it was as good an article to start with as any. Melvin checked his watch—fifteen minutes to kill. He clicked on the headline.

The article was a few years old, barely two hundred words, and to the point: A man was found mauled outside his pickup camper on the outskirts of Wall. A brief follow-up article blamed the attack on coyotes, although there was no explanation as to why the animals would be so close to town and why coyotes would be brave enough to accomplish such an out-of-character deed in the first place. Or why the guide's loaded rifle lay right by his mutilated side when discovered, not a single shot fired. But no matter. Seven coyotes were exterminated the week the man died, case closed. Westerners did not get as stirred up, it seemed, by wild animal intervention in their communities as the folks back East. They were used to it, accepting the wilderness as their neighbor and stomping it out if it dared to trespass.

Melvin checked his watch again. Now he was late, five minutes. But curiosity got the better of him. He did a quick search in an almanac back issue and there it was: The date of the guide's death coincided with a full moon. He had not really expected it, and the sight of the date in the book and that by the flashing cursor on screen left him blank for a moment.

The deputy closed the almanac and sat up straighter in the orange plastic chair, which was better suited for an eighth grader than a grown man. Coincidences or serendipity or the work of fate—Melvin believed in anything that brought confusing elements of the cosmos together in a paradigm that made sense. A thousand miles away in a little town called Wall, a mauling had occurred under the full moon.

For the next few hours, long past the end of his lunch break, Melvin slurped on Tums under Prudy Township's owlish gaze and the winking bulb of his desk lamp while uncovering a trail of news that followed Ivy from state to state. The deputy had checked Los Angeles newspaper archives next, but the city divulged nothing to shout about. A town that big could swallow up missing persons and turn a year before anybody would notice. Thousands of pieces of information poured in, but there was nothing relevant on animal attacks. He moved on to the smaller city Ivy had mentioned, promising to recheck Los Angeles when he had more time. He typed in *New Orleans Times-Picayune* and an approximate year to search.

New Orleans, with its influx of tourists and its backbone of voodoo was an ideal place to settle nefarious wings. It was here in New Orleans when Melvin's notebook made its appearance and notetaking on Doe Springs connections was made. A full-moon killer, nicknamed "the Werewolf of Burgundy," terrorized the French Quarter off and on for two years before the mutilations mysteriously stopped. No suspects, no clues, no traces of evidence left at the attacks, but authorities were sure a large predator was to blame, perhaps trained and guided by a man with ties to the black art of witchcraft. The killings were concluded as the ritualistic work of Satanists, fitting for the area and crafting more character for the city's already dark allure. Melvin found the Werewolf of Burgundy had even turned up in vacation pamphlets. Visitors could tour Burgundy Street by horse-drawn carriage and see the site where the first two bodies were discovered.

But it was the article from Germany that interested Melvin the most. Ignoring the stares and whispers from Prudy Township and Verna at the circulation desk, Melvin scoured foreign newspapers on the Internet until he came upon more than he'd hoped to find: an article from a little girl's tragic past. The Cole family in a rural area outside Cologne . . . a hellish attack on Christmas Eve that stunned neighbors in the quiet community . . . a mother, torn apart by a giant wild dog . . . her child, badly injured, hospitalized, *traumatized.* Melvin imagined the small blond girl, lying in the hospital bed, reliving what she saw over and over. Then, a cold father—an adulterous father—swooping in to take her back to the States before the dirt on her mother's grave had even settled. And, sicker still, hiring his mistress to care for the motherless child.

The latter he gleaned not from the article but his own assumptions, and today the Widow Pritchard had all but confirmed it. Melvin blew right through a stop sign as he recounted in his head all he'd learned about Ivy Cole. After finding the news articles, a follow-up cross-check in the vehicular records database at the station confirmed Ivy's whereabouts over the past years. She'd lived in Rapid City when the mauling occurred in Wall. She was in a New Orleans suburb during the time of the Burgundy attacks. And William and Una Pritchard Cole had gone missing eight years after moving to New York, right after Ivy's eighteenth birthday. Although the exact time of their disappearance was sketchy, they were first noticed missing from their vacation chalet in the Hamptons during the week of a full moon. Under a full moon, when Ivy lost her mother.

Melvin now understood Ivy's fascination with the moon, with dogs, with moving every few years. Melvin now completely understood everything.

"You poor kid." The deputy shook his head. He had no real evidence, just a string of coincidences, and Ava's testimony was no testimony at all. Her loyalty shouldn't surprise him, though; there would be no reason for the elderly lady to suspect that a young girl, part of her own family, could commit such atrocities. And, again, that was just a hunch too, one he wasn't sure he believed himself. Cases could be built on hunches, but hunches didn't stand up in court.

And that, Melvin thought, was a good thing.

Chapter 40

It couldn't be true. It was crazy, this thinking. Not her.

Melvin, accordion-folded to some degree between the edge of his desktop and the flimsy back wall of his cubicle, pondered impossibilities as he stared into the waxy green leaves of his office plant. The new, livelier plant had replaced the wilted one before it managed to completely succumb to a thirsty death. Shirley, without a word about it, had scooped up the ailing greenery, and this larger replacement, whose leaves resembled shiny lily pads of striated plastic, had shown up to sit in its spot and continue the wilting process. Melvin hoped Shirley would understand, but he had more on his mind than caring for foliage.

As facts and dates and sun freckles across the nose of a green-eyed blonde jitterbugged in a mad cacophony on the back side of his mind's eye, Melvin's chin dipped forward onto his chest. He snapped upright and looked around quickly to see if anyone noticed he'd started to nod off, but the office was empty, save for Shirley and Delores at the front. One tapped away on her ancient typewriter while the other fussed a little too loudly about the inappropriateness of junk mail coming to a police station. Typing and ripping and a disapproving snort from time to time were the only sounds.

Melvin was glad the sheriff and Meeks were out for the afternoon. He'd wanted more time alone to think about his meeting with Ava the day before and what to do with the paperwork still stored *(hidden)* in his trunk. Two a.m. came and went last night and he was still out, driving around and thinking things through. Not in the cruiser this time. He'd backed out of the garage in his black Dodge and melted away into the night. Without realizing where he was heading, the engine cut and the headlights dimmed on the Lutsky property.

Melvin made his way through the slippery grass and down the short slope to the creekside, where he and Ivy had enjoyed a summer day together with food and peach wine and each other. She had avoided talk of herself then, and turned it to simpler things—the moon, the hawk, the scar below the cleft in Melvin's chin from a childhood softball toss gone awry. He felt special under her attention, as if Ivy lived only for that moment and their presence in a flower-dappled valley, relishing each second of their time as it ticked by. He felt that is how she chose to live a lifetime, so unlike other people he had known. How freeing, he'd thought and envied, to not plow through the day in some personal uphill struggle toward the future, nor become mired in the quicksand of a past one could not let go. To only live for that day . . . Ivy, with her lazy glances at the sky, and the silky ripple of her voice when she said his name. The day with her was like a slow, ebbing, pleasurable sigh, and he left it feeling he'd already lived life too hard and too quickly with no time to be still, to just be.

Melvin had sat by the creek for a long time, its babbling revealing nothing but woodland secrets he could never understand. Much like the woman herself. Ivy. His sweet Ivy. She was nothing he was looking for, and everything.

Melvin left thoughts of the creek and a picnic to return to the problem at hand. In front of him on his desk, laid open with accusatory ballpoint scribblings exposed, was Melvin's notebook. The battered little book, filled with notes predating Ivy Cole. But now she'd become the main character in its crinkled pages. A story was there: a beginning, a middle, but no end. Undetermined. The sheriff would take care of that if she had more to go on. He'd heard Gloria and Tee behind the closed doors of her office, wringing out ideas and concocting different scenarios until a finger was already starting to swing around and point in Ivy's direction. With Tee off somewhere on his own private witch-hunt, Gloria had slowed down a little. But Melvin knew the sheriff wouldn't wait on Tee long before moving ahead without him. What that meant, exactly, he didn't know. What it meant to him exactly, he knew even less.

The notebook was open, and Melvin had to deal with it. There was a name. And a phone number. Would it prove anything? No. But it could give him some peace of mind. Last night had rewarded him with none of that.

The telephone was an ugly gray thing, hunched on his desk pad like a fat toad. He loathed to touch it. Melvin picked up the receiver and dialed anyway.

"Yo! Dakota Backcountry here. This is Cody. What can I do you for?"

"I'm calling for Nate McKinley. Is he around?"

"Nope, he's heading up a trip till next week. But I'd be glad to help you. Let me get the reservation book out. Are you calling about a weekend excursion or something extended? We're running a special on weeklong camping trips through September."

"I'm not calling about booking a camping trip. I need some information. This is Officer Melvin Sanders from the Doe Springs Sheriff's Office in North Carolina."

"Whoo-ee. What's ole Nate gone and done now? I hate that S.O.B. I'd be glad to tell you anything you want to know."

Melvin heard a chair slide out and the unmistakable *fwwwt* of a match striking up. A breath exhaled long against the receiver, and Melvin pictured Cody settling back with a smoke, eager to sling some mud on a fellow coworker.

"He hasn't done anything. I'm working on an animal attack case and I understand Mr. McKinley's brother, Gabe, was killed in a similar manner."

"How'd you get wind of that? That happened—what—five years ago at least. *Y'all* got a coyote problem down there in the *Sou-outh*?"

Melvin ignored the mocking Southern drawl. Mingled with the Western twang, it sounded kind of nice. Melvin decided to ignore the question as well. "Mr. McKinley gets back in next week?"

"Uh-yuh."

"I'd appreciate it if you'd have him call me at this number." Melvin started to recite his home phone when Cody interrupted.

"I can tell you right now, Officer Sanders, Nate won't call a cop back unless he knows the what-for ahead of time. This is just about his brother?"

"Yes, and a lady he might have known, Ivy Cole. I-V-Y C-O—"

"Ivy? Well, I'll be danged. Is she all right?" The man's tone fell from bluster into genuine concern.

"She's fine, actually. You know her?"

"Ah, shoot, know her? She was the sweetest little lady ever come through our roughneck patch of the woods. She only worked here a summer, helping out with the pack horses, but we could never forget Ivy. Lord, how she loved them horses. All animals, as it turned out. How is our Southern belle?"

"Miss Cole is fine. I'm guessing she knew Gabe McKinley as well, then?"

"Sure she knew him. And let me tell you something," a long draw of silence, followed by the breathy whish of smoke released across the line, "if anybody in this world hated Gabe and Nate worse than I did, it was Ivy. The stories I could tell you."

"Oh yeah? Tell me a couple. I've got a minute." Melvin flipped to a raw page in the notebook and ran his hand over its blank lines. There was more to the story coming. His stomach lurched slightly, and his eyes darted around looking for the Tums.

"Uh, all right. Sure. I ain't much busy right now either. Hold on a sec."

Melvin heard a can top pop open and the fizz of something pouring into a glass. Ice clinked as Cody took a big swallow. By the sound of the whole exchange, Melvin guessed the man was drinking a cola of some kind—a good thing. Melvin didn't like beer guzzlers, a throwback to hauling the broken body of Randy Mabe in after his drunken fall from a bridge, back when this whole Devil of Doe Springs trouble got started.

"The problem," Cody said with a dramatic pause, "was Gabe. He liked Ivy and couldn't let go of it. Hell, there's eight of us worked here and we all were in love with her,

Nate too. But he was only mildly afflicted with the curse—
you know, running after women out of his league—and he
backed off when he saw how crazy Gabe was about Ivy and
how crazy acting he was starting to get when she'd have
none of him. When she kept putting him off—now, mind
you, she was always nice about it—Gabe's stomped-on ego
swelled up into meanness. He started picking at her, doing
things to piss her off or maybe even get her fired. But he was
like that. Nate ain't much different. I kind of wish a couple
of coyotes would pay him a visit, but that'd probably be too
good for him."

"What things would Gabe do?"

"Juvenile stuff. Ivy'd get the horses packed up nice for
our greenest greenhorn customers, and Gabe would go behind her and loosen all the girths so halfway down the trail
all the gear would be hanging off the horses sideways. And
he locked her in the tack room one time for an hour before
Garrett finally heard her yelling and let her out. Stupid tricks
like that. She never reported him or complained about it, just
went on about her way, doing her job with the horses and being as sweet to the rest of us as ever. The way things were
going, we thought she'd weather ole Gabe's teasing right up
to the end of our camping season. But she didn't. We hated
to see her leave, let me tell you. We were all mad as hell
Gabe ran her off with that last thing he did."

"And what was that?"

Cody didn't answer right away, and Melvin feared he
would hang up without revealing the gold nugget of this
drawn-out conversation. The man obviously enjoyed a good
yarn, and Melvin regretted calling from the station. Explain-
ing this call to Sheriff Hubbard would not be easy. Finally
Cody said, "We're up here in Custer, the state park. Do you
know it?"

"No. Never been."

"Don't matter. Suffice it to say, big country and wide-
open spaces don't describe the half of it out here. We're an
outfitter, taking people from all over into the backcountry to
camp, see wildlife, get back to nature, whatever. This particular excursion was just a day trip, though, which we don't

normally do, but some company out in Jersey paid big bucks for us to show their bigwigs and wives a good time for an afternoon.

"Now, Ivy never went out with us for overnighters—something about she had a million dogs to take care of at home—so this was a special treat for her, getting to finally go on a trail with a group. Nate had a fit about it because he got stuck here at the lodge, but Gabe shut him up in a hurry. He put himself right beside Ivy from the get-go.

"We lined up fifteen riders nose to tail with Gabe and Ivy leading the outfit and yours truly bringing up the rear. We were crossing a creek about an hour out from the lodge when Gabe looks up and swears he sees a wolf just down from us going the other direction. Now I'm thinking he's been breathing too much trail dust—wolves are a rare sight even in these parts—but we all start rubbernecking and damned if there on the riverbank fifty yards away ain't standing the finest-looking animal I've ever seen. It was a wolf all right. He was a tawny color, like he'd been poured in sand and maple syrup. Beautiful animal. All the years we'd packed in and out, I'd never seen a wolf. Our riders are pulling out cameras fast as they can, but Gabe steps off his horse, smooth as redeye gravy, and unsheathes his Remington. Before any of us know what's happening, Gabe shoulders the rifle. Ivy sees him first and she starts yelling 'no!' I take my eyes off the wolf, who is watching us now like he's thinking about hightailing it. Ivy's all tore up, I mean, I see pure terror in her. She's screaming at Gabe, screaming at the wolf to run, and all the while Gabe's aiming that gun. He cuts her one of his mean little grins, squints one eye, and . . . *Boom!*"

"Gabe shot the wolf."

"Hell no. Ivy knocked him flat on his ass in the creek. She ran him over with her horse, can you believe it? His gun went off straight up into the air, and all hell broke loose after that. Wives were screaming, horses were wheeling around, and I think a couple of the Jerseyites managed to get a picture of Gabe sprawled in the river. I laughed till I about peed myself."

Melvin silently cheered. Despite the creeping sadness

that a real connection was finally made between the woman he cared about and a dead man, he could not help but feel a sudden prickle of satisfaction at her besting this jerk.

"Gabe's pride smarted worse than his cold-cocked butt for weeks after Ivy outdone him in front of all of us. He got chewed up by the boss man too. Almost lost his job over firing that gun in front of the Jersey crowd, but somehow he swung it to stay on with the outfit.

"After that, Gabe seemed to change. Left Ivy alone. We thought she'd cured him. But no." Cody was quiet again, and when he spoke to finish the story at last, his voice was weighted by a sentimentality Melvin felt the cowboy would rather another man not pick up on.

"I was the one who found her," he said. "She was kneeling on the floor of the tack room, rocking back and forth and not saying a word. Just rocking, with something tucked to her stomach in her arms. She was kind of curled around it." Cody lingered over the thoughts. The words came slower, as if the dread of that day were upon him again and he'd rather not relive it. But Melvin was patient. Finality was arriving, and Melvin felt as caught up in the story as if he were there to hold Ivy himself. He would pry away whatever she held wrapped in her arms and comfort her with the strength of his own.

"It was that wolf's head, Officer Sanders," Cody said quietly. "Must have taken Gabe all that time to hunt the wolf down, but damned if he didn't and left its head on her gear to find. Same sandy coat, there couldn't have been another one like it up here.

"I'll never forget the look in that girl's eyes as long as I live. It's like she'd left us altogether. They were cold, kind of glassy. I thought she was in shock, but when I said her name and shook her shoulder, she looked up at me and the sadness I saw in her touched me hard. I never told anybody this, but you don't know me and it was a long time ago—I lost a lot of sleep thinking about Ivy rocking that bloody wolf's head.

"She was gone before the boss man got back to the barn to talk to her. Gabe got fired, which was way overdue. He moved down to Wall, and that, sir, was the last thing he ever did. You know the rest, if you believe it."

"About the coyotes? You don't believe that's what killed him?"

"I'm not saying they did or didn't, but I can tell you this. Me and my buddies spent plenty of hours around the campfire speculatin' on this thing. Coyotes wouldn't do what happened to Gabe. Shoot, you stamp your foot at a coyote and it'll run off most the time. Nope, I'll be honest with you: We all feel the score's just a bit more square, thinking that wolf came back and gave Gabe what he was asking for. Hokey, I reckon. But I tell you, Officer, out here we believe there is a balance to the world, an order of how things are s'posed to be, and Gabe was one of those agitators who liked to go around upsetting the natural scheme. Like with Ivy, a good little gal, and that ole wolf, who didn't hurt a thing either.

"But that's enough on my philosophies, and that's about all I can tell you on Gabe McKinley. But do this for me, would you? Tell Ivy to give some old dusty cowpokes a jingle from time to time. The trail's a lot lonelier without her."

Part Four

"It's not the wolf that makes the killer.
It's what lies in the heart of the man."

Chapter 41

Moonlight marked the path ahead of the woman as she fought low-hanging branches out of her way. The woods were thick and holding her back. Or protecting her in a cradling embrace, she wasn't sure which, but she blundered forward anyway, the trail hopelessly endless in front of her. She was in a gown, a sheer, filmy thing she would never wear, and like gossamer it floated around her bare feet as she stumbled on her way to a destination she knew she must reach but not sure why. The path became thick like the woods themselves, and mud caked her feet and flecked up her calves. The bottom of the gown grew heavy with splattered muck and the soiled, clinging fabric made a sucking sound each time it slapped her ankles. But she pressed on, ignoring the stems that poked through her hair and tore at her cheeks and the ruined hemline dragging around her legs.

The path broke at last; she could see the cold blue light of the full moon spilling through a hole in the wall of trees. She moved toward the light, her destination arrived.

It was the logger's cabin, huddled dark and small against the mountainside. Moonlight scraped the black beams of its rotted wood, resembling petrified bones on the frame of a long-dead animal. The door was open. She moved toward it, knowing all the answers were inside this place and she could rest.

She stood in the doorway, a halo of blue light silhouetting her and blinding her to what crouched inside. Her vision cleared. Two wolves flanked the woodstove, one black, one white. They peered at one another, entranced, lost in a primal language the woman could not understand. The guttural utterances were punctuated by slight squeaks and clicks of teeth.

"I know you," the woman said. The wolves turned. . . .

Gloria sat upright in bed, her sheets twisted in knots around her arms and legs, the obvious woodland she'd been battling in her dream. Sweaty and perturbed at another ruined night of sleep, Gloria kicked the covers to the foot of the bed and got up. Her feet hit the hardwood and a shock of icy cold quickly dissipated any remnants of the recurring dream. The house could be chilly at night, even in August, and Gloria pulled sweatpants over her nude legs, leaving the flannel nightshirt to hang over them. A pair of heavy socks later and Gloria was padding toward the refuge of her kitchen, where a pot of coffee would complete the wake-up and start her day. It was four in the morning; no point trying to sleep again now.

The kitchen was nearly lit from the moon, and Gloria's hand hesitated over the light switch. A near-perfect bluish-white orb shone through her window, an almost imperceptible sliver missing from its round arc. The following night the piece would not be missing, the circle would be complete, and another full moon would be filling the sky and haunting her community.

While the aged coffeemaker gurgled and spat, Gloria sat down and slid up to the growing mound of paperwork dominating her only eating space. Buried under all the photos and reports rested her grandmother's antique dining table. But she hadn't seen the top of it for some time. All this work should be at the station, but she and Tee had been making all-night work sessions in her kitchen a habit. As romantic as the possibilities may have been, she and Tee were both too consumed with the Devil to move beyond it into the realm of the personal. But there had been moments. Hints at possibilities. Both of them, perhaps, thinking maybe, after the case was done and all this was over, there could be time for gapped bridges to mend. . . .

But no. Tee was gone again. Just like after Annie, when

he'd left for Montana and never looked back. Were they getting too close, and he'd closed the door on it before old hurts could come calling?

Where the hell did you go this time, Tee? There's so much left to do.

Gloria picked up the manila envelope on the top of the stack, labeled from the forensics criminal laboratory and postmarked two days ago. After talking with the lab herself, Gloria had asked them to bypass the office and mail the DNA results directly to her home. What gut instinct demanded she do that, she was not sure. But Tee had become insistent they work the details of the case at her house and keep most of the information between them. Gloria did not like keeping anything from her deputies, but Tee's mistrust—unexplained mistrust—had seeped into her as well.

And then this report on the hair and metal samples her department submitted finally arrived. The most predominant hairs provided in the first sample, the lab stated, although by coarseness and texture did appear to be canine, matched no canid DNA host samples on record in their vast database. They broadened the search comparisons to include other animals in the Southeastern Appalachian region with no success. The answer, the lab concluded, was one of two things: The Blue Ridge had acquired a new unknown species, or the samples submitted by the Doe Springs Sheriff's Office were contaminated. The stiffly formal letter accompanying the nonconclusive results clearly indicated belief in the latter.

Gloria would make sure no one ever got a hold of that letter. "New unknown species" written in an official document was all the locals needed to fan the werewolf rumor to uncontrollable proportions. It was the proof and validation they were looking for, and they'd completely overlook the scientific opinion of contaminated sampling. Someone like Artie Crimshaw from the *Doe Springs Gazette* would have a field day.

At least the lab had been able to determine some things with certainty. From an exclusionary analysis they found that none of the hairs from the cot were synthetic, like from a wolf suit as one of Sanders's theories would have it, although some of it could be credited to typical nocturnal prowlers (rats mostly) as Meeks suggested. The unidentifiable hairs, labeled "contaminated sample: caninelike," were black in color. Black, like the shepherd Ivy Cole sported about.

The coffeepot perked to a long, whistling sigh and one final, rude burp—the signal the last of the caffeine had brewed. Gloria reached behind her to pour a cup. The coffee burned its way down to her stomach in an eye-opening stream, but she barely noticed the fire in her throat as she pulled the second report from the envelope, this in regard to the gold metal found at the Largen farm. Identifying that had been easy. Tee was right, of course. It was a gold cap for a human tooth. *Wedged into the eye of a brutalized pig. What sickness is this?* Gloria would be pulling Ivy's dental records the same day she plucked hairs from the woman's dog. Which would be, most likely, right after the sun came up.

Gloria dropped the report and poured a second cup of coffee. She swiveled back around and put her mug in the center of the forensics letter, where it set up a ragged brown stain around the words *DNA typing error.* The solution to the error was no big deal. Gloria would send in another hair sample from the cot herself—not via a deputy—along with another batch of hair to type and analyze for a possible match. And there would be no mistaking the host of that second sample. By the size, weight, and conformation of Ivy Cole's dog, Gloria estimated a high-percent wolf infusion in the shepherd's blood. A hybrid wolf, with enough shepherd to make him trainable.

If the hair matched that taken from the cot . . . So what? It proved absolutely nothing other than the animal frequented a banged-up logger's cabin for whatever excuse Ivy Cole could come up with. But on the map stuck to Gloria's office wall was a web of pins and red lines connecting them. The pins were the attack sites, the red lines cow paths and roadways joining them. Near center in the web, where the spider might sit, were the Lutsky/power company properties and the logger's cabin. Just outside the inner perimeter lay Ivy Cole's cottage.

Deputy Sanders had conducted a background check on the Cole woman at Gloria's request, but he came up with nothing other than two passed-away parents and a hefty inheritance, which explained how she bought her house for cash. But now, after the fouled lab report and Tee's guarded behavior regarding the office, Gloria wondered if her youngest deputy could be completely trusted. He was a man, after all, a man who just might be in love with the most promising suspect of their case.

Gloria put the envelope back on the table and rose to stand by the window. She looked up at the sky, her face bathed in the cold blue light from her dream. Tonight a full moon would be upon Doe Springs, but this time its sheriff would be ready.

Chapter 42

The woods were beautiful at this early morning hour. Ivy walked through them silently, reverently—a druid worshipping in an ethereal place. Velvety darkness caressed her skin as she meandered along the creek bed. Aufhocker kept pace with her every step, occasionally stopping to sniff the air or take interest in something along the path. August was already bringing changes to the mountain. Colors peeked from fading greens during daylight hours, and a few early signs of leaf fall lay under Ivy's bare feet. In two months, the ground she trod upon would be littered with mottled colors of every hue, palomino golds and bruised purples and blushes of reds foremost among them.

Ivy stopped in the special glade she'd discovered after first moving into her cottage. It was a ring of cleared space amid the heart of clustered hemlocks, ferocious trees with

roots like claws grabbing fistfuls of dirt out of the forest
floor. They surrounded the clandestine dell like protective
overlords, and it was in this safe haven that Ivy came to
think, reflect, and, sometimes, kill. But all traces of Clifford
were finally washed away. The creek's water ran clear of any
pollutants from his blood; the ground had swallowed up any
specks of him the police left behind. The glade was restored.

Ivy settled by the stream and the stand of mushroom um-
brellas marching along the creek's mossy bank. The cool
mud between her toes felt good and the sound of the rushing
water even better. Its flow picked up her most worrisome in-
trospections and carried them downstream, toward the valley
in which she and a kind deputy had picnicked one bright
summer day. Her thoughts could not let go of the tall, dark-
haired policeman. Ivy admitted she had never felt like this
before, had never let herself feel like this. But Deputy
Sanders was different. His aw-shucks, straight-laced ways
had charmed her; Melvin was the side of her she lacked and
she was drawn to it.

But therein lay the greatest danger. He would never understand what she was, and he would never condone it. She was
perilously close to having to move again. The more she fed,
the more in danger the deputy became. Because he would not
stop. He would not be swayed from his duty. He would never
give up until the Devil of Doe Springs was no more. What
would Melvin have thought, sprawled upon the picnic blanket that afternoon, had he known Clifford Hughes's blood
had flowed not five feet from where the deputy lay, shaken
from the coat of an ivory wolf he shared his peach wine with?

Aufhocker pawed Ivy's thigh, smearing it with black soil
from his nails. She put an arm around her vigilant companion. Dawn would break into a day of uncertainty, then night
would follow—it, too, one of dubious conclusions. That was
why she was here in her special place on the morn of the full
moon. To decide. But she knew in her heart there was only
one thing to do: rid Doe Springs of its Devil and the deputy
of his quest. Tonight Ivy would be hunting for one of her
own, and murder was heavy on her mind. To kill the black
wolf was the only choice she had. Then, afterward, she

could leave no traces of her victims ever again. There were other wolves she'd known who lived this way, without proving points using the dead. They simply hunted, and ate, and lived their lives without grandstanding on good intentions.

Ivy played out the final encounter in the quicksilver rush of stream water. Shadows took shape in the moonlit swirls, and she saw the black wolf and herself through the wavery projection. He was a magnificent wolf indeed. His onyx coat rippled like a pearly oil slick across the water, as she saw him moving through the night, seeking his prey. Or seeking, perhaps, herself.

They meet, and greet in the way of wolves. They approach one another with confidence, tails erect and eyes never wavering from the other's. Then they come together, circling, testing boundaries. The black wolf pushes his nose into the scruff of the female's neck, and she allows this. Then his lips pull back in the half grin of a canine smile, and she returns it. Their backs arch low, forepaws and chests on the ground, tails high in the air, in a bow that suddenly breaks, not into aggression, but a bout of play. They leap around one another, then break into a gallop side by side and dash off through the moonlit trees together, a pair.

"No." Ivy kicked the water with her foot, dispersing the image and splashing Aufhocker, who jumped away. She knew what she wanted to do, what her heart needed. She would go see her sweet deputy whether he wanted her to or not.

Ivy drove slowly down Dogwood Avenue, straining to read house numbers through the charcoal mist of daybreak. She was in an older neighborhood of Doe Springs, but that wasn't saying much. It was all old, this town. There were merely varying degrees of it.

As Ivy scanned the simple wood-framed houses for the number 1521 and an Impala cruiser in the driveway, it occurred to her that Melvin had never invited her to his place. Comfortable with that arrangement, she'd never questioned it—until this morning. Copying his address out of the phone book and then spiriting away before daybreak to surprise

him in his driveway before work did not feel very noble. It
felt desperate. But their last phone conversation did not go
well, and she had not heard from him since. It was sadden-
ing, his sudden avoidance. And disappointing. Ivy had expected him on her doorstep with gifts and apologies, both of
which she would have accepted. But he'd done nothing to
make it right between them. The more Ivy thought about it,
the angrier she started to get. Suddenly, seeing the deputy
for a reconciliation was taking a backseat to a good old-fashioned tongue-lashing for screwing them up, first by ruining
her trust and then for not being dutifully repentant afterward. Ivy felt her pulse quicken and her eyes start to shim-
mer as she imagined ambushing him as he came out the
front door for work. How dare he push her away like this.
How dare he try to cut her loose in such a cowardly, childish
way! *I've got a few things to say to you, Melvin Sanders.*

Fifteen twenty-one Dogwood Avenue rose on Ivy's right.
She sat by the curb for a moment, taking the house in.
Melvin's home was completely unexpected. The small two-
story structure was a gingerbread concoction of dormers,
elaborately designed trimming, and latticework. Stonework
seated the foundation and ivy wound around trellises fram-
ing the front door. This was not a bachelor pad by any
means. It was a nest for a family—the wife and children
Melvin hoped to have some day.

Ivy's anger wavered and dissipated. Here was not the
home of a deceiver, and she knew the deputy was no coward.
Whatever his reasons for the change in behavior, well,
they'd talk it out and work through it. Looking at this charm-
ing place, reminiscent of her own cottage, reminded Ivy of
why she cared so much for Melvin in the first place.

Ivy left her van on the side of the road and walked across
the neatly mowed lawn. She rang the doorbell and waited.
No answer. Missing from the driveway was Melvin's police
cruiser, so she walked around to the garage but could not see
inside. Ivy rang the bell once more, but she already knew the
deputy was gone. She had missed him. Too late. It had felt so
important to see him now, before tonight and whatever it
might bring to her fate. Ivy turned to go home. She could try

another call to the station, but earlier thoughts of desperation pushed the idea away. The lady who always answered the phone seemed so aggravated when she called there for Melvin anyway. Perhaps a note would be enough, a token offering to cross their invisible barrier back into friendship. He could read it at his leisure and give consideration to the appropriate reply. If there was one.

Ivy walked to her van and pulled a scratch pad from the glove compartment. With a pencil from the cup holder, she jotted a brief note: *Dear Melvin, I've realized some things from your absence. Namely, that I can't bear it.* Ivy stopped. She ripped the paper out and threw it on the floorboard. On a clean sheet she tried again: *Dear Melvin, Even though you lied about my book and how you would take care of it, I have forgiven your poor judgment.* He'd never call her after that one. A second wad of paper hit the floor. *Dear Melvin, Came by to see you. You were gone. Call me. Ivy.*

It would have to do. Ivy folded the paper into a thin square, then walked back to Melvin's front door with it. She wedged it into the space between the doorknob and jamb, where it protruded like a tiny white flag of surrender.

Surrender. Ivy was halfway to her van when she wheeled around and marched back to Melvin's door. She grasped the note and with a tug, pulled it free. A mechanical click followed the release of the paper and the door swung inward.

Ivy stood there, note in hand, horrified. She had broken into a police officer's home, completely by accident. *What kind of policeman uses such a shabby lock as this anyway?* She was mad at Melvin for a whole new reason. She was now inconvenienced with having to explain a breaking and entering if any of the neighbors spotted her. Ivy looked around but the houses across the street sat quiet. She peered around the garage to Melvin's backyard. It was shielded by a thick row of cypresses. Clean and sparse like the front yard.

Satisfied no one had seen her, Ivy went back to the front of the house. She reached to lock and close the door but found herself slipping inside the living room instead. A thick tapestry rug the color of desert sand welcomed her feet and hugged the center of the hardwood floor almost from corner

to corner of the room. Upon it squatted a heavy chocolate
leather couch, which faced a rough-brick fireplace in earth-
tone beiges. A restored shipping trunk divided the couch
from the fireplace, serving as a rustic coffee table. Black bears
and foxes and other mountain wildlife roamed the taupe
walls in various sizes of prints, alongside tintypes of turn-
of-the-century farmers posing amid Blue Ridge landscapes.
It was obviously a man's room, without the soft touch of feminine lace that would no doubt find its way there one day. But
it was tasteful and comfortable and warm. Ivy would have
liked visiting Melvin here. New hurt pinched her too sharply
to ignore.

Ivy trailed a hand along the back of the leather sofa and
allowed the path to carry her onward into other parts of the
house. A cream-colored kitchen, everything in order, one
dirty coffee cup waiting to be washed in the sink. A carton of
milk in the refrigerator, with a pack of bologna and what
seemed to be a pitcher of grape Kool-Aid below it. Not much
else. In the hallway, a half-bath, its gleaming porcelain obviously tended to regularly with a sponge and Pine-Sol.

Ivy wandered from room to room, upstairs and down, relishing the smells of the deputy and how they altered from
place to place. Coffee beans and shaving cream and a hint of
cologne. Laundry detergent and furniture waxes and cleaning foams. Soap and shampoo and minty toothpaste. He was
alive in the house at this very moment, and she smiled in
spite of herself.

The last room on the tour was in front of her, and she
knew what it must be. Melvin's most private place—his bedroom. How upset she would be to learn someone had snooped
through her house without permission, yet curiosity quelled
the guilt of wrong-doing. Ivy pushed the door open and entered onto heavy eggshell carpet. The bed was simply made
with a white comforter, two oversized pillows (no shams),
and a solid oak headboard. Two wood end tables embraced
the bed between them, and a darkly stained dresser stood
watch over it all. A picture of Melvin's family sat on top of
the chest of drawers along with a four-by-six framed photo
of a dog he must have once loved.

A large book lay facedown on the dresser along with the photographs. Curious as to Melvin's taste in literature, Ivy turned the book over. Her eyes widened and the book trembled in her hands. She steadied herself before dropping it. The deputy's record of transgressions had just filled up. *Thief! Liar!*

Tears flooded Ivy's eyes. The title of *Lykanthrop* blurred into nonsensical symbols. She folded the book to her chest and fled the house, leaving the door standing wide open behind her.

Chapter 43

Deputy Sanders had come to some conclusions. Number one, he was in love with Ivy Cole. Had been since the day he saw her walking down that dusty road in a torn skirt, clutching an injured dog like her life depended on it, not the dog's. Number two, Melvin would get her the help she needed. He could no more turn his back on Ivy than she could have left that terrier by the roadside. And number three, he would continue to protect her in the meantime until he could figure out exactly what "getting help" meant.

And that was why the deputy was here on her doorstep at this inappropriate hour. Melvin skipped his morning run, downed a bad cup of coffee, and drove to Ivy's before heading into the station. Once the sheriff got a hold of her men, there would be no letting up until daybreak tomorrow. What the sheriff's strategy of preparation for tonight's full moon might be, he had no idea, but he knew there would be no time later on to divert Ivy from her task if his suspicions were correct.

Melvin could prove it to himself, easily enough. He could

follow Ivy tonight and settle what his heart still denied was
true. But if he were not alone, if Meeks or the sheriff were
with him, if he could not lose them somehow and handle the
confrontation without unwanted backup, he feared what
could happen. To Ivy. To his partners. To himself. Melvin
would be forced to choose.

The best solution, he decided, was the simplest of all. He
would sit Ivy down and ask her straight out about her mother,
about Una and William, about South Dakota and New Orleans
and the nature of her black shepherd. He would confess to
having *Lykanthrop* and ask her to explain Toomey's rubbing,
initialed I.V.

Melvin rang Ivy's doorbell. An explosion of barking
greeted him from the backyard, the sudden break in morning
silence harsh to Melvin's ears. He noticed the van was gone,
odd at this hour, but he rang the bell again anyway, then
opened the screen door and started banging. Rex's head
popped into view at the living room window.

"Good morning, Rex. Where's Ivy?"

When the little dog answered only with an angry yap,
Melvin stepped off the porch and headed around back. He
rounded the corner, only to find the black shepherd already
at the edge of the fence, waiting for him. While the other
dogs barked, the shepherd stared silently at the deputy, ears
perked and head lowered.

Melvin knelt eye level with the dog. He took him in,
every inch of him, from grizzled nose to the slight ring of
emerging gray around his neck to the powerful shoulders
and hindquarters. How could Melvin have missed it before?
This was no ordinary shepherd. He had not seen, perhaps,
because he'd chosen not to.

"You're the one," Melvin said softly. "The Devil of Doe
Springs."

At Melvin's words, the ridgeline of fur along Aufhocker's
broad neck rose erect and traveled like a reverse course of
dominoes, rising instead of falling, to stop between the animal's shoulder blades. His lips quivered above ivory canines, and a guttural growl rumbled up from the dog's chest.

The deep-pitch eyes never left the deputy's, and Melvin found himself leaning toward the slats in the fence, straining to hear the primal voice, so lulling, reassuring, like the subtle sound of stones tumbling in a child's hand, or distant thunder from a summer storm, but getting softer, ever so softer. A purr, a kitten's purr, mellow, calming, those black eyes, lost in those eyes, deeper and deeper, Melvin could fall forever. . . .

Aufhocker lunged at the fence, his teeth tearing at the weathered slats like they were toothpicks. Splinters of gray wood tore the dog's gums, but he only fought the barrier harder. Flecks of blood flew into the deputy's startled face and he fell backward into the grass. The dog gnashed at Melvin's feet as a hole big enough for the shepherd's massive head finally gave way.

Melvin scuttled backward and fumbled for his holster. He pulled the automatic and tried to get a good aim on the dog's brow as it worried the fence harder, fighting to get the rest of his body through. Melvin's finger rested on the trigger. He squeezed slightly, and stopped. *Ivy.* The deputy saw her coming home, rushing to the backyard to greet her animals, then finding her dog shot dead by the very man who loved her. Melvin let out a howl of his own as he fired the gun straight up into the air, emptying six rounds into the ruined quiet of the morning.

The fresh hole in the fence was vacant. A few other curious faces poked through to stare at the deputy, then warily drew back. Melvin rose to his feet. He held the gun to his side, the nose of the Glock tapping against his thigh as his hand shook. Aufhocker stood in the middle of the backyard, watching him. Bloodied foam dripped from the dog's muzzle.

Melvin raised the gun again, but this time he slid it into the holster. Brushing off his pants, he walked around to the front of the house, only to be nearly knocked flat by Deputy Meeks.

"Jesus Christ! What are you doing here, Meeks?" Melvin let go of the man's shoulder after regaining his balance.

"I heard shots. Are you all right?" Meeks's gun was drawn and ready.

"Yeah, yeah, everything is fine. The dogs were going crazy back there. They were fighting and I fired some rounds to break them up. What are you doing here anyway?"

"The sheriff sent me here with this." Meeks held out a search warrant. "She's on her way too. What are you doing here already? I couldn't reach you on the radio."

"I . . . you're out of luck. Miss Cole's not home."

"Too bad for Miss Cole. C'mon." Meeks was inside the house before Melvin could stop him.

"Door wasn't even locked. What do you make of that?" Meeks said. They stood in Ivy's living room, shoulder to shoulder. Rex squared off in front of the men, barking. Meeks approached the little dog.

"Ferocious one, ain'tcha? I can see why Miss Cole wouldn't lock up with you around." Meeks reached out his hand. Rex backed away uncertainly, then relieved himself on the hardwood floor. The terrier whined, turned, and disappeared down the hallway.

"I'm glad I'm not the only one he doesn't like," Melvin said.

Meeks raised a brow. "Over here that much, are you?"

Melvin ducked the question. "What are we looking for exactly?"

"Anything. Notes, letters, diaries, a smoking gun. You don't seem too surprised we're here to search your girlfriend's house." *And you haven't asked why yet either, old son. You know something, don't you?*

"I'd appreciate it if you'd keep my private life out of this. She's just a friend." Melvin felt attacked again, this time by someone he feared much more than a four-legged aggressor. To have his own department doubt him was unthinkable. What happened to the honorable law enforcement officer he used to be? He'd wrestle with that one later. Right now he had to search this house before the sheriff showed up. *Lykanthrop* was in a safe place for now, but who knew what else Ivy had lying about. "Why don't you look around outside? I'll get started in here."

"No, it'll go quicker if we both clear the house first." Meeks turned toward the direction of the stairwell. "I'll start up there." He didn't miss Melvin's frown, but the younger deputy would just have to suck it up. There was a new man in the house now, and he was on the hunt. An interesting smell emanated from upstairs, and Meeks didn't need the woman's boyfriend breathing over his shoulder while he investigated. He turned his back on Melvin to avoid a protest if one was forthcoming and quickly bounded up the stairs.

Ivy's bedroom was pleasantly feminine with a grandmother's attic feel that was older than her thirty-one years. Meeks turned full circle in the small room, taking in the crocheted pillows, the corner crammed with stacks of hatboxes overflowing with ribbons and yarn, the jars of fading flowers on the sill of the open window. He ran his hand over the patchwork quilt, and his fingertips tingled. Here's where she lay to sleep. Were her dreams peaceful, or the stuff of nightmares like his own? Meeks held one of the pillows to his face and took a long, deep breath. He knew the white wolf's scent, but it was not the one that drew him to this room. Meeks threw the pillow back on the bed and walked to the aged dresser by the window. A blond child with hollow cheeks, wide bright eyes, and long pale hair stared at him from a photograph. "Hello, Ivy. Where is it, your secret stash?"

Meeks abandoned the picture to once more stand in front of the bed. He closed his eyes and focused only on his nose and the perfume that drew him up here—the scent of old, flaking blood. Dead blood. "Where is it, where is it, where is it?" he said through clenched teeth. Then his jaw relaxed, and he smiled.

Meeks looked straight down at his feet. The colorful braided rug was picked and worn in places. He kicked it back and tested the planks underneath with the toe of his boot. One popped loose too easily.

The deputy reached into the hole and pulled out Clifford Hughes's jewelry and a dog-eared journal. He held a ring to his nose. Soap residue mingled with the traces of blood she'd missed in her efforts to cleanse it. Here was an evidence gold mine worthy of a promotion. Meeks pocketed the jewelry and journal, then replaced the plank and rug.

Sheriff Hubbard spoke from behind him. "Find anything?"

Meeks turned to face his boss. "No, Sheriff. Everything looks clean in here."

"Where's Sanders? I saw his car outside."

"I guess he's in another part of the house."

"Good. I'm going to check the kitchen." Gloria started to walk back downstairs, but Meeks lightly caught her arm.

"Uh, Sheriff? I have to tell you something. I didn't want to say anything, but I guess I should."

"What is it?"

"Sanders was already here when I arrived. And the door to the house was unlocked. I just thought you should know."

Gloria nodded slowly. "All right. Let's get back to work."

The officers finished the search of the house, finding nothing of interest. Gloria expected as much. As clean as all the crime scenes had been, she doubted a mind as sharp as the one they were dealing with would be sloppy enough to leave evidence in their own home. Nevertheless, she confiscated the "ten-ounce" silver platter from the kitchen, then headed for the backyard. There was one occupant of this house she was particularly anxious to see.

Seven pairs of eyes glared at the approaching trespassers, but thankfully the barking had stopped.

"What happened here?" Gloria knelt to investigate the hole in the fence.

The deputies shrugged.

"Black hair all around this thing." Gloria glanced over the fence to see the black dog's injured muzzle. "Looks like the shepherd was planning a jail break. That works out well for us. Meeks, get me a bag. I'm taking this hair and some wood splinters." Gloria glanced up as Meeks went to the car to retrieve her things. "Something wrong, Sanders?"

"No, ma'am. Why?"

She squinted up at him, gauging the officer's expression. "You looked pale for a minute."

"Here's the bag, Sheriff." Meeks handed her a pair of gloves as well. The deputies watched as Gloria collected samples around the flicking pink tongue of a golden retriever who'd decided to make friends. The other dogs played a game of chase up and down the fence line, the newcomers finally accepted as harmless. But the black shepherd sat off to himself, his gaze never wavering from the officers in Ivy's yard.

"He's staring at you, Meeks," Gloria said, standing. She carefully sealed the bag of hair and wood, then pulled off her gloves. "Gentle as lambs, isn't that how Doc Hill described these dogs to you, Sanders?"

"Let's find out," Meeks said before Melvin could answer. He walked around the fence to get closer to the shepherd and his vigil under the shade tree by the back of the lot.

"Hey, Meeks, wait. Don't get them stirred up again. They just quieted down," Melvin said.

"No, let him go," Gloria said. "I want to see what happens."

Meeks leaned forward against the fence, then slowly extended his hand. Aufhocker stood, and the hairs on his neck began to stand as well. Melvin watched from across the yard as hackles rose all the way down the dog's back to his tail.

"Oh man, oh man, oh man," Melvin said under his breath. His hand inched its way back to the automatic's holster.

Auf put his nose into the wind and sniffed, his eyes never leaving the man at the fence. And he knew.

Meeks chuckled at the animal's recognition. "You want to play with me, puppy dog?" he said quietly. "I could rip out your spine before you knew what hit you."

Aufhocker's lips drew back into a snarl, and he shook his head angrily from side to side. Then he stepped toward the man, and Meeks grinned. "That's right. Come on. Show the nice sheriff what you can do."

"That's enough, Meeks," Melvin called. "You're getting him worked up. Look at his nose—he's hurt. Dogs are more liable to bite when they're hurt."

Gloria's head whipped around at Melvin, irritated. But he was right. She couldn't use her own deputy as bait in a test. "Sanders has a point. Let's go. I've got what I need."

The grin fell from Meeks's face and he snatched his hand back. "It's your lucky day, wolf. I'll be seeing you later."

Meeks rejoined Melvin and the sheriff. "Not too friendly, I guess."

"No, I don't think he is. A call to animal control might be in order," Gloria said. She turned to Melvin: "And Sanders,

I want to speak with you when we get back to the station."

"Yes, ma'am. Is something wrong?"

Gloria didn't answer him. To both officers: "We're done here. Let's go."

"Sheriff, I need to run back in for a minute. I think I left something in the house," Meeks said.

Meeks observed from the window as the sheriff and Sanders drove away. Sanders pulled out like he was leading a funeral, and Meeks watched the man stall as long as he could before his car finally, painfully, made it over the hill and out of sight.

The deputy left the window and went into the kitchen. A small, shaggy shadow tailed him from room to room, but he left the little terrier alone. He had more on his mind than playing games with inferior canines. A form lay on the kitchen countertop, next to where Ivy's silver platter once rested, and Meeks picked it up. It was a notice, left by the sheriff to inform Ivy Cole that the item had been removed from her house. The deputy folded the form and stuffed it in his shirt pocket.

That accomplished, Meeks moved to the living room and the stairwell. He sprinted up the stairs and into the bedroom once again. Deputy Meeks unzipped his pants and, standing over Ivy's rose-colored patchwork quilt, left her a little something to remember him by.

The new alpha had claimed his home.

Chapter 44

The Widow Pritchard sat on her grand front porch, rocking quietly to the rhythm of the waking morning. A neighbor's dog barked somewhere down the road, too far for her to see. A rooster's hoarse crow rose up right after it, announcing the beginning of the day. Behind the Victorian a quarter mile away, Ava heard the bellowing of another neighbor's cows, herding into the dairy barn for milking. And in front of her, stretching across the horizon of her wildly blossoming front yard and wrapping around the blunted Blue Ridge peaks, was the glow of a rising sun. The sky was still the low-lit orange of a simmering mulled cider—or perhaps the intense gaze of a wolf she knew.

Ava sipped sun tea, the chilly liquid bringing the cold of the outside air within. This was the last batch of sun tea she would make this year. The drink no longer felt right when September rolled in. The widow shivered and pulled her shawl tighter about her shoulders. But it was not the ice in her drink nor the frosty promise of summer's end in the air that caused it. The full moon was arriving, and there was work to be done. Ivy was in danger. Her youth and recklessness were weaknesses that had worried Ava for a long time, and tonight there would be consequences.

Ava had thought about it all night, then wandered to her front porch at last to find solace in the stars. The morning had sneaked up on her, but her mind was made up. It was a hard, hard decision. One she did not come by easily. But she had a record of enforcing hard decisions. Jeb could attest to it.

Jeb. Her sweet Jeb. Ava held up the last of her tea and watched the colors of the sun morph into streaks of ambers and golds through the glass. It was the color of Jeb's hair when they'd met, two teens working a farm for modest wages, but finding something so much more valuable in each other. They'd courted for less than a year and married on this very porch.

The house outlasted Jeb and all of Ava's brothers and sisters. It would live long past Ava's last days as well. But there were no young ones to take up residence once the house was alone. It bothered Ava, to think of her family home plundered at auction by strangers. No, that would never happen. The house belonged to the closest thing to a daughter Ava ever had. She willed it to Ivy right after Jeb died. No one knew it, including Ivy. At eighty-seven, Ava knew the gift would not be too long coming. Ivy would live in Doe

Springs happily and healthily until that day arrived, if Ava had anything to do with it.

The widow finished her drink with a final ladylike sip and patted her lips with a linen napkin. Then she walked inside and dialed the telephone. An answering machine picked up.

"Deputy Sanders, this is Mrs. Pritchard. I need you to come by today, sugar, any time at all. There are some things I'm ready to tell you, and I'm certain you'll want to hear them. Good-bye."

Jeb's picture stared impassively from its place on the wall, but Ava felt the weight of accusation in his dead gaze. She turned away from it to watch the rest of the morning awake outside her window.

"Forgive me," she whispered, as the day moved steadily forward to a full-mooned end.

Chapter 45

The station was quiet when the sheriff returned, but she knew the newspaper's front page headline of the day would busy things up: "Full Moon Tonight, Curfew at 8 p.m." Gloria hoped the Doe Springs citizens would heed the curfew, but there would always be a few yahoos—like that group of teenagers—who would feel the need to court danger.

"Not tonight, Sheriff." Deputy Sanders stood just inside Gloria's office.

She looked up from the newspaper. "What's that?"

"I know what you were thinking just now. You're wondering if folks will be out despite the warning. They won't. Everybody's shook up now. They're taking the Devil of Doe Springs seriously."

"Are you?"

"What do you mean, Sheriff?"

Gloria folded the paper and laid it aside. She had been thinking about how to handle this since the drive back from Ivy Cole's house. There was no easy solution, and drawing it out with long explanations seemed unnecessarily cruel. Gloria preferred the doctor's approach: Keep it short and direct, like getting a shot in the arm. Dealing with the real pain would come later. "Shut the door, Sanders, and sit down."

"Uh, yes, ma'am." The deputy did as he was told. He sat across from the sheriff, waiting.

"I'm taking you off the case."

"What?" Melvin sat up straighter, like a man who'd just been doused with ice water. "Why?"

"Don't look so surprised. You know why. It's a conflict of interest. Meeks told me where you were this morning. I know you spent the night at Ivy Cole's."

"I didn't—"

Gloria held up her hand. "Let me finish. I never get involved in my deputies' personal lives, but this time is different. Ivy Cole is a lead suspect, and I don't want your heart getting in the way of your duties."

Gloria paused, waiting for a response, a defense, even a tirade, but Sanders merely sat there, shock and disappointment competing with professional composure on his handsome face. The Adam's apple in his throat rose and fell, but no words emerged from the effort. Gloria came around her desk and leaned against the wood's worn edge.

"You're a good police officer, Melvin. I don't want to see you screw that up. And I think you're about to, whether you realize it or not. It's my job to protect the citizens of this town, but it's also my job to protect my deputies. This time, Melvin, I'm protecting you . . . from you. Turn over all your paperwork to Meeks."

Melvin looked up at the sheriff standing in front of him. His voice finally found its way past the Adam's apple. It came out calm and even, but a tinge of watery red in his eyes gave him away. Gloria focused on the deputy's forehead to avoid seeing the pain she had just inflicted.

"Am I fired?"

"Leave of absence until this is over. You'll take your time off, starting immediately. I understand you have family in Asheville and West Virginia. I think it would be a good time for a visit." Gloria went back to her seat and crossed her hands on the desk in front of her. Her fingers sought to begin their familiar dance, but she quieted them. "That will be all, Sanders."

He stood and walked out, surprise and anger holding his backbone ramrod straight.

Gloria hit the intercom as soon as the door closed. "Meeks, it's done. Keep an eye on him. If he heads straight to Ivy Cole's, I need to know about it."

She hated it had come to this, hated she always had to do the hard, right thing, and hated the Devil of her nightmares for causing it all. It would be a long, impatient day. For the first time in over a year, Gloria Hubbard looked forward to the coming of the full moon, but now she would be facing it shorthanded.

A quick rap on the door brought Delores into the office. "Sheriff, you busy? There's a man here to see you."

"And so it begins," Gloria mumbled. Concern for Melvin went straight to the back burner. "Name?"

"It's Musket, from the trailer park."

Gloria's ears perked up. "Send him in. Oh, and Delores, call the police chief over in Pine Knot for me. Tell him I may need some help tonight, if he's got anybody he can spare. I'll call him later with the details."

Delores's lips pursed disapprovingly. She'd seen Deputy Sanders stride out of the station without a word to anybody. It did not bode well at all.

Poor Shirley's heart would be broken.

Musket Dobbins, chew in his jaw and a spit cup concealed within a paper bag in his hand, entered the sheriff's office. "Morning, Sheriff. Sorry to bother you, but I figured it was time for me to get on down here to see you."

"What's going on, Musket? Have you heard from Tee?"

"No, Sheriff, Mr. Hubbard ain't been back around. Wish he had, though. Would have saved me a trip down here."

Gloria unleashed her restrained fingers onto the desktop. Da-da-da-*da*. "Okay, what's up?"

"Well, when my wife cleaned Tee's trailer there was—"

"A lot of dog hair, right?" Da-da-da-*da*. Da-da-da-*da*. She couldn't believe this man was bothering her today, of all days, with a rental concern. "If there's an extra fee, I'll take care of it. How much is it?"

"Nah, nah, nothing like that. Mr. Hubbard left the house spic-'n'-span, not a dog hair or speck of dirt anywhere." Musket took a discreet spit into the paper bag. "What I'm saying is when Nettie cleaned the trailer she found something peculiar. I kept meaning to get over here with it, but . . ." He shrugged, as if that explained everything. "Anyways, I kind of forgot about it after a while, but I came across it this morning in the change dish." Musket dug into his overalls pocket with his free hand and fished out a small key. He laid it on the desk.

"What's so peculiar about a key?" Gloria said.

"It's not the key that struck me funny, it was where Nettie found it. It was under the stopper in the bathtub. Sure enough ain't one of mine—we don't go putting stuff like that in the tub. It must have been Mr. Hubbard's."

Gloria picked up the small piece of metal. It looked like it belonged to a safety deposit box. There were letters and a number on the side: HARV 138. Not a safety deposit box after all.

"Thank you for bringing this in, Musket. I'm sure Tee will be looking for it. You wouldn't mind me riding back over there to take a look around his trailer again, would you?"

"Do what you like. Look under the mat at the front door—that's where I keep my keys."

"Right. Well, thanks again."

Musket nodded, spit in his paper bag, and gave her a tobacco-brown grin. "Nothing to it, Sheriff."

Gloria sat alone in her office, turning the key over and over till it warmed in her hands. She hit the intercom. "Delores, I need you to make some calls. We're looking for a storage unit rented to Tee Hubbard. Start your search in Doe

Springs and fan out. The business name may begin with the
letters *H-A-R-V,* or those might be the initials." Gloria released the button, then pressed it again. "Oh, and Delores,
I'm going to be out for a while. Radio me as soon as you
know anything."

It was early still, but already the morning was getting away.
A quick run by the trailer park was in order, followed by a
trip to whatever Delores turned up. The sheriff glanced at
the sky on her way to the Jeep. Another beautiful day in the
mountains, and it could not be wasted. Tonight the full moon
would arrive to shroud it all.

Chapter 46

Deputy Meeks sat in his patrol car down the street from
Sanders's house, which was the first place the man headed
after the unfortunate morning with the sheriff. The rigid
posture Sanders maintained out of Sheriff Hubbard's office
had collapsed the minute he rounded his cubicle's corner.
After gathering up some files from his desk and dropping
them without a word onto Meeks's, he'd shambled out of the
station like a man who'd just lost everything he had.

Meeks hated to rat out a fellow policeman that way, especially one as good as Sanders. Putting a dent in the young
man's career was the last thing he wanted to do, but it was a
necessary evil. The relationship between the human and female wolf could not last. It was not meant to.

Meeks watched now as Sanders carried two suitcases out
of the garage and dusted them off in the yard. Then he disappeared back into the house.

Going on a trip, buddy? Meeks didn't believe it for a
minute, but he admired the effort. Whatever Sanders was up

to, it was his job to sit here and watch him. In the meantime, there was something else he'd been eager to do since the impromptu "search and seizure" at Ivy's house that morning. Meeks reached under the seat and pulled out the woman's ragged journal. It was old, with newer pages tucked inside the aged ones and loose notes stuffed in between all of those. Meeks opened the small book with its crayon-colored cover, careful to hold it intact. It was precious, these passages representing the inner workings of another wolf's mind, and he cradled it with the care of a father holding a newborn child. Ivy would fret when she discovered her thoughts had been plundered, but he would return the diary in good time. For now, it was an opening into a world he'd never gotten to observe, a viewpoint outside his own dark broodings. *The better to see you with, my dear . . .*

Ivy's story unexpectedly began in the dark corners of a closed closet, the fearful child crouching behind boxes and coats. Weeks passed before another entry told of her struggle in the hospital, not so much from the wounds to her injured body but from the trauma of what she'd seen. *She's managing it well, considering,* the psychiatrists told the girl's father before sending her home.

Meeks skipped ahead, grazing entries as if tasting bits of the woman's life on her path to adulthood. There was no peace on that solitary trip, until she'd left (*fled*) New York and finally accepted a life alone, traveling from place to place with little more than dogs for companions.

"June 10, 2000—It is lonely in these Black Hills, rising away from me in the quiet of dawn. I am up to see the sunrise after the set of a moon far fuller than the sun could ever hope to be. But there are no wolfen voices calling to me over the mountains and plains, only the beautiful nothingness of vast open spaces. I howl to no one, and no one answers. Someday, perhaps, another voice will hear me and echo its return. But for now, on this day, the sunrise lifts my spirits just the same. . . . "

Blah, blah, blah. Meeks flipped ahead, looking for substance. He didn't care for poetic drivel. It made him impatient. He was searching for facts, something he could wrap his mind around and hold on to tonight when he met Ivy again face-to-face. Her hunting strategies, her tracking techniques, what she looked for in her victims. He scoured pages until the end. Only one entry was of any interest—and a rage began to build in him as he read it:

"I pitied him. I cleaned up his mess and removed all of his sloppy evidences. I let him go, and have endangered my extended pack in doing so."

I pitied him. The journal shook in Meeks's hands, and loose pages sprinkled between his legs to the floorboard. The words Ivy wrote after her encounter with the black wolf in the campground trembled into illegible scrawl. Indentations from the deputy's clasping nails marred the child-illustrated cover. *I pitied him.*

Meeks threw the journal across the car, smashing it against the opposite door. More pages exploded out of the notebook and scattered over the seat.

Sanders's garage door opened, and Meeks's head jerked up. A black Dodge pickup backed onto the street. Sanders jumped out, and a few minutes later he was slinging suitcases into its bed.

Meeks followed Sanders to the edge of town, the direction away from Ivy Cole's. He was sure the other deputy knew he was back there, but Sanders shouldn't expect anything less. Just doing your job was an idea the young man understood all too well.

"So long, Sanders. For now." Meeks checked his reflection in the rearview. He swiped a rough hand through his black hair and smiled pleasantly. The distraction of police work had mellowed his temper momentarily. There was time for rages, and time to be in complete control. Right now, he needed control. For as his fellow deputy's truck drove away from Doe Springs and a certain country cottage, Deputy Meeks was turning his car around and heading right to it.

Chapter 47

The blinking answering machine—Melvin almost ignored it when he stormed into the house. His anger rekindled itself on the drive home when he spotted Meeks tailing him with an obviousness that rankled him. Suddenly he felt he'd crossed the line to the other side of the law and his own department had turned on him.

The red light finally got the best of him. Downing the last of this week's Tums bottle, Melvin punched the play button to alleviate the irritating red flashing more than anything else. The polished accent on the machine was unmistakable, but disappointing. He'd hoped it was Ivy—it was the Widow Pritchard instead.

So now she wanted to talk. A lot of good it would do him. He was banished to the company of relatives, feeling thrown to the wolves instead.

Melvin replayed the message, then replayed the conversation with Sheriff Hubbard in his head. It was hard to think of anything else at the moment. Was the leave of absence really temporary? Or was the sheriff pushing him out peacefully for now, only to do the real dirty work of firing him at a more convenient time? Her dance card was full up for the day—firing somebody under protest could get messy and distracting. He would not go as gently under those circumstances as he did under these, and Sheriff Hubbard knew that. Either way, temporary leave or leave until termination, his promising record was marred.

Melvin glanced through the curtains. Meeks's patrol car was parked down the street, ever the vigilant watchdog. As infuriating as that was, Melvin could not blame the other deputy. If circumstances were switched, he would be sitting there doing the exact same thing. Orders were orders, and

getting Melvin out of town and away from Ivy was precisely
what the sheriff and Meeks meant to do. Melvin wouldn't
disappoint them.

He loaded two empty suitcases into the truck and drove
the direction a dutiful police officer would go: away. Meeks
predictably turned back at the edge of town, and Melvin
continued on to his real destination.

"Come in, sugar. I knew you'd be along directly." Ava,
wrapped in a lavender shawl, waved the young man inside.
She eyed him up and down, noting the plain clothes and
truck in the driveway, but said nothing. Soon they were
back in the sunroom and seated around the same table they'd
visited across on Melvin's first trip to inquire about Ivy
Cole. Today, instead of sun tea, shortbread cookies awaited,
arranged on a porcelain serving dish accompanied by two
delicate china saucers.

"I thought you might like a snack, Deputy. I didn't know
what time of day you'd be arriving, and shortbread seems to
go with every meal. Are you hungry?"

"No thank you, ma'am. I'm fine," Melvin said.

A brow lifted above the rim of Ava's glasses. "You don't
look fine. You look like the bleached-out side of a frog's
belly. In fact, I think I've seen frog bellies with better color."

"It's nothing. An ulcer maybe. I'll get it checked when I
have time."

"Too busy for the doctor? That's not good business for a
policeman, is it? I'd think you'd need to stay in tip-top shape,
especially with what you're up against. But no matter—you
don't have an ulcer and you don't need medical attention.
Your problem is up here," Ava tapped her head, "and I'm
about to help you with all that. Are you sure you wouldn't like
some shortbread? It's very good." She offered him the platter.

"Mrs. Pritchard, could you please tell me why I'm here?
I've had a really bad day already so forgive me for being
short, but what is going on?"

The widow looked offended. She pushed the cookies
away, leaving the space between them empty. She gave the

shawl a brisk tug, then crossed her hands in front of her on the table. "Fine, Deputy Sanders. We'll cut right to the chase. I like that in others, it's fair for you to expect it from me. But I need you to do me an itty-bitty favor first. I want you to clear your head and open your mind because what I'm about to tell you is far beyond your wildest imagination."

Ava took a deep breath and began. . . .

"A long time ago, my niece, Ivy, was a normal, happy little girl. She had a beautiful mother who adored her and a successful father who loved her by being a good provider. They moved around a lot, however, and even then, with Catherine and Ivy tagging behind William from this place to that place, he still managed to be away from them most the time. Wasn't his fault, I suppose. The man was born driven. I'm guessing Ivy didn't tell you a whole lot about her father, did she?"

"No, ma'am."

"Ambitious to a fault, he was. But that takes its toll on a person, being away from his wife and child so much. Long hours on planes, in hotels. My sister Una just happened to wander into the right situation at the right time. She met William on one of those trips and managed to fall in love with him."

"I was right—there was an affair. Why didn't you tell me that before?"

"Everything comes out in its own good time, Deputy, and yes, you were right. There was an affair. The only catch was Una wanted more than the title of mistress, and there was a wife in the picture that William wasn't keen on leaving. But Una never did let little things like marriage stand in her way, and on her travels across Europe she acquired a particular talent for eliminating troublesome problems."

"A talent? What does that mean exactly?"

"Hush up and listen. It'll all fall into place in a minute. Now, Una knew Catherine would be alone late Christmas Eve that year, just her and Ivy. Christmas Eve was distasteful timing, even for my sister, but no one has control over the appearance of a full moon, least of all those who are ruled by it. She killed Catherine, yes, she surely did, but that's as far as it went. Una might have been a lot of things—jealous-hearted, overzealous, a bit of an aggressive go-getter, bless her heart—but one thing she was not was a child murderer. Una loved children, and later she worked hard to be a good mother to Ivy. . . . "

Ava looked over the top of Deputy Sanders's head and through the wall to a not-too-distant place tucked within the mountains. It was Lake Lure, a day years ago spent with Una and the girl. William was in Vancouver, and Una came calling on her family for the week. Ivy was twelve by then, but she barely spoke a word as they unpacked lunch across the back of a broad gray boulder and watched the pontoon boats drifting by. While Una chatted and laughed with her sisters, Ivy quietly got up and walked to the beach, where she sat alone the rest of the afternoon.

"What a shame it didn't work out like that," Ava said, the sigh in her voice revealing her own wistfulness at what might have been. "It was all wishful thinking on Una's part, though, the possibilities of her having the Cole family and living happily ever after. Ivy was certainly young enough when Catherine died—she could have bonded with Una. Ivy could have come to love Una like the perfect mother and wife she so desperately sought to be—"

"Mrs. Pritchard, what you're saying doesn't make sense," Melvin interrupted again. "I've researched this myself. I don't know about Una and Ivy's relationship, but I do know Catherine Cole was mauled by an animal in her kitchen. All the police reports verified it. And there is no record of your sister or any person being at the house that night after the relatives left."

"The police reports were bunk and the media reports were full of twaddle. I'm telling you what happened that night. Now are you going to keep jabbering or are you going to let me finish my story?" Ava gave her shawl a good yank. "Where was I? Una's mistake in judgment. You see, Una wasn't the only one to come to the house that night, and therein lay her fatal mistake. She didn't count on Stefan Heinrich running back over to get the wallet he'd left Christmas dinner without. He's Ivy's uncle, the one with the special dogs. Does Ivy ever mention Stefan and his canids? You've met one of them."

"Aufhocker, you mean. The dog with an unusual name. I looked it up."

"Oh yes, the German legend of the aufhocker. Well, that's Ivy's sense of humor for you. Auf wouldn't hurt a flea—unless he felt Ivy was in danger. What else do you know about him?"

"Not much, other than he was a gift for Ivy to protect her."

"Ever wonder from what, Deputy Sanders?" Ava leaned closer to the young man. The table grew small between them, and her breath caressed Melvin's face. Her eyes sparkled behind her diamond rims. "I'll tell you. From Una. From others like Una. They can't be trusted, Melvin, no matter how much they claim to love. It's a bitter lesson for some people to learn. Stefan despised Una's kind. And that's why he did what he did to Ivy that night." Ava leaned back and resumed her casual seat, two hands clutching each other as if at prayer.

"He found her first, Stefan did. She was lying in a ruined house with an injured back and leg that left marks on her for life." Ava stopped talking and squinted at the deputy. "Don't overthink it. I can see smoke coming out of your ears right now. You're wondering why you've never seen the scars. Well, you wouldn't. Ivy's very clever at keeping them hidden, even from those she's been—how do I say it?—familiar with. She's a healthy girl now and can heal up without a stitch anymore, but those two scars will never heal.

"But Stefan knew a way, not to heal the injuries on the outside, of course. But there are deeper scars than those of the flesh, Deputy, and that's what Stefan had to decide. At that moment he was faced with two options. He could call the ambulance right away, the paramedics would come save the child, and she would grow up into some dark and miserable thing he detested. He couldn't let that happen, not to his only niece, the only thing left of his butchered sister. . . . "

And then Ava told Melvin of the second option Stefan chose, one no less difficult than, perhaps, just letting the child die at his feet, her blood puddling around his holiday loafers and collecting in the shards of ornamental glass from the destroyed Christmas tree. He'd come back that night with the excuse of a forgotten wallet, but that was only an excuse. He missed his sister and her child. William would pack up the rental house and move his family again before

too long, and Stefan planned to enjoy every last minute he
could with them before that happened. It was the first Christmas Stefan had had with Catherine since she married; it
could be a long time coming around again. As late as it was,
the holiday spirit had moved him. There were things he
wanted to say, moments he wanted to share, lost time he felt
the need to recover on this night. He knew his sister well
enough: She would be up cleaning. An untidy house would
never let her sleep until the last dish were cleaned, the last
crumb swept from the dining room floor.

Stefan parked on the ice-crusted street. He stood by his
car, wrapped in a heavy wool overcoat and looking at the
stone and brick cottage. The lights were out. Maybe they had
gone to bed after all. It was past midnight; he felt foolish to
have come back so late. Tomorrow, then. Stefan started to
get back into his car and stopped. He couldn't help the way
he felt. The house was wrong.

Stefan slipped and skidded across the walkway to the front
door. It opened easily onto the aftermath of murder. The work
was unmistakable. It would mystify only those who refused to
believe, but for others in the outskirts of Cologne, they would
board their windows at night and whisper of the creature with
trembling voices when the moon circled full.

There was no saving Catherine, she was beyond him now.
But the heart still beat in Ivy's chest. Her ripped dress fluttered in the wind that still blew through the shattered window, and Stefan watched the emerald cloth—the injured
wings of an innocent butterfly—and made up his mind.

He was back with the van this time. He pulled behind the
house and unloaded his secret cargo. They stole inside and circled the prone little girl, a tall man in a dark coat and six black
dogs too large to be mere shepherds. Six pairs of ears pricked
in Stefan's direction, heads and tails held high, iridescent eyes
gleaming with silent, expectant intensity. With a wave of his
hand, he loosed them. The beta male took first, and the others
followed. Fenris, the alpha, hung back, watching. Then he,
too, joined his pack. They ate of her gingerly, small nips torn
from the already opened tears in her body. And while their
heads were lowered into the flesh of the child, Stefan, with

tears streaming down his bearded face, moved quickly from one animal to the next, plunging a knife deep into their throats. Fenris was last. He did not run, only studied his master with the confused hurt of an ancient soul that had already endured countless centuries of torture and betrayal by man, let alone from one who loved him and had been loved so deeply in return.

The deed was done, and the knife fell from Stefan's hand. Tears hung frozen from his beard but fresh warmth covered his hands and splattered his clothing. The packs' mingled blood bled into the wounds of the child. They had taken her flesh, and now they shared their blood as payment. As it surged through the girl's tiny arteries and veins, mixing and churning with revitalizing strength, Stefan returned his six lifeless companions to the van and drove away.

Ava took off her glasses and wiped them with the shawl. They had misted up with tears of her own during the telling. How Stefan had mourned those losses that night. Catherine, dear Catherine, and his beloved—

"How do you know all this?" Melvin said.

Ava reseated her spectacles. "I was there, Deputy. Oh, not in person, but Stefan's talked with me about this so much over the years, it's as vivid to me as if I could reach out and stroke Fenris's back right now. Stefan and I became good pen pals after Ivy came to America, and we're still in touch off and on. He calls to check Ivy's progress, keep track of her whereabouts. The girl refuses even to speak with him now, but I've kept his memory alive. I tell Ivy things, whether she wants to hear them or not."

"And you're saying these animals gave Ivy their blood? That seems medically impossible. What are these dogs?"

"Now that is the truly interesting part of all this, Deputy Sanders, and the simplest. They're from a specialized line Stefan's family developed over centuries. Fenris was the epitome of the breeding program, with an intelligence and longevity that bordered supernatural. He was Stefan's heart. Auf is one of his puppies, if you haven't guessed already."

"But what is he? A wolf?"

"Took you all this time to figure that out? Yes, a wolf, but a special kind of wolf, Deputy Sanders, from a lineage that traces back to what some believe is only mythology. These wolves were once said to walk on hind legs. As the legend goes, they copied humans and took up with their ways. But the wolves became ashamed of humans, who only take and take, using everything up and replacing it with nothing. So they reverted to walking four feet upon the ground and hunting what only needed to be hunted and caring for their packs with a loyalty us two-legged creatures rarely ever get to know. Ever hear of how a whole pack will tend for one litter of puppies, Deputy? Or bring food to an elder wolf who can no longer hunt? They are amazing, misunderstood animals." Ava tsk-tsked and shook her head.

"Why would the Heinrichs breed wolves? Did they use them to hunt?"

"Did they use them to kill, is that what you're after? No. They protected them, starting centuries ago."

"From what?"

"Murderers. Armies of them, rampaging across Europe with nothing on their minds but eradication. The Heinrichs gave the wolves refuge. In the remotest villages and tiniest forest caves, these wolves flourished, bred specifically to look more like dogs as a camouflage to protect the species. Primitive conservation—that's all it was! And the wolves are returning the favor. They are the protectors now, and in Ivy's case, the saviors. She is one of them, Deputy Sanders, and different from Una."

"Are they? Different, I mean?"

Ava was disappointed at the implication. "It's not the wolf that makes the killer, Deputy. It's what lies in the heart of the man." Ava smiled. "Or woman."

The floor was wide open for Sanders's reaction, but beyond the random comment, the young man did not speak. Ava had shocked the deputy into incompetence, it appeared. He had not even taken out his notebook to record the important things she was telling him. Exasperated, the widow resumed her soliloquy.

"You had questions for me the last time you were here, Deputy, but I can see you've come up dry all of a sudden. I'll state it all real clearly for you to sum up my storytelling in a tidy package. Yes, Ivy killed Una and William. I don't hold a grudge over that. Una was my sister, but she took a risk killing Catherine, and then another stronger wolf came along and killed her in return. It happens that way in nature sometimes. Has Ivy killed others? Yes. But she only takes what is needed, and she only seeks out the ignoble. You probably think nobody asks to get killed, but I'm telling you there are people who are just begging for it. Wolves in the wild cull the weak and the sick from the herds they stalk, and it improves the genetics of the population. That's all Ivy is doing, Deputy. It's natural selection at its finest."

The story seemed to be over at last, and Melvin sat motionless. He stared at the woman in her crocheted wrap and neatly pinned hair. Her gaze was steady, and there was not a twitch or an awkward glance or an overly casual way about her that would indicate lying. The widow's clear hazel eyes never left his. She was waiting. But he wasn't sure what she expected. This went beyond the need for a clear head and open-mindedness, the favor she'd requested of him before starting this fantastical tale.

Melvin took a deep breath, debating what words would be most fitting under the circumstances. He shifted in his seat, ready to sprint as soon as he could free himself from the obligation of polite good-byes. "That was quite a statement, ma'am. I'm going to give what you've said a lot of thought. Thank you for having me this morning, and if I think of any other questions, I'll let you know."

Melvin began to rise. The widow's hand shot across the table and clamped down on his arm, pinning it to the glass.

"It's true, boy," she hissed. "There are wolves in your woods of a preternatural kind. Always have been, but some take their business out of town. And now I'm going to suggest you do the same, if you know what's good for you. But if you don't and you want proof, follow Ivy tonight. Follow her, and you'll find both your devils."

The grip released and Melvin fell backward, nearly upsetting his chair. He stood up, surprise shaking his balance worse than the near tumble. He opened his mouth to speak, but the widow had already turned her back to him. She faced her wall of windows, her shoulders square under the knitted shawl.

The deputy hurried back to his truck, the unsettledness in his stomach unfamiliar this time. It was not from the suspected ulcer at all. Melvin just had a brush with something dangerous and unexpected. The Widow Pritchard was completely insane.

Chapter 48

Rex peeked around the sofa, checking the all-clear. It was Ivy this time who stood in the middle of the living room. She was still, her head cocked to one side. The little terrier bounded to her, eager to report the invasion of their home. While Rex yipped and yapped and clawed at Ivy's leg, the woman slowly turned full circle, her eyes raking over every corner of the room. The mantel clock was still there. Nothing seemed out of place, and yet . . . Ivy dropped *Lykanthrop* on the coffee table and then moved to the kitchen with Rex skittering on the linoleum after her. A quick glance over cabinets and appliances, then her gaze fell on an empty spot on the counter, a wispy line of dust marking the outline of a missing silver platter.

Ivy's steps quickened as she neared the bedroom, taking two steps at a time up the stairs. She flung open the door, half expecting to see someone—a deputy, perhaps—still there, rifling through her things. She fell to her knees and tore at the rug, splintering the plank when she jerked it loose from the floor and wedging a sliver well into her thumb. She paid the wood little attention. The hole was empty.

Ivy's head dropped into her hands. "How could you, Melvin? How could you!" Ivy threw the plank across the room where it shattered against the whitewashed wall. She heard Rex's nails spinning on the hardwood as he fled the room. Her shoulders hitched as the sobs finally came, and she let them. But only for a minute. Ivy wiped her eyes with the back of her arm and steadied herself against the bed to rise. She pulled her hand back. It was moist. And suddenly the smell was like a jackhammer in the room. In her concern for the journal and jewelry, she had completely ignored the most obvious intrusion of all.

Ivy stood over her bed, her clean hand covering her mouth and nose. A scattershot sprinkling of urine dotted the rosy quilt, and bile rose in Ivy's throat. This smell was not Melvin's. It was *him*.

"The dogs." Ivy ran down the stairs, her feet slipping and stumbling on the steps and her hands grappling for the rail. She careened around corners and down the hallway, Rex picking up the chase and yapping at Ivy's heels. She exploded out the back door and stood there, chest heaving. Canine ears perked up from a mid-morning naptime, all seven pairs accounted for. The dogs broke in unison to crowd around their mistress. Ivy knelt and hugged them all, new tears streaming down her face.

Aufhocker pushed through the mob to greet Ivy. He licked her tears, leaving a swipe of red across her cheek. Ivy drew back, clasping the dog's jowls.

"Auf, what happened here?" Dried blood caked around the wolf's muzzle. Ivy pulled his lips back to examine the ragged gums. The big dog's eyes shifted to the hole in the fence.

"Were they trying to get in, or were you trying to get out?" By the look of things, it was the latter. Whatever had come here had gone, taking her personal items but leaving the dogs unharmed. Aufhocker had protected them. Ivy hugged him tightly, so thankful he was safe. She debated calling Doc, but thought better of it. Right now she wasn't sure all of the blood belonged to her dog.

Ivy gave Auf a final squeeze. Glancing again at the red-rimmed hole in the fence, the woman slowly stood. The time for tears was over.

Chapter 49

The gate to the chain-link fence surrounding the property was open. A sign pointed straight ahead, to a small modular with gray siding. Another sign hung crooked off a nail hammered through the center of a vinyl slat beside the door. It read "Office." Gloria approached the modest building. Delores had found the place before the sheriff had even made it to the trailer park—Harvey's Hangar, Personal Storage, in Pine Knot.

The key in Gloria's pocket seemed to grow heavier as she walked. Whatever it might reveal, one thing Gloria already knew for certain: Tee would never take off and leave something so careless as a key hidden in the bathtub drain. But that was the only thing he did leave, apparently. The revisit to the trailer park had turned out to be a waste of time—for now. The house was as she'd seen it last: clean. Maybe too clean. Gloria knew Musket's wife, Nettie. The lady would do little more than rinse the tub and sink basins, vacuum the floor, and strip the beds before calling it a day. Finding no dirt in the house whatsoever was circumspect, even for a compulsive housekeeper like Tee. It seemed unlikely there would not be even one stray dog hair lying around, and she wondered if the same could be said of fingerprints. An interview with Nettie and a fingerprint check of the trailer were in order. There just were not enough hours in the day.

Gloria found herself at the office door. A heavyset man with jowls that reminded Gloria of Zeke stepped around the side of the modular before she could go inside. The frown dividing his face migrated farther south when he saw the badge.

"You the sheriff that called this morning?"

Gloria kept the hand she would have extended hooked in her belt loop. "That was my office, yes."

"I got a bone to pick with you." He uncurled a sausage finger and pointed it at Gloria's chest.

Gloria sighed. Time was wasting but there was more to her job than chasing four-legged menaces. Two-legged ones required attention too. "Let's hear it."

"Freeloaders. I've complained to your office twice and haven't heard a word back."

"Who did you file a complaint with and what is this about?"

"I don't know who with. One of your deputies, I guess. But now I'm really bent. You ignore my calls and then this morning I hear you're coming over for information on one of the very clowns I been calling about."

"Tee Hubbard?"

"Yeah, that's him, along with about six others. I don't know what people think, renting storage and expecting me to keep their crap for free. Now by law I can't throw their stuff off a cliff like I'd like to, but if you won't do anything about it—"

"When was the last time you heard from Mr. Hubbard?"

The sausage quit pointing at Gloria and hovered to scratch the thinning hair raked over top the man's head. "Best I recollect without seeing my records, it was June when he set up the account. He missed the July payment—I sure remember that plain enough—and now he's late for August too. Let me get my records and I can give you all the names of the late accounts, the balances due, everything."

"I'm assuming you're Harvey?"

"Yeah. Mack Harvey."

"Okay, Mr. Harvey, first of all, the sheriff's office does not handle collections. But I am interested in those names. Call the station and give your information to a woman named Delores. We'll see what we can do." It was a hunch, but Gloria wondered if a few of those delinquent accounts might belong to missing persons tacked up on her bulletin board. And behind that notion, a grimmer thought drifted to the forefront at last, one she'd kept securely held at bay for a while now. Would Tee's picture eventually find its way onto that board along with them?

"You're not blowing smoke up my butt, are you, Sheriff? I don't like being put off."

"I said we'll see what we can do. Right now I'm interested in Tee Hubbard. I need to see his storage rental. I've got this." Gloria held out the key.

Harvey took it and turned it toward the light. "One thirty-eight. That's in what I call my warehouse row. But this key won't do you any good. I put a padlock on all the unpaid units. Hubbard wants his stuff out of there, he's got to go through me, with some cash, to get it."

"I need to see the unit right now, Mr. Harvey."

"This Tee fellow—he's wanted by the law? Because I ain't responsible for whatever he's got stashed in there, you know. What people put in storage is their business."

Gloria's patience was thinning like Harvey's hair. "I assure you, you will not be held liable for anything I find."

"Well," Mack Harvey said, scratching his head again. A sprinkling of dandruff snowed down on his shoulders. "All right. Let me get my key."

Five minutes later, Gloria and Harvey were walking down a row of beige aluminum buildings. They stopped at the last unit on the far end.

"This is the biggest one on the place. Ten by twenty," Harvey said. "It was the last thing I had available, but he wanted it."

Harvey bent and unlocked the padlock that held the garage-type door closed against a cement pad on the ground. He heaved the door upward and sunlight flooded the deep space.

"Well, what do you make of that?" Harvey said.

Gloria squinted inside, unsure she was seeing right. But she was. The unit was empty, except for one leather suitcase in the middle of the floor.

"What a waste," Harvey continued. "He owes me full price just the same, Sheriff."

"I can take it from here, Mr. Harvey. Thanks."

Mack Harvey hesitated and then walked off, grumbling.

Gloria knelt next to the suitcase. It was black and well weathered. She had seen it before, the day Tee packed his things and boarded a plane for a different time zone. He had tried to hug her good-bye at the house, but she'd pulled away. The suitcase was the last thing she saw of him, being loaded into a taxi while she stood watch by the window.

It was a moment she'd relive for a lifetime. It was the day she told her husband to leave.

Gloria ran her hand over the worn grain. She opened the case with a slight flinch, as if something unexpected might leap out. Inside was a stack of manila folders. Gloria pulled out the first thick file and thumbed through its contents. Her eyes widened as the name Annie appeared again and again. "Oh my God, Tee, you're still working on this case." Gloria picked up the second file, and the breath caught in her breastbone as if she'd just been punched there. A picture of Sheriff Hubbard's deputy stared up from her lap.

Chapter 50

A floorboard creaked. Ivy opened her eyes beneath the hot water spray and listened hard. The pounding of the water could only dim what she knew she'd heard plainly enough. Someone was walking around downstairs. Ivy stepped from the shower, a cloud of steam rolling out after her. She wrapped a terry cloth robe around her damp skin and twisted her dripping hair into an out-of-the-way knot. Neither Rex nor any of the other dogs had warned her of a presence in the house, an even more worrisome thought.

Ivy slipped to the top of the stairwell. A shadow moved below the bottom step, then floated out of view around the corner. Perhaps the person who had raided her home earlier had come back for more. She wished she'd brought Auf inside before taking the shower. And where the heck was Rex? He should be barking his head off by now.

Ivy glanced back into the bathroom for a suitable weapon.
A can of hair spray and a toilet bowl brush seemed to be her
greatest defense. She opted out of either one. She was not a
jumpy person under ordinary circumstances, but since coming home to find her things stolen, her dog injured, and her
bed defiled, the rules of the game had changed. Nevertheless, none of that helped her now. She had no weapons and
no dog backup.

Clattering in the kitchen. Something crashed to the floor.

Ivy stomped down the stairs toward the noise, anger overriding caution. She hadn't lived in fear since she was ten
years old, and she was not about to start now, especially with
somebody ransacking her house while she was still in it. Ivy
burst into the kitchen.

"Who are you and what do you want?" she screamed.

"My goodness, sugar, I was just scaring us up a snack is
all." The Widow Pritchard stood over the trash can, holding
a dustpan. Rex was at her feet, wagging his tail. "I'm afraid
I've made a mess, though. I broke one of your cups." Ava
paused, noting the distressed look on her niece's face.
"What's the matter, dear? Did I give you a little fright? I
poked my head through the door and when I heard you in the
shower, I came on in."

Ivy slumped against the wall, relief evaporating her tension. "I'm sorry, Ava. I didn't mean to yell at you. What are
you doing here?"

"Can't a lonely old lady visit her niece on occasion? Here,
come sit. You look completely frazzled." Ava patted a chair
and Ivy slid into it. Ava retrieved a pot from the stove and
poured the creamy contents into two mugs. "It might be early
in the season yet for cocoa, but I say it's good year-round for
treating whatever ails us. You look like you could use some
chocolate today."

"I think I could use a sedative, Ava. You wouldn't believe
what all I've been through lately."

Ava seated herself beside her niece and patted her hand.
"Oh, I think I could more than believe it."

Ivy looked at her aunt over the rim of the mug. "You've
come to tell me something."

Ava nodded. "I have." Her voice was saddened and the smile on her face waned.

Ivy sat her mug down and leaned toward her aunt. "What is it, Aunt Ava? Are you all right? Tell me." It was a day Ivy had dreaded since she was young—something happening to her beloved aunt. She was wrong before, when she claimed she'd not lived a day in fear. There had been plenty of fear in her life: fear of losing the only surviving member of her family that she cared about. Cancer, Alzheimer's, artery blockage . . . all the classic evils of old age raced through Ivy's mind.

"It's about your deputy, Ivy. Deputy Sanders."

Ivy wasn't sure whether to feel relieved again or even more concerned than before. Confusion won the toss-up. "What . . . Melvin? What could you possibly know about Melvin?"

Ava stiffened. "That's a very good question, considering how tight-lipped you've been the last few months. I swear I think we were closer when you were writing me letters from a thousand miles away. At least then you kept me informed about your life."

Ava was right, and Ivy felt ashamed of herself. She was so accustomed to releasing her feelings onto paper, having a living, breathing, loving person right in front of her and ready to listen was an alien idea. She would have to adjust. Seeing the hurt in her aunt's face and knowing she put it there was another unbearable event to add to the miseries of the day. "I'm so sorry, Ava. I didn't mean anything by it."

Ava was satisfied. The girl looked properly chastened. "I know you didn't, sugar, and you can hold your apology. I'm the one who may need to apologize after what I'm about to tell you. Just understand I've been trying to protect you as best I can, but it's gone beyond me now. You're going to have to protect yourself."

"I don't understand. What are you talking about?"

"Your deputy has been making house calls. About you, Ivy. I should have told you sooner, and now I'm furious with myself that I didn't. But I thought it was harmless, just him being a nosy boyfriend. After this morning, I knew it was much more serious than that. The first time he visited, he was full of questions. This morning he came by full of accusations. He knows everything, Ivy. *Everything*."

Ivy's healthy glow from the shower blanched to flour-white. "It's impossible," she whispered. "How could he know?"

Ava snorted. "You're the one who loaned him *Lykanthrop*. Did you think he was a simpleton when you wantonly handed it over?"

"No, of course not, but you took the final pages out and even those don't tell the whole story. Oh, but wait . . . "

The journal. It was Melvin after all!

"You remember something, dear?"

"My journal was stolen this morning, among some other things. I had no explanation for it, but now . . . now I have no doubt."

It was Ava's turn to feel relief. A suitable explanation had presented itself. She would not have to play her ace after all and blame Stefan for betraying his niece. "That explains it, then."

"Did he—did he believe what he read?" Ivy pictured it, Melvin in his patrol car, reading the shaky handwriting of a child as it evolved into the swirly script of a woman, story after story recounting what to him would only be horror. Could he ever see it another way?

"Oh yes, he believed it, at least about the murders. He was particularly interested in what happened to your parents. Look, Ivy, it breaks my own heart to see yours torn apart this way, but you know these relationships don't work. You were fooling yourself if you thought you could continue your life here the way it is and make Melvin—a policeman, of all things—a normal part of it. Don't make the same mistake I made, Ivy, and be forced into a difficult decision. I don't want to see that happen to you."

"Like Uncle Jeb." It was a hateful thing to say. Ivy regretted it immediately, but Ava did not flinch.

"Yes. Like Uncle Jeb."

Ivy had known it all along, but she'd never heard her aunt admit it aloud. It was something unspoken between them, accepted. Uncle Jeb had come in for his sun tea after gardening and the paramedics had carried him out, dead. From a heatstroke or a heart attack, they'd assumed. Considering his age, no autopsy had been necessary. Ivy remembered the call well—her aunt, resolute, telling her of the death and the funeral arrangements. There were no tears, only a hard-edged defiance in the way she reported the information, as if daring someone such as Ivy to judge her.

"It could be different with Melvin," Ivy said at last. "Or I thought it could. I'm so angry and confused right now I don't know what to think anymore. There's one thing I am fairly certain of, though, for good or bad. I'm in love with him, Ava."

"You're not in love, dear, you're in heat. Channel it elsewhere. There is another wolf, so I have heard, that is lurking about these parts. He's one of your own, Ivy, or at least as close as you'll ever find. You don't like his indiscriminate ways—then show him another way. Be his teacher. He *needs* you." Ava smiled softly and clasped Ivy's hand between both of hers. "Think about something for me, sweetheart. Think about how easy living could be from now on. No more lying. No more hiding. Someone to stand beside you, helping you, protecting you, loving you for what you are instead of loathing you for it. Can you imagine how that life could be? Can you?"

And Ivy did see it, for a brief moment, as the pine boughs bent beneath an autumn night's wind and the murmur of rustling leaves sighed her name. She and a mate, running across mossy paths and fording through current-wrinkled streams, the splash of the water over their shaggy sides shining like diamond drops in the full moon's light. The crest of a ridge slows their journey and she stands tall at the cliff's edge. The Blue Ridge stretches out in front of her with night-blackened rises and fog-cloaked valleys below. She would throw back her head and call for the sheer joy of her voice, a howl to be heard miles away, and he would answer, right from her very side. No more loneliness, no more silence in the wooded paths of this solitary life . . .

"That's right, Ivy. You can feel it, can't you? The freedom?

The happiness of a true soul mate? You can grasp it all. What I wouldn't have given . . . "

Ava's words floated like mist in the distance as Ivy swayed slightly in her chair, the trance of eventide music and melancholy howls lulling her, calming her frayed nerves, steadying her.

"Yes, my child. You know I'm right because the situation at hand with your deputy won't do." Ava leaned toward Ivy slightly. The lids over the elderly woman's eyes dipped to hood their sparkle and her voice hoarsened into the guttural coarseness of a woodland thing. "It just . . . won't . . . do."

Ivy looked up at her aunt. The rushing mountain streams from her vision were replaced by the water from her wet hair trickling down her back. It felt cold, like dead fingers tickling her spine.

"What are you saying, Ava?" she whispered.

"I'm saying it's time for a little self-preservation, sugar. I'm saying it's time to go hunting."

Chapter 51

"Hello, Ivy? It's Patricia. Pick up. I know you're screening; I hate it when you do that. Pick up!"

Ivy groaned and shuffled to the phone. "Hi, Patricia."

"Wow, you sound terrible. What's wrong?"

"Nothing. I'm fine." Not really. Ava was gone, it was well into the afternoon, and Ivy still sat in her bathrobe, knotted hair and all. She'd not moved from the kitchen table, until now. "What's up?"

"I know you haven't read the paper or turned on your television—you never do—so I'm calling to tell you the latest. It's a full moon tonight and the sheriff has called for a mandatory curfew at eight o'clock. She and the mayor just held a news conference."

"Oh. Thank you for the update. I'm not usually out past six anyway, so I should be okay." It was as good a news as any. The fewer people out and about tonight, the better. Ivy glanced at the rooster-shaped wall clock (thankfully silent) and ticked off the scant hours between now and nightfall. It was about time to be pulling herself together and focusing on the job at hand. Patricia was still talking, but Ivy cut her off. "You know what, darlin'? I lied before. I'm really not feeling well at all. Can I call you back tomorrow?"

Patricia shrieked in Ivy's ear. "I knew something was wrong! I'll be right over."

"No! I'm not sick or anything. I need some downtime to-day, that's all. But I'll call you tomorrow, I promise." No re-ply. "Patricia? Are you still there?"

"It's the full moon tonight, Ivy. The *full moon.*"

"It will be all right."

"No, it won't." Patricia's voice cracked as it lowered. A sob lay behind that statement, perhaps. Ivy was not sure she could stand another breakdown from the girl. Not today. Patricia spoke up then, no sob in her voice at all but rather, boulder-hard conviction. "There is something among us, Ivy. Some-thing vile. I feel it every time I step out the front door. I see it every time I drive down the road, past the place they found Cliff. They can't explain it, they can't catch it, but I know the truth. It's evil come calling, Ivy, right at our very doorstep. It won't stop until it's accomplished whatever it came here for. And I've lain awake plenty of a night thinking what that might be. And then this morning in bed, it hit me." Patricia took a long, dramatic pause. "It won't leave until it's killed us all."

"For heaven's sake, Patricia."

"No, I'm serious. Mama and Aunt Thelma left. I'm here in this house alone, and I'm scared."

"None of the people have been killed inside. You're safe."

"None of the people have been killed inside *yet.* I want to come spend the night with you. You shouldn't be alone ei-ther. You've got all those dogs; that's some protection. I don't have anybody."

A shrilling sounded in Ivy's free ear. It took her a disoriented moment to recognize it. "There's the doorbell, Patricia.
Somebody's here. We'll talk about this some more, okay?" Ivy
hung up without waiting for an answer. Patricia would be angry for a time over Ivy's coldness, but perhaps that very anger
would keep her at arm's length for a few days, at least until Ivy
could get her life straightened back out. She'd worry about how
to mend bridges later. Right now someone had "come calling,"
to quote her friend, and evil was exactly what she expected.
She wondered if Melvin would have his gun drawn and hand-
cuffs ready. How quaint that he should ring the doorbell first.

"Hello, Miss Ivy Cole."

Ivy glanced around the stranger on her porch but he was
alone. Then she recognized him, from the newspaper article
about Andy Talbot. There had been a photograph showing
Melvin and another deputy going into the woods.

"Hello, Officer. Is something wrong?" Ivy clutched the
bathrobe tighter around her and then reached to touch her
mussed hair. She must look a fright, lounging about at this
time of day in such a state, but it didn't much matter. She
was prepared for the inevitable encounter with the Doe
Springs force, but not like this. It should be Melvin standing
here, and the mistake of her brazen assumption that it would
be him to try to arrest her made her feel sick. Of course he
wouldn't have the guts to do it himself. And now she'd made
a fatal error by not only staying in her house today but actually answering the door to an indifferent enemy.

"Yes, I'm afraid there is something wrong. May I speak
with you a minute, please?"

Ivy stepped aside, letting the man pass. The scent of too
much aftershave followed him in. And something else . . .

"I'm Deputy Jonathan Meeks, by the way." He held out
his hand and Ivy slowly took it. She gave it a firm squeeze,
noting the roughness of a palm she'd have thought better
suited to a laborer than a police officer. She withdrew her
own hand quickly and pocketed it in the bathrobe.

"I'm confused, Deputy Meeks. I spoke with your sheriff
months ago about the Hughes case. I told you everything I
know."

"This isn't about Clifford, and I'm not here on official business, Ivy. May I call you Ivy?" Meeks walked to the woman's fireplace and traced a finger over the clock. The frozen clock, stopped forever at the time of Ivy's gruesome demise and, ironically, rebirth.

"All right. So what is this about?"

Meeks continued to poke along the mantel and then turned to examine the items on an end table. His eyes wandered to the coffee table where they settled on *Lykanthrop*. "It's about Deputy Sanders. He's in a bit of trouble. Seems like he's been a very naughty boy lately, and it's caught up to him."

Ivy shrugged her shoulders and lowered onto the arm of the sofa. "I'm not Deputy Sanders's keeper. What does this have to do with me?"

"Really, now. Do I have to be crude? The department already knows about Melvin's *extracurricular* activities. Over here, to be exact."

Ivy didn't say anything. What else did the department know? Meeks was clearly not here to arrest her. Was it possible Melvin hadn't told them?

Ivy studied the man's broad back as he walked about the room, the way his uniform stretched taut across it only to loosen as the waist whittled downward. The shiny black hair, the cut of his jaw as it angled into the powerful neck. The smell of . . .

"Oh my god," Ivy breathed. "It's *you*."

Meeks finally faced her again. He spread his arms wide and smiled. "You got me."

Ivy's eyes narrowed, and she slowly stood. He was here, in her very house. The Black as human but less human than anyone could possibly fathom. "You've caught me early," she said. "How brave of you."

The side of Meeks's lip wrinkled upward. The sneer vanished as quickly as it arrived. He smiled again, but the hairs on Ivy's neck bristled at the danger that lay behind it.

"Come on, Ivy, I had to see you before the big showdown. How unsportsmanlike would it be of me to know who you are and you not have the same advantage?"

"I don't count sportsmanlike as one of your qualities, considering what I've seen so far."

"Now that hurts me, it really does, coming from such a hunter as yourself. But I'm catching up to you, and tonight I plan on bagging the ultimate prize."

"Don't flatter yourself. I've seen your work. You're the most sloppy, ineffective killer I've ever come across. And I thank God for that every day since you came into my town and ruined everything. I'd laugh at your ineptness if your choice of victims did not make me so sad."

Meeks crossed his arms and rocked back on his heels slightly. "Early on, yes, I have had some trouble. I've run drunks off bridges, treed a hunter who died anyway (what a waste), managed to drown some poor guy in the Crippled Bend only to lose him in the current. There've been other mishaps, so to speak. But cut me some slack—I'm new at this. I don't have years of experience behind me like yourself. All that aside, I have to tell you, you're the one jumping the gun on self-flattery if you think the prize I'm after tonight is you. Although, what a catch that would certainly be."

Ivy took a step toward Meeks. "Is Melvin all right?"

"No, Ivy, Melvin Sanders is definitely not all right." Meeks crossed the space between them too quickly for Ivy to back away. He stood over her, but leaned down close to her pale face. "I've looked for one of my kind too long, Ivy. When I came here, fate handed me so much more than I bargained for."

Ivy's eyes widened. The aftershave and cologne were a poor mask. She breathed the man in, bathing in his earthy scent and feeling the pull of lunar tides deep in her belly. The sound of rushing wind filled her ears, then the crackling of leaves under swift feet. Her blood pounded as her thoughts raced through a black forest with something terrified and fleeing in front of her. In front of *them*. Ava's words came back: *The happiness of a true soul mate. What I wouldn't have given* . . . Longing tingled behind her tongue, down her throat, in the rapidly beating heart in her chest. *Someone to stand beside you . . . loving you for what you are instead of loathing you for it . . .*

Meeks moved closer still, his uniform barely brushing the terry cloth of her robe. "You stink of real wolves, Ivy Cole. But I think I could overlook it." He reached to touch her face and was pleased when she let him. But the warmth of her skin did not meet her eyes. She pushed him back.

"What's wrong with Melvin? Where is he?"

Meeks shook his head. "Melvin." He spat the name. "Here I stand right in front of you, and all you can think of is him." Meeks clenched his fists by his side. A longing was in him as well, to grab this infuriating woman by the shoulders and shake her until she screamed. "Hate to tell you this, but your boyfriend has played you for a fool. You think he's in love with you, but he's been using you from the get-go. It's all been part of the investigation. He and the sheriff are this close to bringing you in, Ivy."

"I don't believe you."

"Yes, you do. But I'll give you the rundown anyway. They were here this morning searching your house. The sheriff wanted something definitive to use in an arrest. She and Sanders have been watching you for a long time. Hell, Sanders even took a shot at your dog when it charged the fence. I'd say in a day or two animal control will be around for that black mutt you got out there, if the law doesn't come for you first."

"They have . . . the evidence?"

"Not they. Sanders. I saw him take jewelry and a note-book out of a hole in your floor upstairs, but he hasn't given it to the sheriff yet. He wants to bring you in himself, Ivy."

"You're lying." There was no defiance in her voice, how-ever. It came out more as a plea. *Meeks was right; I have been a fool. . . .*

"He told me, Ivy. Sanders thinks you're using Aufhocker to kill people and covering up the tracks. If he brings you in, it will not only save his career, it will launch it."

"What do you mean, save his career?"

"Fraternizing with the suspect so intimately was beyond what the sheriff had in mind for staking you out. He's in a lot of trouble with the big cheese at the station, and bringing in the Devil of Doe Springs would make everything all right, wouldn't you agree? Opportunity of a lifetime—I believe those were Sanders's exact words.

"Tonight your lover will be stalking the wolf, Ivy Cole. He thinks you're the one using the cabin up behind Talbot's woods, and he'll be there waiting for you." Meeks reached out and grabbed the lapels of Ivy's robe. He pulled her close to him again and snarled into her face. "And I'll be there, waiting for him."

Half-moons of topaz iris shown through the emerald of Ivy's eyes. A shimmering orange afterglow like a deep burning fire swirled beneath the emerging amber hue and her voice lowered to a growl. "You forget who you're talking to."

Meeks smirked and let her go. "Yes, you humbled me . . . once."

He strode to the door and turned. "I'll see you tonight, Ivy, at my cabin. I'm sure you can find it easy enough. We can tell Deputy Sanders good-bye in that special way only lycanthrope can. Oh, and one more thing. Sorry about your bed. You can send me the cleaning bill."

Jonathan Meeks winked and was gone.

Part Five

"And fortunate was the man who won the love
of a spirit that could appear both
as a beautiful woman and a wolf."
—Brad Steiger

Chapter 52

Ivy stood in her backyard, the adoring pack licking her hands and thumping her legs with their wagging tails. She hugged them one by one. It was not a new ritual, but this time the routine held a significant difference. Tonight Ivy was not sure she would be coming back.

Aufhocker stared up at her silently and Ivy knelt by his side. "It will be fine, Auf. Don't worry about me." Ivy's blond hair brushed against the coal-colored mane of the wolf. *The Black* . . . Auf felt his mistress stiffen, and he nuzzled her neck. Ivy looked into the wolf's dark eyes and knew he would never let her go alone. As good a guardian as he was, he would be no match against what lay ahead.

Ivy grasped the dog by the scruff of the neck and led him into the house. Rex watched the big animal enter with a wary eye. He'd given up on wooing Aufhocker with his friendly terrier ways.

"It's okay, Rex. Auf is going upstairs to the bedroom." Ivy closed the door as the wolf tried to nose back through. He howled at the barrier between them.

"I'm sorry, Aufhocker." Ivy turned and nearly tripped over Rex.

"You look after him for me, okay?" She picked up the scruffy terrier and hugged him tightly.

The sky was streaked in the vibrant bands of sunset: shell pinks merging into warm tangerines and velvety crimsons closer to the horizon. It reminded Ivy of the colored-sand-bottle projects she made as a child. The joy of those days was far behind her.

Ivy parked her van behind Andy Talbot's house. The dim,

hollow eyes of vacancy stared out from its windows. A For
Sale sign had met Ivy at the top of the driveway and another
lay on its side in the front yard, blown over by a sudden gust
with no one there to right it again. It saddened her to see the
Talbots had pulled up stakes so quickly. She liked the farmer
and his wife, but the rumors about town were apparently true:
Margie, like their one remaining dog, was never quite the
same after the brief encounter with a werewolf in their woods.

The barn loomed up on the left as Ivy climbed the hill.
The ground in and around the corral was uneven, still pock-
marked with the trampling of panicking hooved feet. The
land leveled out as she reached the hilltop and approached
the ridge of boulders that divided sheep pasture from the forest beyond. The musk of the other was forever embedded in
her senses, and she picked up a fresh scent marking at the
base of the rocks. How ironic, she thought, to be revisiting
the very spot where she had asked Melvin on their first date.
It seemed like a century ago.

Ivy hopped over the lowest set of boulders and let her
senses lead her. The "cabin" Meeks described was a shack
supported by the mountainside and protected by giant pines.
He'd been right—she found it easily. Ivy reached for the
cabin's doorknob, then saw only a ragged hole in its place.
She pushed the door open slowly, wondering if an ambush
awaited on the other side.

"Melvin? Are you here?" she said into the swirling dust
and shadows. The cabin reeked of the black wolf.

"I'm here, Ivy."

The woman gasped and wheeled around. For all that she
had learned today—from Ava, from Meeks, from the items
taken from her home—she'd still held on to the hope that it
was all a mistake and that Melvin would not show. Yet there
he stood, tall and straight, silhouetted against the trees in the
quickly dropping night sky.

"You came," was all she could think to say.

"I had to. You know that."

"Yes, I suppose I do."

Melvin stepped out of the shadows toward her. He was in
plain clothes and unarmed.

"What do we do now?" Ivy stepped away from the cabin. The man and woman faced each other under the forest canopy. Night inched steadily over them, like a funeral veil of midnight gauze.

Melvin didn't answer right away. Something flitted across his face, cracking the stern blank expression. It was pain. He held out a hand to her. "Come with me."

Ivy shook her head sadly. She wore the hurt openly. She wanted him to see what he had done to her. Soon he would learn the repercussions. "You traveled light to bring me in. Did you think it would be that easy? Did you think you could lead me out of here like an obedient dog?" Ivy saw Melvin quickly glance around him. "Don't worry—I left Aufhocker at home. It's just the two of us for now. But we don't have much time, and I have some questions that need answers. I think I'm entitled."

Melvin nodded. "You are."

Ivy did not expect him to agree so readily. "Good. The first question. Why did you lie about Toomey and my book? You had it all along."

"Ah, it *was* you in my house this morning. That's a fair turnabout, I guess."

"No, not fair. I took my own property back, but what you stole from my house was far more valuable to me."

The platter from Stefan. Melvin saw it tucked under the sheriff's arm when she'd left Ivy's house. "You'll get it back, Ivy, and *Lykanthrop* was always safe. I didn't want to lie to you but when Toomey translated the book for me, I knew you were in trouble. Especially when I saw the rubbing he'd started."

"What rubbing?"

"Of the missing page. The details provided of an old crime were specific enough, but don't worry—I finished the rubbing myself. Toomey never got to read it and, so far, neither has anyone else. I followed it up with some background investigation to fill in all the gaps. But I'm right, aren't I? It's your confession, *I.V.*, yes? Nothing would make me happier than for you to tell me I'm wrong."

She wouldn't deny it. There was no shame here to distract

her sorrow or take the edge off the anger. "So you hoarded all this information for yourself and this morning you hit the jackpot looking for evidence. It's all pretty solid against me now, isn't it?"

"There is nothing incriminating about the platter, but the hair samples from Aufhocker are another story."

"The platter? I'm not talking about the platter. I'm talking about the raid on my bedroom and your shot at a promotion."

"What? Now I don't know what you're talking about. Look, forget it. It doesn't matter. Listen to me now. I followed you here to help you, Ivy, not hurt you anymore than you've already been hurt. I know that you lost your mother in the worst way a child could, and I know you blamed your father and Una because of their affair. I also know you've had a crazy old woman brainwashing you since you were a girl. God forgive any kid who couldn't grow up normal after what you've been through. But now you are grown, and I see something else. I see that you've let the past chase you from place to place while you continue to relive your mother's death through Aufhocker and what you've taught him to do.

"It has to stop, Ivy. It can end right now, tonight. I've prayed for answers too, on the best way to help you. It's bigger than me, but we can get you a professional. You need a doctor. The courts won't put you away. They'll send you to a hospital where you can recover. Please, let me help you. Come with me now." Melvin's hand hung in midair between them.

Ivy slapped it away. "Liar!" She shook her head angrily. "How dare you use the pretense of helping me as an excuse for your underhandedness. You used me to catch what you think is a criminal. Just doing your job, right, Deputy Sanders? Isn't *that* the real truth? Helping me? How could you think I would be so stupid." Ivy could hold it back no longer. She stepped toe to toe with the deputy, drew back, and slapped his face hard. He did not move and she backhanded him again.

"Ivy," he said quietly. It was like the last breath from a dying man. Regret engulfed her rage, but only for a second.

"Question two, Melvin Sanders, and this is a big one. You

better get it right. Are you sorry for what you've done to me? *Are you sorry?*"

Melvin let the question sink in. Sorry he had risked everything? His career, his reputation, his own integrity for a woman he'd so briefly known? Sorry he'd lied to the sheriff by covering up Ivy's past to protect her? Sorry he'd libeled Professor Toomey with that story about him being a thief, when it was he himself, the trusted lawman, who had essentially stolen *Lykanthrop* in the first place? Melvin thought about those things every waking moment, as his head pounded and his ulcerous stomach churned with guilt. But was he sorry?

"No, Ivy, I'm not."

Ivy covered her face with her hands. A wail escaped through her fingers, and her shoulders hitched with grief. How many times had her own intuition, the solid voice of reason in her gut, said to keep away from this man? Even Ava, the woman she loved like a mother—and Meeks, Melvin's closest colleague—had warned her of him. Yet she'd held on to hope. A fool's hope, she saw now. He'd taken all the uncertainty away with that one reply. The sobs shook Ivy until she thought nothing of herself could possibly remain.

But finally, they stopped. The woman's hands dropped to her sides, her limbs as dead and leaden as the look in her red-rimmed eyes. She spoke at last, her voice choked with heartbreak. "Did you love me at all?"

"Ivy, let me explain—"

"Everybody hold it right there!" Sheriff Hubbard emerged from the trees, gun drawn. "Nobody move till I tell you to."

Ivy looked from the sheriff back to Melvin. "I guess your plan failed. You won't be bringing me in alone after all."

"I'm not here for you, Ivy," Gloria said. "I'm here for my deputy. I followed him up here. Where's your gun, Sanders?"

Melvin turned to his boss. "What is this, Sheriff?"

"Here I am, Gloria." Meeks stepped into the clearing. He looked at Melvin. "Sanders, you made it. I knew you couldn't resist following Ivy tonight. But hate to tell you,

buddy, you should have taken the sheriff's advice and gone
to see family."

"What the hell is going on?" Melvin demanded.

Gloria trained her gun and her gaze on Meeks. "Sanders,
I'll ask you again, do you have your weapon? We are arresting
Deputy Jonathan Meeks for the murder of Clifford Hughes."

"Whoa, whoa, whoa, Sheriff," Meeks said, advancing
slowly toward her. "Aren't you being a little hasty? That's a
big allegation."

"Come again, Sheriff? I'm not following you," Melvin
said.

"Recognize this?" Gloria fished something out of her
pocket with her left hand, her right still holding the gun
pointing at Meeks's chest. "It's a Harley Davidson biker ring
and a wedding band with an inscription inside: Love forever,
C. and P. H. I found them along with a gold chain in your
desk, Meeks, lying right there beside your pens and paper
clips. And this isn't the half of it."

Meeks crossed his arms. "Oh, really? I can't wait to hear
the rest."

"Okay, try this on for size. Tee's got enough paperwork
on you to start a library. After I found it, I paid Dr. Tuttle a
visit. You know who Dr. Tuttle is, don't you, John?"

Meeks rubbed his tongue across the bridge of his perfect
teeth. "You know I do."

"Seems you've had some dental work done on a molar.
Seems you lost a gold cap back there last winter. In January,
the same month Dennis lost his pigs, to be exact. Quite a coincidence, don't you think?"

"Would you look at this?" Meeks said. "Our little Glory
here has done some fine sheriffing while I wasn't looking.
Paperwork, dental records. You've been mighty busy today,
haven't you? What else are you hiding in your bag of good-
ies, Sheriff? Surely you're not finished."

"Oh, no. I'm just warming up. The strangest thing of all,
Meeks. Tee thinks you had something to do with killing that
little girl down in Uwharrie a few years back too."

"Is that so? Uwharrie, huh? Let me think back." Meeks
propped a finger under his chin, a playful effort at mockery

that seemed to be lost on his audience. "Why, you must be talking about little Annie Hobbs. Now, if I'm remembering correctly, wasn't that the little girl you and Tee, two of the biggest hotshots around, failed to find, Sheriff? You took some hard press over that, as I recall. How are you sleeping these days over our long-lost Annie? Not too good, I'm guessing. I'll bet you a dollar you even carry a picture of her around in your wallet, don't you? A morbid reminder, if you ask me, but to each his own taste."

Meeks waited for a tirade, a denial, something, but the sheriff gave him nothing. The gun still pointed with a cool hand directly at him. It was one of the things he'd loved about Gloria, before this uncomfortable predicament, anyway: her unflappable strength under pressure.

"Oh, that's all right," Meeks continued. "You don't have to be embarrassed. We're all friends here. But now that I'm reflecting so hard on it, seems Annie does ring a personal bell with me too. A sweet girl, she was." Meeks crept closer, until the barrel of the sheriff's gun almost touched his chest. "I know you're dying to know what happened, Sheriff, and what the hell—I'm going to tell you. Consider it my gift to you. Annie left her tent for a tinkle and got more than she bargained for. I saw her, I *smelled* her, out there all alone in the woods like she'd been put there just for me. How could I pass up that opportunity?

"But that's all it was, Gloria, I swear it. Opportunity. I didn't set out to kill a child, in fact I prefer not to. But you never know what you're going to run across when you're out in the woods at midnight, and age isn't really a factor when hunting under my particular circumstances. It was karma, that's how I saw it for a long time. You see, that's how I first discovered you, Gloria. You don't remember me, but I was there the whole time. My job was controlling traffic around the Uwharrie campground the day you and your husband showed up to do the important police work. I watched you when I could, stole moments to observe when you didn't know I was around.

"I was so impressed with how hard you worked, turning over every leaf trying to find this poor dead kid. The look you had, all that passion for your job, all that persistence and determination. I was drawn to you immediately. I figured we were alike that way, you and me. You see, I recognized another hunter. When the job came open at your office, how could I pass it up? Of course, after I got here I realized I'd misread the signs completely. Fate was not bringing me to you, Gloria. It was bringing me to *her*."

Meeks looked at Ivy, but the sheriff paid no attention. Annie was hot on her mind, the hours—the years—spent wondering, beating herself up, mourning. She'd lost the case and she'd lost a marriage because of it. And now, she feared, she'd lost something else permanently, a man she drove away but secretly dreamed of finding again. Notions of reuniting with her ex evaporated with dusk's last light, and a horrible truth dawned with all of Meeks's revelations.

"You killed Tee, didn't you? Answer me, or I swear I'll blow your head clean off your shoulders."

"*You* killed him, Gloria. If you'd left him in Montana where he belonged, he'd be alive and well today. As for blowing my head off, I'd believe that, if I didn't know you so well. But sadly for you, you're too good of a cop to lose your cool like that, so save your threats. We're just talking. Last I checked, that's not a shootable offense."

He was right. Damn him. "Melvin, come over here and get my cuffs. Then we're going to read Meeks his rights." Gloria looked at her younger deputy, then seemed to really notice Ivy for the first time as well. "What are you two doing here anyway?"

No one spoke. Ivy could not put words together. It was Meeks who had the jewelry, Meeks who lied about Melvin waiting for her here at the cabin. She needed time to sort out this tangled web of confusion. *More time* . . . Ivy's eyes drifted upward to the sky. "It's too late, Sheriff. You're too late."

"That's right, Chief," Meeks said. "Prepare to meet the Devil."

Chapter 53

Patricia clipped the last of the newspaper article and laid it aside for her scrapbook. So far she'd accumulated fifteen pages of mass media speculation about the creature roaming Doe Springs. Since the death of her husband, the stories had only grown bigger, and since Andy Talbot's terrifying sighting, the ghostlike animal was reaching mythical proportions. The stories had not been sensitive to the needs of a grieving widow, and Patricia shivered as the details of her husband's demise played again through her mind. She'd read everything there was to know about what happened to him—and laminated every single word to be pasted into her book.

I wouldn't have wished that on anybody, Cliff, she thought. *Not even you.* But behind that thought lay another: Did anyone ever truly succeed in lying to themselves?

Patricia walked to the bedroom window and stared out through the treetops from the second floor. The sun was down already, and although it was only August, outside it looked cold. Patricia turned to check the time, then remembered her clock had disappeared. It had been a pretty little clock, and Patricia idly wondered if Clifford took it to give to a girlfriend. No matter now. Clifford's time had run out.

"I don't want to be alone tonight," she announced to no one. The creaking of an old settling house was the only reply. Ten minutes later Patricia was in Clifford's El Camino, an overnight bag on the seat beside her and the wheel pointing toward Ivy's. Three minutes later she was pulling up in front of her friend's white picket fence.

"Great." Patricia jammed the car in park and stared at Ivy's empty driveway. Not a light shone in the house anywhere, and judging by how dark it was, the curfew was surely already in effect. Patricia cut the engine, then bounded up the porch steps to pound on Ivy's door. She tried the knob and it easily turned.

"Hello, Ivy? Are you home? It's Patricia!" The young woman entered the house. The usual alarm of barking sounded outside, joined by a forlorn howl from upstairs.

"What in the world is that? Ivy, are you here? Your door was open; I came on in. Hey!" Patricia jumped back as a streak of gray fur brushed her legs on its way out the door.

"Oh no! Rex! Wait, Rex! Come back!" Patricia chased the little dog outside, but he dashed through the gate she'd left open and disappeared around the corner of the house. The last she saw of the terrier, he was running into the dark woods, the dogs in the backyard howling after him.

Chapter 54

Melvin, Gloria, Meeks, and Ivy stood motionless in the small clearing before the cabin. A whisper of wind moved leaves, and shadows slithered up branches and across the treetops. The creeping darkness stopped abruptly as the full moon's light showered the conifers and the four pale faces of the circle.

"Run, Melvin," Ivy said, her voice low, hoarse.

"Ivy?" Melvin thought she looked sick all of a sudden. He moved to grab her in case she fell, but Gloria called to him again.

"Sanders—my cuffs. Everybody else, stay where you are." The gun still held steady on Meeks. He smiled one last time at the sheriff, and then his head reared back with his mouth wide open, his teeth amazingly white in the dark. A faint grumble followed by a groan escaped from the deputy's chest. Then the sound erupted into a piercing howl that cut the stillness. There was nothing melancholy or forlorn about it. It was agony and excitement bundled into an inhuman tenor. The man lowered his head and glared at the sheriff through orange-burning eyes, then his body dropped to the ground and began to writhe.

The sheriff lowered her gun and knelt by Meeks's side. Melvin ran up beside her. Meeks continued to moan and twist at their feet. White foam spilled out the side of his mouth and puddled by his cheek.

"He's having a seizure, Sanders. We've got to—" A hand shot out and grasped the sheriff by the throat, choking off her final thought and killing her air supply. Sharp points like talons dug into the back of her neck as she struggled to free herself from the man's grip. Her mouth gaped open as she fought to draw a breath in, then her gun hand instinctively aimed at the deputy's head before she realized her palm was empty.

Melvin grabbed Meeks's arm and strained to pull him away from the sheriff, even as under his own hands, Meeks's arm bulged and new hair pushed its way through Melvin's grappling fingers.

Gloria broke free, a searing pain ripping down the side of her shoulder as Meeks's nails drug over her flesh trying to find new purchase. She scuttled backward, away from the misshapen form.

My gun, my gun, where's my gun? Gloria raked through the leaves and dirt, searching for the lost weapon knocked away during Meeks's attack. Another howl cut the night, this one very human, as Melvin flew past the sheriff and hit the ground heavily behind her. Gloria looked up at the creature hunched before her.

"John?" she whispered. The figure was motionless, a huge black form on the forest floor.

"Ivy?" Gloria looked around the clearing, but the other woman was gone. Slowly, Gloria began to stand, her eyes locked on what could only be the Devil of Doe Springs.

The creature lifted its head at the motion. Eyes the color of the sun at twilight smoldered above a long black muzzle.

A rough, bristled mane shrouded a neck that led into massive shoulders and a muscle-banded chest. The animal crouched low on powerful haunches, then pivoted on giant clawed feet to face the sheriff.

"This isn't possible," Gloria said, the heartbeat in her ears loud enough to drown the words. The rustling of rumors traveled through her mind, whispered by overimaginative townspeople . . . *a werewolf, Sheriff, plain as the nose on your face, that's what you're after* . . . It was impossible, ridiculous, absurd. And rising to stand over her at this very moment. Everything Gloria thought she knew fled in the face of terror, and she grappled to pull her logic back together, put the pieces into an order that made sense. But this was no wolf suit, no crazy person unleashing dogs on unsuspecting victims or convulsing into multiple and murderous personalities. No, she had seen Jonathan Meeks change into a beast right in front of her, had felt his claws tear the flesh of her shoulder, had seen him fling her two-hundred-fifty-pound deputy like a bag of leaves.

Gloria cautiously took a step backward toward the prone man, praying he was not in too bad a shape. "Sanders, get up," Gloria said, her gaze never leaving the thing that was once a man she'd respected and admired. The werewolf took a step forward, its head low and eyes locked on its prey.

"Sanders, please . . . get up," Gloria hissed. The man remained motionless. "Oh God, help us both," she said under her breath. Then, to Meeks: "Come and get me, you son of a bitch." Gloria ran, away from Sanders's still body. Behind her she heard the snap of twigs as the wolf dropped to all fours and launched itself in pursuit.

Gloria ran blindly down the trail, following the specks of moonlight that dotted the path. She prayed this was the way that led to the main road and not one of the loops that would take her right back to the cabin. The trail snaked left ahead, a sharp bend ringed by wide-trunked pines. She could veer off the trail on the other side of the curve and follow it parallel through the thick cover of trees. Gloria ran harder, propelled by a new plan and the knowledge razor-edged claws tore up the earth somewhere behind her.

The sheriff rounded the corner, and felt herself falling in slow motion as her feet betrayed her. She landed hard on her left hip, the jolt knocking away her breath and a chip from a front tooth. Her shoulder screamed in pain, and a trickle of blood wound down her chin. *Get up, get up, get up!* Gloria scrambled about in the leaves, her panic and injuries making her clumsy. She regained her feet . . . and stopped cold.

The path in front of her was not vacant. Something large sat on the trail twenty feet ahead, unmoving. Then its head swiveled, and the unmistakable eyes fixed on her own.

"No!" Gloria spun around, her face suddenly clouded by a black mass of fur. Saliva dripped from four-inch fangs onto her forehead and ran down her cheek to mingle with the sweat and blood on her chin. Gloria slowly looked up, her gaze following first the thick chest, then the massive shoulders, then the face of the animal leering down at her.

Gloria backed away from the demon in her nightmares. The other wolf padded closer, a silver-white ghost in the moonlight, and Gloria's heart froze in her chest. The silver wolf rose up on its hind legs to walk the rest of the distance between them.

The woman stood still, the giant wolves on either side of her. Tears streamed down her face as the animals pressed closer. The stink of the black wolf was overshadowed by the intoxicating musk of the silver. Images of Chester playing in the mountains filled Gloria's vision as the smells engulfed her. She began to drift away on another calm thought: *It's okay, Glory, you're going to be okay.* Tee's face filled the void left by retreating fear. The tenseness in her body flowed out on a wave of a sigh, and the desire to lie down and sleep alongside Tee was becoming very strong. Gloria looked up dreamily. The wolves stood muzzle to muzzle, moist noses touching and exploring each other. Their quiet growls rumbled like a distant thunder overhead. Gloria marveled at her surreal predicament, but for some reason, it didn't matter anymore. Nothing did. She studied the creatures from a faraway precipice, where she and Tee could watch the ferocious beauty of the wolves like observers studying the wonders of the galaxy.

The Black and the Silver faced one another, the woman

forgotten and only canine instinct between them. The draw
of the pack was strong inside, the loneliness—for this one
instant—abated as the full moon drew the wolves together.

The Black nuzzled the female wolf. Her white canines,
hanging long from heavily serrated jowls, brushed his cheek
as he pushed his nose into her neck. The wolves dropped to
all fours, beside the intrusive woman, and continued the exploration of one another. The Silver reciprocated the male's
touch with a playful paw down his side. He bounced away,
then leaped toward her again to rest his chin across her back.
She allowed this for a moment, then reached around to grasp
his muzzle gently in her own. The Black whimpered slightly
until she released him, and then he pointed his nose to the
moon and loosed one long, soulful note—a song for his
newfound mate.

"Sheriff, run! Get out of there!"

The wolves paused in their courtship and two heads
whipped toward the sound. The haze in Gloria's brain
cleared at Sanders's voice. He stood on the trail behind the
strange triangle, holding his side and the sheriff's gun.

Gloria, free from the spell, fled toward the trees and out
of the line of fire as gunshots and a hellish cry filled her ears,
whether from a wolf or her deputy, she couldn't tell. Gloria
stopped, the urge to flee overridden. She bent down and
grasped a sturdy stick. It would have to do. Hefting it like a
baseball bat, Gloria charged back onto the trail with a
fiendish cry of her own.

She saw Melvin standing as tall as his broken ribs would
allow and firing point blank at the giant black wolf charging
on all fours toward him. But it came on, unfazed. Melvin
emptied the last of the chamber, then threw the gun at the
wolf as its jaws opened wide to greet him. It launched itself
airborne and hit the big man in the chest, knocking them
both backward in a tumble of legs and leaves and flying
blood as the wolf sliced through Melvin's arms raised to
protect himself. Melvin grabbed the ruff of the animal's
neck, its teeth gnashing inches from his face.

Gloria raised the stick overhead and ran toward Melvin's
attacker. But the Silver hit her from the side and knocked the

woman flat. Gloria swung the stick, but the wolf caught the wood in its mouth, snapping it in two and showering them both in rotted splinters. Gloria gritted her teeth, expecting to finally feel the clamp of the animal's jaws on her flesh, but the pain never came as the wolf sprang away. Gloria rolled onto her stomach and grappled for another weapon. Rock in hand, she rose to her feet to go save her deputy. But the sight before her quelled the sudden adrenaline fire in her veins.

The Silver galloped toward the battling man and black wolf. Her long, loping stride never faltered as she plowed into the Black's side, knocking him off his prey. A surprised yelp erupted from the black wolf, then he scrambled to his feet and whirled to confront the new attacker.

The wolves faced each other again, but the frivolous game they'd shared minutes ago was over. The two stood their ground, heads lowered, sizing up the situation. Then the Black watched as the female turned her back on him to nose the man. She would feed first, it seemed. These pack rituals were new to the werewolf, but his need for the mate he'd so desperately sought out kept him in check. He would wait.

The Silver stepped over Melvin to straddle him. His legs paddled against the ground and his nails dug into the dirt as he tried to pull himself backward, away from her. He panted with each painful draw of breath and each searing scrape of earth on his ripped-open arms. The wolf cocked her head, then lowered her nose to his ruined shirt, to the blood collecting in the bend of his elbows, to the throat that pulsed with a weakening heartbeat. Melvin felt the last of his strength gather as the wolf's eyes settled on the vulnerable curve of his neck. His fists bunched. He might die at this moment, but the wolf would feel one last sting from him before the end.

The silver-white head dipped lower, filling Melvin's field of vision like a cloud of brilliant snow lit by a blizzard moon. The deputy felt the first tips of her teeth graze the skin beneath his chin. His eyes met those of the wolf's as he readied himself for a final assault. The wolf's hard gaze locked steadily onto his, and a luminous flicker flared behind the orange irises, an emerald spark that the deputy recognized.

Melvin saw a sparkling smile and heard a sweet voice then, laughing with him in a meadow. He saw blond hair fanning out around the woman as she lay back with him on a blanket, their hands clasped as they watched a hawk flying across a perfect blue sky. It was a day he'd relived a thousand times, and a day he regretted they'd never had a chance to repeat.

Melvin's fists opened and fell limp by his sides. *"Ivy . . . I loved you. . . . ,"* he whispered and closed his eyes.

A loud crack sounded, followed by a sharp jab to the Silver's hindquarters. Another painful blow hit her shoulder. Both wolves' attention snapped to the direction of the onslaught. Gloria, down on one knee, took aim for her third shot, the rock discarded when she came across her gun again. This was the only reload she had; she would make it count. The silver wolf's forehead was an easy target between the shiny orbs marking it in the dark. She leveled the barrel, her blood-slicked hands steady. The trigger began to yield under precise pressure, then something small and furry hurdled out of the trees toward her. Gloria's arm was knocked to the side, the shot gone haywire somewhere into the underbrush. A small terrier stood defiantly in front of the sheriff, its sudden appearance somehow more bizarre than the wolves. He barked twice and then scampered off into the darkness. Gloria jerked her gun back toward the wolves again, but they were gone.

Chapter 55

"Sanders, do you hear me?"

Melvin opened his eyes. "I'm hurt bad."

"You're still alive, now get up. That's an order."

Gloria looked for a place to grab the deputy to haul him

to his feet. His right bicep was ripped into a sinewy flap, and his shirt was black with blood. A moist bubble burst at the end of his nostrils with each ragged breath. As bad as the external injuries seemed to be, Gloria feared the internal ones could be worse. Moving him was the last thing she needed to do, but leaving him here would certainly prove fatal. The wolves were gone, but for how long?

Melvin rolled onto his side and began the painful climb to his feet. Gloria grasped his waist to help steady him. His skin was spongy under her hands.

"We've got to get you out of here, Sanders. Can you walk?"

Melvin nodded. Even the bob of his head made him wince. "I can't make it that far. Take me back to the cabin. I can wait inside until you get help."

Gloria didn't want to leave him, but he was right. At least the cabin provided some shelter. "All right. Lean on me. We'll go back."

The cabin and woods around it were still. Gloria holstered her weapon and took Melvin around the waist again. They staggered like drunken partners to the shack's door, the man's weight taking a hard toll on Gloria's own wounded body. Thankfully, she kicked the cabin door open and Melvin hobbled inside. The sheriff's spine seemed to float upward a few extra inches as the weight lifted from her screaming shoulder and hip.

"Looks a little short on amenities," Melvin said. He tried a smile, but it twisted into a grimace. Gloria helped him lower onto the floor. She knelt beside him. "Take this."

Melvin pushed the gun away. "You need it."

"Take it, Melvin. I don't want to leave you here alone as it is."

"I'll slide up against the door. Nothing can get in. They'll find you out there, Sheriff, and if they do, I'm good as dead anyway if you can't protect yourself. Please, take the gun with you."

"Dammit, Sanders." Gloria stared into the dusty half-light

spilling through the moonlit doorway. It arced just beyond Melvin's feet, then petered away into pitch black at the back of the room. Gloria thought she could make out the bulky shape of the woodstove on the far wall, but that was it. The murky ink of night offered no clarity to her dilemma. Abruptly, she thrust the gun into its holster and stood up. "You hang on until I get back, you hear me?"

"Yes, ma'am."

Gloria waited outside the cabin until she heard Sanders wedge himself against the other side of the door. Then she stepped off into a brisk, unsteady jog, praying she could make it back before it was too late.

Melvin slumped against the cabin door. His eyes were blind to the dark of the empty room. Shallow breath whistled past busted ribs and the torn flesh of his chest and arms. Light-headed, Melvin rested against the wood panel at his back but struggled to keep his eyes open. "Stay awake, Deputy. You stay awake," he commanded himself, but the dark felt as soothing as velvet to his exhausted body. As more blood ebbed into his saturated shirt, a satisfying sleep probed behind his eyes and lay heavy across his lids.

A scratching. A scratching on the other side, behind his head. Melvin stiffened, his back an iron rod up against the door. The noise stopped. A billow of air puffed through the hole left by the stolen doorknob, unsettling the back of Melvin's hair. He slowly leaned away from it, as quietly as possible. Something sniffed hard, then snorted another gust through the opening.

Melvin drew up his knees and dug his heels into the floor, shifting all his weight backward. He waited, and listened.

The scratching again, this time slow, like an obnoxious child raking his nails down a chalkboard. Wood popped and splintered, then was still. A gentle thump followed. Something testing the door, testing the integrity of the old, weathered wood.

The deputy shored up even closer, until the seat of his jeans no longer met the floor. A minute passed. Two minutes.

Three. Melvin's knees began to warn him, and the edges of his heels started to numb. Four minutes passed, and a tingling in the deputy's calves threatened to knot into a cramp. But the bombardment he expected still didn't come. Melvin released his locked position. He pivoted to look through the doorknob hole. It was too dark. Drawing closer, the deputy placed his cheek right up against the splintered wood. One bright blue eye met only night—nothing was there.

Melvin leaned against the door again, relaxed this time, his relief overriding the pain pulsing up and down his entire body. He would make it. He was safe in here. The wolves were at the door, but they couldn't get in. And if they were here, that meant they were not out stalking the sheriff. They could run around the cabin all night, for all he cared. The sun would rise, and Melvin would still be here to see it.

Something shifted in the far corner of the cabin.

Melvin's last smug thought retreated with a new prickling of concern. He bent forward, trying to see into the darkest side of the room. The only light was the faint cast of moonglow coming through the doorknob hole. He strained, trying to discern any lines, shapes, anything at all. There, he could see something. The bulk of the woodstove; it was the only thing the looters and souvenir seekers had not been able to carry out of here.

It moved.

Chapter 56

Gloria ran down the trail as fast as her spent body would allow. The dry night air reached into her lungs and throat, clasping them in a chilly ache. Her side endured one kidney punch after another as a spasm found its way there as well, jabbing her after each step. Yet one foot fell in front of the other religiously. Melvin's blood on her hands and clothes kept her moving.

The trail snaked through rhododendron thickets and around embankments taller than her head. She climbed and tripped and slapped away branches, fighting to keep her direction straight. The trail gradually dwindled to no more than a cow path, until Gloria was not sure she was still on it at all. The moon was of little help—it continued to dip lower in the sky as she ran, and the leaf canopy overhead had only gotten thicker. It did not seem right, and yet, everything looked the same out here at night. She could be fifty feet from her Jeep, or be looped back around to within fifty feet of the cabin. It was impossible to tell.

Gloria stopped and bent over double to catch her breath. She counted to ten, then stood upright again. All around, the forest was quiet. No birds, no insects, only the moan of an occasional breeze. More than once she had mistaken the innocent rustling of leaves for footfalls sneaking up behind her.

The sheriff moved to resume her jog, then suddenly stopped a few feet away. Her toes rested on the edge of a ravine. Grasping a tree trunk for support, she lowered on shaky knees to peer down the edge of the shallow cliff. It was impossible to determine its depth. The sound of water trickled to her ears from somewhere below.

Gloria sat back, incredulous. She was lost. The maze of lumber trails crisscrossing these godforsaken woods had wound her God knew where. Her Jeep was on the shoulder of Route 7, not far down the road from where she had followed Meeks onto the power company's property. She had not gone anywhere near this ravine or a creek bed coming into the woods at dusk.

Over the still night air and the murmur of rushing water, a howl broke the night. Far away, but not far enough. At . . . the cabin, perhaps. The sound drug Gloria back to her feet and she fled the other direction, hoping to find another trail soon. *In Jesus' name, please soon . . .*

Chapter 57

"Are you here?" Melvin said to the darkness. Only the creaking of the pines above the tin-roofed shack answered him. The planks in the walls groaned and settled as a night wind stirred, but those were the only sounds, the only motion as far as Melvin could tell. The movement on the far wall had stopped. He was no longer even sure it had happened. Were hallucinations common with blood loss? He didn't know, but for the first time Melvin wondered if he were dying. It must be true, because in some small place in the back of his mind, indifference to that fact was taking over. He thought of his mother then, her apron dusted in flour and her kitchen smelling of bread when he came home from school. And his father, his booming laughter filling up the house, his scratchy beard tickling his young son. So this was dying. Going backward to childhood. Going back to innocence.

Scuttling now, in another corner. Melvin's eyes darted from the woodstove, following the sound from one dark wall to the other. Then it stopped again. Melvin's eyes ached from straining to see in the lightless room. Something was there, just feet away from him, and he could see nothing outside the scant light from the doorknob hole. Clicking again, rapidly, as it scurried at the deputy too quickly for him to move away. It stopped at the edge of his shoe, whiskers twitching as it sniffed the blood on the man's ankle. It was a rat. *A rat!* The deputy took a deep breath and released it. He started to laugh but his ribs cut the moment of relief short.

"So, I'm not alone after all. It's good to have some company. But not so close now, okay?" Melvin wasn't sure he spoke the words or merely thought them. Nevertheless, the rat was too interested in the exposed skin showing below his pant leg. He lifted his boot to push the rodent away, when a claw reached out of the darkness and grabbed it. The rat's surprised shriek choked off as blood squirted from its mouth and nose. Melvin thought he heard a man screaming as well, then realized it was his own horrified voice alongside the dying squeals of the animal. Orange eyes flared just beyond Melvin's legs and the rat burst into a mass of gore in the werewolf's claw. The rodent fell to the floor in two moist heaps.

Melvin's hand reached for his gun, then he remembered he had no weapon, giving the sheriff the only firearm between them. He came to take Ivy away at her will and had never considered arming himself to be necessary. He believed her feelings for him would save them both. He believed wrong.

The werewolf crept closer to Melvin, its belly so low it nearly scraped the uneven flooring. Whether it was from blood loss or defeat, Melvin remained motionless, his aching legs sprawled in front of him like the lifeless limbs of a puppet. The wolf paused at the man's feet to survey the damage, much as the rat had done. Melvin felt its breath through the leg of his jeans as it crept up an inch more, its nose climbing the scent of blood closer and closer to Melvin's chest. Finally, the great chiseled head rested level with the deputy's own. A black wolfen face stared dispassionately into the deputy's. There was no sound from it, no threatening growls, no expressions of anger. It was a blank slate, cold. And Melvin knew he was about to die.

A long, mournful howl erupted from outside the cabin, and then an animal's heavy bulk slammed into the shack. The cabin shuddered on its frame a second time as something monstrous exploded through the far wall, sending rotting boards and shattered posts flying into the room.

Melvin raised his battered arms to block the debris. When he lowered them again, a new form had risen up from the darkness. It stood tall and lethal in the jagged remains of the cabin wall.

The black wolf started to rise, but the Silver charged, launching them both into Melvin and through the cabin's door, unseating hinges and all. Melvin fought to breathe under the weight of the two wolves rolling over him. Pain screeched through the crevices of his broken rib cage, and his own cry joined that of his attackers. The trio came to a stop in the dirt. Melvin lay pinned underneath the Silver and staring past her head straight into the muzzle of the Black. Fangs snapped inches from Melvin's face as the dark and pale wolves gnashed at each other. The Silver writhed atop the broken man, trying to unseat the male wolf. She paddled with all four feet against his stomach and finally sent him sprawling ten feet away.

Both wolves regained their feet and spun to face each other. The Silver blocked the black wolf from the man once again. The Black crouched low, the spines of his hackles rising down the center of his back. His lips drew upward, exposing sharp teeth in a warning to the female. *Enough with waiting. It is time to feed.* He sprang at the silver wolf and knocked her aside. Then he dove for Melvin's leg and locked on hard.

Melvin bellowed when the wolf's teeth sank through the meat of his calf, then the animal began dragging him toward the trees. The silver wolf ran at them, but the Black kept Melvin's body between the two as he pulled the deputy closer to the underbrush.

The Silver paced just beyond Melvin's head. He stared up at her helplessly as the Black continued the determined haul out of the clearing. The pain in his calf was gone; there was only numbness below the knee. Were he not still steadily moving away from the cabin, the deputy was sure his lower leg might be missing altogether. Melvin glanced upward again, but the Silver was no longer by his head. A jutting root was. He grabbed onto it with his left hand and the only remaining strength he had. The wolf's teeth ripped down Melvin's shin, raking the flesh to the bone, but still Melvin held on. The Black drew back, shaking his head angrily and tossing strips of denim into the air. He opened his jaws to clamp down on the man again, when a sharp pain stabbed into his own leg. The Black's head whipped toward his flank to see the silver wolf, her teeth buried deep in the hair and muscle of his thigh. He snapped at her nose clinched against

him. The Silver pulled back and repositioned the bite into
the thick muscle of the wolf's hindquarters. He bent hard
around trying to reach her, but she stayed out of his range,
her teeth firmly embedded and pulling him away from the
deputy.

In front of the cabin again. The silver wolf released the
Black. Behind her lay the man, the prey, the feed that she refused to allow him. The moon would be down soon, and the
hunt was still not fulfilled. The Black stepped to the right,
and the Silver stepped with him. To the left, the same. Their
dance could continue all night, until sunrise, when it would
be too late. This was what she wanted? This was the great
hunter he sought as a teacher and a mate? Had he wasted
most of this night, running through the forest with the silver
wolf after the sheriff's pitiful assault, only to come back
here and not kill them both? Frustration and disappointment
maddened the Black even more. He would not walk away
from another full moon hungry.

The Black lunged at the female, slamming her onto her
side and losing his own balance with the momentum. He was
first up and with lips pulled back over daggerlike canines, he
plunged all his weight toward the Silver's throat. But something broadsided the Black in the head before his teeth could
connect. It latched onto his ear and sent him rolling to the
side. The little gray terrier held firm, his needle teeth digging deeper into the tender cartilage. The Black stood upright and staggered backward, clawing at the unexpected
animal clinging to his head. Rex dug his paws into the
wolf's thick mane, then worried his adversary's skin like he
would the vermin he was bred to catch. The ear began to rip
and the terrier grabbed hold even tighter.

The Silver regained her feet, slower this time. Splashes of
crimson smeared the fur of her cheeks, jowls, and chest. She
watched as the wolf in front of her clutched the terrier with
both clawed hands and pulled. But the dog clamped harder
onto the delicate tissue. Blood clotted the small attacker's
nose, choking his breathing, but he held fast—until a hot
pain like the slice of razors tore down his side.

The little dog yelped, inadvertently releasing his hold.

The Black removed his claws from the dog's soft belly and tossed him aside.

The Silver saw the shaggy gray body thud against the ground. He lay there, unmoving, a wisp of a dog come so far to protect her. The Silver's eyes flared brightly. Hotness like a falling curtain of fresh-spilled blood began to shroud the rational places left in her canine brain. Thoughts jumbled into a red, cloudy haze and one instinct emerged through the rage.

She roared toward the other wolf and leaped onto his back, smashing him into the ground in a pile of broken ribs. Claws and teeth slashed in a fury and blood-rain poured down around her. Black fur and chunks of flesh flew to litter the ground. *The blood, so good, so good, SO GOOD!* With head thrown back the silver wolf released a howl that shattered the night and reverberated to the heavens. Then she plunged her head into the Black's chest and with one final rip, tore the cavity wide. Black blood and viscera spilled down the werewolf's sides. A weak moan beneath the flurry of teeth and claws brought the Silver to pause. The Black stared up, already the veil of death glazing his eyes. But for one moment, he focused, before the moon pulled the last tide of life away.

Ivy, why . . . ?

The thought drifted along a sea of green calm into the Silver's enraged mind. And then it was gone. She buried her muzzle deep in the flesh once more, her orange eyes feverish with triumph.

Chapter 58

Melvin drifted in and out of consciousness. Time was passing quickly, or not at all. He strained to open his blood-gummed eyes as something nudged him repeatedly. The silver wolf stood over Melvin, its face a horror mask of red. The jaws opened, but a delicate tongue dipped to lick his wounds. . . .

Melvin woke once more, the full moon no longer blazing in his face, but settled lower now, resting within the branches of the trees. He turned his head and felt a pleasant warmth against his cheek, then noticed the soft warmth against the length of his body. Melvin's slitted vision saw the pale fur nestled against him, and he buried his face in it, grateful to sleep again.

Chapter 59

It was easy to find in the daylight, even with a sour gray mist enveloping the forest and dripping from the leaves to wet her jacket. Gloria had only to look at the sky and see the death ring of vultures—a dozen of them at least—circling in formation overhead. But the trail was plain enough, here in the dull light of the early morning, and she ran ahead of the policemen behind her, adrenaline and dread rejuvenating her wearied body. She had wandered about for hours last night, finally finding her way. The old Cherokee loomed dark on the roadside, and she'd staggered toward it, exhausted, bloodied, and grateful. The police department from Pine Knot had rallied quickly at her emergency request, the chief on alert the whole afternoon awaiting a call from Doe Springs that never came—until this morning, when dawn arose to provide no comfort for the one who had struggled to outrun it. The new day was only a reminder to the sheriff that they all may be too late.

"Over here! Over here!" Gloria pushed through the undergrowth, finding the cabin at last. The officer on her heels burst through the brush right behind her, then drew up abruptly. "My God . . . "

Flapping wings startled and resettled at the humans' intrusion. Ravens picked among the dirt, their feet leaving thornlike impressions in the damp earth. Damp, not from the mist. Blood was everywhere, muddying the ground and splashing up the sides of the cabin. Two bodies lay within the carnage, one in pieces. A stringy line of intestine spilled from his eviscerated torso. Two ravens quarreled at the end of it, pulling the tissue taut between them. More ravens tore at the rest of the body, snatching at the ragged holes in the flesh and then flapping a few feet away to eat. Their desolate caws floated across the morning. Four German shepherds dragged their handlers into the clearing, and their excited barking scattered the large birds.

Gloria ran to the other still body. His clothes were in tatters, adhered to his skin by dried layers of blood. The muscle of his calf was nearly severed from the bone. "Sanders, can you hear me?" She felt his neck, expecting nothing under her fingers but the confirmation of death. The artery pulsed faintly, and tears flooded the sheriff's eyes. Melvin's fingers twitched, and Gloria took his hand gently. Pressure no greater than a child's squeezed in reply. "Sanders, it's Gloria." No more words. Sorrow for what had happened and relief for the same held her silent. The sobs collected and she let them quietly come.

"Excuse us, Sheriff. We need to tend to him now." Two

paramedics stood over them, a stretcher waiting. Gloria gave
the deputy's hand a final squeeze, then she placed it by his
side. She wiped her tear-streaked cheeks and could finally
speak again. "You're going to be all right now, Melvin.
Thank you for hanging on." Gloria peered into his face one
last time and for an instant, she thought she saw the faintest
afterglow of orange. She blinked and looked again, but the
deputy's eyes were closed.

"Sheriff? We need you over here."

Gloria stepped to the second body, behind Officer Reid.
Two black body bags had not been necessary after all. Only
one, to collect the scattered remains of what Gloria and Officer Reid examined together now: the disemboweled torso
of Deputy Jonathan Meeks.

"Is this your other deputy, Sheriff Hubbard?" Reid asked.

She nodded. Identification was easy; the silver wolf had
left enough for that.

"Damn, damn, dammit to hell. A good officer ending up
like this." Officer Reid's gun itched to unholster and fire out
of angry frustration. "Wolves in Doe Springs, I never would
have thought it. Turns my stomach, that's what it does. You
can count on us for support, Sheriff. I can spare a couple extra men. We'll catch your devil, I swear it. Sheriff?"

The sheriff didn't answer. Overhead the vultures circled
closer, waiting for the policemen to leave. Gloria watched
them, gliding silently, welcoming death. There had been too
much of it in her lifetime. It came with the job, but not like
this. Not this.

Officer Reid looked at her expectantly, waiting for a reply. But she was not thinking of devils at this moment, but
rather, of loss. Loss of time, loss of life. Not just Tee's, or
Annie's, or even Meeks's. But her own. She would get them
back. Time. A life. How does one begin to leave the familiar
road of anguish? Perhaps the answer to her own question lay
not in the center of something as large as the universe, but
rather, in smaller things. Perhaps she would have that picnic,
drink all the rich coffee she wanted, watch the stars from a
mountaintop. Maybe, someday, she would love another
man. Perhaps . . .

Officer Reid still stood beside her. "It will be back, won't it, Sheriff?"

Gloria came back to earth, leaving the sky to the vultures and the spirits of wistfulness. She stared off into the trees. Finally, she turned to face the policeman.

"No," she said. "It's over. The Devil is gone for good."

Chapter 60

"What's all that racket?"

Doc Hill rolled over in bed and groped for his specs. He squinted at the clock on the nightstand, trying to assess the time from its fluorescent dials. Six fifty-seven a.m. The "office" wouldn't be open for another two hours, yet Samson barked as if the parking lot were full of patients already.

"What's wrong, honey?" Betty leaned up on an elbow, her face green with an avocado facial mask.

"Dunno. Sounds like the dog's raising the roof over something, though." Doc pulled pants over his blue plaid boxers and walked to the stairs. Bonnie poked her head into the hallway. "Daddy?"

"It's okay, Punkin. Go back to bed."

But Bonnie pattered down the stairs after her father anyway, followed by Betty in her housecoat.

Downstairs Samson bayed at the front door, his tail wagging wildly. He clawed at the welcome rug, scooting it behind him, and then continued the assault on the doorjamb. Doc put a hand on the dog's head to cease the paddling paws. He looked out the door's diamond-shaped window onto the front yard.

"Who's out there, Jacob?" Betty stood tiptoe trying to see over her husband's shoulder.

"Good Lord. You won't believe it." Doc pulled open the door and stepped onto the porch. His little family crowded behind him. In front of them on the lawn, six dogs of varying sizes sat quietly in a single row. They stared expectantly at the people who studied them just as hard.

"Daddy, look!" Bonnie pushed past her father. A cardboard box sat at the foot of the steps. Doc Hill crouched beside his daughter and together they pulled back what seemed to be the remnants of a rose-colored quilt. Underneath the coverlet lay a heavily injured terrier, its breath whistling through blood-caked nostrils. A torn piece of paper lay beside it. Doc fingered the note:

Please take care of my babies, Doc. I no longer can. Thank you. For everything.

Doc looked up. "This is Simple Rex. We know all these dogs. They belong to Ivy Cole."

Betty came down the steps and stood by her husband. "What do you make of it, Jacob?"

Doc looked at the note, then looked in the box where Rex struggled for each breath. "We'll figure it all out later. Right now I've got a lot of work to do."

"Well, in that case," Betty said, wiping avocado from her cheeks with tissue pulled from her housecoat pocket, "I better get some chow out. I bet these guys haven't had breakfast yet." She turned to go inside and start gathering bowls.

Doc Hill lifted the box with the terrier.

"Is he going to make it, Daddy?" Bonnie looked up at her father through moist lashes.

Doc pursed his lips. "He's been in bad shape before, but you know what? He's a scrappy little fella."

Rex thumped his tail once, and the vet smiled. "Let's get to my office and patch this guy up."

Bonnie followed her father and the terrier inside.

Epilogue

The train clicked and clacked down the rails in a soothing monotony. Outside, the countryside passing by the window gradually changed from mountains to rolling hills. Fall was beginning to peek through the last of summer's greenery, and the occasional rusted tree stood out brilliantly.

But the blond woman sitting alone saw little of it. Though her eyes looked through the pane of glass, they saw another moving picture, one of dark woods and darker creatures among them. Bright eyes flashed suddenly in the black void, and a voice rang out. It was not the song of the wolf, however, that called to her this time. The eyes in this fantasy were blue, and the voice was the gentle timbre of a man she would never see again.

No, outside this window lay only memories. There was a new life awaiting ahead, new journeys to unfold, new adventures to discover. She had wanted none of that. All she wanted she had left behind, in a town nestled within the folds of the mountains. A cottage slept there, bare and lonely, its walls the vacant shell of an abandoned home. Home. There was no such place. It was as it always had been for her. For the wolf.

Ivy leaned against her seat and let the rhythm of the train slowly rock her. A simple whine carried to her ears. It was neither the train brakes nor the shrill of the engine's whistle; it was a black "shepherd" stored away in the cargo hold. He would be miffed about his uncomfortable confinement for some time, but even wolves had to follow the rules occasionally. Auf would forgive her, as he always did. It was the extraordinary mark of his loyal nature.

The train clattered on, toward the unknown. Night had followed the train and caught them at last. The dented globe of a waning moon hovered above the horizon, and Ivy laid a cool hand on her stomach. There was a stirring there, she instinctively knew. A small life gathering, a part of herself. But would the child be born with the kind heart of one deputy, or the unconscionable soul of the other, she did not know.

But Ivy did know this: The child would be born a girl. And she would call her Luna.

Author's Note

I have always had a lifelong love of animals. Being a mountain girl and particularly aware of wildlife, there was one voice I noticed to be strangely absent from the Appalachians where I grew up: that of the wolf. That notion has stuck with me from an early age. Then, on a writing sabbatical off the Blue Ridge Parkway back in 2002, I sat down to hammer out some ideas for a new horse novel I was kicking around in my head. After a few hours of writing as the winter wind howled outside my loosely shuttered window, I should not have been surprised to find that a wolf—a *were*wolf—story had emerged.

In welcoming Ivy Cole into my life, I knew I did not want her to be an ordinary werewolf. Wolves are not ordinary, and neither is my heroine. I wanted to move away from the typical Hollywood monster version, so I spent a year studying real wolf behavior to implement into my character development. However, to really capture *Canis lupus* on my pages, I found I needed more than textbook research. So in October 2004 I went to Wolf Park, an educational facility in Battle Ground, Indiana, to interact with an actual gray wolf pack. I walked away with a feeling I'd encountered something spiritual in my hands-on contact with these noble, remarkable animals.

In the two and a half years it's taken to write this novel, I have learned a lot. In fact, I would like to tell you that *Ivy Cole and the Moon* is a true story. To a large degree, it is. The details about wolves, werewolf legends, wolf peoples, and deranged souls who succumbed to historical evil are all accounts based on research. Likewise, the horror that wolves have endured over that same historical period is also fact. It was disheartening to discover that the settlers who arrived in America undid in a few hundred years the balance of prey and predator that Mother Nature had set in place for centuries. The wolf was nearly hunted (oftentimes tortured) to extinction in the lower forty-eight states. Thanks to a small recovery effort emerging in the West, beginning with the return of wolves to Yellowstone National Park in 1995, the melancholy song of the wolf may someday be heard echoing over our mountains and plains once more. But while fragile protections are in place, they are sometimes not far-reaching, and although the methods of cruelty may be disguised as more humane, that definition is up to the reader. Today helicopters soar above the Alaskan landscape so hunters can pick off many wolves at a time (as Meeks recalls in chapter 34) and we must ask ourselves, Is this fair sport or a coward's game?

As you leave *Ivy Cole and the Moon*, I hope you walk away having enjoyed an entertaining story. But beyond that, I hope you come away with a little bit more: some insight, perhaps some curiosity, maybe a creeping uneasiness that man and beast are truly closer in nature than we'd like to believe. However you want to view Ivy or her rival or the story in general, please know this: The werewolves who walk among us do not need our protection. I assure you that real wolves do.